PRAISE FOR JEAN JOHNSON
AND THE SONS OF DESTINY NOVELS

"Jean Johnson's writing is fabulously fresh, thoroughly romantic, and wildly entertaining. Terrific—fast, sexy, charming, and utterly engaging. I loved it!"

—Jayne Ann Krentz, *New York Times* bestselling author

"Cursed brothers, fated mates, prophecies, yum! A fresh new voice in fantasy romance, Jean Johnson spins an intriguing tale of destiny and magic."

—Robin D. Owens, RITA Award–winning author

"A must-read for those who enjoy fantasy and romance. I . . . eagerly look forward to each of the other brothers' stories. Jean Johnson can't write them fast enough for me!"

—*The Best Reviews*

"[It] has everything—love, humor, danger, excitement, trickery, hope, and even sizzling hot . . . sex."

—*Errant Dreams Reviews*

"Enchantments, amusement, and eight hunks and one bewitching woman make for a fun romantic fantasy . . . humorous and magical . . . a delightful charmer."

—*Midwest Book Review*

"A paranormal adventure series that will appeal to fantasy and historical fans, plus time-travel lovers as well . . . Jean Johnson has created a mystical world of lessons taught, very much like the great folktales we love to hear over and over. It's like *Alice in Wonderland* meets the *Knights of the Round Table*, and you're never quite sure what's going to happen next. Delightful entertainment . . . An enchanting tale with old-world charm, *The Sword* will leave you dreaming of a sexy mage for yourself."

—*Romance Junkies*

continued . . .

"An intriguing new fantasy romance series . . . a unique combination of magic, time travel, and fantasy that will have readers looking toward the next book. Think *Seven Brides for Seven Brothers*, but add one more and give them magic, with curses and fantasy thrown in for fun. Cunning . . . creative . . . Lovers of magic and fantasy will enjoy this fun, fresh, and very romantic offering."

—*Time Travel Romance Writers*

"The writing is sharp and witty, and the story is charming. [Johnson] makes everything perfectly believable. She has created an enchanting situation and characters that are irascible at times and lovable at others. Jean Johnson . . . is off to a flying start. She tells her story with a lively zest that transports a reader to the place of action. I can hardly wait for the next one. It is a must-read."

—*Romance Reviews Today*

"A fun story. I look forward to seeing how these alpha males find their soul mates in the remaining books."

—*The Eternal Night*

"An intriguing world . . . an enjoyable hero . . . an enjoyable showcase for an inventive new author. Jean Johnson brings a welcome voice to the romance genre, and she's assured of a warm welcome."   —*The Romance Reader*

"An intriguing and entertaining tale of another dimension. It will be fun to see how the prophecy turns out for the rest of the brothers."   —*Fresh Fiction*

THEIRS NOT TO REASON WHY

AN OFFICER'S DUTY

JEAN JOHNSON

ACE BOOKS, NEW YORK

THE BERKLEY PUBLISHING GROUP
Published by the Penguin Group
Penguin Group (USA) Inc.
375 Hudson Street, New York, New York 10014, USA

Penguin Group (Canada), 90 Eglinton Avenue East, Suite 700, Toronto, Ontario M4P 2Y3, Canada
(a division of Pearson Penguin Canada Inc.) • Penguin Books Ltd., 80 Strand, London WC2R 0RL,
England • Penguin Group Ireland, 25 St. Stephen's Green, Dublin 2, Ireland (a division of Penguin
Books Ltd.) • Penguin Group (Australia), 250 Camberwell Road, Camberwell, Victoria 3124, Australia
(a division of Pearson Australia Group Pty. Ltd.) • Penguin Books India Pvt. Ltd., 11 Community
Centre, Panchsheel Park, New Delhi—110 017, India • Penguin Group (NZ), 67 Apollo Drive,
Rosedale, Auckland 0632, New Zealand (a division of Pearson New Zealand Ltd.) • Penguin Books
(South Africa) (Pty.) Ltd., 24 Sturdee Avenue, Rosebank, Johannesburg 2196, South Africa

Penguin Books Ltd., Registered Offices: 80 Strand, London WC2R 0RL, England

This is a work of fiction. Names, characters, places, and incidents either are the product of the author's
imagination or are used fictitiously, and any resemblance to actual persons, living or dead, business
establishments, events, or locales is entirely coincidental. The publisher does not have any control over
and does not assume any responsibility for author or third-party websites or their content.

AN OFFICER'S DUTY

An Ace Book / published by arrangement with the author

PUBLISHING HISTORY
Ace mass-market edition / August 2012

Copyright © 2012 by G. Jean Johnson.
Cover art by Gene Mollica.
Cover design by Annette Fiore DeFex.
Interior text design by Laura K. Corless.

ISBN: 978-1-937007-69-0

ACE
Ace Books are published by The Berkley Publishing Group,
a division of Penguin Group (USA) Inc.,
375 Hudson Street, New York, New York 10014.
ACE and the "A" design are trademarks of Penguin Group (USA) Inc.

PRINTED IN THE UNITED STATES OF AMERICA

10 9 8 7 6 5 4 3 2 1

ALWAYS LEARNING   PEARSON

ACKNOWLEDGMENTS

I'd like to thank my beta editors Alexandra, Stormi, NotSoSaintly, and Buzzy for putting up with my manuscript delays; Mysti and Lanzlo for their insights; my friends and family for occasionally putting up with my plot-bunny-driven insanities (or at least inanities); and my editor, Cindy, for insisting so very firmly on my behalf that this series is *not* a romance series. (*Psst*, it isn't!) I would also like to thank you, my readers, for knowing that authors *can* write engaging stories in different genres. Any errors or oddities in procedures and so forth are my own creation.

This book is a continuation of the events in *Theirs Not to Reason Why: A Soldier's Duty*. I have done my best to make sure it can be read and enjoyed without having access to the first book. Still, to fully understand what's going on, if you haven't read the first novel, you might want to buy it online or at your local bookstore, or check your nearest public library for a spare copy.

As always, this series is dedicated to the many men and women out there who risk their lives for their countries in willing military service. It doesn't matter what post you hold or what country you defend; it only matters that you are willing to hold and defend it. On behalf of those you protect and defend, I thank you.

Jean

CHAPTER 1

Thank you for letting me take that quick break from this interview. It wasn't anything serious, just some new orders and a course correction. I do appreciate the opportunity to share some of this background information with everyone, though of course much of it is Classified and you are—ah, forgive me, I'm starting to use "military-speak" and "military-think" again, aren't I?

During my first trip back home after enlisting, I had that same problem with my family. The military has counselors for this sort of thing, they give you lectures and advice, but . . . For a soldier who's been away for months, even years like myself, it can be a bit of a system shock to come back to civilian life. Things are organized almost down to the minute in a military setting, because they have to get done at a certain time in a certain way, or everything descends into chaos. Things don't always get done in civilian life, because they often can be "done later" or "done some other way."

A lot of soldiers have difficulty making that transition back to civilian life. Even those of us who merely go home for a short visit sometimes have difficulties. Both sides need to remember to slow down, take it easy, and readjust to each other. Don't throw a pot of cold water on the cooker and expect it to instantly boil; even in this day and age, that won't happen right away. There's always a period of readjustment. Sometimes it's quick, and sometimes it's slow, but it's always necessary.

~Ia

JULY 18, 2492 TERRAN STANDARD
OUR BLESSED MOTHER
INDEPENDENT COLONYWORLD SANCTUARY

"This is so exciting!"

Ia glanced over at the woman settling into the next seat. The orbital shuttle was nearly full, and the crew were urging passengers to take their places. The woman who was Ia's seatmate fished for her restraint straps. Her efforts at pulling the three-point belt into place were somewhat hampered by the added bulk of her gravity weave. Nudged a few times by the brown-haired woman's elbow, Ia rolled her eyes and held out her hand, silently offering to latch it.

"Oh, thank you. Wait—where's your gravity weave?" the woman asked as Ia slotted the tab into its latch. "You're taller than me!"

Ia's rare sense of humor surfaced. Since she was clad in camouflage Browns, the speckled, mottled uniform of the Space Force Branch Marine Corps, she flashed a brief smile and stated, "I'm a Marine. We don't *need* gravity weaves."

The woman blinked, her brown eyes widening in shock.

Ia rolled her eyes. *Really, some people will believe anything about the SF-Marines.* "I'm also a native. Born and bred on Sanctuary. I'm coming home on Leave."

"*Ah.* Um . . . thank you for serving," the weave-wrapped woman finally offered.

"It's an honor to serve, meioa," Ia murmured in reply. Now that her seatmate had settled in, her mind was elsewhere, busy going over her schedule for the next three weeks. Some things would have to take place at exactly the right moment in time, while others would be more fluid. Like the problem of her tainted sword-turned-anklet.

The crew finished checking and securing the cabin. The woman at Ia's side said nothing for a long while, paying dutiful attention to the safety procedures lecture. Then, as they detached from the space station with a slight bump, the woman muttered once again, "This is so exciting!"

Sensing the woman was one of those sorts who just had to talk or burst, Ia sighed and asked the most obvious question, rather than dipping into the timestreams. "Is this your first trip to Sanctuary?"

The woman nodded quickly and smiled. She also held out her hand. "Amanda Sutrepya. And yes, it's my first time to your homeworld. I'm here on a missionary trip. And you are . . . ?"

"Lieutenant Ia." Ia shook the other woman's hand as briefly as possible. The closer she got to her homeworld, the more she feared her precognitive gift would turn unpredictable again. Plus there was the fact that physical contact always enhanced her ability to read another sentient being's plethora of potential futures. The combination held too much danger to risk it, though there wasn't much else she could do to avoid brushing up against someone in such crowded conditions. At least the other woman was wearing a purple, long-sleeved shirt under the lumpy web wrapping her limbs.

"Missionary trip?" The question came from the short, balding man on the other side of the aisle. He gave the woman, Amanda, a derogatory look, snorting, "Great. Another godless heathen," before returning his attention to the reader pad in his hands.

"Excuse me?" Amanda asked, her tone and her expression both taken aback. "I am *not* a godless heathen, I am a Christian!"

The man gave her a look somewhere between disdain and pity. "Even worse, then. A deluded *polytheist*."

The woman started to protest. Ia quickly reached over and touched her sleeve. "Don't."

"But he—"

"Just don't," Ia murmured again, cutting her off. "See the corona pin on his jacket lapel? He's a member of the Church of the One True God."

"I . . . don't understand," Amanda muttered. She glanced back and forth between Ia and the man, finally settling on Ia. "Aren't they Christians, too? I thought their worship was based on the same general beliefs. One loving God, Abrahamic teachings . . ."

"So are Muslims and Jews, if you measure it by that method, but no, they are not Christians, they are not Muslims, they are not Jews," Ia told her, flicking up one finger per listing. "In fact, if you must get technical, their dogma actually began as an offshoot of *The Witan: The Book of the Wise*."

"We are *not* an 'offshoot' of anything. *We* are on the *true* path," the man across the aisle corrected tartly. His eyes were on the text of his pad, but his ears were clearly listening to his neighbors. "Not my fault if the rest of you have been misled by the sweet-sounding poison of the Devil's books. The Bible, the Koran, the Torah . . ."

"Well, I never!" Amanda gasped, visibly upset.

"Meioas."

Ia's tone, more sharp than actually loud, cut across the missionary's sputterings, and caused the Church man to look up at her once more. A few others in the nearby seats glanced her way as well, but they didn't protest. Ia kept her eyes on the Church man. When she was sure she had his attention, she had her own say, leaning forward slightly while she held his gaze.

"I am on Leave from two years' worth of fighting on the far side of the known galaxy." That was a slight exaggeration, but she wasn't going to bother with the full truth. "It has taken me three weeks of travel to get this far. I have exactly three weeks, one day, and four hours from the moment we land, precious, precious days and hours to spend with my family, before I have to go back. I would therefore like to finish this last, tedious leg of my journey in peace and quiet."

"You'd be better off spending those three weeks on your knees in one of Our Blessed Sanctums, confessing the sins of spilling blood on some godless heathen's orders," the balding believer retorted.

Ia gave him a not-smile. "And I say unto you in reply, from Book Nine, The Righteous War, Chapter Three, verses four and five: 'Succor the weary and wounded soldiers who claim Sanctuary and take shelter among you. Give them rest and peace, and honor them for the sacrifices they make for the betterment of all.' "

He reddened a bit, having his own holy words flung in his face.

"I am a weary soldier of Sanctuary," Ia reminded him,

speaking softly, but with enough point to cut to the bone, "and I am here to take shelter among my people. Give me my rest and peace, and honor me for the sacrifices I make . . . or spend your weeks on *your* knees, for failing to follow through on God's Own True Words."

Holding his gaze, she stared at him until he backed down, subsiding into his seat. He refocused his attention on his pad. Only then did Ia settle back in hers. Just in time, too; they hit the atmosphere with a jolt and a rattle that made her grateful for the cushions supporting and sheltering her body. A few jolts later, the cabin screens came to life, showing the smiling face of their middle-aged Human pilot.

"Greetings, everyone; this is Captain D'Sall. We are currently traversing the edges of the local early evening thunderstorm, so a bit more of this mild in-flight turbulence is to be expected. Please remain in your seats with your restraint belts firmly fastened. However, our flight will be short, as we will be landing at Our Blessed Mother Inter-Orbital Spaceport in approximately twenty minutes.

"As a reminder, all passengers wearing gravity weaves should have their weaves set to Adaptive Gravimetrics on the Low Strength setting so as not to interfere with the integrity of the shuttle. Do not adjust them back to Full Strength until we are fully on the ground and the Gravity Weave permission sign has been turned on. If you need help fighting the gravity to do so, please remain calm, press the button on your armrest, or alert your seatmates, and the cabin crew will be by to check on you shortly," the captain added politely. "Once we land, only the flight crew are allowed to move about the cabin until we have reached the terminal, so please remain seated.

"If at any time you experience difficulty in moving, breathing, or even thinking, or feel like you are going to black out during your visit to Sanctuary, these are the primary symptoms of the onset of adjustment sickness, which can lead to more serious complications. If you suspect you are about to be ill at any point during your visit to Sanctuary, contact the emergency Nets immediately, and go straight to the nearest medical facility to be checked out for the possibility of gravity sickness.

"The government of Independent Colonyworld Sanctuary wishes to remind all visitors and returning natives that it assumes no liabilities, fiscally or legally, for the complications of gravity sickness or any related injuries. Neither does Gateway Inter-Orbital Transit, of which you were advised before boarding this flight. However, we thank you very much for flying with us. We hope you'll have a safe time while on Sanctuary, and wish you a good day."

The shuttle jolted again. Ia winced as the woman next to her grabbed at her forearm.

"God Almighty!" Amanda exclaimed, bouncing in her seat with the next jolt of turbulence. "*This* is *mild*?"

Prying the woman's hand off the sleeve of her brown camouflage shirt, Ia pressed it to the armrest and tucked her own hands into her lap. "Since we're due to arrive at the equivalent of near-sunset, yes, it's just one of the mild, daily thunderstorms. If it were a *real* storm by Sanctuarian standards, the pilot would have delayed the flight. This one isn't nearly as risky as you'd think."

"Oh."

The other woman started to relax, then yelped a little as the ship bucked again. A flash of light and a not quite muffled *boom* beyond the porthole windows made her yelp a second time, along with a handful of the other passengers. The rest were either too busy enduring the ride, or like Ia and the balding believer across the aisle, weren't fazed by the local weather. Certainly this turbulence wasn't as bad as some of the planet-falls she and the rest of Ferrar's Fighters had made, riding to the rescue of various colonyworlds.

Now I'm riding to the rescue of my own world, in a way. Though my efforts won't bear results for a few more years at the earliest. Enduring the bouncing with stoic patience, she absently rubbed her left hand over the hard cuff hidden beneath the mottled browns of the opposite shirt sleeve. *Presuming all my speculations on the trip out here are in any way accurate, that is . . .*

I wonder what my brothers are going to think when I ask them literally to shed their blood for me, this week?

Thorne was the easiest of her family to spot. He stood literally head and shoulders above everyone else waiting on the far side of the Customs Peacekeepers, as tall as a local doorway and as broad as a tank. His dark brown hair had been trimmed with bangs in the front since she had last seen him in person, though it looked like it was as long as ever, pulled back in a ponytail.

She'd seen the change in the timestreams, but seeing it in person was another matter. It struck her just how much everything had changed back home. How much she had changed, even though Ia had known it would happen.

His hazel eyes met hers within moments, drawn to her thumb-length white locks and mottled brown uniform. There were other tall-by-comparison people arriving, mostly visitors from light-gravitied planets who were wrapped in gravity weaves, but she wasn't lost in a crowd; the others had spaced themselves out so that their personalized repelling fields, now set to full strength, wouldn't conflict and cause each wearer to stagger off balance.

The only thing that made her want to stagger was the full resumption of her home gravity, which she hadn't felt in over two years. Weight suits and artificial gravity could compensate somewhat, but she could tell she was out of shape by home standards. Until she saw her mothers.

Aurelia Jones-Quentin had gained a few fine worry lines between her brows and at the corners of her eyes, but her straight, dark brown locks were as grey-free as her son's. Amelia Quentin-Jones had picked up a few more streaks of silver among her lighter brown curls, but no extra lines on her face. They were clad in the same soft pastels the two women had always favored, and both their faces lit up with the same delight as they spotted her in the queue. Just the sight of her parents banished most of the annoying drag of the planet on her body. Gravity could not stop the lifting of her spirits.

As soon as she cleared the last checkpoint, Ia hurried forward. She dropped her bags to the plexcrete floor as her family moved up to meet her, and swept both of her mothers into a hug. Both older women laughed and sniffled and hugged her right back. She'd forgotten how stooping to hug them could put a crick in her back from the awkward angle, but Ia didn't care. Given everything that had happened since she had left, the pain was an old, revived pleasure by comparison.

For a moment, she let herself be a young woman again,

saying good-bye to her family before heading to her destiny. Then one of her brothers ruffled her hair; from the downward pull of his palm, it was Fyfer, too short to have been seen immediately, compared to their elder brother.

"Look at that hair, all short and ugly, now!" Fyfer crowed, ruffling it again.

"Fyfer!" Aurelia scolded.

As her mothers released her, Ia pushed his hand away, then pulled him into a half hug and rubbed her knuckles over his brown locks. He squirmed and spluttered a protest, then twisted into her grip and pinched her inner bicep in the spot she had taught him. Even toughened up by her life in the military, it hurt like hell. Grunting and flinching, Ia released him. Then *oofed* as he flung his arms around her ribs in an enthusiastic hug.

Chuckling, Ia hugged him back. Unlike their elder brother, Fyfer was normal for a Sanctuarian. Naturally muscular, but short and not nearly the brick-walled body that Thorne was. So she squeezed and sort of picked him up. Just a few inches, but enough to prove she was still stronger. He *oofed* in turn, then laughed and slapped her on the back.

"Slag, Ia! You used to pick me up higher than that! What happened to you in the Army?" he joked.

"It was the *Marine Corps*," Ia shot back, dropping him gently onto his feet. "And I've been living in lesser gravity. I've been working out as heavy as I can get it for several hours a day, but still *living* in lightworlder spaces."

Releasing her younger brother, she faced her half-twin. They had different mothers but the same father, both of them born barely half an hour apart. Both were anomalies in a world of gravitationally challenged heights. Thorne just held open his arms, and Ia walked into them, nestling her head on his shoulder and her arms around his waist. He didn't threaten her ribs, just hugged her back.

"*Mizzu,*" he murmured, his voice a quiet bass rumble. *I missed you.* The word was the shorthand speech from their childhood, raised like full-blooded twins, treated like twins, thinking like twins, until her gifts started developing in earnest.

"*Mizzu tu,*" she agreed. *I missed you, too.* She hugged him, relaxing for a long moment . . . until her skin crawled, warning her that her precognitive gift was trying to open, trying to read all the possibilities of his future. Thankfully, the moment she shifted back, he released her. It might have been two years, but he still remembered how touchy her abilities could be.

"You okay?" Thorne asked her as she stepped back. He wasn't the only one giving her a concerned look.

Ia nodded . . . then shook her head. This was more than just the timestreams prickling at his proximity. Holding up her hand, she squeezed her eyes shut and focused on strengthening the walls in her mind. *No. Not right now. Not here and now, among all these people. I will* not *succumb to the Fire Girl Prophecy right now . . .*

Pushing it away, resisting, she breathed hard for a few moments. Someone else screamed, making her jump and snap her eyes open again. It wasn't a member of her family that had collapsed; instead, it was a familiar, purple-wrapped body. The Christian missionary, Amanda Something-or-Other, had dropped to her knees.

"Fire!" Amanda screamed, startling the mostly Human collection of tourists into wide-eyed, wary looks. "Fire! Birds in the sky! A girl—fire in her eyes! Fire in the world! A . . . a cathedral—a wall in the sky—*aaaaaaah!*"

Those who were native to Sanctuary looked at her, too. They, however, weren't confused by her outcry. Instead, they were broken into three groups. A few concerned-looking spaceport personnel hurried forward, mostly to ward off the few concerned tourists who were about to touch her—never a good idea, since the Fire Girl attacks tended to spread on contact more often than not. The rest were either blasé about the attack, looking for a few moments in curiosity before shrugging and moving on, or they hastily backed up, sketching corona-circles on their foreheads and muttering under their breath, no doubt prayers warding off any evil influence from the "demonically possessed."

Since it looked like the missionary would get some of the help she needed, a sketchy explanation of the phenomenon and suitable reassurances from spaceport staff, Ia herself settled into the non-Church category of natives and ignored the poor woman's plight. Stooping, she picked up her kitbag and the locked travel case stuffed with her writing pad and all the postdated letters she had printed out during the journey home. "I'll be fine. We have a lot to do. Move out."

She didn't miss the look her mothers exchanged, nor the glance they shared with Thorne, but Fyfer immediately started chatting about all the things she had missed, his graduation half a year early and subsequent enrollment in an acting school, Thorne's fast-paced progress in his space station governance degree, and of course questions on what her own last two years had been like. Ia did her best to listen and respond, but Fyfer didn't cease the steady stream of chatter until they were at the family ground car, and he finally noticed that Ia wasn't moving to put her things into the vehicle parked on one of the tiers of the spaceport's garage.

Instead, she had stopped, closed her eyes, and was simply breathing. Deep, steady breaths, the kind that sought to fill every last corner of her lungs.

"Hey," Fyfer admonished her. "Are you falling asleep already? I thought you Marines were tough!"

"I'm not *that* tired. I'm just enjoying the smell of home. You don't get ozone like this on other worlds, unless you deliberately go around creating sparks. Or the dampness, or the flickering of lightning pressing through your eyelids like little feathery touches . . ." She sighed and opened her eyes, smiling wryly. "It's just not the same, elsewhere."

"So what *is* it like on other worlds?" Thorne asked her, taking her bags and tucking them into the boot.

She held up her hand and gestured for the others to climb into the car, then took the front passenger seat, her preferred spot so her gifts didn't trigger. Thorne took the driver's seat; with his broad, muscular shoulders, it was either let him drive or be squished in the backseat as he took up half of the space usually meant for three people. Once the doors had slid up into place and they were moving, Ia answered his question.

"What's it like on other worlds? Bouncy, until you get used to the gravity. The air can smell like a million different things. Recycled and dusty if it's a mining domeworld. Slimy and moldy if you've set down in a rainy spot on an atmospheric world, like that planet where we helped out the flood victims. And then there's the recycled air of a starship, with cleaning products and sweating bodies in the gym, lubricants and hydraulics fluids in the mechsuit repair bays . . . and of course the greenery in lifesupport, but they limit access to that part of the ship. The Motherworld didn't smell bad," she added. "Lots of flowers and green growing things. Not enough thunderstorms, but not bad."

"Ooh! Tell us about the Motherworld!" Amelia interjected.

"Yes, please," Aurelia urged Ia. "What's it like? I've always wondered."

Smiling, Ia complied. "My first view was from orbit. It's really not that much different from Sanctuary, except the night-side glows with a million cities, and not from crystal fields and the few settlements we have. And only so many lightning storms can be seen, and only so many aurora curtains and sprite jets . . . You can't really see the lightning on Earth from space unless it's in a really big storm. And then of course my first stop was Antananarivo, on Madagascar Island. It's very tropical in the lowlands, but where I was, which was up in the hills, it's a bit cooler. More like around here."

"That was at the Afaso Headquarters, right?" Thorne asked her, directing the car into the flow of traffic skirting the capital city.

Ia nodded. "That's right. Grandmaster Ssarra says hello, by the way. They have a lot of land, much of it established as a nature preserve as well as farmland for self-sufficiency. There are *lots* of green plants there, compared to here — yes, the grass really *is* greener, on Earth." That made her family laugh. Enjoying their humor, Ia smiled and continued. "They have none of the blue plants like we have, not even as imports, and very few that look even vaguely purple. There are some yellow ones— grass when it's dry, for one—but the first impression you get of a nondesert landscape on Earth is of a million different shades of green . . ."

A door opened down the hall. It was followed by shuffling foot-steps, which were not quite lost under the soft, rhythmic grunts coming from Ia as she measured out a set of sit-ups, toes hooked under the living room couch for counterbalance. Her biomother, Amelia, squinted at her in the light from the reading lamp.

"Gataki mou?" Amelia shuffled a few steps closer, her bare

feet tucked into worn pink slippers and her body wrapped in a fuzzy green bathrobe. "What are you doing, child?"

A little distracted by being called her old, Greek nickname of *my kitten*, Ia struggled to finish the set. Uncurling her stomach after three more crunches, she relaxed on the springy, rubbery floor, breathing hard. "I'm doing my morning calisthenics . . . and I'm really out of shape. I did what I could on the flight from Earth, but . . . I had to leave my weight suit behind. It would've cost too much to transport all that mass."

"Well . . . can you keep it down a little?" her mother asked. Behind her, the door opened again. "And maybe not start so early? I know we changed the beds in your old room so your brothers could have a little more room, which means you have to sleep out here, but . . . well, the floor here in the living room kind of squeaks, and . . ."

"Have you lost all sense of common courtesy?" Aurelia demanded, coming up behind her wife. Being slightly taller, she glared at Ia over her partner's shoulder. "It's five in the morning! Not even your brothers get up until seven at the earliest, and only because Thorne goes to school that early."

"Sorry." Sitting up, Ia shrugged. "I'll go for a run or something."

"In this neighborhood? At *this* hour?" Amelia asked.

Pushing to her feet, Ia arched her brow, looking down at her mothers. "Would *you* mess with someone as tall as me, who can comfortably jog in *this* gravity?"

"No, but we're not talking about vagrants or gang members," Aurelia reminded her daughter. "The Church has been moving more and more converts into this area. They're not going to look kindly on some . . . some solitary weirdo jogging around the block at this hour. Anything that isn't in Church doctrine, they won't like it."

"*And* they'll let you know," Amelia agreed.

Rolling her eyes, Ia swept her hands over her hair, raking back the sweaty locks. "I *do* know, Mother. But I'm going straight into the Naval Academy after this, and they'll be expecting me to stay in shape even while on an Extended Leave."

It didn't matter which one she was addressing. Amelia was Mom, Aurelia was Ma, but both were forever *Mother* to all

three of their kids, and usually addressed as such when the pair
were tag teaming said kids.

Aurelia lifted her finger. "Don't sass us, *gataki*. If you're
going to go jogging, then go. But go *quietly*. Your mother and
I need our sleep. We closed the restaurant for your homecoming
yesterday, but we'll have a busy day of it today, since it's the
end of the week."

"I'll go put on my cammies," Ia offered, holding up her
hands. "Even Church members have seen the occasional episode
of *Space Patrol*, so they should know what a soldier looks
like . . . and I'm just as sure that, by now, everyone who came
into Momma's Restaurant in the last month knows that you've
been expecting me home from the military."

"I suppose that'll have to do," Aurelia muttered. She pointed
a tanned finger at her daughter. "And no more getting up at 'oh
dark hundred,' you got that? That's an order." She folded her
arms across her chest as Amelia turned to eye her. "A mother
always outranks her little girl."

There were several retorts Ia could've made to that, but she
refrained. Her mothers were trying to reduce her to the little
girl they knew and loved—and they were succeeding to a
point—but Ia's universe had changed. It was an uncomfortable,
unhappy realization, acknowledging that her parents were no
longer the center of that universe.

Instead of replying, she sighed and grabbed her kitbag, tucked
at the end of the couch where she had been sleeping. Fishing
out a set of mottled browns, she headed for the bathroom. Amelia
and Aurelia let her pass, then returned to their bedroom.

Her parents had never had much room in their apartment
above the small but popular restaurant: just the two bedrooms,
a bathroom, an office, the living room, and a small nook of a
kitchen, which was rarely used to cook any meal other than
breakfast. Sleeping on the couch wasn't any worse than sleeping
in a tent, and she was already in the habit of tidying her bed,
so folding up the blankets right after waking and rising hadn't
been a problem.

It was the getting up part that seemed to be the problem. *I
forgot to adjust my hours to Mom and Ma's hours, not Sanctuarian hours, on the trip out from Earth. I forgot they don't*

get up until almost 9 a.m. and don't go to bed until midnight—
though I'd think I would've noticed last night how "late" every-
one stayed up, catching up with all the gossip I never bothered
to scry for in the timestreams . . .

Speaking of which, I should check the timestreams, see
what I need to do versus what I should do, while waiting for my
family to wake up again. Better yet, I'll take my writing pad
with me and work on jotting down yet more prophecies elec-
trokinetically while I jog, she decided, slipping out of her plain
brown T-shirt and shorts. It was a little chilly outside, the
weather more autumn-like than late summer, so jogging in long
pants and a long-sleeved shirt wouldn't be too warm. *Three*
hundred years go by awfully fast when you're dead and can't
tell anyone how to stop a galaxy-wide war.

JULY 20, 2492 T.S.

"How much longer?" Fyfer asked, his tone bored.

"If I can put up with Mom and Ma throwing that surprise
welcome home party for me at the restaurant yesterday . . . and
then making me wash all the dishes afterwards," Ia muttered
half under her breath, "*you* can put up with a little drive into
the countryside this morning."

"The question is, how far of a drive?" Thorne asked her.
Once again, he was driving, guiding the family ground car over
the ruts in the unpaved, barely graded road they were following.
Hovercars strong enough to counteract the local gravity were
too expensive for most settlers to afford on Sanctuary, but that
didn't mean the government sank a lot of money into high-
quality back roads, either.

"Yeah, you said you're looking for a crysium field, but we've
already passed three," Fyfer added, shifting forward as far as
his safety restraints would allow, bracing his elbows on the
backs of their chairs.

"One where we won't be interrupted. What I'm about to do,
no one outside of the three of us is to ever know about, and I
do mean *no one*—turn left up ahead," Ia ordered Thorne.

He complied, carefully turning between the red-barked,
purple-leaved trees. The side road she picked wasn't even really

a road, more like a leafer-path. Aquamarine grass had sprung up in the leafer's wake, along with small bushes, making him slow the car. "How much farther? I am not damaging Ma's car on one of your quests if it can be avoided."

"Quarter klick, no more. There's a small clearing of crystals off to the right. Up there," Ia added, pointing ahead at a gap in the growth. "You can just turn around right there. Point the car outward."

"Ia . . . pointing the car *back* the way it came is the new version of the archaic handkerchief-on-the-doorknob trick," Fyfer warned her.

"All the more reason the few who might make it this far will back up and find another spot," Ia countered.

Thorne sighed and carefully jockeyed the ground vehicle around so that it faced back toward the dirt road. "At least with a path this wide, the leafer isn't likely to wake up until late winter at the earliest."

"Another thing I'm counting on." Disentangling herself from the restraints, Ia opened her door and climbed out as soon as the panel had tucked itself beneath the floorboards. Steadying herself against the hard, half-forgotten tug of high gravity, she faced the other way. The partially recovered path ended about a hundred and fifty meters away in what looked like a brush-choked, grass-strewn slope, a modest hill that rose a good twenty-five meters at its crest, twenty or so meters in width, and probably extended for five times that in length. But a leafer was no hill.

Thankfully, it wasn't a carnivore, either. Instead, it was the largest land-based herbivore in the known galaxy. If the beasts could have been tamed and trained, the government of Sanctuary would have done so, but the few times they had tried had proven too disastrous. Leafers were too dumb, too interested in the recyclable plastics and elastics known as plexi—a common prefab building material—and too prone to torpor and months-long hibernation after only a kilometer or so of feeding, depending on the size.

Her brother's assessment was fairly accurate; a quick probe into the local timestreams showed that it wouldn't bother them, so long as they didn't try to climb up and dig a hole through the outer patina of dirt hosting all those bushes on its back.

Closing the car door, she looked over at the field bordering the leafer-path. Rocky outcrops poked up through the ground to the east, a rugged clearing too stony to permit the growth of many trees. A few bushes did their best to cling to pockets of soil, but there was plenty of evidence that this little meadow flooded whenever a heavy rainstorm came through. The back-and-forth cycle of dry-and-drowned kept most plants away from this area, making it the perfect zone for a different sort of growth.

The real growth, slow as it was, came from the sprays of crystals dotting the field, pastel and glowing faintly, just bright enough to be seen even in the light of midmorning.

The predominant color among the shafts was transparent gold, not quite amber, but here and there, other hues could also be seen. Mint green, aquamarine, lilac, and rose. All of them were clear enough to see through. They also ranged in sizes from tiny, sharp-edged sprays no bigger than her head, to towering, conifer-like shapes four times her height. Heading toward them, she stopped when her younger brother gasped, dropping to his knees.

"Fire!" he yelled, clutching at his head, eyes wide and focused on things that weren't there. *"The Phoenix rises! The cathedral on fire—golden birds covering the sky!"*

The attack startled her. She hadn't felt anything building up around her. Normally, those who were the most psychically sensitive suffered the most from the phenomenon, and her brother Fyfer was about as mind-blind as any second-generation resident of Sanctuary could possibly claim to be. Slightly more sensitive than the rest of the Humans in the known galaxy, but only slightly.

Thorne rolled his eyes and aimed a kick at his brother's rump. "Get up. Your acting isn't *that* good."

Laughing, Fyfer dropped his hands and pushed to his feet. He grinned at his siblings, brushing the dirt from his knees. "*You* know I've been practicing . . . but I'll bet I had *her* fooled!"

"If I weren't so sensitive to the buildup of precognitive KI— or rather, the lack of it this time—then yes, I would've been fooled," Ia agreed. "You were good in every other detail I could see."

"Annoying is more like it," Thorne snorted, eyeing his younger brother. He returned his attention to their sister. "So, why are we out here? I'm supposed to be studying for my second big test in Economics."

"We're here to experiment." Ia removed the cuff from her right arm. Not the left one, which was her military ident unit, but the one hidden under her right sleeve. Molding it with a touch of electrokinetic energy to soften the material and a nudge of telekinesis to shape it, she formed it into a round, pink peach sphere. Unlike the sprays, it wasn't completely transparent, as the pink infusing the gold clouded the material. She held it out on the palm of her hand, displaying it to her siblings. "Do you know what this is?"

"A holokinetic illusion?" Fyfer asked, dropping his jester's attitude with a shrug. Underneath the charming jokester, he was quite bright for such a young man. "Or maybe some sort of psychic gelatin? At least, I'm presuming it's one or the other, either holokinesis of something that doesn't exist, or telekinetic manipulation of something that does. Except the last I checked, you weren't a holokinetic."

Thorne, for all that he looked like a walking mountain of muscle, frowned at the sphere on her palm, then looked at the sprays. "It sort of . . . That *can't* be . . . can it? Is that crysium?"

Ia drew out energy from the sphere, making the solid ball sag. She poured energy back into it, enough that her palm crackled with miniature lightning, and the ball crystallized. Literally, it grew crystals, turning into a miniature version of the much larger, cone-spoked spray around them. Both of her brothers swore under their breath, eyes wide.

"How . . . ?" Thorne managed.

"Special abilities," she dismissed, carefully staying vague even in front of her own siblings. "The next person to be able to do this won't come around for another two hundred years . . . and she will *be* Phoenix, the Fire Girl of Prophecy. The thing is, *this* stuff isn't your standard crysium."

Drawing energy out, which destabilized the otherwise tough mineral, she reshaped it as ball, then tossed it at Thorne. He caught it on reflex . . . and stiffened and stared at nothing. Blinked. Breathed. Blinking again, he focused on her. "You . . . this . . . what . . ."

She crossed the few meters between them and plucked the sphere from his palm. "What did you see?"

"The . . . time moved. The day sped up and raced by. The evening lightning storm came by . . . but I *knew* I was still standing here in midmorning," he finished, confusion creasing his brow. "Ia . . . I saw the *future*."

She nodded, and held out the ball to Fyfer. He quirked one of his dark brows but took the crystal ball—and sucked in a sharp breath, as real as the previous one had been faked. He didn't drop to his knees, but he did shudder. Taking pity on him, Ia took it back.

"What did *you* see?" she prodded him when he just blinked and breathed.

"Uh . . . the crew, the other students from school . . . they're going to call me on my wrist unit . . . ask me out to dinner with the group," he revealed.

Ia probed the future, and nodded. "Go ahead and accept . . . but tell them you plan to shift majors at the end of the semester."

"Shift majors?" Fyfer protested. "Why would I want to shift majors? I'm great at acting! I actually enjoy it. Besides, *you* told me to go into acting school."

She pinned her brother with a firm look. "Because I also told you that you would need to shift majors. You're going to start studying law—"

"Law!" he protested, throwing up his hands. "Why me? Why law?"

"And politics," Ia finished. Sphere cupped in her right hand, she ticked off three of the fingers on her left hand. "Rabbit is studying sociology, psychology, and behavioral sciences. Thorne is studying economics, business management, and logistics. *You* need to study law, acting, and politics. I've *told* you this, Fyfer. Over and over and over.

"Rabbit will be in charge of organizing the Free World Colony and its resistance movement. She can write a very moving speech, but she is *not* a public speaker, and thus not a public motivator. We all know that the adults wouldn't take her seriously just because of her size. Thorne will be in charge of the FWC's physical needs, making sure the cities are well-planned and well-provisioned, with strategic defenses, housing and feeding, powering and cleaning needs all carefully considered and arranged. *You* will be the face of the Free World Colony, but you need to be *more* than just a face to motivate people. You need to know the difference between wrong and right, just and unfair, and that means studying acting, politics, and law."

"Only Church slaves study law and politics. All those classes at Thorne's college are filled with forehead-circling fanatics." He wrinkled his nose in disgust, then mockingly scribbled his finger on his forehead, making a face.

Ia gave him a disgusted, sardonic look. "How else did you think the Church was going to take over the government? They're going to do it *by the book*, Fyfer. The Church's leaders have been planning this since they funded their half of the push to find a new heavyworld to settle. It may have been a cosmic accident that they ended up on *this* world along with the saner contingents from Eiaven and the other heavyworld colonies who contributed, but they are here, and we have to deal with them. *Your* job will be to stave off the too-rapid degeneration of Sanctuarian society from within the political and legal framework."

"Isn't there some other way?" Fyfer protested, throwing up his hands. "*Any* other way? You're supposed to be able to see all the twists and turns for a thousand years! Isn't there some other way than . . . than to turn me into a Kennedy, or a Mac-Kenzie, or some other historically big-named *politarazzi*?"

She wished there was. Ia clenched her hands and closed her eyes. She searched on the timeplains, the great, amber-hued prairie of existence crisscrossed by a thousand million life-streams. What she *needed* was a way to show him what his best future path could be, without the trauma of actually dragging him into his own timestream and holding him there. Fyfer had the grace to stay silent while she dipped into stream after stream in rapid, practiced succession, but pouted when she opened her eyes and shook her head, fingers tightening on the ring in her grasp.

"I'm sorry, Fyfer. But I need you to do what I'm telling you. You're very charismatic and quick-witted when you want to be, and you know how to skirt the fine line between believability and showmanship. *You* are going to save a lot of people from slipping into the madness of believing the Church's doctrines and dogmas in the coming years." Ia held his gaze, though she softened her expression. "I *need* you, Brother. I need you to do what I myself cannot.

"*Everyone* on this world needs you . . . and they will need you to study law and politics, so you can *use* those as your sword and shield in the fight against the fanatics of the One True God!" She flung out her left hand in the direction of the city . . . and realized her right hand was no longer clutching a sphere. Instead, it now held a pink peach bracelet, a wrist-sized torus of rippling, stiffened crystal shaped something like either a turbulent stream or a fluttering veil. Confused, Ia stared. She hadn't consciously tried to shape it . . . or . . . had she?

Acting on impulse, Ia grabbed Fyfer's wrist with her free hand and dropped the torus-bracelet-thing on his palm. He shuddered, eyes widening much like they had when it had been a mere sphere, but this time dropped to his knees as well. Sagged, more like it. Thorne hissed and shifted forward, ready to catch Fyfer in case he didn't fall safely, but Fyfer ended up merely kneeling. Rather than touching his brother, Thorne stopped next to him, glancing up in confusion at their sister.

Unsure what was happening to him, Ia extended a finger and brushed his temple very lightly, intending to use her minor telepathic skill to probe his thoughts. What she got instead was swept onto the timeplains next to her brother, who stood waist-deep in the waters of his own stream, his gaze fixed on the surface as scene after scene rushed past. Hissing, she hauled herself out and snatched the overgrown ring from his hand, freeing him as well.

Fyfer sucked in a deep breath and let it out again, coughing a bit. "God! God above!" He blinked and looked up at her. "Is . . . is *that* what you always see? Like a series of 3-D movies, snippets of . . . of moments . . . ?"

Wary, Ia merely asked, "What, specifically, did you see?"

"I . . . saw myself going to law school. It was hard—I could see myself hating you at times, but . . . then I saw what you were talking about. I was in a debate over some council position . . . and I turned some Church woman's arguments upside down and in her face and . . . and I was winning, and it was a rush to win . . ." Fyfer shook his head. "I *never* would've thought I'd like politics. Politics are . . . *ugh*! But, this?"

Patting him on the shoulder, Ia left him to deal with whatever it was he had seen. Whatever it was, it hadn't harmed her cause.

Turning to her other brother, she held out the bracelet. Thorne backed up, hands raised out of accepting range.

"No, no, not me; that's not necessary," he protested. "Honest. I remember all too well my last visit into your timestreams."

"And normally I wouldn't subject you to that again," Ia promised. "But unlike Fyfer, you *know* what that's like . . . and I need to know if *this* is like *that*."

Holding it out, she waited. He shifted, clearly uncomfortable, then wrinkled his nose and held out his palm. Dropping the bracelet onto his skin, she waited. He, too, gasped and sagged to his knees. His eyes blinked, flicking this way and that, no doubt viewing the same timestream images that Fyfer had seen. Or maybe not. After several seconds, her curiosity overwhelmed her, and Ia touched his forehead as well.

What she found shocked her. He *wasn't* seeing his brother's life-choices. Some of them, yes, but only from his own perspective, wherever their lives crossed. Most of what he was seeing were his own possible paths. Since they would continue to live and work together, the two stepbrothers' lives intertwined quite a lot, but the perspective was purely from Thorne's life and its choices. Plucking the bracelet from his hand, Ia waited while he shuddered and recovered.

"Okay . . ." Thorne finally murmured, head nodding slightly. "*How* did you do that, Ia? You weren't even touching me, yet you put all those images in my head!"

"That's what I'm here to find out," Ia confessed, shrugging. She eyed the bracelet on her hand, then set it on the grass-trampled ground. As soon as she released it, the ever-present lurking of the timestreams in the back of her mind diminished just a little bit. Barely enough for her to notice, but it was just enough to detect. Picking it up again, she could hear the faint, psychic "hum" of the crysium, and could once again feel the timestreams crowding a little closer than usual.

Whatever she had done to the bracelet had changed it. This wasn't a brief look into the immediate future by a few minutes, or a few hours. This was a look into the future by months, even years.

The strange, semi-alive biocrystal already defied logic. It was literally the discarded matter of the Feyori. The only known sentient race to have evolved as beings of energy instead of matter, they were the only race in the known galaxy who could manage to convert energy to matter and back at the squared speed of light.

They did so by traveling faster than the fastest spaceship, whether it traveled through normal space by greasing the laws of physics through faster-than-light panels, or by siphoning itself through a hyperrift via other-than-light travel. Because the transformation from one form to the other was never 100 percent complete, it was the Feyori who had introduced psychic abilities—using energy to manipulate matter, rather than the other way around—into the sentient races they had secretly bred with over the millennia.

The converse was also true. When they shifted back to energy-based bodies, the Feyori took a little bit of matter across with them. The easiest way to shed it and "purify" themselves was to find a world with a high enough gravity to pull it out of their bodies. By preference, they preferred high-energy worlds where they could "snack" at the same time. Sanctuary, with its churning core of both molten iron and gold, had a natural electrosphere as well as a natural magnetosphere. Lighting was nothing more than candied popcorn to the Feyori, making it a favorite dumping ground.

That dumped matter, discarded in the form of dust, combined itself with rainwater and the constantly generated energies from the storms plaguing Sanctuary every day. Seeded on bare rocks like the ones scattered through this field, the solution crystallized into sprays, with growth dependent upon just how much energy each shaft received. It was too tough to be cut, too difficult to break in all but the thinnest of shafts, and too bizarre for anyone to figure out how to use . . . unless they knew the secrets of both its origins and its strength, as Ia did.

But what to do with it? How to do it?

"Ia?" Thorne finally asked, catching her attention. She looked down at him. He shrugged. "What's going on?"

"I'm not sure, but . . . I *think* this is the solution to my not being able to be in two, or three, or five hundred different places at once. Follow me," she ordered, tucking the bracelet into one of the pockets on her brown military pants.

Without looking back, she headed into the middle of the

field, looking for an easily overlooked spray. Selecting one, she touched the shaft. This time, the humming resonance was louder in her mind; this was a full-sized shaft on a spray twice as tall as her body. She only needed some of it, however.

Concentrating on the flow of energies, she siphoned off just enough to pull away a chunk barely the size of her head, then carefully reshaped the end of the shaft so that it looked whole and untouched. Only someone who intimately knew each and every shaft would be able to tell this one was now shorter. Settling on the ground, Ia prepped the lump she had separated. Carefully dividing it into eight fist-sized chunks, she shaped them into balls with a thought, then looked up.

Fyfer and Thorne had followed her, thankfully. She held out a sphere to each of them. Both hesitated. At the arch of her brow, each of her half brothers settled on the ground across from her and took a clear pink sphere.

Tense, they waited for the future to once again drag them under.

CHAPTER 2

All throughout my early career, I knew that there would be more than one war we'd have to fight. Everyone could see the Salik were going to work free of the Blockade, sooner or later. That one was a given. That it had worked as well as it had for roughly two hundred years was a small miracle—not to say it worked perfectly, but it did work well up to a point. However, there was another war brewing, one back home.

Fanaticism is dangerous—oh, laugh if you must, given my reputation and all, but it is dangerous. Fanaticism paired with a power trip is what really shakks the universe . . . uh, can I say that? You'll edit it out if needed? Good . . . Part of the problem with fanaticism, you see, is that people tend to get so blinded by their zeal that they lose their way. Often quite badly, to the point where they pave that path not only straight to hell but via the scenic route of violence and destruction, becoming just another variation of what they usually claim they oppose.

In my case . . . I can't lose my way. It's shoved in my face every single day. Whether I'm awake or dreaming, it doesn't matter. I have to double-check every single centimeter of the path I'm taking, over and over and over. One tiny deviation left uncorrected could throw off a hundred years' worth of preparations.

*So yes, I knew there was a civil war brewing back home.
I knew every trick the other side would try to use. And
somehow, I had to find a way to counter that, so that there
would be some hope of my people surviving long enough
to escape the coming destruction. My biggest problem,
however, was convincing people what to do when I wasn't
even there . . . and contrary to popular belief, I am mortal,
and will not live forever. Certainly not for the full three
hundred years my messages need to survive.*

~Ia

After several silent seconds, Thorne shook his head slowly.
"Nothing is happening."

"Yeah," Fyfer agreed, frowning. "Aren't we supposed to be
seeing the future again, or something?"

Ia shook her head. "That's not what raw crysium does,
though I'm glad to see it confirmed. No, it was during the battle
to free my superiors and fellow sergeants that something strange
happened to my sword."

"The crystal one we shipped to you?" Fyfer asked.

She nodded and patted the lump hiding in her thigh pocket.
"The one and the same as the bracelet-thing you just held.
I kind of had to reshape and hide it after . . . Well, what happened was, I kind of lost my grip on it, dropping it, and one
of the Lyebariko guards got ahold of it just as I grabbed the
blade."

Both men hissed. Fyfer wrinkled his nose. "How long did
it take for the Marines to reattach your fingers?"

"He didn't actually cut them off," Ia corrected, flexing her
fingers absently. "Luckily, I had managed a pressure-grip on
the sides to stop him from slicing completely through, and I
reshaped it so that *I* had the hilt. But . . . I think some of my
blood was incorporated into the crystal when I reshaped it. So.
We are going to test this theory."

Picking up one of the clear crystals from the ground, she
reshaped it with just a few thoughts into a short, sharp blade.
Fyfer's eyes widened, while Thorne's narrowed.

"You're going to cut yourself again, only this time deliberately?" her older brother asked.

"More to the point, I'm going to ask *you* to cut yourselves. Hand me the spheres," Ia ordered.

"Are you out of your mind?" Fyfer protested.

Ia leaned over and plucked the spheres from her brothers' hands. "I need control samples." Softening and prodding each one with her fingertip, forming a small divot, she handed Thorne his sphere and the blade. "Just a few drops, that's all I need."

He gave her a dark look, but accepted blade and ball. "You're asking a lot."

"I know." A beeping interrupted her before she could say more. All three of them jumped. Fyfer's wrist unit beeped again. Feeling foolish since she'd forgotten about it already, Ia lifted her chin, giving her brother permission to answer the call.

Knife in hand, Thorne addressed her under his breath while their brother flipped up the battered grey screen and greeted his caller. "Are you going to heal this when I'm done?"

"Of course," she snorted. "For one, you know where I'm currently sleeping. For another, you'd probably sic both our mothers on me."

"Nice to know you didn't lose *all* of your wits when you joined the military," he quipped back, carefully cutting into the edge of his palm. Ia shifted forward again, rocking onto her knees to help catch the trickle of crimson seeping from the wound in the crystal. Pinching the crysium shut over the sample of blood, Ia concentrated, molding the crystal with her gifts until it was a homogenous shade of translucent pink.

Covering the cut with her free hand, she closed her eyes and concentrated on her brother's body. It wasn't easy to heal others, particularly as it was a matter of "convincing" his body to speed up the natural healing process, but her brother was familiar, despite the last two years of separation. That, and his body responded well to psychic stimulation, given how they shared a father. It didn't take long for her to pull her hand away, showing a sealed cut instead of a seeping one.

Fyfer ended his call, snapping shut the viewscreen of his cheap plexi wrist unit. "Okay, so they know I'll be there tonight, and that I have some unspecified news to share." Sighing, he raked his free hand through his dark, shoulder-length curls. "But honestly, Ia, a lawyer? Me? Why not him?" he asked, gesturing at Thorne. "I could've been a spaceport organizer, you know. I *am* quite brilliant."

Both Ia and Thorne quirked their brows skeptically at that. Fyfer flushed and grumbled under his breath. Shaking her head, Ia corrected him. "Both of you are brilliant, but in different ways. Thorne is better at organizing things, keeping track of business details, handling the accounting and the economizing. You are better at public speaking, rousing enthusiasm, and keeping track of people-based details. There are reasons for every choice I am asking you to make . . . and reasons for you to accept and embrace them. Now cut yourself."

Thorne cuffed her, making her yelp and rub her bicep. "Say 'please' and 'thank you.' You're not in the military right now, you know."

"Or rather, *we're* not," Fyfer amended, accepting the blade from his brother. He wiped it on the grass, then on his dark blue trousers, then carefully cut his hand in more or less the same spot as his brother had his. "If you're right about me knowing how to handle people, then here's some advice. Nectar catches sticker-bugs faster than vinegar or water."

"*Please* cut yourself and donate a few drops of blood to my experiment, Brother." Ia helped him collect the blood, then molded it into his sample sphere, too. "Thank you."

"Aren't you going to heal him?" Thorne prompted her.

Ia nodded, setting down the second sphere. Covering Fyfer's hand, she focused her kinetic inergy into the wound, that peculiar not-electromagnetic energy all psychics could tap. When she pulled her hand away, his cut was clotted, though not quite as healed as Thorne's now looked.

"Okay . . . now what?" Fyfer asked when she sat back.

"Now we see if there's anything unusual about your sphere." Picking it up, she tossed it at her younger brother.

He caught it in his cupped hands, blinked, then held it, rolled the ball between his fingers, and finally shrugged. "It's crysium. Pink, slightly cloudy crysium. *How* you made it a ball, I don't know, but it's hard and cool to the touch, and that's it. No images, no future impressions, nothing."

He lobbed it at Thorne, who caught it, held it, and shrugged as well. Thorne tossed it back to their sister. "Crystal. Nothing more."

Ia caught it and set it down by her right knee, the side Fyfer was sitting on. Picking up Thorne's blooded sphere, she tossed it at Fyfer first, wanting to see what his reaction would be. He bobbled it for a moment, trapped it against his chest, then held it. Fyfer started to shrug, then paused, frowned, and scratched at the edge of his left hand . . . then looked at his skin, frowning.

"What the . . . slag? Look at that, it's healing faster." He shrugged and scratched his head. "At least, it itches like it's healing fast."

"Pass it to Thorne. Please," Ia added. He complied, and their eldest sibling held it, frowned softly, and rubbed at the side of his hand. "Well?"

"I'm not sure, but . . . I think he's right. Maybe. Here," he said, handing it back to Fyfer. "You hold it in your left hand, and if your cut heals faster than mine, we'll know it's the crystal. I've always healed faster than you, naturally."

"Thanks to a very minor biokinetic propensity," Ia murmured, nodding in agreement. Both of her brothers looked at her. She shrugged. "It was nothing strong enough to bother with getting you trained, but I knew it was there—don't go there," she added, lifting her finger to cut off Fyfer's indrawn breath. "That's the wrong line of inquiry, and it would be dangerous as well as fruitless if you tried to look for the right one. Let it be, Brothers. *No one* must know how to manipulate and amplify crysium until it's the right time. No one but me."

"You know, you'd *think* it would be great, having a sister who could literally foresee the future . . . but no. It's more of a pain in the *asteroid*," Fyfer quipped sardonically. "Will there ever come a question where you give us the full answer?"

"Maybe." Her lips curled up in a wicked grin as he groaned.

"So, what now?" Thorne asked her. "Are you going to cut yourself, or is that torture reserved just for us?"

"Hush, I'm developing a theory," she muttered, thinking. Picking up one of the untainted, clear pink spheres, she studied it. "I think first . . . I should try and turn this into another torus. Bear with me. And don't touch me."

"Trust me, we know better," Fyfer muttered.

With the sphere gripped lightly in her hands, Ia focused her mind down and in, flipping it fully onto the timeplains. The blue and purples of the forested hills around them, the golds and pastels of the crystal sprays, and her brothers, Thorne in shades of dark green and Fyfer dressed in dark blue, vanished from view. In its place, a sunbaked, grassy plain undulated in all directions to the far, far horizon.

Stepping up out of the waters of her own timestream, Ia focused on finding the right path. Off in the future, downstream by three hundred or so years, most every life-stream ended, destroyed by the invading might of the Zida"ya, or the Soor, as they had been nicknamed by their ancient enemy. One stream, however, one convergence of actions and destinies, broke through that desert, saving and restoring the rightful lives of all those future generations.

Skimming the waters, their surfaces glimmering with glimpses of different moments in time, she followed that path, or rather, tangle of paths . . . then came back to herself with a deep indrawn breath. Ia opened her eyes as she exhaled. She knew her gift was strong, too strong to risk anyone touching her when she ventured fully onto the timeplains. The bracelet-like object now cradled in her hands told her that, combined with the peculiarities of crysium, her precognition could activate her other gifts as well, and do so without conscious thought.

Specifically electrokinesis, drawing energy out of the crystal to soften its otherwise impermeable surface, and telekinesis, shaping it into this rippling ring thing. Her battle precognition had without a doubt been trained by her efforts to work in tandem with her other abilities during combat, dodging shrapnel, firing at targets, whatever it took. But this was proof it could happen outside of any conscious need as well.

Ia picked Thorne, offering him the ring. "Here. See if you can sense anything."

Taking it from her, he started to say something, then hesitated. Thorne blinked and stared at nothing. After a long moment, he shook it off. "It's . . . not as strong as the ring. The first one, I mean. But . . . I could see things. Little hints of things. I couldn't place them in time though. Nothing pinpointed to a specific hour or date."

He offered it to Fyfer, who took it, hesitated, and stared. It took him longer to come back to himself, and when he did, their younger brother quickly dropped the ring on the ground. It *chinged* off a piece of rock and thumped into a patch of dirt.

"Something wrong?" Thorne asked.

Fyfer scrubbed his right hand, then quickly shifted the translucent pink sphere out of his left hand. "*Ah* . . . yeah. Sort of. The cut's almost healed . . . and whatever this trick is, Ia, you *have* to put in some sort of time-limit modifier," he warned his sister. "This one wasn't as strong as the first ring, but it took effort to pull away from the images I was seeing. The previous one . . . it was too intense. I couldn't stop looking."

Thorne nodded.

"Duly noted," she murmured. Leaning forward, Ia picked up both the clear ring and the blade. The ring, she put into her other thigh patch-pocket. Then she carefully cut her hand and bled onto a clean sphere, molded the blood into the ball, and flipped her mind onto the timeplains.

This time, she limited herself to key moments—nothing specific, just whatever caught her eye in the shifting images of the streams she passed, soaring through the amber-hued skies in her mind—and limited herself firmly to just a few minutes. When she pulled out and came back to herself, the pink-clouded sphere had become more of an oval-shaped ring.

This time, when Fyfer tried it, he stayed enthralled for only a little while. Glancing at the chrono on the bracer-style wrist unit covering her left forearm, Ia timed it. Two minutes and thirteen seconds Standard later, he came back to himself and set the ring on the ground. Thorne tried it as well . . . and came back to himself after only one minute forty-nine seconds. The moment she announced that in a puzzled murmur, both her brothers frowned. Fyfer snatched up the ring again.

"Time it again," Fyfer told her.

". . . Two minutes, two seconds," Ia told him when he blinked out of whatever it was he was seeing. While Fyfer recovered, Thorne tried it a second time. Ia monitored the length of that session as well. "And your trip was two minutes, thirty-six seconds this time."

Thorne frowned, rubbed at the nape of his muscular neck, then shrugged. "I suppose that makes sense, since I saw something different this time. It was important, but not the same. You?"

Fyfer nodded. "Something different each time," he agreed. "The question now is what good is this peek-into-the-future ability for anyone else? We know what *you* can do with it, but anyone else?"

"Well, I'm *hoping* to make use of it in convincing people to follow me when I'm no longer around to give directives," Ia admitted. "But . . . I have very little clue as to what I'm doing. I know I've seen something *like* this in the timestreams," she added, lifting the latest, wrist-sized ring. "But it was sized to fit on someone's head, and there were two types: one to encourage people, and one to discourage them."

"So just ask your future self how to make them!" Fyfer groused, rubbing at the edge of his palm. "Why bother experimenting on us?"

"Because I *can't* ask my future self how to make them. It's like . . . like watching a vid with the sound turned off," Ia offered, groping for an analogy her brothers could understand. "You can kind of get the gist of what's happening in the show, but without the words and the noises, you're just as likely to get only parts of it right and parts of it wrong. Only in this case, I can see the sights and hear the sounds, but I cannot *be* inside my own head, listening to my own thoughts, when crafting these things.

"Which I'll do at some point in the future. Even my abilities have their limits." Dropping the ring on the ground, she sighed. Idly, she touched one of the remaining, undifferentiated crystal balls. The transparent sphere didn't do anything special, other than look pink and round rather than crystalline and fractal.

"Predestination paradox," Fyfer offered, making her look up. He shrugged. "You're the only one who knows how all of this weirdness works, so you're the only one who could possibly crack open the mysteries of it . . . which means you actually have to do the work." Leaning forward, Fyfer smirked and poke-tapped her on the forehead a couple of times. "*No* cheating by copying someone else's notes on *this* life-test, Sister."

She stuck out her tongue at him. He stuck out his in return. Thorne raspberried them both, breaking up their silent fight with a bout of snickering. Calming down, he shook his head, his braid sliding across his shoulders. "Enough. This ground is hard, and my asteroid is growing numb. I'd like to get moving again soon. Besides, a handful of bracelets, or circlet-things, won't be enough to go around. You're asking me to plan for a population base of several million. We barely have a third of a million people on Sanctuary right now, and that's only because Population Expansion is subsidizing large families, with every wombpod in every crèche producing full time."

Fyfer sighed and propped his elbows on his knees, plucking at a tuft of something greenish blue attempting to grow up through the dried mud coating the rocky ground. "I would've loved to have had a few more siblings. A pity Mom and Ma decided they couldn't handle another round of pregnancies, and couldn't afford any more mouths to feed, even if Pop Ex footed the bill."

"You'll have plenty of kids of your own to look after," Ia promised him. "Both biological ones and ones from wombpod manufactories."

"Yeah, with what money?" Fyfer shot back. "You also said Pop Ex will be in the hands of the Church by then, and all their wombpods with them."

"I told you, you'll get the numbers when the time is right," she admonished him. "Just keep buying tickets, handpicking each and every set of numbers. Then you'll be able to afford your own version of Population Expansion."

A quick exchange of looks with her older brother promised Thorne that *he* would get the right numbers first, and be the one to dole them out at the right moment. She knew the many burdens she was piling onto his shoulders, but Ia had little choice. Fyfer was still too young for the heavy responsibilities waiting for him. How ironic that she, who had so little time to spare, was being forced by Time to be patient.

Changing the subject, Ia gathered up the rings. "Obviously, something in my blood is enough to trigger precognitive episodes. And something in the shape of these lumpy rings does it as well, if not quite to the same degree. But combining the two makes it far more effective than either one alone.

"The question is, how much of a combination will make it effective? I can't exactly open up a vein and bleed myself to death; that's counterproductive," Ia stated, mulling through the problem. "I'll have to experiment to see what size dose of blood is an absolute requirement, and experiment to see what size and shape of crystal is the best. Not to mention the differences between positive and negative reinforcement. And I'll have to pull it off *before* I leave . . . and then figure out how to get *enough* blood into them . . . I don't know. I don't know how I could possibly fit enough blood into the few windows of opportunity I'll have, the few times I'll be coming back here."

"Not without bleeding yourself to death," Fyfer agreed. "I may grumble and gripe, but I really don't want to lose you. Particularly to something stupid."

She gave him a wry half smile. "Thanks."

Thorne shrugged, rubbing his chin. "Why not . . . make a whole bunch of tiny little spheres, and just have us ship 'em to you? Standardized sizes, each one dosed with a few drops, and you mix 'em up, resphere 'em, and ship 'em back to us? That way you can donate a few drops every day without worry about massive blood loss."

"Uh, presuming the blood doesn't go bad in transit, that is," Fyfer cautioned both of them. "That may be a factor you'll have to consider."

Ia shook her head, fishing out her original bracelet from its thigh-pocket. "I bled on this one months ago, and it hasn't changed color, let alone lost strength as far as I can tell. Not that *I* can tell much, since I can barely sense it augmenting my abilities . . . but based on your reactions, it's still quite strong."

"A literal drop in the bucket of your abilities, no doubt," Thorne agreed, eyeing her from head to toe. He lifted his chin at the rings in her hands. "Figure out how much blood you need, and how big a crystal ball or bubble to preserve it, then go from there."

"A ball, I'd think. And . . . only a marble in size. I can always combine little spheres into large ones, but a bubble would only let the blood spoil. Blending it is what seems to preserve it." Lifting her gaze to the crystals surrounding them, she tried to calculate how much she would need. "I'll need to convert several dozen mature sprays, at the very least . . . but that's a task for another day."

"Have you given any thought as to how you'll explain shipping all those beads back and forth?" Fyfer asked his sister.

Ia shrugged. "Something along the lines of 'holy beads' shaped and blessed by an active-duty warrior, something-something local religious beliefs. I *am* listed as a Witan priestess in my Service records, for all that I'm not serving as a chaplain."

"We'll back it up, if anyone calls home and asks," Fyfer dismissed, flicking his hand.

Thorne nodded in agreement and pushed to his feet, stretching. Ia, still seated on the ground, started gathering up the tainted and clear scraps of crysium, stuffing them into her pockets.

Fyfer stood and stretched as well. He scratched his stomach, then shrugged and tipped his head. "Watching you mold that stuff while you were in your little trance reminds me of an old saying . . ."

"Oh? Which one?" Ia asked, looking up at him. The slightly bloodied, crystalline knife they had used finished dulling and turning into an oblong, safe-to-handle blob in her fingers.

"That any sufficiently advanced science is indistinguishable from magic. I know you said—or rather, implied—that it's some sort of special psychic gift," he told her, holding up his hands. "And that we're not supposed to ask questions or speculate or whatever, but . . . it looked more like magic than science, just now."

"Well, maybe I could've made a great stage magician," Ia quipped, smiling. "You never know, we could have some Mankiller blood in our family tree. Speaking of magic, and thus vanishing acts, I need to make sure I contact Rabbit today. You'll need a safe place on Sanctuary to store all my 'blood beads,' for lack of a better term. I figure the best place for that is deep in the caverns, down where the Church won't find them."

Fyfer lifted his chin at her. "When you do, tell her I said hi, and that I'll call her soon, alright? Unlike *some* people who never use their wrist units to *call* anyone . . . or rather, didn't bother to ask for her number."

"I did ask, but I rarely call her because she rarely *wears* her wrist unit," Thorne retorted. "Which you'd know if you ever bothered to talk *with* her, instead of just *at* her."

Ia rolled her eyes. "Stop it. Both of you. She likes you *both*. She *will* like you both. This is not a competition for her affections, nor can it ever be. The three of you working together as one unit is a force not even Time can stop, and I need you to *be* that united force."

"Well . . . you could've at least picked out another woman for one of us!" Thorne protested.

"The only other women out there are ones who would resent

the demands of your tasks. Rabbit believes as much as both of you do. Be grateful that you *will* be able to get along so well, and that you'll all have each other for company. Some people aren't that lucky."

Fyfer smirked. "Careful, Sister, you sounded almost jealous, there. Haven't you picked out someone for yourself, yet? You've got an infinite number of possibilities to choose from, after all."

Ia merely quirked a brow at him. "*When*, exactly, would I have time for a relationship?"

"Oh, that's right, I forgot. The Prophet of a Thousand Years is a slagging *martyr*. Maybe they should've nicknamed you the Virgin Mary, instead of Bloo—*OW!*" Wincing, Fyfer flinched back from a second backhanded blow. He rubbed his bruised bicep and glared at his stepbrother.

Thorne lifted his arm in warning of a third attack, his stare now focused on the youngest of the siblings. "Get in the car. And *think* before you open your mouth again!"

"It's alright, Thorne," Ia muttered, pushing to her feet. "He's not saying anything I haven't thought, myself. I *am* female, Little Brother," she added, fixing Fyfer with a sardonic look. "I do have urges and needs. I just don't have the time to spare. Or the energy. I do not, however, look upon it as an act of *martyrdom*. All I'm doing is giving up sex with someone else, not to mention avoiding the risk of that someone being dragged onto the time-plains with me during intimate contact. That's hardly a life-altering loss, which is what martyrdom requires."

"Says someone who's clearly never *had*—I'm going, I'm going!" Fyfer yelped and skipped back as his older brother swung at him again. Not with his full strength, of course; Thorne was readily capable of breaking bones without breaking a sweat. He was also normally quite gentle. Just the swipe of his hand through the air between them was enough warning to make the younger man retreat.

"Leave him alone, Thorne," Ia muttered, dusting herself off. "In the first place, he's upset that I'm making him go into law school instead of continuing as an actor. In the second, he's unhappy that I'm encouraging you to flirt with Rabbit. Just like *you're* upset that I'm letting him flirt with her, too." Walking with him toward the ground car, she raised her voice enough so that Fyfer would hear as well. "Just . . . both of you, would you *try* to keep your heads out of your pants for at least a few more years? Please?

"See?" she added, pressing the latch button and waiting for the door to swing down out of the way. "I *do* remember common courtesies. It's just that usually they have a rank attached to them. The only problem is, you don't have any rank."

Thorne snorted. "Maybe you should *give* me a rank, given how I'm supposed to be marshalling all these impending resources for your little colonial survival scenario."

"Dibs on General!" Fyfer called out, ducking into the backseat before either of them could protest.

"Don't be ridiculous," Thorne snorted, climbing in across from Ia. "One look at your scrawny frame, and they'll flock to *me* for war field leadership."

"Ha! They'd be flocking to you to *hide* behind," Fyfer shot back.

"Oh, please," Ia groused. "*I'm* the one in the military, remember? *I* get to be the general in this family. Just . . . not yet. Besides, you'll need a Security Chief long before you'll need a General of the Armed Forces, and that spot is already reserved for someone else. Now, take us back home, Thorne. Please," she remembered to add.

He looked at her, not yet activating the generator. "Didn't you want to go get a larger chunk of crysium to experiment with, first?"

She didn't quite slap her forehead, but mostly because she was fumbling with releasing the restraints instead of buckling them in place. "Right! Right . . . I'll be right back."

"And shape it so it doesn't *look* like a chunk of crysium?" he called out after her, his voice following her into the crystal patch. "Since it's supposed to be a big *secret*, and all!"

Ia flicked her hand over her shoulder, silently acknowledging and dismissing the rather obvious advice.

Unlike Thorne, who constantly wore his wrist unit, but disliked using it out of some silly fear of accidentally aiming the video pickups into his nostrils, Rabbit didn't like wearing hers very often. Rabbit believed that Church-planted members of the government were attempting to infiltrate the emergency services systems, which used a wrist unit's transponder to track the movements of each citizen. It was just one more step, she felt, that the Church of the One True God was taking on a path toward a coup of the colonyworld's government, and a totalitarian level of control over its colonists.

Ia had never disabused her friend of that seemingly wild idea. She knew better. So she knew that Rabbit didn't always wear her wrist unit. Thorne might not *like* using his to talk with people, but he did wear it every day. Then again, he had classes to attend, public transport to catch, and myriad responsibilities requiring identification and a link to his bank account. Rabbit was independently wealthy, thanks to a little help from Ia and a sizeable winning lottery ticket, and preferred walking wherever possible. Then again, her lighter mass made it easier for her to walk everywhere.

So Ia knew better than to call Rabbit on her wrist unit. Instead, Ia dipped into the timestreams once she was done creating a small pile of marble-sized beads back home. Ia carefully verified that her friend hadn't changed her mind and gone spelunking in the many ancient lava caves and tunnels under the plateau on which the capital city, Our Blessed Mother, had been built, and headed into the heart of the city.

Rabbit's gang wasn't hanging out at the old haunts anymore. Ia didn't bother to probe the past as to why. It could have been an economic downturn; it could have been pressure from the Church which closed the previous business, or whatever reason, but it didn't really matter. Rabbit and company had moved their hang-out location from a restaurant serving spicy V'Dan-style cuisine to a Terran Italian restaurant named "Frrrangelico's" . . . with a triple *R* for a reason.

Frrrangelico, the owner, was a Solarican: a furred, bipedal, tail-bearing, claw-fingered, felinoid sentient race. It was rumored they had colonies scattered all across the Milky Way, not just in the unfashionable sub-arm containing the region colloquially referred to as the "known galaxy." It was known, however, that their home system was located as far above the flat plane of the galaxy as Earth was located out from its core; the only reason why they had managed to colonize other worlds was because of a peculiarity of space, or rather, hyperspace, near their home system.

As a race, they were almost as careful as the spider-like K'katta in getting along with others. Most people assumed it was because the Solaricans were so powerful, they could afford to be polite. Ia knew it was simply a matter of logistics. The Solarican Empire was so widely spread, each pocket of settlement had to be as autonomous as possible when it came to self-defense; they simply couldn't afford the large fleet everyone assumed they surely must have, not without stripping vital protections from the other pockets of settlements around the galaxy.

The spider-like K'katta, with their dual skeletal systems, bones on the inside, and chiton on the outside, had evolved in 2.3Gs Standard. The four-armed Gatsugi, amphibious Choya, and the equally amphibious but blockaded and interdicted Salik couldn't tolerate more than twice the Standard measurement for habitable-world gravity; their physiology simply wasn't capable of withstanding that much compression.

Solaricans had evolved in gravity just a little above 1G Standard; like Humans, they could tolerate three times as much gravity *if* they were bred for it, which always took a few generations per half-G. In fact, most of their colonyworlds in the known pocket of the galaxy were above the dividing line of 1.5Gs Standard, classifying them officially as heavyworlders in the Alliance lexicon, since that was the majority of their local population. So while it wasn't common for an alien to live on Sanctuary, with its gravity of 3.21Gs, it wasn't unheard of, either.

Not that the non-Human residents would be here for much longer, Ia knew. It was a fact not only underscored by her forays into the timestreams, but by the presence of a middle-aged diner attempting to lodge a protest in the front lobby as Ia entered. Frrrangelico, his grey and cream ears flattened so low that the earrings piercing the back edge couldn't be seen, was attempting to keep his teeth from showing as he patiently dealt with the vocal woman.

"—if I'd choked on it?" the middle-aged redhead was grousing, flicking her hand through the air. "Not only is it unhygienic, I could've died!"

"Meioa . . . perrrhaps in your agitation, you are exaggerrrating?" the Solarican male asked patiently.

"Well, maybe I'm allergic!" she snapped. "It *was* a cat hair!

I demand a refund—and you can bet I'll get this place shut down for health code violations, too!"

Rolling her eyes, Ia stepped in. Literally, between the two. That forced the woman to look up, since her eyes were at the level of Ia's brown-covered breasts, and that meant she had to take a step back to save herself from neck-strain.

"Meioa," Ia stated calmly, "the odds of you experiencing an allergic reaction of *any* sort are as high as a meteorite successfully striking Our Blessed Mother Cathedral. *Every* Human on this world, native or traveler, has been inoculated with the *jungen* virus. As for the health code, it's clearly posted outside this restaurant that there are Solaricans on staff . . . and I can see a row of certificates on the wall in here guaranteeing they passed inspection earlier this year, and have passed them every year."

Ia smiled, a polite curve of her mouth, and waited.

With a twist of her mouth that wasn't anything near polite, the red-haired woman turned and headed for the door. She muttered an insult as she left, though, glancing briefly, darkly at Ia before shoving open the door. "*Animal* lover . . ."

While there had been quite a lot of religious turmoil among each of the sentient races after finally contacting and confirming the existence of other extrastellar intelligences, such turmoil had died down within a century or so. Particularly after each religious faction had compared notes across species, which was what the Unigalactan movement had been all about. God, it was finally—if grudgingly—admitted by most faiths, had created a wide variety of sentient races, beings who were smart enough to ask the ultimate question of *why*, smart enough to codify similar actions as immoral, unethical, or unjust, and smart enough to be able to compare and find more similarities than differences across the xenodivide.

Calling an alien an animal in this day and age was therefore an ugly accusation, beneath the vast majority of sentientkind. It also squarely pegged the woman as a Church follower. Then again, the muttered growl from the proprietor, spoken in his native dialect, wasn't entirely nice, either. Chuckling, Ia turned to face him.

"Anatomically impossible where *that* particular meioa is concerned," she quipped, smiling with her lips covering her teeth. "But I thank you for the laugh."

Frrrangelico's ears flicked up. "You speak my language?"

He asked it in Terranglo, the trade tongue of the known galaxy. Ia replied in the same, shrugging. "Understand, yes. Speak? Not so much. I'm told my accent is terrible. Like I'm talking with a mouthful of topadoes."

The owner lifted a finger, foreclaw slightly extended. "Human orrr Solarican, you're not supposed to talk with yourrr mouth full. Now, for your help, dessert is on the house. Dinnerr, you'll have to pay forrr . . . since she'll probably be back. Or someone like herr."

"I know they'll be back. For dessert, I'll have the chulia nut and chocolate cannolis," Ia told him, nodding at the menu posted on the wall. "For dinner, the chef's special, rauela in a Frangelico sauce with topado noodles, Sanctuary size. No mushrooms, though. And I'll take an extra tall ice water, and some garlic bread to start."

"You got it, meioa," he promised. He flicked his hand, with its five fingers and thumb, bare skin on the palm and velvet-short fur on the back, gesturing forward another Solarican hovering in the archway between the restaurant's corridor-like foyer and the kitchens. "Marranna will show you to a good table."

Ia held up her own hand. "Actually, I'll be eating with the kids. Just bring it to the back when it's ready."

Both Solaricans eyed her from head to foot. Frrrangelico flicked his ears, making his rings chink against each other. "On yourrr head, Human. If you get into any fights, dessert is no longerrr on the house."

"You'rrre wasting your time. They won't listen to a rrre-cruiter," the waitress added, shaking her head. Like Frrrangel-ico, her ears were decorated with rings, though hers were black-tipped, matching her hands and arms; the rest of her fur was a plush grey. "I'll show you to a table in frrront."

"I'm not here to recruit, and I don't start fights. I'm actually one of Rabbit's friends," she explained. Both Solaricans perked their ears in surprise, and comprehension. Frrrangelico blinked a moment later.

"Militarrry? You must be Ia! Marranna, this is Ia, the Seerrrr girl!" He added a spate of words in Solarican, then turned back to Ia. "If you can answerrr my questions, *dinnerrr* is also on the house!"

"I'll be paying for it," Ia told him. "Because you won't like my answer. You will have four, maybe five, more years, then you *must* leave. All of you," she added, glancing not just at the other Solarican, but at the archway to the kitchens, including the rest of his staff in her gaze. "Stay six years, and it won't be safe."

"Five yearrrs?" Frrrangelico protested, ears flattening again. "Isn't therrre anything we can do? This worrrld is as much *my* home—"

"Not at the expense of others, it isn't," Ia stated, cutting him off. He started to protest again, as did his waitress. She flicked up both hands, fingers spread and curved like claws. Both Solaricans stilled at the signal. Ia snapped her hands together, one inverted over the other, fingers forming a cage in front of her sternum. *"Arrraoull rrrall sinn ah!"*

Frrrangelico wrinkled his muzzle-like nose. "You'rrre rright. Your accent *is* terrrrible. But the Starrrs Have Spoken, eyah?"

"The Stars Have Spoken," Ia agreed. It was the Terranglo translation of the ancient oath used by the Seers—the psychics—of the Solarican race. She shrugged. "I'm sorry I can't give you any better news."

He grunted. "About what I'd expect, consulting an orrraclc. As forrr the otherrr thing . . ."

"Your progeny will be healthy; that's all you need know," Ia stated bluntly. "Now, if you don't mind, I need to go have a talk with Rabbit and her friends."

"Eh, go. But no fighting," he ordered, lifting a claw again. "And worrrk on yourr accent."

Nodding, Ia headed down the hall. To the right were the kitchens, and to the left the main part of the restaurant. Straight back and around the corner to the right, past the lavatories and a storage closet, was a room big enough for a modest-sized banquet. It was used in the evenings for business meetings by various groups, but during the afternoon hours, it was the latest place for rebellious teens to gather. Rebellious quasi-gangmember teens.

They might've turned themselves into an actual gang, if it weren't for Rabbit. In fact, three gangs had started to form about six years back . . . but all three considered Rabbit to be a sort of honorary mascot. Shy and sweet, as adorable as her namesake, she had taken ruthless advantage of that fact to take over all three groups and meld them into one. Ia had been there for some of it, but the shock of her gifts awakening in full had dragged her into a completely different path for her life. She did remember it involving teary-eyed looks, snifflings, and everyone caving in, not wanting to hurt Rabbit's feelings by fighting against one of her "other friends." The rest had been lost in the flood of preparations for the future.

Not only had Ia been busy getting ready for the future, for three of those years, she had also been off-world for the last two of them. The moment she pushed open the door and stepped inside the banquet room, over two dozen unfamiliar faces turned her way. There were another two dozen who would recognize her, but unfortunately, the closest ones were the ones who didn't know her. Three of the nearest Humans, two males and a female, shoved to their feet and stalked toward her, blocking the views of the rest.

"I'm sorry, meioa," the male in the middle growled, giving her a menacing look, "but this is a *private* meeting. I'm afraid you'll have to leave. One way or another."

"Yeah, we don't like *military* types, around here."

"Military—Ia?" The call came from farther back in the room as one of the older girls stood up. "Is that you?"

"Ia?" An explosion of bodies tumbled out of the way. They made way, some involuntarily, for a very petite figure who scrambled literally over tables and chairs and bodies in her way.

Ia gave her would-be menacer a slight smile. "White hair, unnaturally tall, and no gravity weave? *You* should've paid closer attention whenev—*Oof!*"

She barely managed to catch the pint-sized projectile, supporting Rabbit long enough for the much smaller woman to get her arms around Ia's shoulders and her calves around Ia's waist. She endured the smacking kisses on both of her cheeks, returned a couple of them, then lowered the other woman to the floor . . . and got squeezed again around the hips and waist.

Even for a heavyworlder, Rabbit was short, barely a hundred and twenty centimeters to Ia's hundred and seventy-five. She was proportionate, however, and if one looked past her baggy clothes, had the curves of a fully grown female. Then again, the petite woman was five years older than Ia, who was now twenty. Like a lot of people with Terran blood in their background,

Rabbit also had an Asiatic cast to her features, though hers were more prominent than Ia's. Her face was moon-round rather than Ia's more heart-shaped one, her eyes more almond-shaped than Ia's, and her nose, if dusted with a scattering of freckles, was flatter and broader.

The moment she pulled back and grinned up at Ia, her other prominent physical feature was visible. Like her namesake, Rabbit had two buck teeth with slight gaps on either side, emphasizing them in a very rabbity way. The grin transformed her from somewhat plain to adorably cute. It was also an infectious smile, as unavoidable as a bright sunny day. Even knowing about it in advance, Ia found herself grinning back.

"Look at you!" Rabbit exclaimed, flipping her hands at her friend. "You may be stuck among lightworlders, but I think you added a muscle or two—ooh, your poor angel hair!" Her sunny smile switched to a pouting frown, and the implied sunlight went away as surely as the shadow of a thick cloud. "I can't believe it's all gone! It used to be so long . . . I have to touch it."

Another flick of her hands beckoned Ia down. Obliging the petite woman, she dropped to one knee and let Rabbit run those small hands through her locks. Her hair was no longer a waist-length mass of soft white with a slight curl. Though it had grown out somewhat from the buzz cut all new recruits received, she had carefully kept it trimmed to the bottom of her ears.

Thankfully, before the constant contact could threaten to rouse her precognitive senses, Rabbit withdrew her hands. She pinched thumb and forefinger close together and wrinkled her nose. "You need to grow it at *least* one more centimeter, because it just looks wrong that way. It's too short. And I'm not too keen on the fringe in front."

"I'm a combat soldier. It's not supposed to touch my collar or it'll get caught in my p-suit's o-ring, and I also can't risk it getting in my eyes when I'm suited up," Ia told her. "This is the longest I can grow it."

Rabbit flipped her hands. "Well, just get an angle cut that's shorter in the back and a little longer in the front, and . . . and, oh, a widow's peak cut for the bangs. Something to break up that awful straight edge. You're not a plexi toy or a robot, you know. You're a woman. You should *look* like one."

Ia started to protest. The timestreams filtered into the back of her mind, showing what she would look like if she made the alterations, and how it would affect the futures ahead of her. The effect was negligible, so she settled on a sigh and a shrug. "I'll see what I can do."

"Good!" The sun came back out, beaming with the approval in Rabbit's smile. Turning, she waved her hands over her head, fluttering her fingers. "Okay, everybody! For those of you who don't know? *This* is Ia. Do everything she tells you to do!"

What a way to put the spotlight on me, Ia thought wryly. *Unfortunately, I do need it.* Quickly, while the others were still studying her, she skimmed part of her mind into the timeplains, touching and connecting lifestreams to faces.

"You want *us* to obey *her*? Slag that!" one of the teens scoffed, slashing his hand through the air. He was one of the boys from the clutch that had first risen to face her.

The boy next to him, similar enough to have been a brother or a cousin, flicked his hand at Ia's brown T-shirt and brown pants. "Look at 'er! She's *military.* That means she's *government.* I don't pay no attention to no military *skut.*"

Ia had no idea what a *skut* was, other than some local slang that was apparently now in fashion. The dark mutterings of those who knew who she was told her it was an insulting term, as did the scowl pinching Rabbit's brow. The petite woman whirled on the two boys, hands going to her hips. Ia stopped her verbally.

"Enough." Left hand pointing out to the side at a pair of bodies in her peripheral vision, Ia started listing names. "Cassia McWhorten. James Chong-Wuu." She pointed with her right hand, also at people not in her direct line of sight. Her gaze remained on the two cousins. "Aru Nahasman. Luke Pettima-pinneska. And the two of you, Zezu Brown and Leuron Brown-Smotz."

"*Hm?* What do you want done with them?" Rabbit asked her.

"Line up, right here." Ia drew an invisible line across the floor in front of her. Then remembered her brothers' complaint, and added, "Please."

She stepped back as she did so, leaving plenty of room between herself and the clutch of furniture dotting the banquet hall. The older members—older in terms of how long they'd been around Rabbit, long enough to have known Ia before she had left—herded the six named bodies into place. Surveying them, with expressions ranging from puzzled on Luke's part to wary on Cassia's and sullen on Zezu's, Ia nodded to herself. Stepping up to Cassia, who was only three years younger than her, she smiled gently and lifted her hand, placing it on the other girl's brow.

Cassia's wary look deepened. "Uhhh . . . what are you doing?"

That was a good question. Telepathy wasn't her strongest gift, but Ia insinuated it into the other girl's head. Not as anything overt, but as a background murmur, emphasizing certain thoughts.

These people are weird . . . and boring. Useless. Freaky, too . . . It was fun to rebel, but now it's just getting too weird. Mom's going to point and gloat about how she was right, but . . . she was right. These people are just idle tools waiting for the Devil's hands—I don't want anything more to do with them . . .

"I said, what are you doing?" Cassia asked, her tone sharpening.

Ia smiled at her, a plexi sort of smile, fake and recyclable. "Why, giving you my *blessing*, of course."

I don't want to get blessed by this white-haired freak! She's no deacon of the Church! Mom was right—if I hang out with these people, they'll induct me into some freakish cult! I'll be damned for eternity!

Cassia pushed Ia's hand away from her forehead, frowning. "*No*, thanks. I'm out of here!" Breaking away from the line, she quickly gathered up her things, a few schoolbooks, a portable writing station, a few pieces of candy, and stuffed them into her bag. Slinging it over her shoulder, she flipped her hand. "You *k'toks* can do what you want. I'm *out*."

"Cassia . . ." One of the males stepped out of line, hand held out toward her.

"No, let her go, Luke," Ia said. "I'm more concerned about you . . . and the fact that you're reporting to the Church."

CHAPTER 3

Until I had that means—which I will not divulge at this time—I had to convince people the hard way. In person, which was a bit of a time waster . . . and I never had a lot of time to spare. Suffice to say, my methods were sometimes subtle, but more often, they were rather blunt.

~Ia

"What?" Luke gaped at her. He wasn't the only one. Several others stared, too.

Rabbit was the first to recover. "Right. Luke, you're banished. Pack up, get out, and don't come back."

"You can't be serious! I'd never report to the Church!" he protested.

"You can't just take the word of this . . . stranger!" Zezu argued, eyeing Ia with disgust.

"You were wearing a green hooded shirt and brown pants yesterday. You exited the northern door on the west side of Our Blessed Sanctum of Pialla Square at five thirty-nine in the morning. You stopped to adjust your shoe, because it looked like your toe was starting to poke through the side of your sneaker—black, grey, and white sneakers, though I can't be completely sure about the white, given how ratty they were," Ia stated flatly.

Luke glanced down at his running shoes. So did the others. They were black and brand-new looking. Leuron frowned at him. "You said you went and bought those shoes yesterday, 'cause you just found out they were comin' apart at the seams!"

"How would *you* know anything like that?" Luke asked, eyeing Ia warily.

"I was out jogging at that hour," Ia told him. "You had your hood up, but the streetlamp showed your face when you straightened and turned down Settler Avenue. I have a good memory for faces . . . and you looked rather furtive when you left the church."

"You're crazy," Luke protested. "Okay, I'll admit I did stop in and use the restroom, but that doesn't make me a Church *skut*! It's all just coincidence!"

"It doesn't take much to put all that together," a girl named Diselle muttered. Ia remembered her from over two years ago. "Looks pretty damned suspicious to me, too."

"I trust Ia's judgment, Luke," Rabbit told him, moving up and patting his arm. "You might as well follow Cassia and help her feel better about her decision to leave us. She's probably feeling pretty bad right now."

He gave Ia and the others—the ones who had been around longest—a dismayed look, then frowned and shook his head. "She's right. You *are* mad. You'd turn on one of your own just because of some . . . ?"

Rather than finishing that statement, he shook his head a second time and turned to go collect his own things.

Zezu looked like he would protest. Ia held up two fingers, cutting him off. Rabbit's own solemn look kept the others quiet. A moment after Luke passed through the door, it opened again, admitting the Solarican waitress from the hallway. Balancing the serving platter on shoulder and hand, she eyed the cluster of youths.

"Wherrrre do you want yourrr food?" she asked Ia.

"Third table on the far left, the empty spot next to the pink bag," Ia directed her. Again, Zezu started to protest, and again she held up her fingers. Only when the waitress had left, shutting the door behind her, did Ia lower her hand. "*Never* argue about our business in front of outsiders."

He frowned. "What is this, some sort of cult? Is that what that 'blessing' *shakk* was all about?"

"More like a resistance movement, albeit in the preplanning stages," Ia corrected him. Stepping forward, Ia pressed her hands against his and his cousin's foreheads. "Watch, and learn."

Both shifted to move back, but it was too late. With a simple touch of her fingertips, Ia pulled them onto the timeplains. Since both young men were close friends as well as cousins, it was economical to show both of them at the same time. It would also reassure them that they hadn't hallucinated, since they would later be able to compare notes.

This time, it wasn't a fade or a flip. It was a snap, and a mental yank to get them up onto the grass. Zezu blinked and looked around. Ia was no longer touching his forehead; instead, she gripped his hand. She did the same for his cousin Leuron, immersing both of them—all three of them—firmly in the timestreams, making this moment as real as she could for them.

"What the hell?" he gasped, peering around the undulating, sepia-toned prairie, with its Earth-yellowed grasses and criss-crossing streams.

"Where did the restaurant go?" Leuron demanded. He rubbed at his chest. "Man . . . my heart is racing!"

"It's still there," Ia reassured them. "And your heart—the real one, in your real body—is actually only beating once for every two or three minutes you spend in here. It's all relative."

"And where is here?" Zezu demanded, glaring at her. "Take us back!"

"Not until you've seen what Rabbit and I are really doing. What we're working for. As for where we are," Ia stated, lifting her chin as she looked around, "welcome to my world. Everything you're seeing right now is what I see . . . and what I see, gentlemeioas, is *Time*."

The word rumbled across the plains, grumbling and echoing like thunder. It disturbed everything in its path like a gust of wind, making the leaves of the scattered bushes rustle, and the blades of grass sway.

"Whoa," Leuron muttered, brown eyes widening.

"Don't say that word carelessly while you're here, or you'll stir up a storm that would put one of Sanctuary's to shame," she cautioned them. "You wanted to know what I'm doing? Why

Rabbit is willing to follow me, and have everyone else do so as well? More to the point, why here, and why Sanctuary? Come see what I see."

A tug of her mind slid them up forward, the grass racing past their floating feet. Zezu gasped and clutched at her with his free hand. Leuron swallowed and braced himself. She nodded at the streams, now looking like rivulets, cracks, tiny shining hairs on the never-ending plains spreading out beneath them.

"Each one of those streams is a life. Where they cross and touch, they strongly influence other lives. Your lives travel almost side by side," she told them. "At least, for now."

"What's that up there?" Leuron asked, looking at the blighted desert approaching in the distance.

"The destruction of our galaxy." The casual way she said it made both boys glance sharply at her. Ia shrugged. "More to the point . . . the source of that destruction is one which both of you will find very familiar."

Drifting them down to the edge of the grass, to the point where the life faded from the timeplains, leaving cracked, dead dirt and rocks in its place, Ia dropped all three of them into one of the timestreams near the edge . . .

They were a Terran pilot named Terrence, suited up and seated at the controls of a starfighter . . . and they were afraid. In front of them lay a wall of stone and metal, impossibly huge. For five hours, they had flown at top insystem speeds, the kind that could cross half a star system in that amount of time, and they were still a long, long ways from that grey and brown surface. It could just barely be seen curving in the distance, and they knew, having seen it upon their arrival in this part of space, that it was nothing more and nothing less than an unbelievably huge sphere.

A sphere with tiny, tiny baby spheres, ones the size of gas giants themselves. Those satellites had been sent out, and were swarming around a real gas giant. Devouring it. In just the span of a handful of minutes, the gas giant had shrunk perceptibly.

The real horror was, Terrence knew there was nothing he or his fellow Humans could do to stop it. No one had the resources to stop these extragalactic predators. Not even if all the sentient, star-faring races in the whole galaxy somehow miraculously combined.

It would also be another day or so before he got anywhere near the surface of that mind-boggling wall of a sphere. Three months, and the aliens would reach Earth, the Human Motherworld. His own home colony would be gone within three and a half. And the experts all agreed that within one hundred years, there wouldn't be a star left in this entire section of the cosmos, because they were already tearing apart the nearest stars as well, sucking up their fusion fires to fuel their rapacious hunger. Nothing would be left to light up any stray dust particles the invaders might have missed.

The entire galaxy was as doomed as that gas giant . . . which was shrinking even faster, now that the outer layers of atmosphere had been siphoned away . . .

Ia lifted them out of that numbed pilot's lifestream. Setting her passengers on the ground next to it, she waited for them to recover from the shock of living someone else's life. At least she had been kind, dipping them into the memories and awareness of a fellow male.

"What . . . what the slag was that?" Leuron muttered, staring once more at the bone-dry desert ahead of them.

"That was the Wall, wasn't it?" Zezu asked her. "That's the Wall from the Fire Girl Prophecies! I've seen it before. That was the Wall!"

"That was, is, and will be the Wall," Ia confirmed. "More specifically, it is a Dysun's Sphere, built by an extragalactic sentient race of beings who treat other galaxies the way locustbugs treat forests and fields. They are swarmers; they live inside their giant hive until they outgrow it, then they find a galaxy, strip it bare—the *entire* galaxy—and build a second hivesphere. Then the two groups part company and head off across the intergalactic void in different directions, each in search of new material for their hive-homes, uncaring that they've destroyed thousands of sentient races, millions of inhabitable worlds, and billions of stars. Including our own."

"Shakk," Leuron muttered. "That meioa-o . . . he didn't think anyone could stop it. Who *could* stop something that huge?"

"I can."

Her calm statement caused both young men to choke. Zezu was the first to regain his voice. "Like a Church hell, you can!"

She gave him a sardonic look. "Well, not on my *own*, no. I'll need your help."

"Help for what?" Zezu demanded. He swept his left hand at the barren, lifeless desert beyond them. "If all those streams are lives, then all those lives are dead. This *can't* be stopped. That guy, he was thinking there wasn't an army created that could stop these . . . these things!"

"Not an army, no," Ia agreed. Lifting them again, shifting the timestreams beneath their feat, she readjusted their position in the future. When they landed, it was beside a stream planted with bushes. She tightened her grip on their hands, particularly Leuron's, who had shifted toward the stream and the images visible beneath its ripples. "Do not touch the waters of this life. I don't have the time to put your brains back together, if you do. Even I get a raging headache when I try. Just stay on the bank and walk beside it with me."

They gave her wary looks, but followed her. She carefully expanded the timeplains, focusing down so that there was plenty of room to move between the streams. Several of them intersected and mingled with the bush-marked stream, and broad footbridges appeared, allowing the trio to cross each companion creek.

Zezu, peering at the waters, finally shook his head. "What are we looking at? This stream is exactly the same as all the rest. I think. The vidshows in the water are running by so fast . . ."

"Shhh . . . just follow it a few more meters."

Leading them up to the edge of the barren zone, Ia guided them right next to the water. The air felt thicker here, looking as warm and viscous as amber glass. She pulled them through . . . and stepped onto a vibrant green lawn latticed with healthy, flowing streams. It was probably aqua blue, the color of the Sanctuarian equivalent of grass, but the amber golden light pouring down around them continued to give everything a sepia hue.

"How . . . ?" Zezu asked, peering at the grass, the streams, the vibrant signs of life.

"What this one person can do—just this one person, at the

right time and the right place—can stop the coming invasion. Everyone continues to live, and the galaxy is even better off than before." She slid them backwards, back through the barrier. Back behind the view of the lifeless desert looming in their future. "All of this takes place roughly three hundred years in the future. And now . . . for a different view."

The streams shifted, rippled, and changed. They moved physically, and they altered visually as Ia turned them around. She pointed them now into the past.

"See all the purple waters? Those are all one lifestream. One person's life—the one person who can stop the invasion. All the blue ones, another life. All the green ones, so on and so forth for each color. The different channels, though, represent different choices. Only one choice leads to the right hole through that barrier of death and destruction behind us . . . and that means the blue life and the green life and the pink and so forth all have to influence the purple life to make the right choices at the right points in time."

"So . . . what? What can we do?" Leuron asked her. "If this is all three hundred years in the future, what can *we* do about it?"

"There's nothing we can do!" Zezu dismissed.

"On the contrary, there's quite a lot you can do." Tightening her grip on their hands, she lifted them up and sent them forward, soaring over the multihued waters intersecting and interweaving. "All you have to do is look at the water. Some channels are deeper than others; some choices are more obvious and likely than others. Each person's actions influence those after them, just as each person is influenced by those who come before them. It's all a great chain. We just have to set up the dominos in advance, and tend to each junction as it comes to pass . . . and encourage those who follow us to tend each choice in the coming paths.

"I don't know about you, but having seen all of this, I can't turn my back on it. I can't walk away." Ia shrugged, surveying her stream markers. "Those who see the problem, and know of a good solution for it, *those* are the people who are responsible for fixing that problem."

Leuron shook his head. "This is too much, meioa. I can't take it in right now . . ."

"I got a question," Zezu stated, glancing over his shoulder. "That life . . . the one that punches through the desert and saves everybody from the Wall? Is that the Fire Girl?"

Ia shook her head. "No. She comes along in about two hundred years, give or take."

"*Shakk,*" he muttered. "Are we gonna keep suffering from the Fire Girl Prophecies for two hundred more years?"

"The answer to that question is a resounding 'yes,'" she returned dryly. "Sorry to be the bearer of such annoying news, but there it is . . . and there is nothing which can be done to stop it, save abandoning the entire planet. Of course, if you do that, the Savior won't be in the right places at the right times, won't make the right choices, and won't save the galaxy from complete annihilation."

"Well, what the *shakk* can *we* do about it?" Leuron demanded.

Ia lifted her chin. In a moment, they had zoomed back to a moment close to their entry point. "I'm glad you asked. Both of you have a talent for martial arts. Increase your training. Zezu, I need you to go into mining as soon as you graduate. You're going to need to learn how to operate sandhog drills, and learn them well enough not only to operate any kind of deep ground drill you can get your hands on, but also teach it to others. Leuron, you have an untapped gift for aquaponics. You need to apply for space station lifesupport training as soon as you graduate."

"Space station lifesupport?" Leuron asked, wrinkling his nose. "You want me to go into space?"

"Actually, I need you to go underground. Everyone will have to go underground . . . everyone except for the Church and its followers, that is," Ia amended. "Look, you've both seen it. They're already trying to tighten their grip on this planet. Trying to spread and enforce their fanaticism on everyone. They will succeed in taking over. The problem is, the Savior is bound to head for this world, and if the Church is still in control when she gets here, the wrong things will get done, and all that will be left is death, destruction, and an endless, empty desert."

"So, what? We have to fight a war with the Church and win?" Leuron asked. He flexed his shoulders a little, tilting his head until his vertebrae cracked. "I can fight 'em!"

She gave him a quelling look. "Save it, Leuron. If the Church loses at the *wrong* point in time, it will be just as bad as if they win in the end."

"So what is the right point in time?" Zezu asked, exchanging a look with his cousin.

The answer made her smile. A wry smile, but a smile all the same. "About two hundred years in the future, when the Fire Girl arises and sets their biggest cathedral on fire—the Fire Girl Prophecies are exactly that: prophecies of the future. And the Church fears them. It doesn't fit in with their doctrine, save as the works of the Devil . . . and we have to go."

"We have to go?" Zezu asked her, while his cousin peered at the water-crossed, sunlit prairie surrounding them.

She nodded. "Unfortunately, I don't have a lot of time to spare . . . and you need time to think about what I've shown you. Unlike the Church, who will be trying to brainwash everyone into following their directives blindly in a couple of decades, I and the others who will be opposing them expect you to think for yourselves. To choose of your own free will. But choose quickly. And I hope you follow through on what your conscience tells you to do.

"Remember, do not discuss any of this anywhere near a member of the Church. They will mark you as rebels and heretics, and come after you with a self-righteous vengeance that neither hellfire nor damnation will stop. In fact," Ia added wryly, "they'd consider it God's True Work to destroy you. Including anyone associated with you . . . and that includes Rabbit."

"How do we know you didn't brainwash her into following you?" Leuron asked.

Her mouth twisted once more. "Even the most sophisticated brainwashing technique breaks down over time, Leuron. People wise up, or they grow resistant, or the illogical inconsistencies in the neurotic dogmas of their would-be programmers eventually trip them up. The only way I can convince you to put in a true long-term effort is if I have your full, free-willed cooperation. Particularly *you*, Leuron, since I know for a fact you've studied martial arts. I'll need you to train others, to form a bodyguard for key members, such as Rabbit.

"Now, brace yourselves. I'm bringing you back to your bodies. Keep your mouths shut while I deal with the other two.

They need to see for themselves, and to decide for themselves," she warned them.

They nodded, and Ia reached *out* and *up* with her mind, flipping them back into their bodies.

Both young men drew in deep breaths, opening their eyes. Once more, they were surrounded by the plebian décor of the Italian-themed restaurant. Removing her fingertips from their foreheads, Ia stepped back. A glance at the chrono on her wrist unit showed that only half a minute had passed. She nodded solemnly to the two cousins, then turned to the remaining two, James and Aru.

James eyed her warily. "What was *that* all about?"

"I'm glad you're so willing to volunteer and find out, James." Stepping up to him, Ia lifted her hand to his forehead.

So tedious, having to do this over and over . . . I really, really have to figure out how to make those crystalline wreaths work. Maybe if I take one into the timestreams with me, the next time I do this? It did seem to work—at least to shape it—when I took myself onto the timestreams. But to . . . program it, for lack of a better term . . . I'll have to try it after today. As soon as I handle Aru, I'll need to eat. Traversing Time doesn't happen for free, after all. Not even for me.

Gently, she touched James's brow with the pads of her fingers, connecting her meager telepathy and her major precognition with his unsuspecting mind. Between one breath and the next, reality dissolved around her and James Chong-Wuu. The world turned amber gold and grassy in undulating, stream-crossed plains. Patiently, Ia hauled her companion out of the waters of his own life, before the images of his potential-possible futures could overwhelm and drown the poor boy.

Once more, she led another hopeful, potential helper on a heavily edited exploration of the horrors lurking in the future. "Come and see what I see, James, and see what Rabbit knows we must do."

JULY 24, 2492 T.S.

The average Human body can recover about forty milliliters of blood a day . . .

Ia set the measuring shot glass on the bathroom counter, along with a small box and an eyedropper. The room was kept very clean; life on a triple-gravitied planet was hard enough without risking a careless infection by some local or imported disease. Counters, toilet, sink, and knobs were wiped down every day, the floor and showering tub scrubbed every week on the one day the restaurant downstairs was closed. Her parents had never been afraid of hard work, particularly when it came to caring for family.

Anyone who donates blood on a regular basis, particularly in small, consistent amounts, needs to increase the iron and other nutrients in their diet . . .

Today's lunch had been a generous serving of medium-rare roasted slices of q'al, a salad of chartreuse butter-mung leaves, and a colorful casserole of topadoes *au gratin*, with the bright blue tubers sliced into medallions and layered with orange-hued, tangy-sharp cheeses. So she had eaten her protein for the day, plenty of other vitamins and nutrients in the topadoes, plus the local equivalent of leafy greens to process all that protein and iron with folic acid.

The extraction of blood is still a somewhat primitive process medically, particularly in doses larger than a fraction of a milliliter . . .

Scrubbing her hands at the sink, she carefully wiped them on a fresh towel, then rubbed antiseptic sanitizer on her skin from the pump dispenser for added safety. The stuff smelled like crisp apples, an exotic, imported treat on Sanctuary, where real apples and other fruit often ended up falling off the tree before it could ripen. Local scientists were still working on breeding varieties with stronger, sturdier stems, but even with advanced horticultural techniques, it still took years to mature, breed, and crossbreed enough trees before anyone could come up with a healthy, viable variation.

Not to mention the original extraction equipment often had to be discarded after each use, wasting resources and clogging disposal facilities . . .

The contents of the small box she had set beside the shot glass hadn't been easy to get. Not without someone tracing the transaction back to her. A little luck and a bit of digging through the timestreams on Ia's part had allowed a friend of

Rabbit's to acquire it for her. Expensive in terms of time, but worth it.

And of course with the advent of interorbital travel, it became prohibitively expensive to send fully trained medical personnel along with each and every spaceship . . . which is why the Triple-S, or Subdermal Strap-on Sampler, is the best friend of doctors, nurses, paramedics, and ship medics. For any sample larger than a few drops but smaller than a quarter of a liter, this tool, made from completely recyclable, easily cleaned and sterilized, environmentally friendly, medical-grade plexi, will be your new best friend . . .

Opening the box, Ia followed the instructions both written on the box and recited in the back of her mind. The words of the lecture came from herself, albeit from a far-removed possible life wherein she had taken up a career in medicine, instead of gone into the military. A life wherein she lectured younger nursing students on how to draw blood for various tests. A large number could be done with the blood still safely inside the body, but there were still certain kinds of medical procedures where it had to be placed in a vial or a beaker before it could be experimented upon.

Or in her case, in a shot glass.

Most importantly, so long as the body involved has a functional cardiovascular system, it requires no power setting to withdraw the blood once you have set the volume marker to indicate how much you wish to extract . . . and since it works on the vacuum principle, it can work in free fall as well as our local Sanctuarian gravity . . .

Carefully centering the crosshairs over one of the blue veins on the back of her left hand, Ia strapped it in place, set the volume marker, and depressed the accordion-folded container on the back slowly, pressing the air out of the extraction chamber. Once it was depressed to the right depth for forty milliliters, she braced herself.

Ia hesitated, thumb on the puncturing lever.

Oh, this is ridiculous! Scowling, she glared at her reflection in the mirror. The same face as always scowled back. Almond-shaped amber eyes, brown eyebrows and lashes, crone-white hair that needed a good combing, and probably could stand to be a little longer in front, as Rabbit had suggested. *Did you or did you not unflinchingly take a damned kitchen knife through your palm last year? Through your palm? Stop being such a wimp, Iantha. It couldn't possibly hurt any more than an overcharged laser through the shoulder, you know.*

Yeah, the fear flinching behind her glaring eyes replied, *but those were one-time pains. This is something you'll have to do again and again and again and again, day after day after day after day . . .*

Closing her eyes, Ia gritted her teeth and pictured the barren, lifeless desert of the future. *Failure is not an option. It never was, and it never will be.* Opening them again, she looked down at her hand and shoved the little lever. Once past the tension point, it snapped into place. Pain pinched the soft skin on the back of her hand, and the compressed extraction chamber started expanding again. The translucent white plexi turned darker, redder as she watched.

When it filled to the right depth, the lever snapped back into position. Unstrapping the peculiar little machine, Ia grimaced at the blood trickling from the back of her hand. A few drops made it to the countertop. Again, she closed her eyes, this time to flex her mind and seal the injury. It worked faster than it had for Fyfer and Thorne, but that was only natural; her biokinetic abilities worked best on her own flesh, drawing far greater power from the direct application of her own peculiar energies.

A slow, deliberate count to one hundred, and she opened her eyes, reaching for the sink faucet. Scrubbing and drying her skin, she found the wound sealed and mostly healed, just a pink dot not much bigger than the head of a pin. *Painful and unpleasant . . . but bearable. Though I don't know how people like diabetics and such went through this day after day, back at the beginnings of modern medicine . . .*

Right. The next step. Picking up the Triple-S, she extracted the container from the back of the device—and yelped as the door swung partway open. It quickly shut again, followed by the sound of her mother's voice.

"Ia? Is that you? I'm sorry, kitten," Aurelia called through the panel. "I didn't hit you, did I?"

"Uh, no . . . no," Ia called back, quickly gathering her supplies. She could stuff the eyedropper and the shot glass into her shirt pocket, but the Triple-S and the extraction vessel were a little more awkward. She managed to get the mechanism back into the box, but her mother opened the door again, this time by a handspan.

"What are you doing, *gataki mou*? Wait—is that *blood*?" She pushed the door open further, poking her head through. "Ia, are you *cutting* yourself?"

It wasn't the container that had caught her mother's eyes, but the drops on the counter, which she hadn't cleaned up yet. Worse, her precognitive instincts twinged, warning her of the coming, headache-sized conversation.

"Mother, *no*. No, I am *not* 'cutting' myself. I am *not* emotionally depressed, I am *not* thinking suicidal thoughts, I do *not* need to go into psychiatric therapy *again*," she stressed, rolling her eyes at her mother's reflection.

Aurelia rolled her own eyes. "Then *what* are you doing bleeding all over our bathroom counter, young lady?"

"I'm performing an *experiment*. It's nothing you need worry about." Grabbing a tissue from the dispenser, Ia mopped up the stains. She scrubbed the counter with a second one and a little water, then tossed them into the recycler. Snatching up the squeeze-box of blood, Ia gave Aurelia a pointed look of her own. "Shouldn't *you* be working down in the restaurant right now?"

"The restrooms downstairs were full. What sort of an experiment?" Aurelia asked, pursuing it anyway.

Ia knew that Thorne's biological mother was where he had gotten his stubborn determination. Once Aurelia Jones-Quentin sank her teeth into something, it took finesse to get her to let go. Unfortunately, Ia had inherited some of that bluntness as well. Lifting her chin, Ia replied tartly, "Obviously, a *prophetic* sort of experiment? It's just one more thing I have to do to prepare for the future. Now, if you'll get out of my way, I'll exit the bathroom, and you can do your business and get back to work. Don't forget to wash your hands."

"Impertinent . . . !" Giving her daughter a sardonic look— one which mother and daughter shared, since Ia had learned it from her—Aurelia moved back, letting her exit the bathroom. She softened her look, hand gently cupping Ia's shoulder. "You *are* doing okay, aren't you? I know all those nightmares still kept bothering you long after you stopped screaming each night . . ."

Uncomfortable with even her own mother touching her, Ia's answering smile was wry at best. She patted her mother's fingers and slid out from under them. "Trust me, I'm fine. I had the Marine Corps looking out for me while I was gone. Not to mention a chaplain named Bennie who took a personal interest in my mental health and welfare."

Aurelia tipped her head at that, giving her daughter a speculative look. "Is he cute?"

"Actually, *he* is a *she*," Ia corrected her mother.

"Is *she* cute?" Aurelia persisted. "I wouldn't say no to either a son- or a daughter-in-law one of these days."

Unable to help herself, Ia chuckled. She leaned down and kissed her mother on the cheek. "Look to your sons for grand-children, Mother. Or to the Free World Colony's wombpods. I won't be carrying any of my own. At least, not personally. I do plan on donating some eggs at some point, though."

The older woman grumbled under her breath. "Oh, sure, ruin my plans for spoiling your children in person, why don't you?"

Kissing her mother again, this time on the top of her sleek, dark-haired head, Ia stepped through the door to her old bed-room. "I'm giving you an entire colony . . . well, half of it . . . to dote and fuss over, Ma. Be content with that. Now, if you'll excuse me, I have weird, bizarre, future-probing experiments to conduct in secret . . . and no, I am *not* going to 'cut' myself again today."

She closed the door before her mother could interrogate her further. Turning around, Ia faced her old bedchamber. It still looked banal, if not quite so crowded. There were two twin-sized beds in here now, instead of a twin and a queen. That meant there were almost two full meters between the two beds, plenty of room to move around. The foot of each bed still served as seating for a built-in desk counter with drawers, and it was to the foot of Fyfer's bed that she moved.

On the counter were two large boxes. One was empty, while the other had been filled with carefully hollowed thimble-beads crafted from transparent, pastel chunks of crysium. They were pure beads, too, clear and tinted. Some were pale pink, some pale blue or pale green, but most were a pale, clear gold.

At least I could see approximately how many drops per bead I was using, through the timestreams, she acknowledged, settling everything in place. Squeezing the blood from the container into the shot glass, she picked up the first bead and the eyedropper, dipped the dropper to fill it, then carefully measured out four drops. A pull of energies with her mind softened the bead, and a rolling mush of her fingers mingled the blood with the mineral, until she had a translucent peach bead. *Too much destabilizes the crysium, threatening the decay of the blood and the inability to reintegrate the beads with more of the crystalline medium. Too little dilutes the precognitive resonance between my Feyori-enhanced biology and the Feyori-discarded mineral.*

I will need . . . approximately two milliliters of my blood per wreath. Four drops per bead and twenty per milliliter mean I need ten beads per wreath. I think . . . Dipping the eyedropper into the next bead, she squeezed out four more drops. A knock on the door interrupted her. Quickly pinching the bead shut, she rolled it between her palms. "Yes?"

Aurelia opened the door and peered in at her, but saw nothing but Ia rolling something between her hands, looking over her shoulder at her mother. "You do know we moved the wall harp down into the restaurant, right?"

"It was hard to miss," Ia said, plucking another bead from the box. From the doorway, she could hear the faint sounds of people chatting and tableware clattering; the later dinner crowd was still going strong, downstairs.

"Could you . . . you know . . . play it tonight?" Aurelia asked her. "I've missed the sound of you practicing on it."

Ia sighed. "I don't like people knowing I have these abilities, Ma. I'm freakish enough just from my hair and my size."

Aurelia pushed the door open wider. "My daughter is *not* a freak. Do you hear me?"

Rolling her eyes, Ia sighed. "Fine, I'm not a freak. But I still don't want people to know I can play it telekinetically. Particularly now that I'm in the military. It's too soon for that."

Her mother lingered in the doorway. Ia molded three more beads before sighing and giving in to Aurelia's unspoken plea.

"Okay. But I won't play it while I'm in the same room. And I won't take requests . . . mainly because I won't be in the same room, but also because I don't want anyone to know that I'm the one playing it." Tossing the latest translucent bead into the nearly empty box on her right, Ia glanced back at her mother. "You *do* realize that having someone play the wall harp will only pinpoint you all the harder as heretical demon-lovers in the eyes of the Church, right?"

Aurelia snorted and folded her arms across her chest. "No more so than for being an 'unnatural man-hater' or whatever. I don't actually hate men. I just fell in love with a wonderful woman, and that was that. Anyway . . . when are you coming down to play the harp? And where will you be, if not in the same room?"

Sighing, Ia closed her eyes and concentrated. "I only have to know exactly where it is in relation to myself, and be within about five hundred meters of it, Mother. I could even go for a run around the block and still be able to play it, that's how good I've grown. Now, where are the picks?"

"In a basket on the credenza under the harp. *Um* . . . left corner as you look at it, but back by the wall, not the front corner."

"Five of them?" Ia asked, attention turned inward and outward, looking in the timestreams for the spot her mother mentioned.

"I think so," her mother offered. "Four, for sure. Are you really going to play it from all the way up here?"

She nodded. "I've expanded my telekinetic abilities in the last two years. Mind you, it's nice to use them for something peaceful this time around." Faintly through the open door, the first few notes could be heard. It was just a simple arpeggio to warm up her half-forgotten skills, but it still sounded good, just barely audible over the tops of conversations, cutlery, and cooking wafting up from below. "If you swing by the music store tomorrow and get me a dozen, I can play a full concert later. I'll just play a four-pick melody for now—thank you for keeping it in tune."

"We've had a few psis stop in and try to play it. And for a while, we had a dulcimer harpist performing on the occasional weekend. He brought his own hammers and used them by hand. He ended up being hired by an upscale restaurant in the downtown core, though—could you play 'La Partida' for me, *gataki mou*?" Aurelia asked her daughter. "Then whatever else you want, but make it something pretty and lighthearted? I have to get back down. Weston isn't bad as head waiter, but I really should get back to work."

"I'll play it," Ia promised her. "But it'll take all five picks and then some—I'll play a simplified version for now."

"Thank you, kitten." Blowing her daughter a kiss, Aurelia retreated. She left the door open behind her. Ia didn't bother to shut it, but instead just picked up another bead and the eyedropper, trying to get a feel for this new process manually so that she could replicate it telekinetically later. She would have done so now, but didn't want to mess up one of her mother's favorite songs.

The faint strains of strings being plucked in the up-and-down waves of an arpeggio shifted, turning much more melodic. Rising and falling with the song, the notes sang at rhythmic intervals, depending on how strongly or subtly she plucked them. The arpeggio had served its purpose, by adjusting her mind to the physical location of each string. Now she could play it in earnest as she worked.

Wall harps were not uncommon among telekinetics; it was considered a primary test just to be able to pluck the strings with the force of one's mind, let alone waft a pick into the air and flick it across the metal lines. The real benefit, however, lay in practicing it like one practiced a normal instrument; the more a telekinetic could flick and pluck and play, the stronger they could train their abilities.

Of course, there were limits to psychic training. Everyone— at least among Humans—could train into themselves a baseline level of raw empathic, clairsentient, gut-instinct level sensitivity, with time and effort. For the flashier abilities, one had to be born with them, and then discover them—usually in the puberty years—and then master and train them. Raw ability could rank someone at a certain baseline, and training could push them a few ranks higher, but there were limits. Raw strength could lift and move a heavy weight, but wielding something as tiny as a string pick with enough deftness and dexterity to play a song took practice, practice, and more practice.

She hadn't lied in telling her mother it would be nice to use her abilities for something peaceful. Nor had she lied about being a lot better at subtle manipulations by now. Still, there

was a difference between telekinetically guiding the outcome
of a battle in her favor and plucking a charming tune from harp
strings strung on a frame two meters wide and mounted on the
wall of the dining half of the restaurant downstairs.

The noise of the diners had muted a bit during her warm-up.
Now the melody soared and danced, growing a little louder as
her mother slipped through the door at the bottom of the stairs,
leaving it, too, slightly ajar. Pots and pans rattled in the kitchen,
and she could hear her birthmother, Amelia, ordering someone
to clean up a spill, but over all those noises, the wall harp
played on.

Ia picked up another bead and carefully measured four drops
of blood into the hollow at its center. She worked in time with
the tune, thumbs squishing and kneading, palms rubbing and
rolling. *Four drops of blood per bead, twenty in a milliliter . . .
that's eight hundred beads before I run out of blood. As soon
as I've gotten a good rhythm and habit established up here,
and I've played enough music for a set . . . I'll be able to return
the picks to their bowl downstairs and use my abilities on these
beads instead. Then things should go a lot faster.*

*A pity I wasn't born a Gatsugi, with four arms instead of
two. Then I could've done this twice as fast by hand . . .*

As much as part of her wanted to stay with her family, to
be on hand to help Rabbit and the rest in their coming underground war against the Church, Ia was all too aware that her
time here was running out.

CHAPTER 4

One of the requirements of being a bona fide psychic is to be registered with a duly authorized organization that can help train and monitor the activities of psis, as a reassurance to the general populace. The most widespread one, of course, is the PsiLeague, but the second largest, if less known than most people realize, is the Witan Order. Where the League is very much a scientific organization, devoted to the study, dissection, training, and improvement of paranormal abilities with a careful methodology and a healthy— but not excessive—dose of skepticism, the Witan Order is very much a religious organization. In fact, only a small part of the Witan Order actually deals with psis, with the rest being devoted to what it's really known for, the unification of wisdom and worship across religious and secular boundaries. But they do deal in psychic abilities on a larger scale than most people realize.

This is not to say they don't use the same training methods as the PsiLeague, since they are indeed effective. It's just that, as a religious order, the Witan Order is capable of doing more things than a nonreligious one like the League. For instance, for certain subsects of the Witan Order, you have to be a psychic in order to be ordained as a priest or priestess for that sect. Others, you can be, and are presumed to be, but it isn't necessary to actually be

one. More than that, the Witan Order may be required by
law to keep files on who is psychic, so on and so forth . . .
but those files can be sealed to the subsect of the Order if
someone is a duly ordained priest or priestess of that sect,
revealable only upon a court order. And they don't always
talk about which subsects within the Order have these
requirements . . . because to the Witans, that falls under
the confidentiality of the confessional.

In my case, it was listed in my military application that
I was a duly ordained priestess of the Witan Order, subsect
Zenobian. And there actually is a Zenobian Sect of the
Witan Order. It's just a very, very small one, confined to
Sanctuary itself, which at the time contained no more than
a couple dozen duly ordained clergy. And yes, you do have
to be a duly registered psi to be a priestess of the Zenobian
Sect. They just don't talk about the requirements.

So the information has been there all the time, which
by law it has to be . . . but also by right of privacy law, I
didn't have to go around blaring it to everyone that I was
indeed a psi. Provided, of course, that I was duly registered
and that I underwent the required yearly ethical exams by
duly authorized telepathic examiners . . . which, conve-
niently, the Zenobian Sect just happened to possess.

~Ia

AUGUST 3, 2492 T.S.

"No, no, and no," Ia admonished the group of grimy, gritty,
coverall-clad youths lined up in front of her. "You do *not* go
into any of these side tunnels alone. I know it *seems* more
efficient, but it isn't."

She was just as dirty as they were, with good reason. For
the last three hours, they had been climbing, rappelling, sliding,
scuttling, and otherwise surveying yet another stretch in the
maze of lava tube tunnels beneath the foothills of the Grampnell
Mountains east of the capital. Some of it had been done in the
wall-climbers Rabbit had bought just for this, but much of these
tunnels had to be surveyed on foot for accuracy. Curved stone
walls surrounded them, some charcoal grey, some reddish

brown, and many streaked with either mineral stains, water marks, or the local equivalent of mold spores.

"You will *not* violate the basic laws of spelunking," Rabbit added. She held up one petite finger per point, lecturing them. "Nobody goes caving alone, nobody goes without a beacon transponder in case of an emergency, nobody goes anywhere down here without a pack carrying enough emergency rations to sustain them for two days . . . and nobody goes down here without telling someone else in the gang."

"We do need these three-dimensional surveys," Ia added, pointing at the wall-crawler vehicles waiting to be manned again, "but we will *not* be careless about it."

"I don't feel comf'ble, lyin' to my uncle," one of the girls mumbled, arms crossed tightly over her chest. "What if he needs to get down here? And gets lost tryin' t' make sense of the maps we're givin' 'im?"

"As much as it pains me to have to deceive your uncle, too, Jula, he works for the Department of Geology, and the DoG is one of the places the Church will swarm with a thousand microscopes when it comes to open war between the colony's two main factions."

"I could've fit," the slender boy next to Jula argued. "And Rabbit, too."

"Until we can get the right equipment to widen those side tunnels, it's too dangerous. If either of you got stuck, the rest of us would have a near-impossible time trying to pull you back out," Ia stated.

"And while I'm small enough to go in after you, I'm nowhere near strong enough to pull you back out," Rabbit reminded them.

"So when do we get that equipment?" Leuron asked Ia, lifting his chin. That flashed his headlamp into her eyes, but only for a moment. "You keep promising a bunch of fancy equipment will show up. When?"

"When the time is right. I can't exactly pull a sandhog out of my kitbag, you know. As it stands—" Ia cut herself off, bemused by the beeping of her arm unit. The bracer-sized brown plexi device beeped again. Flipping open the lid, she arched a brow at the sight of the woman peering up at her from the screen inside. "Yes, Leona?"

"There's been a change in our schedule. We're going to have to move up your exams by two days."

That was unexpected. Ia frowned. "Two days early would make it *today*."

"Heddie had an attack of Fire Girl Prophesy, followed by a bout of precognition. She says she has to be elsewhere today, which means she'd be on duty in two days' time. You know as well as I do that sometimes two precogs cancel each other out, which was why she wasn't going to be on duty. But now she is, and I don't think it'll be a good idea for you to be scanned by her."

"She'd blab half the things she hears to her best friend, who will tell her cousin, who just happens to be dating a Church member, you mean," Ia muttered.

"You're the expert on intercausality chains, not me. How soon can you get up here? You're in the tunnels, right?" Leona asked her, squinting at the cavern ceiling beyond her view of Ia's head.

"About two hours out from the city, maybe a little more. I'll need a few minutes for instructions, and a few minutes to get cleaned up, once I'm topside."

"Call me when you're on the surface, and I'll get everything ready," Leona instructed her.

Nodding, Ia ended the call by flipping her wrist unit lid shut. Sighing roughly, she turned to the others. They had spread out a little, murmuring among themselves. "Okay. I'd much rather give you your choice in where to go and what to do for the rest of today, but I'm out of time. While for most things, I can predict certain probabilities with great accuracy . . . they still remain probabilities. So I'm going to *show* each of you where to go spelunking today, and what pitfalls to avoid. Line up and present foreheads; this won't take long."

Thankfully, they obeyed. It didn't take long, either. This wasn't an explanation of her greatest war and the reason why; this was simply a skimming of their immediate futures, showing them which paths were the best to take and which were the ones to avoid.

The volcanoes that had formed these lava tubes in the ancient days of this planet had long since gone extinct, but they had left behind a veritable maze of passages. The Space Force, which had dug bunkers and shelters into the bedrock when it had looked like the Terrans and the methane-breathing Dlmvla were on the brink of going to war, had stumbled across these tunnels. Their solution had been to seal them off with tough plexcrete walls, though the Department of Geology had insisted on doors being added for future spelunking needs.

Ironically, attempts had been made to prospect for ores, but the Terran Space Force had shut that down, locking the bunkers with security codes so that they could only be opened in a genuine emergency. The star system containing Sanctuary also hosted two methane gas worlds, prime targets for the Dlmvla, so the bunkers had to remain inviolate. Naturally, Ia knew the release codes in advance. And just as naturally—or rather, precognitively—she knew these tunnels would form the starting point for sheltering the saner half of the coming civil war.

Leuron hesitated when she reached for his forehead. Ia did as well, arching a brow. "Yes?"

"Why do we gotta build stuff down here?" he asked her. "Why can't we just move people to the other side of the planet?"

"Duh," Rabbit answered before Ia could. "Because the Church will simply bomb the *shakk* outta whatever settlements we have on the surface. Gerald Fortranger runs the Department of Defense, and *he's* one of the Elders of the Church."

"Then why use the Terran bunkers?" another teenager asked. "Fortranger probably has the access codes memorized."

"Because the codes can be changed," Ia told him. "The next time I come back here, they *will* be changed. In fact, the locking mechanisms will probably be updated as well . . . and the new codes, the real codes, won't go to anyone on the Church's side."

"If you wanna keep up, Leuron, you'll have to start following religion and politics," Rabbit stated wryly. Then wrinkled her nose. "Add in sex and sports, and you'll have the Forbidden Four Topics."

One of the other teen boys grinned and nudged the girl next to him. "You wanna go off in that side passage we found last week, and get to 'third base' while the Prophet's handing out assignments?"

His target wasn't the only one to groan at the bad pun. Ignoring them, Ia touched her fingertips to Leuron's forehead, giving him a touch of forewarning on what to look for while he was busy surveying the network of lava tunnels. She finished going down the line, then nodded at the last two, a pair of girls. "You two are with me. The laws of spelunking apply even to myself, so you'll escort me up, then help each other back down before resuming the surveys. Whatever you do, don't drop your scanners. They cost Rabbit a glossy cred chit, and you'll make her cry if you break one."

Rabbit mock-rubbed her eyes, miming crying if they should ruin the equipment, then grinned. Her child-like soprano voice echoed off the rough, rounded walls. "Well, you heard Ia. We have a long, hard slog ahead of us, but it'll be fun! Pizza and topado cakes when we're done, everyone!"

Leaving her to marshal her unlikely, cave-crawling troops, Ia nodded to the two girls and turned toward one of the wall-crawlers with four seats instead of two. "Come along. As fun as it is down here, I have to get back up to the surface."

"You think this is fun?" one of the girls asked, wrinkling her nose. She plucked at her coveralls in distaste. "I'm only down here because Rabbit and you asked me to help."

Ia looked down at her grime-covered clothes, then eyed the younger woman, equally smeared in lava grit. "Compared to being covered head to toe in alien guts? Yes, I *do* think this is fun. Unfortunately, I have to go and get my head cracked open now."

The Witan Church of Contemplation was quiet, peaceful, and well-lit. Not just from the tasteful spiral-galaxy chandeliers in the foyer, narthex, and sanctuary, visible through the large plexi windows separating each section of the ground floor, but also by the lightning flickering outside. It lit up the stained glass windows with their geometric, almost crystalline patterns, and brought the scents of ozone and a hint of rain into the front hall with her, the smells that said she was home.

Closing the door behind her, Ia pulled off the light jacket she had donned to ward off the slight chill in the air. She had stopped long enough at her parents' home to shower and change into clean civilian clothes, a flowery blue shirt and plain dark blue slacks left over from the years before she had left for Earth and the Space Force. They weren't quite SF-Navy blue, but she'd be wearing those colors soon enough.

Leona, an older woman with greying auburn brown hair

and hints of gravity stress-lines creasing her face, met her in the narthex beyond the foyer. Befitting her rank in the Witan Order, and the fact that she was on duty, she wore a white tabard over a blue robe. The Unigalactan sword-in-galaxy had been embroidered in silvery thread on the front and back of the tabard, and she had embellished it further along the edges with stylized flames intertwined with lightning bolts.

On the pommel-nut of the downward-pointing sword, a tiny, gold-threaded Radiant Eye had been stitched. Originally done in black as the symbol for the PsiLeague, it had been adopted by several psychic registration organizations, including the Witan Order. The difference from a standard sword-in-galaxy was subtle, but the Order preferred discretion for its psychic associations. Even in the late twenty-fifth century, there were still those who feared to let others know they had actual paranormal abilities.

Then again, with the Church of the One True God declaring such things an abomination of nature and a sin against God, who could blame anyone for wanting to be a little cautious?

"Are you ready to confess your sins, meioa-e?" Leona asked her. The older woman quirked her mouth up on one side as she did so, acknowledging the irony of those words on this world.

"I am ready, yes," Ia replied, twisting her own lips.

"This way, then." Gesturing, Leona led the way to the stairs to the basement level. Not that Ia needed guiding, since this was the church nearest her family's home, the church where her gifts had first been diagnosed and trained.

There was something new about the place. She eyed the mottled shades of blue underfoot as they descended. "New rugs?"

"A bit of an extravagance if you ask me, since most people take the lifts going back up, but the Church committee insisted," Leona told her. " 'One day soon, our people won't get breathless just going up and down the stairs, so they might as well look good,' and all that."

"If it's any consolation, they do look good," Ia offered.

"Have you gone into fashion and interior design, then?" Leona asked dryly.

"Not in *this* life," Ia retorted crisply. "It's just a nice change from military hues, that's all."

"*Ah*, yes. I received a vid-call from a Chaplain Benjamin,

regarding you," the older priestess told Ia. "She wanted to know if you were handling civilian life alright."

Ia refrained from rolling her eyes. "She's something of a friend, and something of a watchdog. I think the Department of Innovations asked her to keep a closer eye on my mental and emotional stability, considering how I've been constantly deployed in a combat hot spot for the last two years. You're listed on my personnel file as my family pastor, so naturally she'd call you."

"Department of Innovations?" Leona asked, leading her down a side corridor. "What's that?"

"It's part of the Branch Special Forces in the Terran military. They oversee merit-based promotions, and fast-track those with leadership potential," Ia explained. "Or slow the advance of those who have, *ah*, reached their maximum capacity for competence."

Leona smiled. "Then let us hope they do not have reason to slow you down. We're in the east conference room," she told Ia, opening the door. "Your examiners will be myself, Priest Ortuu, and Priestess Kaskalla. Be gentle on Kaskalla, as this will be her first time participating in these sessions."

Ia nodded at the familiar figure of Ortuu. Like Leona, he had the white tabard of the Witan Order arrayed over his blue robes. Like his compatriot, his was decorated around the edges with fire and lightning, symbols of the Zenobian Sect. Unlike her, he was resting in a chair with his feet propped up on a second seat, sipping from what smelled like a cup of caf'.

Beside him, perched somewhat nervously on her own chair at the round, white-topped table, was the young woman Kaskalla. Like Ortuu, her complexion was dark, her eyes brown, and her hair black and fuzzy. Her tabard contained the sword-in-galaxy of the Unigalactans . . . but the edges of hers were marked with fanciful rauela feathers, each long, curving shaft stitched in a different rainbow hue.

"She's . . . not a member of the Zenobian Sect," Ia observed, glancing at the older priestess. She didn't like this second surprise sprung on her. If she had probed the future in more than just a light skimming, if her instincts about the timestreams hadn't remained calm, she would have called an end to this session before even arriving.

"I thought it best that you have at least one 'neutral' observer on record. Don't worry; Kaskalla's one of us in heart, if not in vows," Leona added.

Ia shook her head. "I'll have to scan her, first. Introducing *any* new element, however seemingly benign, can shift the paradigms too far."

"Scan *me*?" Kaskalla asked, brows lifting. "I've already undergone my ethics probes for the year, meioa. In fact, it was just last month."

"It's not that kind of scan," Ia corrected her. She glanced at Leona.

"I haven't told her much about you," Leona confessed. "I figured it'd be best that way. But I'll vouch for her. I was one of the ones who scanned her, last month."

"I'll still have to scan her," Ia demurred. Crossing to the younger woman, Ia addressed her concerned look. "My abilities are a bit . . . touchy, meioa. Oversensitive, I suppose you could say. I need to make sure you and I can interact without triggering them the wrong way. It does not, however, involve reading your thoughts. It's sort of more like scanning your aura than anything else. Do I have your permission to do so?"

Kaskalla looked at the other two. "Is this safe?"

Ortuu shrugged. "Ia *is* a duly ordained priestess of the Zenobian Sect. She's passed all the required psychic ethics and appropriate conduct classes, the exact same as you."

"Do you need me to lower my shields?" the young priestess asked Ia.

Ia shook her head. "That shouldn't be necessary. But I do need you to refrain from reacting psychically to anything you may sense."

That earned her a skeptical look, but Kaskalla shrugged and acquiesced anyway. "Alright, you have my permission."

Nodding, Ia touched her fingers to the other woman's forehead. This wasn't quite like touching the minds of the youths Rabbit had gathered around her. Kaskalla was Ia's age, maybe a little younger, but she was a fellow psi. That changed all the variables.

Back when the kinetic inergy, or KI, machine had first been crafted and proven to be capable of reliably measuring psychic emanations—weeding out the con artists and the merely

delusional from the actually gifted members of society—
scientists had discovered that different people had different
"frequencies" of psychic abilities. Some of these frequencies
could augment fellow psis, while others could negate, counter,
or otherwise interfere with the abilities of two or more gifted
people.

Touch almost always concentrated that effect, though personal effort via mental "shields" could quell some of it, and
the stronger the gift, the more likely it was to overpower or
override a fellow psychic's abilities. But by a quirk of quantum
probabilities—namely, the butterfly effect—even a weak ability
could mess with a very strong one. Highly subjective as most
psychic abilities still were, despite the advances of modern
detection and training methods, they did operate under the
same general rules of physics as other energy phenomena.

So Ia eased her mind open very slowly, very carefully. Leona's
mind, she knew. Ortuu's mind, she knew. Kaskalla's mind was
rife with curiosity and touches of wary caution. It wasn't telepathy, per se, but it was a pathic-level awareness of the other female.
Opening her precognition a tiny trickle, Ia probed carefully into
her timestream possibilities, skimming lightly to minimize the
chance the other woman would sense what she was doing.

What she was looking for . . . she didn't find. Kaskalla
wouldn't betray Ia or her fellow colonists to the Church. Not
on any potential level of possibility, not in the timeplain paths
Ia was trying to guide everyone into. There was a chance Kaskalla's gifts could augment her own a little, since she was apparently a very strong telepath, but she was a polite one, remaining
safely within her mental walls.

Relieved, Ia backed out of her probings. Removing her fingers, she nodded. "I think we'll be compatible enough."

"Good. Then we can get started?" Kaskalla asked, glancing
at the others.

Ortuu put down his caf' cup with a heavy sigh, visibly reluctant to give up the hybrid version of coffee. The Terrans and the
V'Dan had developed it between themselves shortly after the two
disparate branches had been reunited, smoothing out the bitter
flavors and increasing the caffeine content pleasantly. Leona
took a seat at the table, a cup of water resting in front of her. Ia
sat as well, picking a seat between her and Kaskalla.

The younger priestess eyed her. "*Um* . . . I thought we were going to move to one of the testing rooms. You know, where the KI machines are?"

Leona, Ortuu, and Ia all shook their heads. Ortuu, dropping his feet from the spare seat, answered her question. "We can't have an active KI machine in the same room while we do this."

"Ethical Scan regulations clearly state that the psi in question needs to be monitored with a KI machine to ascertain whether or not they're straining away from the probe," Kaskalla argued, tapping the table.

"Yes, but the *cost* of those precious KI machines argue against using them in Ia's presence," Ortuu countered just as tartly. "Her gifts and those machines are incompatible during an ethics probe. Unless you yourself want to pay the twenty-three thousand credits per machine to replace them, we do this without any active ones—speaking of which, I'd better go and double-check the ones in the testing rooms *are* still turned off," he added, pushing to his feet. He snagged his mug as he rose. "I know I checked them earlier, but paranoia is only prudent. I'll be right back."

Kaskalla gave him a confused look as he left. She shifted her gaze to Ia. "I don't get it. How can you damage a KI machine, unless it's done physically?"

"You didn't tell her anything about my gifts?" Ia asked Leona. The older woman shook her head. Sighing, Ia gave the younger woman a brief explanation. "As I said, my gifts are overly sensitive. Particularly when someone is mucking around in my brain. Three of my gifts are telekinesis, pyrokinesis, and electrokinesis, all of which can affect the KI machines. Particularly the electrokinesis, if it's triggered inadvertently by you stumbling around inside my head.

"Unfortunately, while the actors in *Space Patrol* pull down huge piles of creds for each vidshow they make, I'm in the *real* Space Force, and my pay is a laughable pittance by comparison," Ia said, holding Kaskalla's gaze. "I had to save for two years just to be able to afford to come home. I literally cannot afford to replace the Order's testing machines on my salary."

"She killed four of them before we figured out what she was doing, back when her gifts fully blossomed," Leona added dryly. "Thankfully, one of her *other* gifts was precognition."

"Precognition?" Kaskalla asked. "Why be thankful for that?"

"Because I gave the Order the exact numbers to win just enough money in the Alliance Lottery to cover the replacement and shipping costs for four new machines," Ia told her.

The younger priestess opened her mouth, hesitated, then closed it. She shook her head. "That . . . skims the grey lines of ethics rather neatly. You didn't benefit *directly* from doing that, and it is covered under the 'reparations' addendum. Which technically leaves you clean, ethically. Though I wonder how you could pluck the exact numbers out of the air so readily," Kaskalla murmured, frowning. "Or was that a lucky touch of your gift?"

Ia lifted her left arm, checking the chrono display on the lid of her arm unit. "Tonight's local lottery drawings will take place in . . . forty-three minutes. Considering this session will take over two hours to complete, it doesn't violate any ethics to give you the winning numbers for tonight's games, since you won't be free to go buy a ticket. The Sanctuarian Daily Lotto's numbers are 4, 37, 18, 9, and Blue. The Lucky Draw's cards will be Queen of Diamonds, Three of Clubs, Seven of Clubs, and Ace of Spades.

"I'd give you the Alliance Lottery's Power Pick winning numbers," Ia added, smiling slightly, "but those won't be drawn until tomorrow, and *that* would be a violation of ethical use of precognition in predicting gambling outcomes, because you would have time to go buy a handpicked ticket, which in turn could be construed as a bribe to you . . . not to mention it would be a violation of the future, since you're not scheduled to win any of the drawings this week. Sorry."

"You didn't even *strain* to pick those numbers," Kaskalla protested. "How can I know they're real?"

"Write them down, and check them after the fact—welcome back, Ortuu," Ia added as the priest reentered the conference room. "Everything shut off?"

"Everything's shut off, and I have a fresh cup of caf'," he agreed, setting the refilled mug back on the table. "Let's get started, then. Everyone scoot a little more evenly around the table. I'll be the anchor, the one not in direct contact with her mind. Kaskalla, you are only to *observe* in this session. Make sure you do not say or think the word *time* while you are observing, while you're at it. Leona will be leading the probe and the questions. Ia, when you are ready, bring us in."

"Right." Closing her eyes, Ia calmed her thoughts. Running through the grounding and centering exercises was by now an old habit, but she consciously took herself through each visualization step, until she felt stable, calm, and controlled. Opening her eyes, she reached for Kaskalla's hand, gently bringing the Witan priestess into mental contact with her.

(*Hello,*) Kaskalla greeted her. (*By the code of the ethics probe, what is yours will remain yours until the end of this session, where my fellow scanners and I will debate the legalities of your psychic-related actions. You have the right to defend each point of contention during this scan. You have the right to a second scan. If any illegalities are uncovered and sustained upon a second scan, you have the right to legal counsel and legal representation in a court of law. Do you understand these rights as I have explained them to you?*)

(*Trust me, I've been doing this since I was a little girl. Just don't prejudge until you have all the facts,*) Ia warned her. (*Don't leap to any conclusions, and limit your questions. Let Leona take the lead. She knows which questions to ask. Brace yourself; I'm bringing her in.*)

She could sort of sense the older woman already, who lurked beyond Ortuu's thoughts, who lurked at the edges of Kaskalla's mind. When she held out her hand, accepting Leona's grasp, the circle of thoughts jolted. Now Leona was a strong presence on her right and a weaker echo from the left. Kaskalla was strong from the left and an echo from the right. Ortuu was a double echo, anchoring the far side of the ring. Not in direct, physical contact with her, he would remain the clearheaded member of the trio, much more of a dispassionate observer than either woman, who would be in direct contact with Ia's thoughts, emotions, and memories.

(*You know the standard rights and waivers, Ia, so let us begin. Your last probe took place on February 13th, 2492 Terran Standard. Examiners were myself, Priestess Miranda Fyodore and Priest Ortuu Wickenne of the Zenobian Sect of the Witan Order of Sanctuary,*) Leona stated. (*We will therefore start with the day of February 13th of 2492 T.S. Today is July*

27th, 2492. Have you consistently used your psychic abilities every single day between the thirteenth of February and today?)

(*I have,*) Ia stated, putting conviction and honesty behind the mental words. It was exceptionally difficult to lie mind-to-mind. It could be done, if the person lying possessed both very strong telepathic abilities and were a talented method actor, but with three trained and strongly gifted examiners watching her every thought, Ia didn't bother.

(*God, every single day? We'll be here all night!*) Kaskalla protested.

Leona frowned at her. (*Keep your kibbitzing to a minimum, Priestess. It will not take all night. Ia, have you, to the best of your knowledge and honesty, used your abilities in the vast majority of instances with ethical care and consideration for obeying the laws of the Alliance?*)

(*In the vast majority of instances, I have,*) Ia stated. She could feel Kaskalla start to form a protest and squeezed the younger woman's fingers in silent warning to stay quiet. (*I am prepared to show you any example you wish of legally acceptable use of my psychic abilities.*)

Leona nodded. (*We will exercise that option at our discretion. Regarding instances which do not fall firmly into the category of ethical care and consideration for obeying the laws of the Alliance . . . are you prepared to submit those instances for our examination and consideration?*)

(*With the understanding that I have the legal right to call upon the statutes covering* Johns *and* Miskha *versus the United Nations, regarding the rights of precognitives to act or not act in accordance with the betterment and benefit of future lives and their overall safety as foreseen in advance . . . I am prepared to submit all potentially questionable instances of my psychic behavior to this ethics inquiry,*) Ia replied.

(*You're going to use* Johns *and* Mishka *as your main defense?*) Kaskalla asked skeptically from her left. The echo from the right was flavored with Ortuu's amusement and Leona's impatience.

(*If you keep interrupting to ask questions and make comments, this* will *take all night,*) Leona admonished the younger woman.

(*Skipping over the vast majority of the instances in which*

*she used her abilities with a broad, generalized statement of . . .
of dismissal is a violation of procedure!*) Kaskalla argued.

(*In Ia's case, since she* does *use her abilities near-constantly,
examining each and every single instance on an individual
basis would take as long as the entire span of time between her
last probe and now,*) Ortuu retorted. (*Possibly longer.*)

(*Oh, for God's sake,*) Ia muttered as Kaskalla marshalled
her thoughts for another attack of procedures versus expediency.
(*We don't have* Time *for this.*)

The word dumped them onto the timeplains. A jerk hauled
them up out of their individual timestreams. Kaskalla gasped,
clutching at Ia's hand. Metaphorically, she was dripping wet
and shivering, more strongly affected by that brief dip into her
own existence than any non-psychic. Ortuu and Leona, veterans
of the inadvertent effect, merely waited for Ia to stabilize them.

"*Look*, you silly little rules lawyer," Ia stated, impatience
sharpening her tone. "*This* is why I can call upon *Johns and
Mishka* with impunity. This is *Time*." Thunder rolled at the word,
washing across the endless sea of grass and streams. She zoomed
them upward, making Kaskalla gasp and Leona sway. Ortuu
blinked a little, but said nothing as Ia reshaped the timeplains
into a sepia-toned chart on a wall, standing them in an amber-hued
version of the same conference room their bodies still occupied.
"Everything I do is so gods-be-damned *interconnected* with the
future that it would take your mind literally a year to understand
just how much I have to use my gifts every single day.

"Every single day, I spend hours sifting through the future
possibilities and probabilities so that I can find the right path
to ensure that the maximum number of sentient beings have
the maximum possible chance at a good quality of life overall."
Releasing their hands in the vision, though not in reality, Ia
tapped the chart of interbranching lines on the wall, thumping
it to highlight each section in different colors as she spoke. "Do
try to keep up?

"I have *one* shot at stopping the destruction of our galaxy
three hundred years into the future. The Fire Girl Prophecies
have already shown this coming invasion in the symbology of
the great Wall. The physical source of that Wall is a Dysun's
Sphere filled with intergalactic locusts coming to devour the
entire resources of the Milky Way. Since so many of the key

events needed to aim for that one shot will happen long after I'm dead and gone, I must seek out the key focal points and write precognitive directives for people to follow. The right people must be born at the right point in time, the right decisions made . . . and the wrong decisions and the wrong people must be carefully calculated and guarded against.

"Bump into the right person here," she stated, thumping the tangle of lines so that some of them turned blue and streaked toward a star-shaped point on the far right of the map, "and two people will meet, fall in love, have the right kids who will go on to have more of the right kids, who will eventually befriend this person here," Ia added, thumping another section which turned yellow, intersected with the blue lines, and formed green streaks toward the star as well, "who will provide the right focal moment for this line of people to have the right life-experiences to be in the perfect place and time to help *this* person, who will stop the coming invasion.

"But in order to get this yellow line to exist, I have to throw off this person here from their current path in life, or this entire branch vanishes, the blue doesn't turn green, but instead goes purple, and poof, no Savior, no stopping the locusts, no Milky Way and no octillions of sentient lives still able to live free and enjoy their lives four hundred years from now," Ia told her. "If throwing off that one life here at the start of the yellow path means killing that person, I'd say a ratio of one to octillions is worth the stain on my soul.

"But losing that life when it isn't necessary is *also* a sin against the future. So I have to be damned sure that it's the absolute best option . . . because if I can find another option which keeps that person alive and gives them a good quality of life without destroying the future for everyone else, then I *have* to find it.

"*That* is the only ethics I have to defend. Not deciding whether or not Mary and John should get married so that the blue line can be correctly formed with the right kids at the right time. That chain of events is relatively harmless and benign, compared to the fact that, elsewhere, I literally have to decide who lives and who dies."

Ia eased back on the illustration, returning them to the timeplains.

"Your job is *not* to sit on your sanctimonious little butt debating the scale and scope of a problem beyond your meager comprehension. *Your* job is to make sure that *I* comprehend it, and am doing my best to sufficiently agonize ethically over the worst of my decisions before following through on any choices I must make," Ia finished tartly.

"Even the laws of physics can seemingly be bent, though never broken," Leona said as Ia finished, unruffled by the rapid changes in venues. "So, too, can the laws of ethics. This woman *is* one of the most ethical, honorable beings in the known universe. She has proven it consistently time and again in these ethics sessions."

"What if she told you that you had to die? And by her hand?" Kaskalla argued. "What if she said she had to *kill* you?"

"Having already examined her and her ethics several times over the years, I would know she had already spent untold hours agonizing over the decision, searching for any other possible way to avoid such a fate," Leona replied calmly.

"And you'd just . . . accept it?" Kaskalla asked, clearly bewildered by that thought.

"Would you run into a burning building with children trapped inside? Would you do it knowing you would probably die in the attempt to save them?" Ortuu asked mildly. "But still knowing they *needed* to be saved?"

"Well . . ."

"It's the same thing," the priest dismissed, flicking his hand. "The only difference is that Ia asks it of everyone, not just of herself. You should know these things, being an ordained priestess of the Witan Order. The vast majority of known sentientkind, all the races of the Alliance, believe in certain principles of kindness, compassion, and cooperation. These are the trademarks of sentient civilizations, however disparate we may be in physiology. A Dlmvla is as likely to rush into a burning building to save its progeny as any Gatsugi or Human."

"Yes, but we don't go around ordering other people into burning buildings!" Kaskalla protested. "Normal, sane people don't do that!"

"The military does," Ia told her. "That's the burden of every officer, as well as the duty of every soldier. And we *are* normal and sane, all jokes set aside."

"Firefighters, Peacekeepers, and other emergency, safety, and support services also order their fellow sentients into danger," Ortuu reminded the young priestess.

"Those who have the experience to direct the fight against the fires will give those orders to those who have the will to save property and lives. Now, if you don't mind, we've wasted enough . . . seconds . . . on this subject," Leona stated, carefully skirting the T-word. "Ia, please take us to the first potential psychic ethical conundrum you have faced since our last probe in February."

"Of course." She slid them through the timeplains, back into the past, and transformed it into the same presentation display of different colored lines. "The first one took place during a boarding inspection of a Gatsugi merchant vessel, the *Plump-Brown*, at the end of February. I knew in advance that they were smuggling hallucinogenic drugs, which carry the strong possibility of harming people. But I also knew the effects of this particular shipment on the settlement of Ceti Omega IV would positively affect the future in the following ways . . ."

———————

Two hours later, they were done. Ia knew the presentation board visualization dehumanized the impact of what she was discussing. Unfortunately, it was necessary; the sheer scope of time and lives involved required a vastly simplified version. She herself was used to skimming the timestreams more directly and kinesthetically feeling her way through the effects that would happen downstream, but she couldn't do that in this session. Not without traumatizing the others.

At least the pulses from Kaskalla's mind, laced with irritation, confusion, and the urge to comment on anything she didn't understand, had slowly quelled as the session continued. Pulling them fully out of the timeplains at the end, Ia flexed her muscles subtly. The others also shifted in their chairs, stiff from having sat for too long. (*So. That, I believe, was the last of the moral ambiguities on my plate. At least to date. Any questions?*)

(*Yes, actually,*) Kaskalla stated, her thoughts crisp but guarded.

Ia's instincts prickled. Worse, the clarity she could usually sense the future with had thickened, turning misty and obscure.

Not overall, but for the next day or so. Warily, she asked, (*What do you need to know?*)

(*Can we go back to the,* ah, *timeplains, you called them?*) she asked.

Ia didn't trust her motives. Grey patches on the timeplains were often dangerous points of transition. Sometimes it was just a matter of too many choices. Sometimes it was a matter of too much interference from others. In this case, the interference came not only from a fellow psychic, but from the fact that Kaskalla was young enough to want to enjoy her position of power, and young enough to not quite have learned the life-lesson that *having* power was not the same as *wielding* power. Not where true wisdom was concerned.

Partitioning off a corner of her mind from the others, Ia examined the streams which exited the fog. The quick peek showed that whatever happened here wouldn't badly mangle the necessary paths of the future, but if she didn't pick the right choice, the wrong side-stream would increase her workload to lay and strengthen the correct courses for the future.

(*Or are you going to refuse a direct request to view your psychic abilities and activities during your current ethics review?*) Kaskalla added smugly. She tightened her grip on Ia's hand as she projected her thoughts, proving physically that she wasn't about to let go.

Ia did not trust her. It was fairly obvious the younger woman wasn't about to retract the request. She glanced at Ortuu and Leona, who were frowning slightly, but who weren't contradicting Kaskalla's request. Unfortunately, there was nothing Ia could do to probe the young woman directly, since an unasked, unauthorized telepathic scan, particularly of one of her own ethics session examiners, would violate psychic ethics beyond redemption.

There was only one path she had available to safely navigate this grey patch of uncertainty, and that was to do some legal asteroid-covering.

(*If you insist. But I'll remind you that, whatever you wish to see, you are to keep to yourself under the seal of the confessional,*) Ia added, holding her gaze.

(*I wish,*) Kaskalla stated, staring back, (*to go back onto the timeplains and ask one more question.*)

(*So be it.*) Since Kaskalla was determined to make this a

part of her ethics probe, Ia had no choice but to haul all four of them back onto the timeplains. Amber sunlight replaced artificial white, with the walls of the conference room dissolving into waves of wheat and wending streams.

"So. What did you want to see?" Ia asked her, facing the other woman.

Kaskalla lifted her chin. "I wanted to know why you don't like anyone to say the word *Time* while you're here."

Ia winced as the word rolled through their current plane of existence. "Please, don't."

"Why not? It's just a word. *Time!*" she asserted.

Ia flinched again, struggling to control her gifts. The timeplains trembled under their feet, streambeds rippling as alternate possibilities tried to shift into existence.

"Kaskalla, you're a *fool*!" Ortuu berated her, tugging on the younger woman's hand. "Haven't you figured it out, yet? For someone like Ia, word and thought and will are combined. You say that word in this place, and it will trigger her abilities involuntarily."

"That is the *point*, Ortuu," Kaskalla retorted. "If she is not in control of herself, she is a danger to others." Turning, she projected the word right in Ia's ear, deep into Ia's mind. "Time Time Time Time TIME!"

Ortuu and Leona broke their link the moment Kaskalla shouted, ripping their minds and their hands away from Ia and the other girl with a jolt. Kaskalla clung, despite the way Ia tried to shove her away. The other woman was too strong a telepath to be dislodged, her intent too piercing. With that word echoing and bouncing around them in multiple thundering rumbles, the timeplains heaved, lurching up around them like tsunami waves. This had only happened twice before in the early exploration of her newly awakened abilities . . . but despite being much more practiced in her gifts, Ia could only roll herself up in a ball and endure.

Time swallowed her whole, drowning Kaskalla's shrieks as she clung to Ia's mental back. Eons, seconds, months, minutes, centuries, years. Turn right or turn left, the fish in the river no longer had a choice in how to get around the rock in its path; the rock split, the fish split, the waters split and shattered. *Existence* shattered . . .

Children grew, aged, died. Trees shot up, split, decayed. A thousand leafer beasts nibbled new paths through the forests and valleys. Rocks reassembled themselves in reverse from weathered shards and sand. Silver spheres shat golden dust on everything in sight. Fire blossomed in obscene bouquets, volcanoes exploding, starships shattering, flames boiling up explosively from the base of a cathedral where giant projection screens were showing a man whipping a half-naked girl who screamed, not in pain, but a word, a phrase, a name distorted by the warping of Time.

"Iiiiiiaaaaa! Iiiiaaaaa'nnn sud'dhaaaaa'aaaaaaaaaa!"

It was the only thing that could have anchored both of them. Ia could weather anything Time threw at her, but Kaskalla had nothing to help *her* cope with the onslaught of infinite possibilities, save for her limited experience with this one, definitive, local moment. She grabbed at it, still clinging to Ia, dragging both of them into the scene.

The whip rose, snapped onto flesh, fell, swung, disjointed images of too many times, too many tries, too many variables. The girl bled, the girl burned; the girl lived triumphant, and simultaneously died. The Church fell, the Church thrived, a thousand golden birds took flight . . .

At least from *here*, Ia could find her way—their way—back. It felt like she was pulling that ground bus all over again, the one she had hauled on in Basic Training, but she pulled on it. Like moving a thousand, no, *ten* thousand minds back into a semblance of sanity.

Pain *cracked* across her face, mostly in her chin and nose. Groaning, Ia rolled her head to the side, sinuses throbbing from the blow. It was only the edges of the table—indeed, all furniture on Sanctuary—which were padded with the resilient, rubbery, forgiving version of plexi. The main surface of the conference table was hard and white, suitable for writing. Not for smacking into headfirst.

The inside of her skull hurt. Worse, her inner reserves were low. Dreading what that meant, Ia probed cautiously into the timestreams, holding most of her awareness at a safe distance. It took a few moments to make sense of what she saw. When she did, Ia lurched upright. Almost making it to her feet, she dropped back onto the padded seat with a *thump* and another groan.

"Slag!" Grimacing, she gingerly touched her face, then reached over and slapped the dazed-looking girl at her side. "Wake up."

Kaskalla squeaked, the blow more of a sting than a bruise. Ia slapped her again, just hard enough to redden her cheek. When the younger priestess focused on her for a glare, Ia pressed her finger to the girl's forehead. Not to touch the other woman psychically, but to imprint her message *physically*, with focus-grounding pain.

"Congratulations, meioa. Because *you* wouldn't listen, your stubbornness has just caused a citywide *mind-quake."*

"Guh . . . wha . . . ?" Kaskalla asked, blinking.

Ia shoved hard with her finger before releasing the girl. She lifted her fingers to her aching nose and focused her inner biokinetic energies into the bruised flesh, healing the inadvertent damage. Once that was done, she dipped two fingers into Leona's cup of water and dragged them across her brow, trying to use evaporation to cool the heat burning through her forehead, her sinuses.

Slumped back in her chair where she had collapsed, Leona lifted her hands to her face and groaned. "Oh, gods, not another mind-quake . . ."

"Ugh . . . what's a mind-quake?" Kaskalla asked, still a bit dazed but finally regathering her wits.

Grunting, Ortuu lifted his dark head from the table. Like Ia, he dipped his fingers in his drink and streaked them around the bridge of his nose before puffing air upward in the hopes of soothing the mental burn. "A mind-quake . . . is when an especially powerful psi . . . *ungh* . . . affects *everyone* within a set range. You grew up down by the sea, but even *you* should remember the Night of the Prophecy, from four and a half years back? It was in all the news Nets."

"The Night . . . ? I did a report on it in high school, but everyone thought it was just some strange mass attack of the Fire Girl Prophecy!" Kaskalla protested. "No one had ever found a triggering cause!"

Lifting her free hand, Ia fluttered her fingers. Kaskalla gaped and shook her head in denial. She subsided when both Leona and Ortuu nodded in confirmation.

Leona lifted her own hand. The older woman's cheeks turned

a bit pink as well. "I made the same mistake you did just now. Except I at least had Ia's permission, since we didn't know what we were doing at the time. After our second try did the exact same thing that night, we knew better than to try again."

Nose still throbbing but on its way to being healed, Ia gave Kaskalla a hard, dark look.

"People are going to come looking for the epicenter of the mass Prophecy attack, and that means they will come *here*. All three of you will simply say, 'I honestly cannot say what happened' . . . and if you have any qualms about lying, you are *forbidden* to say what happened, so therefore you cannot," Ia stated crisply. She aimed it mostly at Kaskalla, since Ortuu and Leona already knew what not to say. "If anyone asks about me, I was only here for a brief stop to say hello to some old friends . . . and I left over an hour ago. You will put the truth into my official evaluation, because the truth must be put into it, but then you will *seal it*. Got that?"

"*Ah* . . . I . . . guess so," Kaskalla agreed. She half shook her head, still looking a bit dazed. Then quickly grabbed her temples, grimacing. "But . . . I just can't believe that *you* were the source of . . . of *thousands* of people all experiencing a massive surge of prophetic visions! And . . . and you've been offworld for two *years*, yet we've still been having these Fire Girl attacks. How can *you* be the source of them when you're not even here?"

"That's because I'm *not* the source of them, normally," Ia admitted, though she carefully avoided saying what that source was. "However, you are a very strong telepath, and you were hooked into my brain, with *my* gifts. We were in gestalt, which amplified my precognitive visions right across the city. Luckily, most everyone had enough warning to brace themselves . . . but because *you* triggered a broadcasting of my abilities, strong enough that people lost control of their senses, you have directly caused sixteen traffic accidents. Thankfully, none of them were lethal, and everyone will recover with medical aid."

Pushing to her feet, Ia swayed, then slumped back into her chair once more. Grunting, she touched her forehead, then shoved up the lid of her wrist unit.

"Great . . . I'm drained. I can't walk very far." Punching in the numbers for her brother's unit, she waited a few seconds. The moment Thorne answered, Ia spoke. "Thorne, to answer your question, *yes*, it happened again. But I'm in no shape to walk all the way out of here. Meet me in the bunker tunnels under the Church of Contemplation."

"I'm hardly in any shape to carry you, myself," he retorted, hand coming into view at the edge of the screen. He rubbed at his face, then sighed. "*Fine* . . . I'll be there shortly. Stop giving people slagging headaches."

Nodding, Ia shut the lid, ending the connection. "Remember, as far as anyone else is concerned I was here *only* for a short time, and *not* for anything psi-related. I was just here to catch up with my old church friends, and left a while ago. Volunteer nothing, because otherwise you're as clueless as anyone else as to what just happened here. And don't embellish."

Gathering her willpower, Ia pushed one last time to her feet. Head aching, mind throbbing, she shuffled toward the door. Thankfully, the access hatch to the bunker tunnels was only a few doors down from this particular conference room.

"I'm . . . I *am* sorry," Kaskalla offered. She was rubbing the side of her head, which no doubt still ached.

Ia paused at the door, glancing back over her shoulder. "Try to listen a little better next time. Other people *do* occasionally know better than you . . . and some experiments should not be repeated."

Pulling the door open, Ia left them in the room. She had to brace her hand on the corridor wall to keep her trembling body from staggering, but she left. It would be another twenty-plus minutes before emergency services realized the mind-quake was more or less round in shape, and another ten minutes to realize that this location was the focal point of its kilometers-wide radius. She needed to be back home long before then, without anyone seeing her near the church.

On the bright side, the fog has cleared . . . and Kaskalla will indeed do whatever I or Leona or Ortuu tell her to do. She'll rise in the ranks of non-Church religious politics, and be an added touch of leverage for saving everyone when the revolution comes.

So this moment was a literal headache, and I'll have tidying-up efforts to make, based on the few people whose accidents might adversely affect the shift and flow of the future . . . but overall, a net gain. Small, but good.

CHAPTER 5

My mothers never did get used to my rising early for physi-
cal training while I stayed with them. I tried to be quiet,
but it was an inevitable reminder that I was now in the
military and they were going to lose me again. But they did
rise early with me, my last day on Sanctuary that year. It's
never easy when loved ones have to leave you, and doubly
hard when you know they're going to serve in the military.
Even if I wasn't headed for a combat zone at that point,
they knew I'd wind up in one eventually.

For myself, parting from them wasn't easy. I knew I had
to do it, and I did it, but I never once said any of this was
easy.

~Ia

AUGUST 9, 2492 T.S.

Her head ached. Thankfully not from any overuse of her gifts
or face-plants on a hard surface. Lack of sleep made her uncomfortable this time. Rubbing at her tired eyes, wishing she could
just go back to bed, Ia breathed deeply several times. She also
swallowed another mouth of cold caf', and stared blearily at
the last three questions on her Net-based exams. They were
being taken in real time over the hyperrelay channels, despite

the lag between Sanctuary and Earth of roughly one second for every fifty lightyears, and had to be completed on time, or her scores would be docked.

Ia already had a Field Commission as a Lieutenant Second Class in the Space Force Marine Corps. In order to retain that rank, she had to go through training at an Officers' Academy; that was standard military procedure, and smart, since it guaranteed all officers above the lowest attainable rank had the same basic leadership training. In order to advance beyond Lieutenant First Class, however—which she would only get after distinguishing herself through at least a full decade of service, if she didn't play the military's game—she also had to have a Master's degree.

Since she needed to be able to advance at a moment's notice in the future, Ia had signed up for a series of classes on the Nets shortly after boarding the *Liu Ji*, back when she was just a corporal in the Marines. This particular virtual college simply presented the course materials, expected the students to learn on their own time, and then provided the exams online, all for a reasonable fee. It worked well, but it only worked if the students actually applied themselves to their lessons. It wasn't just rote memorization, either; each question in the final exams was different enough from the information provided in the resource materials that a student had to *know* the subject matter to be able to answer them correctly.

The door down the hall opened. Ia answered the question on her screen and hit the send key on her parents' workstation, without bothering to correct the typo in her answer. It might count slightly against her, but that was alright; she didn't want to pass with perfect marks, just pass with reasonably good ones.

One of her mothers shuffled out of their bedroom. Thankfully toward the bathroom, not the living room. Ia focused on the next question on her test; this was her final exam in her chosen Master's field, Military History. Once she was done with it and her scores tallied and registered, she would be eligible for the fast-track program at her chosen Academy. The bedroom door opened again behind her, and she heard her other mother move to wait at the bathroom door, not quite successfully smothering a yawn.

That audio cue forced Ia to smother one of her own, then sip at the cooled remnants of caf' in her mug. By the time she reached the final question, Amelia had slipped onto the sofa next to her child. Wrapping an arm around Ia's shoulders and snuggling her head on her daughter's shoulder, she peered at the screen. With her arm cushioned from Ia's skin by her bathrobe and her cheek on the fabric covering Ia's shoulder, there was less chance for her mother to trigger a precognitive vision, but less wasn't the same as none. Ia slipped her arm around her biomother's ribs, hugging her back, then helped her biomother sit upright again.

"'Who was nicknamed the White Death in World War II, Terran Standard Twentieth Century, and what trick did he use to prevent his breath from being seen?'" her mother recited aloud. "*Ugh*. You couldn't *pay* me to study Military History in that much depth. Did you get any sleep at all, *gataki mou*?"

Struggling against another yawn, Ia nodded. "Some. There's . . . *mm* . . . a Human on the other end of the testing Net at this time of the morning. I've already chatted with her. I need to have this last test witnessed so that when my transcripts arrive at the Academy, the TUPSF will be able to question and confirm that it really was me taking the exams—the voice link is active," she added, tapping the screen. "She can hear everything we're saying. That is, if she's not busy with something else. This is the last question, anyway."

"I trust you know it?" Aurelia asked, headed for the kitchen. "Fresh caf', anyone?"

"*Mm*, that would be lovely, dear," Amelia murmured. She sagged back on the couch, leaving her daughter free to compose her answer.

Ia touched the keys, typing each letter with her fingers, rather than her mind.

"*Simo Häyhä was the 'White Death' of Finland. Fighting in the coldest months of winter, he would often put snow into his mouth and breathe through it, so that the ice crystals would chill his breath with each exhale, preventing any puffs of steam from giving away his position. His military service took place during the Winter War of 1939–1940 Terran Standard, involving Finland versus the invading forces of the Soviet Union, and included over seven hundred confirmed, credited kills with both sniper rifle and machine gun. His career ended March 6th, 1940 T.S. when a bullet disfigured his face.*"

It was a bit more than the question actually called for, but it was an easy question, and Ia wanted to reassure the test examiners that she did, indeed, know historical military facts. *As if I couldn't just dip into the past on the timeplains and pluck the facts from any stream I wanted—the real facts, not just the accounts written down afterward.*

"There. Done." She struck the send key, then tapped the icon for the voice link. *"Thanks for keeping me company, Meioa Giltrers."*

It took a few seconds for the reply to come back. Even at hyperrelay speeds, Sanctuary was a long, long way from Earth. *"Eh, it's not like I have anything better to do on the night shift. You go on and have a good night's rest, or whatever time of day it is all the way out at wherever-the-heck you're from."*

That made Ia chuckle. *"It's now morning, local time."*

"Says *you*," her biomother grunted, still slouched on the sofa, arm over her eyes.

The examiner, Giltrers, spoke up again through the link. *"Then I'll just say good morning to you. Your test will be graded and the results will be posted in three days. If you don't see them by then, contact the Exam Board via the conveniently named Contact the Exam Board link, and include my name, Maria Giltrers, as the test examiner for verification purposes. Now, any questions before we end this undoubtedly hellaciously expensive link?"*

"None—and it's still technically a brand-new colonyworld, so all links certified for educational purposes only are provided for free by the government. Thank you for your patience, meioa, and have a good night." Ending the connection, Ia powered down the workstation. Shifting it from her lap to the coffee table, she sagged back against the cushions. For a moment, all she could see was the bleak prospect of packing up her belongings and boarding a shuttle for the space station that evening. *But I only have nineteen hours left with my family, and some of those hours won't be pleasant ones . . .*

Curling over, she cuddled onto her mother's lap. Amelia stroked her fingers through Ia's short white locks. "My little white kitten . . . How big you've grown. How far you'll roam. I do wish you didn't have to go away . . ."

"*I* wish I didn't have to go back, either," Ia murmured. "That none of this was necessary. That I could be *normal*."

Aurelia emerged from the kitchen, carrying a tray with three steaming mugs of caf' deftly balanced on it. "You'd be extraordinary, *gataki*, no matter what your abilities were like. I have proof of it; you were kind enough to prepare an extra pot, so I didn't have to wait as long for it to brew."

Ia smiled wryly at that. Sighing, she pushed herself upright and accepted the fresh mug. "So . . . anything planned for today?"

"Crying, weeping, wailing, gnashing of teeth, and some breast-beating. Possibly some sobbing, if we can fit it into the schedule," Aurelia quipped, settling on Ia's other side. She patted her daughter on the leg, then sagged back against the sofa cushions with a sigh. "I don't want you to go, either. It'll be, what, two more years before we'll see you again?"

"In person, yes. And it'll be three years; I have to spend one year at the Academy in Sines, Portugal, then two more years of duty before I'll be free to come back home. But I'll be an officer, with more leeway in making hyperrelay calls back home," Ia offered. "Once a week, rather than once a month."

"Scant comfort," Aurelia groused. "It's not the same as holding my baby girl. Not that I can hold you for long, even when you *are* here . . ."

Mouth twisting in wry acknowledgment, Ia leaned onto her other mother's shoulder. Aurelia pulled her close, giving her a cuddle, then patted her on the arm and let Ia sit back up again. Drawing in a deep breath, Ia let it out. She tipped her head back, copying both of her mothers, and looked at the white-painted ceiling. "So. My last day here."

Aurelia patted her on the thigh. "What do you need to do today, kitten?"

"*Mm.* Finish filling up those memory chips so you can print out my precognitive missives once I'm gone . . . experiment on my brothers nefariously . . . and eat Momma's Restaurant's famous triple topado pie." She flashed each of her mothers a grin at that last one. "With ice cream."

Amelia chuckled. "Opportunist."

"What sort of experiments?" Aurelia asked, frowning.

"Just some prototype devices I need to have working and ready to go into production, next time I come back," Ia dismissed. "They're pretty much ready, though I wouldn't mind running one last set of tests. Actually, I really should run them on someone . . . else . . . oh, bother." Ia groaned under her breath, realizing there was one last thing she hadn't covered, yet. "Mom? Ma? We need to have a talk."

"What sort of talk?" Aurelia asked, her brow pinched and her tone skeptical.

"*The* Talk." Sighing, Ia pushed herself upright and edged around the coffee table. Putting physical space between her and her mothers would help. Looming over them would be too aggressive, yet she had to be on her feet, to assert herself visually. Turning to face them once she was a couple body-lengths away, Ia relaxed her shoulders with a shrug. "I love you both, dearly and deeply . . . but it's time to have The Talk with you."

"Alright . . . so, talk," Aurelia told her. Amelia scooted closer to her, cuddling subtly with her wife.

Taking a deep breath, Ia gave it to them. "I am *not* your little girl anymore. I have not been for years, and I will *never again* be your little girl—and I'm not just talking about being a grown-up," she added as Amelia drew in a breath to speak. "I am talking about the fact that I need you to support me as the *Prophet*, from here on out. You are two of the most normal people I know. Everybody *sees* you as perfectly normal."

"Except for the Church," Amelia snorted.

"They're not normal themselves," Ia dismissed. "My point is, I need you to stop seeing me, addressing me, and treating me as your little girl, your daughter, your child. People need to start seeing me as the Prophet of a Thousand Years, foretold in V'Dan folklore and the Sh'nai faith, the master of the Fire Girl Prophecies, the protector and defender of the future. *Our* future, on this world. If they see *you*, two perfectly normal, sane, well-adjusted adults accepting, honoring, and following my directives . . ."

"Look," she tried again, raking a hand through her hair before dropping it to her hip. "There's a certain momentum that needs to build, here in Sanctuarian society. Rabbit has the teenagers covered; the key members have met with me and they now believe in me, and she'll keep them believing. Thorne is working on presenting me to the support services, manufactories, and other businesses, and so forth. Fyfer will be going into the political and legal venues. I need *you* to reassure all the other perfectly normal people that I am a viable, sane alternative to falling in step with the madness of the Church. And you *cannot* do that if you keep calling me 'kitten' and *gataki mou* and thinking of me as your sweet little girl. It will come out in the littlest, subtlest ways . . . and that will undermine everything I need to do."

She eyed her parents, waiting to see how they would take all of that. Amelia twisted her mouth, while Aurelia huffed and frowned. Arms folded, Aurelia retorted, "Well, you *are* our little girl, first and foremost."

"No. I am not," Ia countered. "Not anymore, not ever again. *Think.* You're resisting me right now. You're not taking me seriously now. Hell—you don't even take the fact that I'm in the *military* seriously!" She flipped her hands up, then dropped them back to her hips, hoping and wishing her parents could see why this was necessary. "I would give up *almost* anything to still *be* your little girl . . . but I cannot, and *will not*, give up all the lives that will be slaughtered if I cannot pull off a gods-be-slagging *miracle*, both here and abroad. And *I cannot be here.*

"I need *you* to do what I cannot. I need you to be my hands and my arms and my legs here on Sanctuary. I need you to lead by *example.* You're still very strong figures in the local community. You're business leaders. People look up to you, they like you, they're friends with you . . . discounting the Church's brainwash victims and persecution hounds," Ia allowed. "You need to be *more* active in local business meetings. You need to circulate more, and talk about the things your sons are trying to do. You need to make friends and contacts, and be *the* couple to go to for safe, sane solutions in an increasingly *insane* political environment. And you need to do it with an unshaking faith in both myself as the Prophet and in the future predictions I have made. Which *you* must distribute when the time is right. Not Thorne, not Fyfer, not Rabbit. *You.*

"Which means you must stop thinking of me as your 'little girl.' Stop trying to shelter me, stop trying to protect me, and stop trying to defend your status as my parents and thus 'always superior' to me." Realizing her shoulders were tensing up, Ia shrugged and sighed, relaxing them. "It's like your joke earlier, that a mother will always outrank her daughter. I'm sorry, Mom, Ma . . . but you do not, you cannot, and you *must* not ever think that way again, or it will ruin the things I'm striving for."

Her biomother didn't look too happy. Her other mother looked even less pleased. Aurelia rolled her eyes. "Fine. So we can't call you our little girl anymore. We get the point."

"We'll do what you want, *gata* . . . er, Ia," Amelia amended. "I'm sorry. You can't expect us to give up being your mothers in a heartbeat! I mean, we'll try, but . . ."

Ia didn't have to probe the timestreams to know it was a reluctant, unhappy acceptance. She did anyway, double-checking the probabilities. What she found didn't make her happy, either. Raking her hands through her hair, Ia checked her options. The potential possibilities ended with her angling a hand back toward the hallway. The door to her brothers' bedroom opened silently, telekinetically, and two faintly glowing circlets floated out of the darkness.

"I'm treading a very fine line, here," she told her mothers, catching a head-sized, lumpy ring in each hand, matched pairs of her prophetic circlets. "The Church tricks its followers with its rhetoric and its verses and its dogmatic interpretations. They even do subtle subliminal advertisings already. And they will one day resort to outright brainwashing, and worse. I do realize the irony of what I myself am trying to do in return. I *am* building up my own cult of followers, filling them with my own dogmas and my own demands."

The words hurt to admit, but Ia admitted them bluntly, accepting responsibility to her parents for what she needed to do to the saner half of their homeworld.

"I am, in so many ways, doing *exactly* what they are doing. My methods may be slightly different, and my message vastly different . . . but the end result is the same. Two ideologically opposed camps filled with fanatics on both sides. Their side, and my side. What they do with rhetoric and coercion, I must do with truths and persuasion." She looked down at the lumpy, wreath-shaped, translucent peach rings in her hands. "And, like them, I must use tricks to get my message across . . . and I must use them on my own mothers."

"What are those things?" Aurelia asked her, eyeing them warily. "I know you've been working on them, but . . . what, exactly, are they?"

"Technically . . . I suppose you could call them biokinetically activated, parapsicognitive, temporal consequence feedback enhancers." At her mothers' blank looks, Ia let a touch of humor twist the corners of her mouth. "Don't worry about it. Just call them the Rings of Truth. It's a lot easier to say.

"This one," she said, lifting the one shaped vaguely like a crown of brambles, with lumpy bits suggestive of thorns, "is the Wreath of Pain. And this one is the Wreath of Hope." She lifted the other one, which had rounder, less linear blobs, which, in a certain light, suggested the thought of flowers. Looking back at her mothers, she lowered them, her smile fading. "You will get to try on both."

Amelia slipped her hand into her gynowife's, gripping it. Aurelia eyed the devices warily. "Why does the thought of putting on something nicknamed the Wreath of Pain fill me with deep reluctance, Daughter?"

Aware that both mothers shared that reluctance, Ia answered obliquely.

"The difference between the Church's methodology and my own is that the Church wants to take away the free will of its followers. To brainwash everyone into following its dogmatic beliefs, smothering logic, truth, and free thought. 'You *will* follow the teachings of the Church of the One True God, because God says that there *is* no other way,'" she mocked dryly. "'Every other way is a sin, and to follow any other path means condemning your souls and the souls of those who follow you into the agonies of eternal hellfire and damnation . . .' And for the Church in the decades to come, that eternal hellfire and damnation will become a very real and physical fire for those condemned as heretics. Stop thinking and conform, or die.

"Or be 'reeducated' . . . which for the psychically gifted will include lobotomizing certain portions of the brain in an effort to stop such abilities from forming and being used. After all, if you can read another person's thoughts, that means someone out there is actually still thinking, and isn't being a perfect little sheep in their flock. Or worse," Ia added sardonically.

"The psi in question might find out what the Church Elders are *really* plotting behind the woolly little backs of that flock."

"And *your* methods?" Amelia asked her quietly.

"My methods?" Ia asked. She spread her arms slightly. "I believe in free will. As ironic as it is for *me* to say this, of all people, I have always believed in it. I believe in people choosing the best lives possible, both for themselves and for others. But how can you make a *good* choice if you do not yet know the consequences of your decisions? *These* will show people those consequences.

"Both of the things they have done in the past," Ia stated, lifting the Wreath of Pain, then the Wreath of Hope, "and the things they should do in the future. I need people on my side, working for my cause, because they *know* it's the right thing to do. People who, after having been fully informed, have consciously decided to do the right thing . . . *these* people can move mountains, worlds, and even whole star systems when they put their minds and their wills and their efforts into it.

"So I am . . . I am *asking* you," Ia said, stumbling a little over the words, because these *were* her parents, her beloved mothers, and she *knew* this would change their relationship that last little irrevocable bit, "to put these on. To *see* with your own eyes what I have seen—just a *fraction* of what I have seen—and to choose. I need you to decide of your own free will whether you will follow me as the Prophet of a Thousand Years, and *not* just because I'm Iantha Iulia Quentin-Jones, your very strange, very troubled, but well-meaning little girl.

"You raised me both to see the problems around me, and to step up to the responsibility of fixing them. You raised me to do the right thing," she reminded her mothers. "For that, you should be proud as my mothers . . . but it is time to let me go and let me do it. And it is time for you to decide whether or not you'll do it as well. *After* you have seen the choices and the consequences that await."

Stepping around the coffee table, Ia held up the Wreath of Pain. Her mothers eyed it for a long moment, then Amelia started to reach for it. She hesitated, though. "*Um . . . gataki . . .* isn't this the one you called the Wreath of Pain?"

"I need you to wear both. For the next thirty years, *everyone* will have to try on both. It's the best way to get the right kind of momentum going. And I need you to try the Wreath of Pain first, so that . . . well, so that you'll have the Wreath of Hope to look forward to—don't worry so much," she said, rolling her eyes as that statement made her biomother hesitate even more. "You aren't a mass murderer, so you won't be seeing the points of view of your victims. You'll just see some of the consequences of bad decisions you've made in the past. I won't lie; it *will* be unsettling. But you'll come out of it okay. My Prophetic Stamp on that."

Aurelia let out a short, dry chuckle at that. "You keep saying that, little kitten. I suppose I ought to see if you really mean it. *Ah* . . . is there anything *I* should do?"

"Well, Mom should move away from you," Ia told her, grateful when Amelia complied. "But otherwise, the only thing you need to do is be sitting or kneeling when trying one of these things. I've foreseen that some people might sag a little if they're startled by what they see. Here, let me put it on you, Ma . . ."

The device had a subtly tapered, thicker segment on the inner side. Part of that was to help augment the psychic resonances of the device, but part of it was simply to ensure that it would fit on any head it encountered. Almost any head; the K'katta, the Chinsoiy, and the Dlmvla didn't keep their brains in the same physiologically analogous location as most of the other currently known sentient races. But since her mother was a fellow Human—more so, given who and what Ia's father had been—it was just a matter of aligning the ring so that it settled comfortably onto the crown of Aurelia's skull.

Her mother sucked in a sharp breath, brown eyes widening until the whites could be seen all around them. Amelia eyed her partner warily, then looked to Ia for reassurance. Holding up her empty hand, Ia waited. Trial and error over the last three weeks had led her to this version of the torus rings, which she hoped was the final one. In particular, the Wreath of Pain was the most difficult to judge. She had tried it on her brothers, and Fyfer—who had broken more laws than Thorne—had reacted more strongly to what he saw, but neither of her brothers were lifelong criminals. Neither of them had lived all that long, period.

By comparison, her mothers had a couple extra decades of

life-choices on their consciences; the law of averages dictated they had more things to regret and atone for. They also had calmer natures than either the exuberant Fyfer or his phlegmatic stepbrother. A corner of Ia's mind considered this one part of a proof-of-concept experiment, since the Wreath of Pain was meant to thoroughly punish only those who thoroughly deserved it. The rest of her waited tensely, uncomfortable with making her beloved parent suffer.

Tears gathered in Aurelia's eyes. They didn't spill until she blinked and lifted her hands, removing the heavy, crystalline ring from her head. Sniffing, she held it out to Ia without a word. Ia accepted it, and settled the Wreath of Hope on her mother's dark hair . . . then reached over and placed the Wreath of Pain on her biomother's curly brown locks. Amelia stiffened, eyes wide and sightless. Aurelia sagged, eyes shut and fluttering as she strained to process the new images.

Experiments on her brothers had shown her that the images being seen would be the ones most crucial for Ia's purposes. Truths would be shown about how certain tasks needed to be undertaken, and the consequences of both success and failure. That part was necessary. It wasn't what the wreaths showed that concerned her now, but rather their intensity.

Amelia finished before Aurelia. She reached up and pushed the ring of crysium from her head. Ia stooped and plucked it from the sofa before it could flop over and land on her other mother. Her experiments had also proven it wasn't wise to mix the two; the chaos of the dual effects had given Fyfer a painful migraine for a few hours. When Aurelia opened her eyes, sniffing hard, Ia transferred the Wreath of Hope to her biological mother and waited. And waited. Finally, Amelia opened her eyes as well, tipping her head forward so Ia could remove the device.

Aurelia sniffed again, then nodded. "Alright. I see now what you mean. I mean, I've *seen* some of your visions; you've showed me things in the past, but this . . . This is . . ."

"This is what *we* can do about it," Amelia finished, finding and squeezing her gynowife's hand. Aurelia glanced at her and nodded. Together, they looked at Ia. Looked to her for guidance. For approval.

For the first time, she sensed her parents were finally looking at her as a fellow adult. More than that, they were looking at her as the Prophet. The little girl deep inside of Ia, the one who just wanted to curl up on their laps and let them stroke her hair, wanted to cry at this last loss of her childhood. Instead, that little girl curled up and faded into the shadows of her past. It hurt. Ia acknowledged silently that it hurt . . . and she set it aside.

"I'm glad," she murmured, "because I really do need you. In fact, I'm going to put these rings into your hands. Yours, and my brothers' hands," she amended. Ia set them on the coffee table, two *clacks*. Molded though they were, the peach gold rings were still very much a hard, unyielding crystal. "Use your contacts within the community. Figure out who you think can be trusted with exposure to these."

"What if . . . what if we choose wrong?" Amelia asked her. "And some Church sympathizer gets hold of one?"

Ia lifted her chin. "I've already considered that. If they're really Church agents, or Church sympathizers . . . or anyone who is bound to betray us to them . . . well, they'll just get a dose of the Fire Girl Prophecy. A rather large dose."

Aurelia snorted. "*That* should be enough to send 'em running for the leafer-hills."

Twisting her mouth in a wry smile, Ia nodded at the rings. "I'll be taking them out later this afternoon, once Thorne gets back from college. There's one more person who needs to experience them before I leave, to make sure they're working properly. We'll be back at least two hours before I have to leave for the spaceport, don't worry." She paused for a yawn, and scrubbed at her face with both hands. "*Ugh.* I got up way too early. At least my ship is already docked at Gateway Station, busy with unloading cargo for the colony and arranging for exports to the rest of the known galaxy. I can sleep as soon as I've been shown to my berth."

"Do you want breakfast?" Aurelia asked, leaning forward to pick up her forgotten caf' mug.

Ia stooped and picked up her own. "Not yet. I need to go for a run, first." Swallowing half of the still warm liquid, she set it back down again. "The Naval Academy will be putting us through regimen training, and they'll be expecting me to wear my weight suit, so I need to stay in shape. But I'll cut it down

to half an hour this morning, so you can make me a really nice
going-away breakfast."

Rising, Aurelia lifted onto her toes and kissed Ia on her
cheek. "It'll be hot and waiting."

"*Mm*, good, I can go back to sleep, then," Amelia murmured.
She closed her eyes and snuggled into the corner of the sofa.

Her wife leaned down and slapped her lightly on one
bathrobe-covered thigh. "Oh, no you don't, meioa-e! You're a
far better chef than I am, and you know it. Get into that kitchen
and start cooking, love."

Amelia grumbled something uncomplimentary in Greek,
added an Irish expletive for color, raspberried her wife half-
heartedly, and hauled herself upright. Relieved that her parents
hadn't changed *that* much in the wake of the wreaths, Ia headed
for the door to the stairs. Rain or shine, space or ground, she
had to keep herself in shape.

Edwin V'Sasselli lived in one of the apartment complexes built
during the Terran–Dlmvla tensions. In fact, he lived in one of
the basement-level apartments, formerly a series of storage rooms
and janitorial facilities converted into living quarters. As a result,
he had at the back of his spare bedroom an access door which
led down into the escape tunnels for the Terran bunkers.

Of course, all such doors were supposed to be sealed with
Terran military-grade locks, to reduce the chance of the colonists
pilfering or vandalizing Terran military equipment. Edwin
V'Sasselli had taken great pains to neutralize and remove those
locks. He had taken even greater pains to make sure that the
path to the door was kept clear, and the door itself hidden by a
rather large, showy rug which he had hung up like a tapestry.

He never mentioned the existence of the door to anyone,
never mentioned that it was unlocked, and only used it infre-
quently at best. So when Ia and Thorne opened the door from
within the dusty, musty tunnels and slipped into that spare
bedroom, set up as his office, he had no clue that anyone else
knew of it, let alone intended to use it as the means for committing illegalities. Then again, Edwin V'Sasselli was something of an expert on committing illegalities, himself.

Thorne might have protested at this act of breaking and

entering, save for the facts she had given him when explaining the necessity of this one particular home invasion. When he had heard those facts, when she had sworn they were true with her Prophetic Stamp, he had agreed to accompany her. Coming here on her own would have defeated the purpose of this little visit, after all.

This was something Ia was not allowed to do for her brother. All she could do was assist him just a little bit. Thorne was the one who had to carry it through.

The plexcrete floor under the carpeting was old, but not yet old enough to squeak under the compression of her footsteps. Padding quietly into the living room, Ia held up her hand. Startled by her sudden appearance in his home, the short, balding, wiry Edwin rose from his couch where he had been quietly watching the evening news. Grabbing him telekinetically, Ia held him in place, half crouched, half erect, and unable to move. At least, unable to move his limbs; she hadn't done anything about his mouth.

"What the—! How dare you!" he snapped, struggling in little twitches. "Let me go! I'll call the Peacekeepers for this!"

"I think you'll find that impossible, as I have cut power to the emergency pickups in your apartment," Ia returned calmly. "Just like you yourself have done, time and again."

Glancing at her brother, she nodded. He swallowed, nodded back, and shifted the backpack he was carrying, swinging it around on one shoulder so that he could open the main compartment. Fishing out the thorn-themed ring tucked inside, he lifted it in one hand.

"Edwin V'Sasselli . . . by the authority invested in me by the Free World Colony . . . the paperwork for which is still being processed by the Alliance courts," Thorne stated, clearing his throat, "I hereby charge you with the murders of Vanessa Smythe, Erika Johnston, and Clattica Jjoll, among others."

Edwin twitched at those names, eyes widening. "I don't know what you're talking about. What is that thing? What are you going to do with it?"

"What, this?" Thorne asked, his voice deepening. He lifted the Wreath of Pain above the smaller man's head, but didn't place it yet. "This is Justice. And *it*, not I, will deliver your sentence and your punishment."

Setting it squarely on the man's head, Thorne stepped back. Edwin sucked in a sharp breath, eyes first rolling up, then squeezing shut. Ia eased his half-bent body back onto the cushions of the couch. She loosened some of her mental grip on him, grateful to be relieved of his weight, but still kept some of it in place. It was a good thing, too; he opened his mouth in a hissing, near-silent scream, and started thrashing, trying to beat at his chest. Or rather, trying to beat something away from his chest.

Thorne started to move toward him.

"No," Ia countered sharply, firmly. "He must endure this until he *himself* takes off the wreath."

"He's trying to thrash it off his head," Thorne grumbled, voice deepening in his distress. "Isn't *that* a form of trying to take it off, himself?"

Sighing, Ia stepped around the padded corner of the coffee table. Reaching up, she pinned the coronet-like wreath in place and sunk her gifts into the material, altering its shape slightly. Not just altering the physical suggestion of thorns, but the interior striations of pink-tinged gold, where her blood had been fused to the faintly luminescent stone.

Edwin's thrashings quieted. She removed her touch. He still twitched, but his head lolled back against the cushions of the sofa, the makeshift crown of crysium still lodged firmly on his balding head. His mouth still opened and shut, but it did so with eerie silence.

"The experience has now been intensified internally, not externally. He won't throw it off. Nor will the others—don't stop watching him, Thorne," she warned her brother. "You *have* to watch it. Everyone has to watch this happening with the future criminals you will find. It will become one of the requirements for ascending to adult status in the coming years. *You*, I know, will have the fortitude to apply the Wreath of Pain to criminals. Fyfer won't do it more than twice at most, and Rabbit's too softhearted to do it even once, herself, though she must watch at the very least. Your mother might drop it on someone's head—Aurelia has always been the tougher of the pair—but we both know *my* mother won't.

"You won't have the facilities to incarcerate criminals," Ia reminded him, ignoring the way V'Sasselli continued to twitch and spasm on the sofa. "Not in the long term. You won't have the resources to spare to *build* long-term prisons, let alone maintain and guard them. You also won't have the means to chain your criminals to a topado patch like the Terrans do, either. Instead, you will have to use this technique. Together, the Wreaths of Pain and Hope will be your greatest tools for dealing with criminals. Those who are redeemable, they will work to redeem themselves."

"And if they're not?" Thorne challenged her as Edwin V'Sasselli continued to grimace and twitch. "What if being caught up in a postcognitive loop of the victims' sufferings from *their* point of view isn't enough to convince them to rehabilitate themselves?"

"One of three things will happen. If they have a conscience, they will work hard to make reparations. If they are beyond redemption, they will most likely end their own lives. And if they are *fated* to continue . . . they will continue. After that point," she acknowledged, not even flinching at the hard look her half brother gave her, "if they break the law again and you catch them, you will put them through the Wreath of Pain a second time. If they choose to break it a third time—and I haven't written any precognitive missives countermanding it—then you will execute them.

"I believe the term back on pre-interstellar Earth was 'three strikes and you're out,' " she added dryly, dispassionately watching the man on the couch twitching and suffering in breath-huffing quiet. "Once Edwin here removes this Ring of Truth, if he doesn't head straight for the kitchen and the nearest knife . . . his favorite knife . . . then you will put the Wreath of Hope on his head. There's a roughly thirty percent chance he will kill himself straight away, just from the Wreath of Pain. After the Wreath of Hope . . . it jumps to forty percent.

"However," she cautioned her brother, "*if* he chooses to rehabilitate himself by swearing to follow you and me . . . you *will* use him. Remember, Thorne, your resources will be severely limited when the civil war hits. You will need men and women like Edwin, here. Murderers who will become assassins, thieves who will become infiltration artists and security specialists. Spies who will become counterspies and double-agents."

"You told me," he muttered, slowly shaking his head. "You *told* me, but I didn't believe it . . ."

"The criminal element *must* become a part of the Free World Colony's government. You will need every trick of their trades to counter every trick the Church will try to throw at you," Ia reminded him, word for word. "Cities can be attacked, tunnels can be collapsed, food and water and even clean air may sometimes be in short supply, but your greatest resource will *always* be the people you command. Use. Them. Wisely." She returned her gaze to the man on the couch. "Even if, personally, you think serial killer *skut* like this piece of slag should be thrown into the ocean."

Thorne snorted at that. "What, and poison the devilfish? Ironic as that might be, not even those things deserve to choke on a murderer's flesh."

"If he doesn't kill himself, you'll get five, maybe six good years out of him," Ia told her brother. "He'll itch to kill, so you may need to *find* targets . . . but in five to six years, he'll break loose and try to freelance. At that point, don't hesitate; just kill him, quickly and cleanly. Your alternative option, whether or not this one cracks and goes under now or later, is outlined in the time-sensitive files. You'll encounter him about a year from now—one way or another, you *will* need to remove a couple of key players in the Church's inner circle, in a year and a half, and you'll need the help of someone, *ah* . . . eminently qualified, shall we say?"

That made him wrinkle his nose. "I am *not* comfortable contemplating the cold-blooded assassination of anyone. Even a fanatical Church member."

"I know." She softened her tone with a touch of pity, compassion, and understanding. "Believe me, I do know. No one's life should have to be wasted . . . but if it's a choice between shooting down a rabid stubbie or letting the dog bite everyone in sight, shoot that one dog quickly and cleanly, and spare everyone else. If it helps, you can always put on the Wreath of Hope and remind yourself *why* we're doing all of this."

"Oh, I do know. You made me and Fyfer wear the damned things repeatedly over the last three weeks," he grumbled. "I feel like I could almost write a couple of prophesies myself."

Ia rolled her eyes. "Do try to refrain. Oh, and crack down hard and fast on *anyone* who tries to forge my prophecies," she added. "God knows the Church will try, but so will some of the less stable elements on the Free World Colony's side. I'll be leaving a definitive list with both you and the Afaso Order, so you'll know exactly which ones are real and which ones are being faked."

"Any other last-minute directives, O Prophet?" Thorne asked her dryly.

Unlike her mothers, she didn't expect him to stop treating her like his sister. They were as close as any set of twins born from the same mother, though they only shared the same absent father. He knew she was an adult, and knew she was the Prophet of a Thousand Years, but unlike their parents, Thorne had agreed to help carry out her plans years ago.

"Yeah, I do. Remember me. *Me*, I mean. Your sister," Ia explained. "The woman, and not just the Prophet. I need you to *obey* me as the Prophet . . . but I need someone who'll remember *me*."

"What, you think Fyfer will start worshipping you?" he asked, snickering briefly at the thought.

"More like he'll get so wrapped up in his own life, he won't think much about me. The original me," she clarified.

Edwin spasmed, gasping. He panted for air, eyes almost opening . . . then they rolled up into his head again, fluttering shut.

"Uhh . . . how long will he be like this?" her brother asked her.

"Approximately forty more minutes, give or take a few," Ia estimated, skimming the timestreams with a brief close of her eyes. "Then either he'll run and kill himself, or you can drop the second ring on his head. Then we get to wait another twenty minutes to see if he'll be willing to live and cooperate with us. It's all about free will, Thorne. It's always about free will, and about taking responsibility for our actions—or not—and about making our own choices once we know what's at stake. Even for *skut v'shakk* like this. He *does* have a choice, once the wreath is done with him."

Thorne snorted. He covered his nose hastily, broad shoulders shaking. "*Ow. Please* don't combine those two slang words again. *Owww . . .* They do *not* go together. I almost turned my nose inside out! You're lucky I wasn't drinking anything."

"Awww," Ia mock-sympathized. Hands clasped behind her back, she returned to watching Edwin V'Sasselli suffering through first-person perspectives of each of his brutalized victims. "Remember, if he goes for the kitchen, don't stop him, just head for the bedroom exit. I'll do a sweep for any stray bits of DNA on the way out. If he doesn't head for the kitchen, drop the next wreath on his head."

This really was the most humane way she could think of to deal with someone like Edwin V'Sasselli, given the ethics of the situation. She knew he was a serial killer, yet she knew her brother needed someone with that exact set of skills on his side. Normal on the outside, psychotic on the inside, and fully capable of killing just about anyone, given the right opportunity. Edwin would be a dangerous tool at best, but one which her brother had to learn how to use. This tool, or the next.

If she hadn't needed Edwin V'Sasselli, if she didn't believe even someone him like had a right to life, so long as that life didn't adversely affect the future . . . her personal preference would have been to kill him. Quickly, cleanly, and mercifully. It was far more humane than what he had done to his own victims, and far more than he deserved. It was also why she was willing to risk him committing suicide after undergoing this . . . treatment.

Her next psychic ethics review was bound to be an interesting one, having to explain and justify this to Leona and the others.

———

Skin crawling, gifts twitching, Ia hugged her mothers long and hard anyway. This was her last chance to do so for another three years. If everything went right, that was. If it didn't . . . She hugged her mothers a little bit longer before turning to Fyfer. They mock-tussled a moment, her knuckles rubbing over his dark curls and his fingers trying to pinch her vulnerable points, then they hugged. Patting her on the back, Fyfer let her go to the open arms of her half-twin.

"I'm still not happy that you made me do all that, earlier,"

Thorne muttered into her ear, hugging her tight enough to make her ribs ache.

Ia hugged him back just as hard. "It could've been worse. Keep an eye on him. *Use* him. Above all, give him *no* cause to doubt that your hand and mine are one."

"And give none of the others cause for doubt, either," he recited under his breath. Dropping his cheek on her forehead, Thorne hugged his sister. *"Mizzu 'reddy."*

"Gonna mizzu, tu," she agreed. One final squeeze and Thorne let her go. Ia stepped back, relieved her gifts hadn't triggered while hugging him. Looking at the four members of her immediate family, she gave them a wistful smile. "I will miss you . . . but you are *never* far from my thoughts. I love you all very much. Remember that."

Aurelia waggled one naturally tan finger at her daughter. "I am *not* Jewish, meioa-e; you are *not* allowed to make me *verklempt.*"

"Go on, Sis," Thorne added, lifting his chin at the modest-sized spaceport terminal. "That shuttle won't wait forever."

Nodding, Ia picked up her kitbag and turned away from her family. She heard Fyfer opening the ground car's doors for their mothers, before the rumbling of a shuttle lifting off in the distance covered up any further noise. Crossing the road from the parking garage to the terminal, Ia entered the building. She did not look back. Instead, she looked forward, dipping briefly into her future to make sure everything would be on track.

Three years, and counting . . . Oh, god, she thought, wincing. *It looks like I* am *going to get stuck next to that chatty grandmother type who will want to tell me all about her current medical ailments. I swear, the Creator has a bowl of popcorn as big as a leafer beast nestled at Her side, tonight . . .*

CHAPTER 6

*Why did I enter the Naval Academy, instead of entering a
Marine Academy, after my Field Commission? Obviously
because I needed to be able to both command a group of
soldiers larger than a Squad or a Platoon, and pilot a fair-
sized starship. Short-range starfighters, interorbital shuttle
craft, and other various forms of troop transport, all of
these things can be piloted by a noncommissioned soldier,
all under the guise of the yeoman class pilot programs.*

*Heck, getting a job as an insystem shuttle pilot is one
of the biggest and best-paying employment opportunities
out there, and the military will actually pay you to learn
how to do it. Whether it's cargo, or people, or whatever,
so long as it's a small vessel with a short range in a non-
combat zone, employers are going to want the disciplined
mind-set of a former yeoman on their freight team.*

*Piloting an actual starship, however, requires a far greater
level of responsibility. Anything with a crew compliment
larger than five requires the lead crewmeioa to be a duly
trained officer. Particularly if it's intended to be used in combat in a way that puts more than just a single pilot and his or
her gunners' lives at risk. The military is not in the habit
of wasting lives and resources . . . and the Terran United
Planets Space Force in particular is too huge an entity to
allow its members to "make things up" as they go along.*

Every single soldier, whatever their Branch, goes through Basic Training. In the case of medical and religious personnel, it might be a modified version of Basic Training, with less emphasis on the physical aspects of military life, but they undertake the same mental, emotional, intellectual, and logistics training as everyone else, so that everyone is on the same page.

Whether you're running with a crew of twenty or a crew of two thousand, it's a whole new level of command, and a whole new level of responsibility. The military needs to make sure each of its officers understands what that means, and follows the same procedures as everyone else. Precognitive or not, that included me.

~Ia

AUGUST 24, 2492 T.S.
SINES, PORTUGAL, WESTERN EUROPROVINCE
EARTH

A stiff wind was blowing off the Atlantic when the hovertaxi descended to ground level and glided up to the gates of the Academia de Marinha Estrelas. The driver patiently parked it in the entry arch, holding out his wrist unit for scanning. Seated in the front, Ia had to first unsnap the cuff of her Dress Brown jacket, then reach across her body with her left arm to poke her unit out the passenger window, allowing the guards to hand-scan it.

The sensors built into the entry arch were capable of scanning the identification bracelets from a distance, but since she and the driver were new to the campus, they had to be visually identified by the guards, their faces matched to the ident files on the guards' handheld scanner pads. Thankfully, it didn't take long to confirm their identities, nor for the car to be cleared to proceed. Pulling forward, the driver followed her directions to the administration building.

Though the materials were modern, most of the buildings on the Academy campus had been built with a medieval flavor, echoing the region's strong, ancient, maritime history. The administrative center was no exception. Its crenellated roofline and square, flanking towers evoked comparisons to an era a thousand years before, when the natives of this region had dared to leave their stone castles in order to explore the planet's waters in ancient wooden ships.

Locally, it was considered fitting that the TUPSF-Navy had one of its top Academies here, in the region given as a feudal fiefdom to the explorer Vasco da Gama. They even had a bust of him over the main entryway. Personally, Ia thought it was ironic; the man had committed various acts of brutality against foreigners, that which would have pleased only someone like V'Sasselli back on Sanctuary. *At home, a hero; abroad, a villain. At least I know the instructors here at the Academia do have a sense of perspective, and don't whitewash him into a saint.*

Offering her bracer-sized arm unit to the driver, Ia paid the cab fare and exited the vehicle. The wind immediately tugged at the brown and black dress cap on her head. Yanking it down firmly, Ia ducked the front of it low, facing into the wind.

Leaving the cabbie to extract her kitbag from the trunk, she hauled out the heavy, wheeled case taking up most of the back-seat. Totaling one hundred seventy-three kilos, not including the extra weight of the case itself, the contents were a familiar burden. It contained her exercise weight suit, a webwork of tile-weighted straps that would cover her body from head to foot in order to simulate the strain of heavy gravity.

Technology could create gravity weaves under the floor plates on spaceships, space stations, and even the dome colonies found on asteroids, planetoids, and moons, permitting people a semblance of normal life while traveling and living in space. Gravity weaves could warp the effects of a natural gravity well, giving a lightworlder some respite from the constant drag on their frames. But gravity weaves couldn't add weight, and gravity deckplates were too expensive to be used casually. Certainly, it would have been ridiculous to expect the Human Motherworld to pave its sidewalks and streets with excess gravity just for her.

Yet the benefits of heavyworlder strength and speed couldn't be denied. Nor could it be denied that a heavyworlder's muscles and reflexes atrophied when stuck in a lightworlder environment for more than a few weeks. So, in an elegantly simplistic solution, the Space Force had decreed that all heavyworlders—those whose normal gravity exceeded 1.5Gs Standard—had to wear weight suits while exercising. No matter where she was sent,

Ia was condemned to lug the suit from duty post to duty post. Hauling up on the handle, she lugged the heavy case onto the sidewalk with a *thump*.

When the cabdriver handed her kitbag to her, by comparison, it was negligible. Ia slung the duffel strap over her shoulder and thanked him in the local tongue. Most of her Marine uniforms had already been sent either to storage or to the military's recyclers; the only items she carried in the brown bag were her toiletries, her writing station and supplies, the square of velvet on which she had pinned her various medals and ribbons, and two changes of red-colored civilian clothes. The only items she would be retaining from her time in the TUPSF-Marine Corps would be her service record, her Field Commission, and her glittery, military slang for the various medals and service ribbons she had earned.

Even the Dress Browns she wore, with their crisp black stripes down the brown jacket sleeves and matching trouser legs, would be sent into storage by the end of the day, replaced by TUPSF-Navy blue. Leaving the cabdriver to point his vehicle back toward the gate, Ia tugged her dress cap more firmly on her white locks as the wind tried to play with it again, grasped the handle of her weight suit box, and hauled everything into the administrative building.

Once the automatic doors slid quietly shut behind her, the wind stopped. Compared to the warm but windy weather outside, it was comfortably cool in the broad foyer. Ia glanced up, checked the various signs posted near the tops of doors, and turned to her right, heading down the side hall. Three doors down was the admissions center. Dragging her case in her wake, she approached the front desk.

The Human at the desk was a fellow lieutenant, though his single brass bar meant Lieutenant Second Grade, not Lieutenant Second Class, like hers did. Since she was from a different Branch and clad in her dress uniform, the burden of saluting first fell upon her. Resting her case on its end, she draped her kitbag over the handle, then gave the man a crisp salute.

"Lieutenant Second Class Ia, TUPSF-Marine Corps, reporting for transfer and admittance into the TUPSF-Navy Academia de Marinha Estrelas as scheduled, sir," she stated, holding her pose.

The blond man eyed her up and down. His gaze fixated on her

glittery, pinned to the left side of her jacket. Returning her salute, he lifted his chin at the collection of ribbons and medals. "Welcome to the Academy, Lieutenant. You didn't have to wear your full glittery, you know. You only have to wear the bare minimum when in Dress Colors, even if it's Marine Browns. You won't impress your instructors by dressing yourself up in everything you own. We believe our cadets should earn their respect on merit."

"Actually, I didn't wear everything, Lieutenant," Ia told him, her tone mild. "Regulations stipulate that when traveling between duty posts, an officer is to wear 'half glittery,' which is the bare minimum of one of each type of medal. I have honors in twelve different categories, not including my Field Commission and my Service pins. I am therefore wearing twelve different medals, plus my Border Patrol ribbon, which is the bare minimum of glittery required."

The lieutenant peered at her chest, taking in the fact that there was indeed only one of each type. "Huh. I guess that is half glittery." He returned his attention to his workstation console. "We have . . . two meioa-es scheduled to arrive this week from the SF-MC. What did you say your name was again, Lieutenant?"

"Ia. Spelled I-A, not E-A," she added in clarification. "Just the one, first, last, and only name, no others." Digging into her trouser pocket, she fished out a datachip and offered it to him. "Here is the chip with my official transfer orders, military records, and datafile links."

"Just the one name? You're not actually Conequa or Janniston?" he asked, glancing up at her again. When she nodded, he sighed and tapped in a few commands. "Huh. Looks like you're not listed. Wait, let me check the pending files . . . *Ah*, here it is. There's a flag on your records; it says your name is incomplete, and when it arrived, we didn't have your collegiate degree on file, so we didn't process the paperwork. But . . . it looks like your college credits have come in. Military History? Good choice. So. What's the rest of your name?"

"That *is* my full name, Lieutenant. Just the one name, legally, fully, and duly registered as Ia. Nothing more, nothing less; two letters, two syllables, that's it," she told him patiently. Mostly patiently. Clasping her hands together, she rested them on the counter. "I know the Marine Corps had no difficulty in registering my name exactly as it legally stands."

He took in her mild tone, slight but pleasant smile, and sighed. "Ident number?"

"Ident number 96-03-0004-0092-0076-0002. I am registered as a former citizen of Independent Colonyworld Sanctuary, by Charter rights a duly oathsworn citizen of the Terran United Planets via service in its Space Force." *There, that ought to cover all bases,* she thought, stifling an impatient sigh. The hovercab hadn't taken too long to soar from Lisboa to the outskirts of Sines, but she was going to need a restroom break soon. "I could quote the relevant Charter sections and subparagraphs if you insist, but the rules and regulations governing I.C. transferal of citizenship have already been checked, crosschecked, and covered by the Marines . . . and by the Department of Innovation."

That last bit was a blatant name-drop, but a glimpse into the immediate future gave it a calculated 83 percent chance to work, cutting off a good half hour of tedious extra paperwork processing. The other lieutenant raised a brow, but tapped a few more commands into his workstation. Sighing, he dipped his head in acknowledgment. "Right. Since you have a Master's degree, and you've had more than two tours of duty as a noncommissioned officer . . . and half a tour as a Field Commissioned officer . . . you are indeed cleared for the one-year fast-track program. Provided you can keep up with it."

"Trust me, I can keep up with it, Lieutenant. Attending classes all day long will be like a vacation to me, compared to constantly being shot at on a hot spot Border Patrol," Ia muttered. "And I never give less than my best, sir."

"Then all your paperwork and your transfer orders appear to be in order," he stated. "Lieutenant Ia, ident #96-03-0004-0092-0076-0002, are you prepared at this time to transfer your service contract from the Branch Marine Corps to the Branch Navy of the Terran United Planets Space Force, and enter this Academy for training specifically as an SF-Navy officer?"

"Sir, yes, sir," she agreed. "I am ready to be transferred into the Space Force Navy and its Academy system at this time, sir."

"You'll want to get used to saying 'Aye, sir,' since that's the Navy's way," he quipped, "but we get enough cross-Branch transfers, that they'll take a 'yes, sir' all the same." Swirling his finger through the air, he bopped it onto his keyboard and flashed her a smile. "Congratulations, meioa-e, you are now officially in the SF-Navy. Welcome to the Academia de Marinha Estrelas, Class 1252.

"You're also officially in the wrong uniform, now," he added, smiling to show he was teasing Ia. "Luckily for you, it's a Sunday. Let me call your class trainer, Lieutenant Commander Spada. He'll run you over to the dispensary for a fresh set of uniforms, then to the dorms to assign you your quarters. We still have a dozen more cadets expected to arrive by tonight. That is, presuming the windstorm outside doesn't delay them any further.

"You'd think that by the end of the twenty-fifth century, we'd have gotten the hang of controlling the weather, but no, we haven't yet," the lieutenant mock-sighed. Shrugging, he continued with the introductory lecture. "Be advised that cadets are *not* allowed off the Academy grounds unless escorted by a regimen trainer or a class instructor, or given formal Leave to go into town. Curfews are strict, and the Department of Innovations will be watching your every move. Cadets who lack sufficient drive and discipline will never rise in rank above the bare minimum for their service time and pay grade . . . and before you ask, I merely lack the drive, not the discipline. I like being a lowly lieutenant, and I actively enjoy administrative work. You can't be an effective administrator if you're not disciplined."

"Then I'm glad you have a job and a position you love," Ia quipped back. "The rest of us should be so lucky."

"With luck, you'll get the postings you like, too . . . or at least come to like the postings you get. Be advised that your classes will run twice as fast as standard collegiate quarters . . . which is why we start a new class group eight times a year here at the Academia, instead of four." He finished typing in a few more things, then lifted his chin at her. "Hold out your arm so I can scan your ident unit."

Ia complied, unbuttoning her jacket sleeve once more. "I know; it was one of the few things that gave me enough time to go home to visit my family. Otherwise it would've been another year before I got Leave."

"Where'd you get your Field Commission, anyway?" he asked, setting down the scanner wand.

"The incident on Zubeneschamali." That was all she needed to say. His eyes widened in recognition.

"Zuben . . . *you're* Bloody Mary?" He stared at her as if she had sprouted horns or something.

Ia pulled off her dress cap, revealing the rest of her snow-white hair. She shrugged expressively, setting the cap on top of her kitbag, and gave him a wry smile. "That is my nickname, yes. I'll admit it's not very obvious; I haven't been in a combat zone in a couple months, so I'm fresh out of blood."

The lieutenant manning the admissions desk hesitated a moment, then leaned forward on the counter and asked in an undertone, "Did you really rip off that K'katta's leg and beat him with it?"

Ia leaned forward, smiling back at him. This wasn't the first time someone had asked her that question since the incident at Zubeneschamali, nor would it be the last. "I only *threatened* to rip it off and beat him with it. He wisely decided to surrender, instead."

"I'll take your word for it. I'm Lieutenant Chazter," he added, offering his hand in introduction. "Michael Chazter. So, why the transfer to the Navy? Why not a Marines Academy?"

"I worked well with the crew of the TUPSF *Liu Ji*, and I have the reflexes and spatial coordination to be a pilot. The SF-Navy made sense. Where's the restroom?" Ia asked him.

"Go out the door, turn left, third door down, can't miss it," he stated.

Nodding, Ia left her bags at the registration desk. By the time she came back, three more people had arrived. Two were male and clad in civilian clothes, though their buzz-cropped hair proved they were cadets who had just arrived from Basic Training. The third was also male, but clad in Navy blue dress casuals of navy leather shoes, dark blue slacks, and a lighter blue dress shirt with short sleeves.

Unlike Ia, who was wearing the half glittery required when wearing Dress Browns, the other officer was wearing the absolute minimum required for daily wear, which consisted of the two silver bars of a lieutenant commander, five service ribbons, and his name tag, but no medals. With his grey-streaked dark brown hair cropped almost recruit-short, his face age-lined but graced with a pleasant perpetual ghost of a smile, Lieutenant

Commander Spada looked as confident and knowledgeable as anyone could expect from an Academy training officer.

Since neither of them was wearing a cap and both were indoors planet-side, Ia didn't salute. She did pull herself up straight, nodding to the older man. "Commander Spada, sir. I'm Cadet Ia, duly registered for the one-year fast-track program, sir."

Spada nodded, and eyed the large brown case topped with her matching duffel bag and dress cap. "What's in the box? It's too small to be a mechsuit."

"Weight suit, sir. I'm a heavyworlder. My mechsuit should be stored in the Academy's mechpool. I sent it over two months ago, and did receive confirmation from the Academy on its arrival."

"That's right, your file said you're a heavyworlder. Roll it outside, Cadet. It's taking up space," Spada ordered her. "Go wait in the hallway. I'll be taking all three of you to the dispensary and the dorms in a few minutes."

"Sir, yes—aye, sir," Ia complied, grabbing hat, kitbag, and case handle. The other two cadets, both males, had glanced her way in curiosity when the word *heavyworlder* was mentioned. Lieutenant Chazter was still processing them, however, so they reluctantly returned their attention back to the meioa-o behind the counter. Ia knew that wouldn't be the end of their curiosity, but it was something that would be settled later.

The only thing Ia didn't know was who her roommate would be. Not that she had seen *who* she would paired with, exactly. Sometimes the timestreams were like that. The faceless crowds found in daily life rarely had any impact or influence on her courses of action. If they weren't important to the flow of Time, well, Ia had learned to conserve her energies. She didn't ignore them completely—the incident with Estes and her face-goop came to mind; *that* had been a shock to learn—but mostly they were nothing more than flickers and blurs at the edges of her precognitive awareness. So long as whoever-it-was didn't threaten her work, their presence or absence was immaterial in the end.

At least now her career path in the Navy had been laid. It would take careful tending, but the next year would be a relative breeze compared to the two that would follow.

CHAPTER 7

I only ever made one real mistake when planning for my future—oh, don't get me wrong; I don't mean mistakes in the course of my duties. Everyone makes little mistakes. I've mistakenly entered the wrong information on a form, and I've burned my tongue from trying to drink a cup of too-hot caf', the same as everyone else. No, what I'm talking about was a mistake of arrogant ignorance on my part. A compounded mistake, though it took a year for that mistake to fully unfold and reveal itself.

You see, the mistake was believing I had foreseen everything I needed to know about my life. As it turned out, even the Prophet of a Thousand Years can be blindsided by Fate.

~Ia

AUGUST 25, 2492 T.S.

Hand fumbling out of the covers, Ia slapped at the snooze button on her bedside chrono. It buzzed again. She grumbled and slapped harder; she *knew* she had another seventeen minutes before the slagging thing was supposed to go off. Having stayed awake far too late last night, composing prophetic instructions for the future, she needed every second of sleep she could get.

The noise buzzed again, and the intercom for the door—it

was the doorbell, not her alarm—activated. *"Cadet Ia, this is Lieutenant Commander Spada. You are requested to wake and open this door."*

. . . *Guh—WHAT?* Heart lurching, snapping her mind wide awake, Ia splashed through the waters of her own timestream, floundering in shock. Hauling herself up, dripping with misty, muddied, clueless possibilities, she tried to make sense of the request. The door buzzed again. Scrambling physically as well as mentally, she lurched for the door. Nothing in the timestreams had warned her about this visit last night, and nothing in those same waters *now* warned her about this visit. *God—I know I can sense the Future, so I can't have lost my precognitive senses . . . can I?*

Unlocking the controls, she slapped the door open, pulling herself to Attention as best she could. "Lieutenant Commander, sir!" she managed, doing her best to ignore the fact that she was wearing nothing more than a light blue T-shirt and matching underpants for sleepwear. Heart still thumping, she managed to ask, "Uh . . . is anything wrong, sir?"

Spada curved his mouth up on one side. "Only that you're a heavy sleeper, Cadet."

"Uh . . . it was a very long day, yesterday, sir." Blinking, she glanced at the other figure beside the lieutenant commander. Tallish, naturally tanned, and distinctly Asian, the young man at Spada's side smiled at Ia. She could tell he was trying not to let his gaze dip below her face to the obvious, if muscular curves of her heavyworlder figure, and warded off an unusual urge to blush. Returning her gaze to the training officer, Ia asked hesitantly, *"Ah . . . sir?"*

"This is your new roommate. Your psych profile says you don't care about sharing quarters with the meioa-os as well as the meioa-es . . . and since we have more males entering the Academia right now than females," Spada elaborated with a shrug, "you get a male roommate. I trust that isn't going to be a problem, Cadet?"

Now her precognitive senses twitched, warning her that Spada was going to keep an eye on Ia in this matter, in case Ia turned out to be one of those sorts who insisted on making a fuss over every little thing. But . . . eerily . . . Ia could sense *nothing* about the black-haired, brown-eyed, moon-faced young man smiling wryly at her. Unsure how to handle the peculiarity of his non-ish existence, Ia sagged back onto her only, and therefore best, guess: Treat the moment with proper military protocols in mind.

"Sir, yes, sir," she agreed, stepping back from the doorway. "I mean, aye, sir, I don't mind, sir."

Nodding, Lieutenant Commander Spada gestured for the blue-clad cadet to enter. Hefting his kitbag onto his shoulder, he stepped inside as the commander spoke. "Cadet Ia, meet Cadet Meyun Harper. Harper, this is Ia. You're both heavy-worlders, though Harper is from Dabin, and you're from Sanctuary. Harper here is on the same one-year fast-track program as you, Cadet. However, he's aimed more at a career in Logistics and/or Engineering, whereas you've indicated an interest in Piloting and/or Combat Command.

"Regardless of any philosophical differences you may have in the classroom regarding your majors, gentlemeioas, you will be expected to get along just fine all the same," Spada warned both of them. "Don't forget to report for breakfast by no later than 0700 local. You'll have a long day ahead of you. Your first class in the accelerated curriculum starts at 0730 in room 202 of the Sodré Building. Good morning, and don't be late."

"No, sir," Ia promised. "I won't be late, sir."

Spada started to reach for the door controls, then paused and asked, "Cadet Ia . . . why did you feel it was necessary to engage the privacy lock?"

"I . . . think I just did it out of habit, sir. I guess I just feel more secure behind a locked door," Ia managed to suggest. The real reason was that she hadn't wanted anyone to surprise her while she was busy writing precognitive missives. Instead, she improvised a plausible alternative: "You know . . . after having spent so many tours of duty in a combat zone."

"Well. Just remember that, one, you are required to unlock and open your quarters to myself or any other superior officer stationed at this Academy, leaving them available for inspection at any time of day or night. And two . . . there will be no frat-ernizing of an intimate nature between cadets while you are at this Academy."

"Trust me, sir, that won't be a problem," Ia muttered. No way was she even going to *touch* the man behind her, not even casually. Not until she figured out *why* she couldn't sense him.

Nodding, Spada touched the controls, closing the door

between them. That left her alone with a man who, according to her precognitive senses, didn't exist. Still disoriented from her disrupted sleep, Ia stayed in the nook between the closet door, front door, and bathroom door for a few moments, marshalling her wits. Marshalling them, and trying to sense Cadet Harper through the timestreams.

Nothing. He was a living, breathing grey spot. Not, as she had presumed the night before, someone who was unimportant in the greater scheme of her quests to save the galaxy, but . . . someone who she literally could not predict. A blank spot, an empty space . . . a glass rock parting the waters of the future around his existence, seen only by the way others reacted in his vicinity at absolute best. At least, as far as she could tell without fully flipping her mind onto the timeplains.

Giving up, she scrubbed at her face and hair to try and finish waking up, then padded back into the main room. She couldn't risk immersing herself in the timeplains when she didn't know yet if he would try to touch her while she seemingly meditated. The whole situation had Ia so puzzled, so uncomfortable, she didn't even realize how she was looking at him until he glanced up from unpacking his kitbag and arched one thick dark brow.

"Is something wrong?"

"*Ah* . . . no. No, nothing's wrong. I'm, *uh*, still trying to wake up," Ia improvised. She returned to her bed and sat on the edge, trying to get a grip on her senses.

"Yeah, I guess I can relate to that. I've been up for nineteen hours, myself, but they're not going to hold back the opening class just so I can catch a few winks," he agreed.

His voice was deeper than she expected. Aside from the flat roundness of his face, reminding her somewhat of her friend Rabbit, Cadet Meyun Harper was tallish, thinnish, and youngish-looking. Though she supposed that could've been due to his clean-shaven face. She honestly had no clue as to his age, his history, his origins. Her postcognitive abilities weren't nearly as strong as her precognitive ones, but they were still incredibly strong, all things considered.

Yet . . . nothing. Zip. Zilch. A . . . a grey hole in existence. Not quite a black hole, since he clearly exists and I can see and interact with him physically, but . . . psychically? How can he not-exist like that?

Her bedside chrono beeped, startling her into jumping up. Heart pounding, Ia endured another bemused look from her new roommate. Settling back down, she shook her head briefly to clear it, then leaned over and shut off the machine. "*Ah . . . you need a shower?*"

"You go first," he offered. "You look like you need to wake up. I still need to figure out if I'm folding everything right."

Turning to her wardrobe bureau, Ia opened up the top three drawers, extracting everything but the shoes she would need for the day. She left the drawers open. "Here, look at how I've folded my own. The Navy's way shouldn't be that much different from the Marines'."

"You're from the Marines?" he asked her.

"I'm a cross-Branch transfer. I won't take long in the shower, Cadet, promise," she added, bundling up her under- and outer garments.

"Thanks, I'll look it all over. Oh, *um*, wait," he stated, holding out his hand, first palm up and out, then turning it sideways. "Call me Meyun. When we're alone in here. Obviously they'll have us calling each other 'Cadet Harper' and 'Cadet Ia' out in the halls and such. But since we're roommates . . . just call me Meyun."

"May-yoon . . ." She tested the name. Nothing. Not a single twinge of her gifts, pre- or postcognitive. Again, she was forced to fall back on the only safe procedures she had, the habits of courtesy and military protocol. Except she didn't reach for the hand he offered. "Thank you, Meyun. I'm told I don't snore, though I haven't had to share quarters in over a year. If I do . . . just throw a boot or something at me. From a safe distance. I *did* just come from a combat-heavy Border Patrol, so it might not be safe to be within range if you startle me awake."

"Duly noted." He gave her an expectant look, then raised his brows and flicked his outstretched hand. "And *your* given name would be . . . ?"

This, at least, was familiar ground. She gave him a wry smile, clutching her clothes to her T-shirt-covered chest as an excuse to avoid shaking his hand. "My full name *is* Ia. Nothing less, and nothing more."

"Right. Though I can't see how it could be any less."

"Trust me, I've heard that one before," she managed to quip, edging toward the facilities.

He watched her head toward the bathroom. If he lowered his hand, Ia didn't know. She very carefully kept her attention on the need to hold her clothes to her chest. For the first time in her life, she felt naked, as in exposed. Vulnerable. Not physically, but deeper than that. His quip about her name wasn't the first time she'd heard that, but . . . *Okay, so I do feel a little naked physically* . . .

It wasn't until she was lathering up her hair under the hot spray of the shower that a new thought crossed her mind. One which hadn't been felt in a very long time. A kind of thought which she believed had died in the early dawn hours of an ordinary, banal morning some five years ago.

I can't believe how cute he is . . .

I can't . . . ? I can't believe how cute *he is?* Dismayed at herself, Ia stared at the steam-fogged plexi of the shower door until a trickle of lather threatened to get into her eyes. Scrubbing her scalp furiously, she did her best to wash that idiotic, useless, pointless thought down the drain.

"That, Class 1252, concludes the overview of your daily schedule," Lieutenant Commander Spada stated, tapping his arm unit to advance the image being projected on the wall behind him. "I realize it is a very full schedule, more so than any of the four- or even two-year programs here at the Academia, but between your transcripts, your DoI profiles, and the recommendations of some of your superiors—since most of you are Field Commission recipients—the Space Force believes you can handle it."

His co-teacher for the class and one of their chief testers, Captain Rzhikly, spoke up next. Not everyone spoke Terranglo with a neutral accent; some provinces on Earth still retained their native tongues for everyday use. His accent was therefore thick but his words wise with the years salting his dark hair in stark streaks of grey.

"Of course, dis does mean ve have to break you down and build you up all de faster, since you're being fast-tracked through de accelerated studies program . . . but today, ve'll go easy on you." He smiled wryly. "So to speak. De first task, of course, is to find out vat *you* know about vat it means to be an officer. Ve vill start vit vat it means to be a soldier, de most basic unit of any military organization, because dere is a difference between a soldier and an officer—and by using de term *soldier*, I'm including all de enlisted sailors in de Space Force Navy, de Marines of de Marine Corps, and so forth—you are *all* in de Space Force, derefore you are *all* soldiers. Not just de vuns who serve in de TUPSF-Army."

"So," Lieutenant Commander Spada stated, moving to the next topic. "Cadet Burroughs. Of all your classmates, you've been in the military the longest, serving with distinction as both an enlisted soldier and a noncommissioned officer in the TUPSF-Army for over thirteen years before earning your Field Commission just three weeks ago. What would *you* say are the responsibilities of a soldier?" Spada asked him.

"Commander, yes . . . I mean, aye, sir," the cadet in question corrected himself.

As they had been instructed, Cadet Burroughs stood up next to his desk-seat in order to answer their lead instructor. He also used the approved short-form of Spada's title, as instructed. Spada wasn't a plain lieutenant and he wasn't a commander, but was instead slotted between the two. So, Spada had explained that the default was to use the higher half of his rank, if they wished to shorten the amount of time it took to address him by rank—or to address a lieutenant colonel in one of the other three Branches, or even a brigadier, major, or lieutenant general.

Burroughs was a tall, thin, buzz-cut man in his mid- to late thirties. His skin was only mildly tanned, his hair an indiscriminate shade of brownish something given how short it was, and his eyes were a piercing shade of grey blue. He wasn't the oldest member of Class 1252, but he was close to it.

"In the Army, sirs," he said, "we were taught that a soldier's responsibilities are to obey the laws of the Terran United Planets, to obey the lawful orders of his or her superiors, and to achieve all objectives in the most efficient, effective manner possible. By following the rules and regulations of the TUPSF-Army . . . and the other three Branches . . . a soldier's efforts will be carried out in a suitably efficient, effective manner," Burroughs stated. "A soldier is responsible for whatever he is legally assigned to do, and responsible for doing it in the approved manner. Beyond that . . . the variety of tasks which will be asked of a soldier are too great to list without taking all day, sirs."

"Alright. That's a good start. Cadet Ffulke," Spada addressed next, pacing along the platform at the front of the auditorium-style classroom. The chamber held an additional twenty or so empty seats, but there were only fifty-three people in this current group of officer candidates. "You have never actually served in the military, but between your Military Aptitude Test scores, your college records, and the recommendations of your Junior Reserve trainers on Eiaven, they think you may have what it takes to make a good officer, and to do it in just one year. So. What *are* the responsibilities of an officer?"

"Commander, sir," Cadet Ffulke stated, standing up beside his desk. He was short, stocky, and a fellow heavyworlder. His hair was dark, his skin had that golden cast to it that said he held V'Dan more than Terran ancestry, and his eyes puppy dog brown. He kind of reminded Ia of a stubbie, the short-legged breed of dog found on Sanctuary. "An officer must carry out the same duties and responsibilities as any soldier . . . *and* be responsible for overseeing the duties and responsibilities of those soldiers placed under his or her command. Sir."

"Good answer. A few of you are like Cadet Ffulke: new to the Service, yet full of a great deal of potential and promise, great enough to see how well you can hold up here in the accelerated studies program," Spada stated. "Most of you are more like Cadet Burroughs; you've served for at least half a dozen years on average and have either earned a Field Commission, or have passed the requisite tests and requested transfer to an Academy at the end of your most recent tour of duty so that you can attempt to become an officer. But none of you have served *as* an officer for more than a couple weeks at most . . . except for Cadet Ia."

Oh, great. Here it comes . . .

Captain Rzhikly lifted his chin at her. "Cadet Ia, you earned your Field Commission several months ago over de incident involving Beta Librae V, in de Zubeneschamali System. You den stepped up to fill your Platoon Lieutenant's shoes vhile she vos recovering from her spinal injuries. You served as de Second Platoon Lieutenant of your Marine Company for almost tree months, is dat correct?"

Ia slid out of her seat, standing At Attention. "Sir, yes, sir."

"That's a bit unusual. Normally, a Field Commissioned

officer is shipped off as soon as possible." Spada said, pacing along the platform, hands clasped behind his back. "Do you know why you weren't?"

"Captain Ferrar thought it was best for the Company's morale if we did not appear to 'replace' Lieutenant D'kora with a stranger, sirs. The entire incident was unsettling enough for us to endure as it was, however temporary."

"Well, your DoI file lists a few additions to that reasoning, but we won't get around to dissecting and discussing DoI reports for another five months. Alright, Cadet. Give us *your* opinion of what the differences are between a soldier and an officer, since you've had the most practical experience of anyone in your class at being the latter," Lieutenant Commander Spada instructed her.

"Captain, Lieutenant Commander, in my estimation, the duties and obligations of soldiers versus officers are nearly identical, with three major exceptions, sirs," Ia stated. She clasped her hands behind her blue-clad back in a modified Parade Rest, since her feet were together instead of shoulder-width apart. "In the Marines, we were taught that a soldier's duty is to place his or her weapons, skills, body, and even life between innocent civilians and anything that threatens them. A soldier's responsibility is to do these things by obeying his or her orders in a manner that is consistently legal, efficient, and moral, in compliance with military regulations, sirs."

"And by comparison, Cadet Ia, an officer's duty is . . . ?" Rzhikly prompted her when she paused for breath.

"An officer's duty is to place his or her weapons, skills, body, and even life between innocent civilians and anything that threatens them . . . *and* to use the weapons, skills, bodies, and lives of the soldiers placed under that officer's lawful command. This is the first difference between a soldier and an officer.

"An officer's responsibility is to do these things by obeying his or her orders in a manner that is consistently legal, efficient, and moral, just like any soldier," Ia said. "But it is also to *craft* their own orders to the soldiers placed under them with the same level of care for the legalities, the efficiencies, and the ethics to which all soldiers, commissioned or otherwise, must aspire. This is the second major difference between the two.

"For the third . . . it is the most important difference," Ia stated, lifting her chin slightly. "In the course of enacting these duties and responsibilities, a *good* officer must ensure that those weapons, skills, bodies, and most especially lives are utilized to their utmost with the highest level of care, consideration, and efficiency for the soldiers under his or her command . . . because while an officer's ultimate *duty* is to ensure that a particular job does get completed via the soldiers and resources within their command, their ultimate *responsibility* is to get it done with the least number of wasted resources, the least number of injuries, and the least number of lost lives. An officer must do their best to get everyone back home again, preferably alive. At least, in so far as I myself have observed, sirs."

"Vell said, Cadet. Be seated," Rzhikly added, gesturing at her seat.

Ia returned to her chair. She clasped her hands on the surface of the arm-table and affected a relaxed but sober, serious air. She knew, however, that her classmates were studying her. Some of them had already made the connection with the system name, Zubeneschamali. Others hadn't yet grasped the link, but they would. Ironic as it was, as much as she needed the reputation and to have it be spread, she didn't want it to spread too wild and fast, or for the wrong reasons. Or for it to draw the wrong attention at the wrong moment. She focused her gaze on Spada as he spoke.

"All of these versions are correct. They are incomplete without each other, and without much more besides, but they are correct enough for what they are," the lieutenant commander allowed. "You, the members of Class 1252, are about to learn just how much more. Open your arm units and link to channel Beta 52, to download the data. You can see it on the main screen behind me, but you'll want to have access to it later, since you'll be tested on all of this by the end of this week."

Leaning over the edge of her arm-desk, Ia quietly demonstrated to the newly recruited cadet next to her how to access the data channels on his arm unit. They weren't designed quite like civilian units, though they were close in some regards. Rzhikly moved to help one of the other new cadets on the other side of the room.

Anyone not familiar with the military versions would have

trouble picking through the extra command buttons, particularly as many were merely symbols that had to be memorized. It was meant to obscure their function in case any of them were captured by enemy forces, but made them a pain in the asteroid to use, at least until the symbols were fully learned. Enlisted wrist unit versions were more complex than civilian ones, but simplified compared to the versatility of an officer's arm unit. Certainly the screen was larger.

"It has been said for centuries," Spada lectured as soon as most of the class was ready again, "that the real work of running the military lies in the hands of our noncommissioned officers. This is half true. It is true that the petty officers of the Navy—and the corresponding sergeants of the other three Branches—do tend to ensure that the majority of all work does get done in the end. As officers, should you graduate from this Academy, you *must* keep this in mind, and give your noncoms the respect they are due for all their hard work on your behalf."

Fishing a small silver rod from his pocket, Spada extended it and tapped the projections on the wall with the red-lit tip of the wand. The pickups for the workstation powering the display responded by highlighting each segment of the flowchart and image associated with his lecture. Off to one side, the captain assumed a relaxed version of Parade Rest, his brown gaze surveying the students as they listened attentively to his co-teacher.

"Like officers, they are responsible in part for ensuring the soldiers in their care complete their missions *and* come back alive. But the planning of those missions often rests upon the shoulders and the minds of the commissioned officers above them. Commissioned officers plan what should be done; noncommissioned officers execute what must be done; and soldiers do what they're told. That is, *if* everything goes according to plan," Spada stated. "But it isn't enough to plan, execute, and do. Officers must also motivate, without losing the extent and discipline of their authority.

"Your first series of lessons will be in military history and historical figures of consequence. Concurrent with each example will be a case by case study of military psychology: how each officer led their troops in a given situation, who they led, where they led, what resources they had to draw upon, and why they completed their missions successfully . . . or why they failed to complete their tasks. You can learn as much from a person's failures as their successes," Spada added, tapping a red outlined section of the flowchart, then the green outlined chain of text boxes and images next to it. "But only if you know what to look for, and which questions to ask.

"If you have not yet mastered it, you *will* learn how to think critically and quickly by the time these lessons are through. I will put each and every one of you under a spotlight before you'll be allowed to move on to the next phase of your training." He shrugged eloquently. "Then again, so will the rest of your instructors. I suggest you get used to it. These are the habits that will hopefully allow you to plan *how* to make the most efficient, effective uses of the lives and resources under your command, in a legal and ethical manner . . . and hopefully allow you to plan for ways to ensure those resources and those lives are not wasted while you do so."

Lieutenant Commander Spada paused and swept his gaze soberly over each row of cadets seated in the small auditorium.

"Learning how to make effective, efficient plans is the single most important part of becoming an officer . . . because each and every single one of your 'forces' is a *real* person. With a name, a family, a history, a set of interests and hobbies . . . even a favorite type of sandwich," their chief instructor lectured them somberly. "You must *never* forget that they are *real* people, whether they are Humans, or naturalized K'katta, or Solaricans, or whoever or whatever ends up being placed beneath you in lawfully designated authority."

Ia nodded slowly. That was exactly how it should be. Every single person she encountered, interacted with . . . and even killed in the name of her duty to the future . . . every single one of them had a name, a family, a history. *Except for Cadet Meyun Harper. I still don't know why I can't sense him in the timestreams . . . unless he's some sort of anti-precog. Or a precog strong enough to interfere with my sensitivities . . . though I've never heard of the former. And of the latter, I'm far more likely to mess with* their *psychic reception, than the other way around . . .*

"Thus it is vital for you to learn how to make the best plans and lay your contingencies carefully. One day, you *will* have to order the meioas under your command into a situation that you know is lethal. It will be up to you to ensure through careful planning that the risks to life and limb remain a *potential*, and not a fact. Over the next year, it will be our responsibility to drill the necessary skill sets into your brains, over and over, until they become a flexible reflex. In the chaos and panic of battle, particularly when your plans have been blown to pieces, *you* will be the person your troops will look to for stability, sanity, and strategy. We're here to teach you all of that until it is bone-deep in you, and becomes the foundation from which you will act."

Amen, Brother. Preachin' to the choir, here, Ia thought wryly. *Unfortunately, that does mean I have to sit here for the next year, listening to you and your fellow instructors telling me things I already know. But you're right, Commander. These are things that have to be drilled so deep, I can rely on them even when the mist descends and my precognition temporarily fails. It has before, and it will again, after all.*

———————

Cadet Bruer slid his tray onto the table next to Ia's, settling into the empty chair on her left. "So, you're really her?"

"Her, who?" Cadet Jinja-Marsuu asked, looking up from her salad. She glanced between Bruer and Ia.

"You don't know?" Bruer asked, poking his thumb at Ia. "Man, I thought everybody heard! It made the news Nets everywhere, and like everything. April 11th, a group of Marine officers got kidnapped by this bunch of undergalactic crime lords. And *this* meioa-e goes in guns blazing and gets 'em out! She got a Star of Service for it, from the hands of the Secondaire herself!"

"They were actually kidnapped March 29th," Ia corrected mildly, spearing another forkful of her meal. The steak strips and wheat pasta were excellent, if a little bland compared to topado-flour noodles. "The rescue took place April 1st, and the awards were handed out to several of us on April 11th. For the record, I myself did not go in guns blazing. I allowed myself to be caught, and started a distraction that allowed the *rest* of my Company to go in guns blazing. It was very much a team effort, not a solo fight."

"But, the Star of Service!" Bruer argued. His voice carried past their own table, causing more than one head to turn. "You got a Star of Service, meioa. Surely that counts for *something*?"

"As far as I'm concerned, I was doing my job, which was to rescue my fellow Marines. Bringing them back alive was the best reward I could have earned, and the only reward I wanted," Ia told him.

"Yeah, right," Cadet Jinja-Marsuu snorted, stabbing into her salad. "Tell that to the reporters. What you *really* wanted was a fat medal. Admit it. We *all* do."

"What I *really* want, Cadet," Ia stated, setting down her fork, "is *not* to have had to tell the mother of Private First Class Paul McDaniels that he died under my command. We were running to take shelter in the subsurface emergency tunnels on Oberon's Rock," she explained quietly as more cadets joined them from the chow line, filling up the table. "I had just caught up with the others when the pirates strafed our section of the domeworld. We didn't find him until almost an hour of digging later . . . and we were digging because we were going to suffocate if we didn't find a fresh supply of oxygen.

"War is not pretty. It is not shiny. It is *not glittery*. I would gladly give up every medal I've ever been given to have him still walking around alive," she finished bluntly.

Cadet Harper settled into the seat on her right, unnerving her. She hadn't been able to foresee where he would sit, which meant anything he did or said might derail her plans for the future. His question as he settled into place seemed innocent enough, though. "So, why do you do it, then? Why did you join up?"

"I took up this job because someone needs to do it, and I happen to be one of the ones good at it. If I do it, that means someone else doesn't have to. Someone who may be less skilled, less careful, and less likely to keep the meioas around them safe and alive. Or mostly alive." Picking up her fork, she again stabbed at the strips of steak that had slipped partway off the tines. "Now, if my superiors think that what I do merits awards and ribbons, that's their prerogative. I'm just doing my job, as best I can."

"Yeah, but your nickname, Bloody Mary?" Bruer offered: "Don't tell me you didn't earn *that*. Even if only a *tenth* of all the rumors were true, it's a Marine Corps nickname. Every Marine I've ever talked to said you have to *earn* one of those."

"Hey, I never said it was a *clean* job. But since it isn't, let's change the subject. We *are* eating, remember?" Popping the forkful of food into her mouth, she chewed.

"Well, you're in the Navy now, sailor," one of the other cadets quipped. "You'll have to earn an entirely new nickname. Besides, you might not end up in combat, next tour of duty. You could end up shuttling supplies back and forth, or pushing paper planet-side somewhere."

"She got her Field Commission in combat, Jordan," Bruer pointed out. "She goes right back into a combat position . . . provided she still passes the psychological exams."

"I served several back-to-back tours in a combat-heavy Border zone without too many difficulties, so I'm probably considered quite well-adjusted." Taking a sip of her juice—apple, a rare treat since that particular fruit didn't grow well on Sanctuary— Ia speared another mouthful of pasta. "Actually, I'm hoping to get a Blockade Patrol, after this. Well, after some pilot training, too."

Harper wrinkled his nose at her while she chewed. "You're actively *hoping* for a Blockade Patrol? It isn't nearly as glamorous as shows like *Space Patrol* make it sound, you know."

Ia cleared her mouth with another sip. "Oh, I know. But the tours of duty are shorter because it's so stressful on most people, they can only handle four-month stretches at most, rather than six months at a time," Ia stated, digging into her salad. "If I'm psychologically stable in a combat zone, it makes sense to post *me* there. That reduces the stress on whoever I'm replacing, freeing them up for a more suitable duty, and makes the military more efficient as a whole."

"How can you be 'psychologically stable' for something as dangerous as a Blockade Patrol?" Jinja-Marsuu asked Ia, though she gestured at the others, inviting them to comment as well. "I've heard the casualty rate for it is around eighty percent. That's outright deadly."

"Casualty rates include all injuries serious enough to warrant treatment in an infirmary, not just deaths," Harper reminded Jinja-Marsuu.

"The actual death rate is around thirteen percent," Ia murmured, reaching for the pepper. She dusted her greens with the spice. "But that's taking into account total crew losses from entire ships being destroyed in starfights, not just individual losses during boarding and inspection. They're building better ships all the time, though. And a good pilot can get you out of most problems. I have the reflexes for it, and my military tests agree, so that's the career track I've picked."

"Yeah, but that doesn't explain how you could still be 'stable' after several back-to-back combat posts," Jinja-Marsuu argued.

"I'm a second-generation first-worlder. From the heaviest heavyworld, no less." At her blank look, Ia elaborated. "I'm from an M-class world. You can't put counterweaves in the ceiling of an M-class world because there are no ceilings when you go outside. Mind you, Sanctuary's not nearly as lethal as Parker's World, but we have our own nasty life-forms, both microscopic and mammoth. Plus the local gravity is over three times Standard. Just *falling* from something as simple as tripping while walking can crack your head literally wide open. By the time I turned ten, I had seen or personally knew of seventeen people who had fallen to their death just from running around on the wrong surface.

"The medical facilities are reasonably good back home, but not like here on Earth, and supplies are often limited. Not to mention the local flora and fauna can be quite deadly. Growing up in circumstances like those, you get used to dealing with danger, violence, disease, injury, and death," she finished.

The part about the local plants and animals was a slight exaggeration. The interior, where the capital of Sanctuary was located, was fairly mild. It was the coast, where various species dwelled in the gravity-reducing waters of the ocean, that held the real danger on her homeworld. Still, the other dangers did exist.

"I'm not sure I'd want to get used to that," Jinja-Marsuu muttered. "Death and dying as a daily part of life . . ."

"Then you're in the wrong career, meioa," Harper stated. He glanced at his roommate. "How's the steak?"

"Good," Ia admitted warily. "Salad needs something, but the vegetables are cooked right."

"Do you cook?" Harper asked her, unrolling his silverware

from the napkin provided. The Academy's dining hall was a step up from the mess hall for recruits back at Camp Nallibong. Then again, they were supposed to be training to be officers, not enlisted soldiers.

"Not if I can help it. I can do prep work and some of the non-fancy stuff, but my parents usually had me waiting tables, scrubbing floors, or washing dishes in their restaurant," she admitted. Answering his questions about herself made her uncomfortable. Ia didn't know what his motives were. Instead, she turned the tables on him. "What about you? Do you cook?"

"My cooking's only okay, but I enjoy baking. Not that I get all that many opportunities anymore," he added with a shrug. "Welcome to the military life, and all."

Bruer shrugged. "Maybe you'll get assigned to a head chef position in the galley of one of the bigger ships."

"I doubt it. My degree's in applied engineering," Harper said. "I just enjoy baking. And track. I heard the Academy here in Portugal has a good track program. They had a cadet who was a runner in the hurdles, two Summer Olympics ago. I remember watching the programs as a kid."

"That's right," Ia said, swallowing quickly. "Commander Spada said this morning that you were hoping for a career in either Logistics or Engineering, didn't he?"

Harper nodded. "And your subjects were Combat Command and Piloting. What sort of sport will you be doing?"

Ia shook her head. "I'll probably be running the confidence course in my halfmech. I'm too strong a heavyworlder to get involved in any sort of contact sport with anyone, so it's either do that or run around the track like you. But since I've already been fitted with a suit, I might as well use it. That'll mesh with my interest in getting posted to a Blockade Patrol anyway, since there'll be plenty of mechsuited boarding opportunities. Maybe as part of a base ship, but more likely on one of the smaller patrollers. I don't know yet."

"I'll probably end up on one of the bigger ships, or maybe a Battle Platform, something with its own manufactory department. How about you, Cadet Bruer?" Harper asked him. "What are your interests?"

"Combat Command and Munitions, with side interests in volleyball and skeet shooting. My degree is in chemistry, specializing in things that go *boom*. How about you?" he asked Jinja-Marsuu.

"Lifesupport and Logistics—and I'll see *you* on the other side of the volleyball net," she told Bruer, grinning. "I love the sport. As for my education, I have a botany degree, with a secondary major in cuisine. I'm Cordon Bleu trained. Lifesupport and Logistics means that *I'm* the one who'll probably be put in charge of galley services on a major ship." The female cadet smiled, then her nose wrinkled wryly as she lifted a forkful of pasta. "This food is good, but this ain't Cordon Bleu."

Everyone chuckled. Harper yawned, hastily smothering it behind one hand, before removing it and allowing his other to bring up his fork. "So tired . . . 'scuse me . . . and we still have the rest of the evening to get through . . ."

"Oh, c'mon," one of the other cadets ribbed him. "Those calisthenics before supper weren't *that* hard."

"I've been up for over twenty-eight hours Standard, meioa-o," Harper told him. "Two of the last four systems on my flight to Earth had ion storm problems. We had to hover for hours in the nearest planet's magnetosphere because we were too small to risk that much radiation during the fluctuations in the front of the storm, and we couldn't open a hyperspace rift until the worst of the trailing particle clouds had passed. Courier shuttles have ceristeel plating, the same as any other spaceship, but not quite thick enough for that heavy a storm."

"You could afford to take a courier shuttle?" Jinja-Marsuu asked him, eyes widening.

Bruer stretched his arm over Ia's back and tapped Harper on the shoulder. "Saaaay, can I borrow fifty thousand credits?"

"It was a *military* shuttle. Half the adults in my extended family serve in the military," Harper explained, rolling his eyes. "When I asked my uncle which Academy he'd recommend, he told me the Academia de Marinha Estrelas would probably be a good fit, and he hooked me up for a string of fast flights."

"You're brave, meioa," Bruer murmured, digging into his own salad. "Stringing other-than-light jumps would make me heave up all over the place. I'll stick to faster-than-light, thank you. Slower, but safer."

"Some of us don't have any choice," Ia pointed out. "My homeworld is on the backside of Terran space, over seven hundred lightyears from here. It took me two weeks of swapping between OTL and FTL to get here. I actually started out from the Terran–Gatsugi Border, in a region about thirteen hundred lightyears from home. That's three weeks of stringing mostly hyperjumps with only a few days of FTL in between to recover. If I'd tried to take strictly faster-than-light transport, I wouldn't even have *reached* my homeworld before I would've had to change course in order to get here in time. I was lucky to get three weeks of Leave plus travel time as it was."

"Seven hundred?" Jinja-Marsuu muttered, gaze looking upward and inward, "Backside of . . ." She lowered her gaze to Ia's face and smiled. "You're from Sanctuary, aren't you? That's an Independent Colonyworld, if I remember right."

Ia nodded. "That's right. You're good."

The other young woman smiled. "I almost went into Astronavigation, since I have a real spatial memory for star system placement, but I'm not *that* fond of the math required. I'd rather work with aquaculture systems and hydroponics."

Bruer grinned. "*Aha, so you're* the one I have to butter up if I ever get stuck on lifesupport filtration duty."

Jinja-Marsuu made a face at him. The others turned on Bruer, ribbing him back. Ia focused on her food. She still had to eat about twice as much as the average person just to sustain her higher heavyworlder metabolic needs but had to do it in the same amount of time as all the lightworlders around her. Next to her, she saw Harper was eating quickly as well. Like her, he had worn a specially made weight suit during their exercise period right before supper. Not as heavy as hers, but still a burden meant to compensate for the lighter gravity here on Earth.

From what she was slowly learning about him, they had a number of things in common. It was everything else about him which she still had no clue.

Why can't I sense him in the timestreams?

CHAPTER 8

I'd never encountered anyone like Meyun Harper, before. I had no clue what he was, no clue what it meant that I couldn't foresee anything about him, and I went through a lot of bizarre speculations as a result. I also wanted to avoid touching him, out of sheer caution, but I knew it would only be a matter of time before we ended up colliding, or being paired for exercises. I needed to know everything I couldn't learn about him. So I tried going about it the sneaky way.

Naturally, it backfired.

~Ia

Ia couldn't sleep. Not even three meters away, the biggest blank spot in her life slumbered in near-silent innocence. The one person she couldn't predict. The one person she couldn't confirm existed in the timestreams.

Or is he innocent? Ia wondered. Twisting onto her back, she stared up into the shadows. The nightlight from the bathroom spilled a small amount of illumination into the rest of the dormitory room. With her eyes adapted to the darkness, she could have seen his dark hair on the pale blue of his pillow. She didn't look, though. Nor did she flip her mind inward and out onto the timeplains.

What could he be, then? He's not the Immortal One, I know that for a fact. She's currently lurking on the V'Dan homeworld. I also know I'm going nowhere near her. She'd want to "help" me, and that would ruin the timestreams. I don't have to look for effects to know she'd muck everything up. And she wouldn't leave me alone once she found me.

Her and her silly notions of Fate; she doesn't yet have a clue what it really means . . . Not that I myself understand. I can only See it; grasping it isn't up to me. At least, not in this life . . .

So what is he? Could he be an AI? No . . . he couldn't be. For one, the vast majority were destroyed in the AI War. For another, the only intact survivors are the few remaining loyalist members, but they're mostly resting in shutdown mode in the Immortal One's Vault, waiting either for her next visit, for their turn at dusting and watching over her archives, or for the day when Humans are again willing to accept their help. For another . . . alive or not, truly sentient or merely programmed to think they are, I know I can see their movements in the timestreams. They may not have souls and thus may not be alive, but they are there in the waters. Visible. Meyun Harper is an invisible fish, not a visible one.

Unless . . . could he be a Feyori? They are hard to track. They are living energy beings, capable of shielding themselves from all sorts of detection methods, physical and psychic. But I should be able to sense him anyway. I can most of the other Meddlers, particularly this close to one.

For that matter, why would a Meddler want to go into the TUPSF-Navy? The one I met back at Camp Nallibong, "Dr. Silverstone" . . . well, okay, it could be ruled in the Great Game that the Navy and the Marine Corps are two different areas of influence. Especially since the doctor is outside the direct chain of command . . . They also could be faction members. Or they could be counterfaction, and Harper is making a move against the plans being laid by Silverstone . . . She winced and lifted a hand, rubbing at her forehead. *Ugh, trying to keep up with the Feyori mind-set is a headache.*

Of course, this is all just speculation. Even the most para-noid Feyori can still be seen by me in the distant waters of the timeplains. It's when they get up close that their efforts at cloaking their movements work best. Invisible fish in the local pond, and all that. But . . . not Harper. Why can't I predict him?

She didn't like things she couldn't predict. They were dangerous. Any anomaly in Time could derail her efforts to save the future. Yet it was hard to dislike Harper himself. Twisting onto her right side, Ia stared at the shades of grey making up the shapes of his bed. *He's nice, polite, intelligent, thoughtful, has a good sense of humor, isn't overblown, or over the top, or overly full of himself. I find his company quite tolerable. It's not like he's a monster, or is breaking any laws that I know of. I just . . . cannot . . . foresee him. Or even past-see him.*

The only possibility that made the slightest sense was that he was indeed a Feyori. The silvery soap-bubble aliens were a very strange, energy-based form of sentience. Given that they were the only beings who could accelerate to the squared speed of light, they were the only ones who could transform energy into matter, and vice versa. They didn't have precognitive abilities quite like she did, but they could read the flux of time to an extent. At least, after a fashion, though not in the depth and detail that she could.

Unfortunately, if they can read it, they can hide in it. I think. I don't really know. Or rather, I don't really understand.

I do know that if he is a Feyori, he cannot hide from a touch. There's no way he can hide his past or his future from my gifts, not at a touch . . . and if he is a Feyori, I'll be able to read it in the surface thoughts of his sleep. If he is Feyori . . . then we have to come to an agreement that we are faction, not counterfaction, so that he doesn't interfere with my destiny.

Which means there's not going to be a better time than right now, when we're not under surveillance from anyone else. Stifling a sigh, Ia sat up and slipped out of the covers. Padding across the gap between their beds, she stared down at the blanket-draped lump that was her classmate. He sighed in his sleep, cheek nuzzling his pillow, his face lax and vaguely boyish, cloaked mostly in darkness as it was. Ia stifled another sigh. *I'll have to be careful, so I don't wake him up . . .*

Slowly, she lowered her hand toward his cheek. Hesitating a centimeter from his skin, she finally steeled herself and pressed her hand gently against him. Not lightly, as a too-light touch might wake him up, but gently.

His current dream appeared in her mind, an image of Meyun Harper lounging on a cushioned divan in some ancient Greco-Roman setting. They were in some sort of marble, open-sided temple with lush gardens all around. The details were blurry in spots—it was a dream, after all—but he was barely clad in a modified toga that also kind of looked like the undershorts he had gone to bed wearing. As she watched, he was being fed. The "food" looked like strips of archaic newspaper being dangled by equally scantily clad chickens. Chicken-lady things.

Ia gave up trying to make sense of it. This was a dream, and that was all the sense there would be to it. Except the newspaper strips became flowers and ribbons, the ends of which caressed his mostly naked chest. And her hand was now touching his cheek . . . and her clothes, T-shirt and undershorts, were now gone. Since this was his dream, Ia was bemused to discover he had imagined her with white hair down below as well as on her head. Unsettled, she did her best to quell her reaction. She didn't want to wake him up.

Even more unsettling, he turned his head and kissed her fingers. Not just in the dream-vision, but in his sleep, out in the real world. Strange feelings raced through her nerves. Things she hadn't felt in over five and a half years. The thrill of desire . . . and she wasn't the only one feeling it, too. Around her, the dream morphed. They were cradled in some sort of fur-draped couch, body to body . . . and he was going to kiss her.

Ia slipped out of his dream and out of his mind as fast as she could, without making it an abrupt departure. Snatching back her hand, she turned and padded quickly for the bathroom. Behind her, she heard him draw in a deep breath, the kind that sounded like he was waking up. Locking herself in the bathroom, she braced her hands on the sink and recited her grounding and centering exercises in her mind.

I am not scattered to the four winds . . . All of the facets of my personality are in one place. They are one with myself, blended smooth and whole. I am calm, I am centered, I am controlled. I am one, and whole . . .

. . . And it's pretty damn bad, if he can knock me off my

center, psychically. God! Why him? Why am I attracted to a man I cannot even sense? Hell, why am I attracted to anyone at all? I don't have Time for this!

A soft rapping on the door startled her. Barely suppressing a shriek, Ia panted for breath, heart racing.

"Uh . . . Ia? Are you going to be in there long?" she heard him call through the door. "I woke up and I have to . . . you know."

"Give me a few, I just woke up," she replied. She didn't have to go, but she did turn on the faucet and splash water on her face. *I am not attracted to him. First of all, it's forbidden between cadets. Second, it's not like we'll have the time for it, given our near-continuous workload in the coming months. Third, it's not like I'll have the Time for it, period. And fourth . . . I do know he's Human, but I have no clue what he is, other than a blank spot in my life. And blank spots are dangerous.*

But I can't avoid him. He's my damned roommate. So . . . I'll be nice to him, polite to him, but distance myself from him. Friendly, but not friends. That'll take care of two problems: any potential further attraction, and any potential disturbances of the paths to my goal.

Wiping her face dry on the hand towel, Ia unlocked the door and exited, giving him the chance to enter. The nook where the doors were located was small enough, the two of them brushed in passing. Awareness tingled through her body, reminding her of the flower-ribbons that had tickled both of their skin in his dream. She couldn't see what his expression was from that brief contact, but she knew she didn't want him to see hers.

And no *physical contact. Not unless we're fully clothed, and other people are around. This is just residue from that dream. That's all it is. I'm not actually attracted to the man. I don't even know him—literally, I don't. It's just . . . the last dregs of a delayed adolescence catching up with me. Nothing more, and nothing important.*

Reassuring herself of these things, Ia returned to her bed. According to the bedside chrono, they would have to get up in another three hours, and that meant she needed whatever sleep she could get.

"Gentlemeioas of Class 1252, welcome to the TUPSF *Vasco da Gama*," Lieutenant Commander Spada stated. "Aside from the occasional weeklong break every month or so to permit each class to undergo our special little version of Hell Week—which is what was happening last week—you will be undergoing daily hands-on classes on board the *da Gama*, here."

They stood at Parade Rest in front of the large, long, silvery grey structure occupying a bedrock-dug cavern buried somewhere below the headland east of the beach. The vessel was cradled in a vast array of crane-like pistons and yardarms built into the underground chamber, almost like a starship in a repair dock at a spaceport. Spada's voice carried half to their ears, echoing faintly off the gantries, struts, and vast ceiling surrounding them, and half into the headsets each and every cadet wore.

In Basic Training, the recruits hadn't received headsets for their first month of training. Here at the Academy, the cadets had received them within the first week, and for good reason. In Basic, Ia and the other recruits had worked more in the open air than in close quarters; orders could carry and be heard easily in such conditions. On board a ship, the muffling effects of hatchways and bulkheads, corridors and decks would render many of their instructions inaudible without the use of these headsets.

"Yes, what you see behind me is a real starship. She is a Frigate Class, one of the most common types of vessels run by the SF-Navy. Of course, the FTL warp panels, insystem thrusters, and gunnery pods have all been disabled, and she has been retrofitted with a number of services which will provide you with as realistic an experience as the Space Force can create. This means she cannot *go* anywhere," Spada admitted, shrugging, "but she *is* capable of *simulating* going just about anywhere.

"The support struts and gravitational webbing you see surrounding the hull are capable of re-creating the actual sensations from space travel and space combat. You will experience bumps and bruises in the course of your training, with the possibility of more severe injuries. Medical personnel are included in these simulations, but many of them will *also* be students, stationed here as a part of their medical internship training.

"Any officer you see on board the *da Gama* will be treated with respect, and you will follow the appropriate chain of command for your training positions . . . which can and *will* change from day to day," Spada warned them. "Just like today, you will be given a group number, and that number will be assigned to a specific section of shipboard life. Today, it may be engineering. Tomorrow, it might be gunnery, or plumbing. It might even change midclass, so get used to it."

The man standing next to her, Master Petty Officer Clarke, addressed the cadets standing At Attention in front of them. "You will also see noncommissioned personnel and enlisted personnel aboard the *da Gama*, such as myself. These people technically will not be considered your superiors in rank for the purposes of the simulations, but they *are* your evaluators. They are renowned as specialists in their fields, and they serve this Academy as highly qualified instructors. You will therefore treat them with respect, and get into the *habit* of treating them with respect.

"Demonstrating a basic level of respect for your fellow sailors will carry far greater weight in earning *their* respect for *you*. Respect for your person and trust in your knowledge and authority are the grease which makes the wheels of the military turn," Master Petty Clarke stated. "You can yell, you can threaten, you can scream, but if you don't have that respect, the crew placed beneath you can and will ignore you. The carrot *must* be visible from the start, as well as the stick. It will be your responsibility as officers to make sure the sailors and soldiers placed under you carry out the orders that you will be handing down to them."

"With that said, it is time to enter the *Vasco da Gama* and begin your first Ship Orientation class. Each of you has been assigned a *temporary* department. This may or may not have anything to do with your chosen training track," Spada warned them, "and these assignment positions *will* change. You will need to learn *all* the facets of shipboard life, and be able to pick up the slack at any point to a sufficiently competent degree. Casualties can and will happen in space, and if the officer in charge of lifesupport is in the infirmary with a busted collarbone, *you* may have to put your hand on the reins to make sure the most basic needs of shipboard life keep flowing.

"Make sure your arm unit maps are linked and your headsets are active. You will not be using the ship's comm systems to communicate this time while on board. Class 1252, you now have permission to come aboard," Spada ordered.

"You heard the Lieutenant Commander! Line up, Cadets! You have been given permission to board the *da Gama*, so do not dawdle!"

"Psst, hey, Ia," the cadet behind her whispered as they shuffled into formation and headed up the boarding ramp. "You ever been in one of these things?"

"Frigate Class?" she asked, equally under her breath. "Yes, I was stationed on the *Liu Ji*, which is a Frigate Class, if at the smaller end of the spectrum. The *da Gama* looks like it might be a little bit bigger . . . but then I never actually stood outside the *Liu Ji*. I won't know for sure until I've been inside for a little bit."

"No, I meant have you ever been on one of these simulator ships," he said.

"They use training simulation rooms similar to portions of actual starships in the Marines—namely the sections anyone in the Marines would be expected to know and of course a shakedown tour of a few weeks in space on a real ship," Ia murmured back, "but not a whole ship rigged for simulations, no."

"Cadet, is there something you wanted to share with your class?" The question came from one of the watchful, blue-clad noncommissioned officers overseeing their entrance to the ship.

"Sergeant, no, Sergeant," she answered promptly. Then winced and amended it to, "I mean, no, Petty Officer."

"Were you Army?" the middle-aged man inquired, lifting his brow.

"Marine Corps," Ia told him.

He tipped his head. "Well, at least you didn't call me 'Sarge' . . . or worse, 'sir.' "

She smiled wryly. "They did beat at least that much into my head, Petty."

Her headset came to life, filling her left ear once again with Spada's voice, though he could no longer be seen. *"As you enter, you will remember from your orientation classes that all ships are numbered in decks from top to bottom, numbered from forward to aft, and lettered phonetically from port to starboard. You are currently entering on Deck 8, cross-corridor Juliett, next to corridor 1.*

"Placards on doors and next to hatchways will also indicate what direction you're facing. If it's on a forward wall, the top and bottom edges are trimmed in blue. If in reading the sign you are facing aft, the top and bottom edges are yellow. Placards which are facing the port side of a starship are always red at top and bottom, and the ones facing starboard are always edged green. If you have problems with color-blindness, judge by the blue or yellow found either on the tops, bottoms, or right or left edge of all signs," Spada directed them. *"Remember that port is off to the left of blue when facing the bow, but off to the right of yellow when facing the stern. There aren't a lot of viewports on a military starship, so get used to looking at the various signs for clues on where you are, and where to go.*

"You will be tested on finding your way around a standard TUPSF starship without arm units, headsets, or cheat sheets, before you are allowed to graduate from this Academy," Spada added. Humor colored his voice. *"Mind you, most cadets find the concept of a scavenger hunt a lot of fun . . . except that most of these scavenger hunts will be conducted under combat conditions.*

"Once a week, at some point in that week, we will be placing five vouchers for three-hour-long Leave passes around this ship, usable either Saturday or Sunday evening. That's just enough time to go into town and have a nice meal for supper, and maybe even catch a show. At the end of this hour's lesson, you will have precisely fifteen minutes to decipher the clues we will give you in order to find those tickets and return them to me at a location I will specify.

"Only one ticket is allowed per cadet, and if you tear the edge of the vouchers even by a tiny bit, nobody gets to use that pass. So you'd better pay attention right now to what you are about to learn . . . and decide who you think should win the voucher, if several of you should find it at once. You are future officers, and will conduct yourselves with the appropriate level of dignity at all times."

"I've heard about this," the young woman in front of Ia whispered. "My cousin went through this same Academy, also on the fast-track program, and she said they did this at least once a week. That's plenty of chances for each of us to get an evening's Leave."

The cadet behind Ia nudged her. "I suppose you'll get to the tickets first, since you know the layouts of these ships?"

Ia shook her head. "There are similarities, but while the bones are the same, the muscles and organs vary from beast to beast, so to speak—the actual layout of the rooms on a particular deck in a particular section will often vary from ship to ship within a particular class, even if the major features and main layouts are the same."

Spada started speaking again, telling them more about what they were expected to see and do in the next hour. Ia and the others fell silent, listening to the words transmitted by their earpieces. A corner of her brain idly picked at the timestreams, wondering if she should grab one of the tickets now, or wait until next week. *This week, I think. It'll spur the others to learn faster, especially when I point out that the layout really isn't that hard to learn, if even a Marine grunt like me could learn it. Hm. But if I wait a week, then point out they've had a week to learn the ship that might be better . . . but would that be mean of me?*

Well, I could point out this week that I didn't grab the voucher because I wanted to be fair to everyone who had never been on board a starship before. And then warn them in advance I'll be going for the ticket next week. That'll work, she decided. *I can use the opportunity next week to print out and mail off my prophecies as well as my blood beads . . .*

Once everyone was on board, the order was given to split up into their various tours. Ia had been sorted into the lifesupport group. She knew more or less how it worked, but hadn't had much reason or opportunity to visit that particular part of a ship before now. At least, not when she wasn't being given a punishment detail.

Like most vital systems, lifesupport was broken up into several parts, the largest of which were buried in the heart of the ship. In the event of a hull breach, each ship section could be sealed off and sustain itself with small hydrogenerators, reoxygenators, and backup water filtration systems. Gravity might go offline, the air might stink, and the water taste bad, but life could be sustained hopefully long enough to wait it out until rescue could arrive.

When not sealed off from damage, however, the majority of lifesupport needs came from the pair of brightly lit core chambers on Deck 6. The setup was ingenious. It started with the sanitation system, which flushed biological waste into a system of alternating tanks and beds. The first ones contained algae and bacteria in removable, moss-like filters, with both air and water bubbling through the material, exchanging oxygen and carbon dioxide along with air and waterborne pollutants.

The filters had to be carefully scrubbed every once in a while, mainly so that the larger chunks were broken down. It was a messy, necessary job, one which didn't always look or smell pleasant. That made them perfect for punishment details. The watered-down slurry then passed through stack after stack of vegetation, first feeding the leafy oxygenators, then filtering down to the vegetable beds. From there, the water ran through tanks of fish and the aquatic plants which fed them, followed by yet more beds of vegetation and herbs to remove the ammonia and other wastes produced by the fish, and more tanks of fish after that.

The second influx point included composting soils from the galleys. At the end of each vegetation bed was an extraction point for the water, which passed through secondary filtration systems consisting of biomat filters and aquatic grasses. Air bubbled through these filters as well, scrubbing out additional carbon dioxide and replacing it with oxygen through photosynthesis.

Each ship larger than a courier shuttle, which was twice to three times the size of an orbital shuttle, was guaranteed a supply of fresh food via the plants and the fish, plus fresh water and extra oxygen beyond that supplied as a waste by-product of the hydrogenerators. Smaller vessels had to make do with scaled down versions where the only filtration came from the supplemental algae and bacterial filters, while large ships could eat almost entirely fresh meals on a daily basis. Some even had enough to spare. Battle Platforms and space stations usually grew enough to sell off the excess to passing vessels, and many incorporated other animals, such as chickens and V'Dan water hens.

Frigate Class ships were just large enough to permit the inclusion of four sets of fish tanks and two coops of water hens, divided evenly between the two bays. The clucking and cooing and splashing of the blue-and-brown birds as they waddled and swam in their enclosure could be heard over the trickling of the water and the bubbling of the filters. Fish swam in the plexi-sided tanks, occasionally drifting close enough to peer out at the students before darting back in among the water weeds. The air was rich with moisture and the scents of green growing things, from the bitter of lettuce greens to the prickle of tomato plants, the sweetness of strawberries to the tang of lemongrass.

Compared to the more sterile environments elsewhere on the ship, this section almost always smelled like home to the people these ships carried. The only thing it was missing in Ia's estimation was the spark-like scent of ozone, though she knew the others wouldn't have agreed on that point. She paid polite attention as the instructor in charge of lifesupport gave the cadets in her group an overview of the importance of the various symbiotic cycles, and the vital importance of monitoring, adjusting, and repairing every step along the way.

"For those of you who have lived your lives in an M-class, Human-compatible habitat, such as here on Earth, do not be afraid to drink this water. It has undergone a scaled down version of the exact same kinds of natural filtration you will find here on the Motherworld," their tour instructor, Lieutenant Danvers, stated. "The air you will be breathing, the food you will be eating, and the waste you will be excreting will all become a part of the *da Gama*'s lifesupport system. It must therefore be embraced, not shied away from. Lifesupport is exactly that: the systems, plural, which support life.

"This chamber is the core of that system, which is why it is buried in the heart of all Navy vessels, hopefully deep enough inside that it won't sustain catastrophic damage during a starfight. Speaking of which, you will notice the excessive number of interior safety field nodes, and the excessively strong support structures involved. Any one of these systems, broken free, would cause a catastrophic mess in here, and a potentially lethal one at that," Lieutenant Danvers warned them. "As you can see, every care is taken to adhere to the Lock and Web Law of space travel.

"Plants and filtration bedding materials are held in place with reinforced biomeshes. Most of the tanks are enclosed systems, though they can be opened for maintenance. The floor is perforated to recapture sloshed or spilled liquids. And the hen coop, while open to the air, is wrapped in mesh wire and bears extra suppression fields to cover the water and keep the hens safe in the advent of unexpected maneuvers or impacts—Cadet Phong, those strawberries are *not* for your consumption."

"Sorry, sir." He quickly lowered his hand to his side, swallowing quickly, but the damage had been done.

"Congratulations, Cadet," Danvers told him, twisting her mouth up in wry humor. "You've just earned yourself five demerits, and the right to be the very first person put on biofiltration detail. Of course, *all* of you will learn how to clean the filters and do basic lifesupport monitoring and repair work. This is probably one of the easiest ship systems to maintain and repair, for all that it does require some definite knowledge of aquaponics to maintain perfectly. However, it is also one of the systems that can cause the most trouble. If it gets out of balance, you can poison the water or the food, kill off the fish, wither the crops, starve or dehydrate your fellow sentients, and even cause problems with the breathability of the ship's air.

"The air itself is an important factor. The ventilation system does circulate this air throughout the whole of the ship, passing through various computer-controlled airlock shafts. Under the bulkhead lockdown of combat conditions, it takes an estimated twenty-five minutes for air to circulate from here to the bow and back, and thirty minutes from here through the extremities of the stern," the instructor stated. "However, in the event of a catastrophic breach, it may not be possible to oxygenate a particular ship segment.

"With gravity, your own body heat will continue to circulate all the air in a particular cabin, allowing the heavier carbon dioxide to settle down to the decking. Without it, you can literally suffocate in a matter of minutes as your own exhalations cause the carbon dioxide to build up around your head and torso, clinging to your vicinity. Of course, it only takes a slight movement to stir the air, but it is still a concern. This is why we have miniature, and somewhat more mechanical, versions of reoxygenation systems redundantly scattered throughout the ship, along with emergency hydrogenerator engines in every sector to provide backup power.

"Once we have finished with this segment of our tour," Lieutenant Danvers told the blue-clad cadets standing between the stacks of plant beds and tanks in the long, narrow chamber, "we will go to classroom 6-Beta, which is in the next ship section forward of this. There, you will get to see a series of reoxygenators in various states of assembly and repair. For this week's training sessions, you will learn basic maintenance and repair for lifesupport, hydrogeneration, and communications. These are the three most vital aspects of survival on board any starship. Whatever your specialty may end up being, you *will* learn how to manage and maintain these three parts, just as you will learn how to direct others in their management and maintenance.

"We will, however, start you on the mechanical backup systems for Lifesupport . . . because if you break one part on those, you just order another part. Kill off the fish tanks with a simple, stupid mistake, and the whole system can crash," Danvers warned them dryly. "This is also why most battleships carry two lifesupport cabins, so that in the event of a breakdown in one, the other can be used to reseed the damaged systems. In space, redundancy saves lives. The goal of the modern military, contrary to popular belief, is more about saving lives than in killing them off.

"Do try to keep these top three needs of your ship in mind at all times, since as future officers, you *will* be responsible for the use, or abuse, of the lives under your command."

Aye, aye, sir, Ia silently agreed.

NOVEMBER 7, 2492 T.S.

Sighing, Meyun Harper leaned back in his desk chair and stretched. His blue T-shirt rode up on his stomach with the movement, exposing a stretch of tan abdomen. Ia, curled up on her bed with pillows propping up her back, tried not to look up from her writing station. She failed. There weren't that many men who had that many muscles outside of a heavyworlder or a weight lifter, and her newly rediscovered feminine side was insisting upon noticing each and every one, whenever they were bared in her presence.

Ostensibly she was doing homework. In actuality, she was composing prophecies, with her homework already electrokinetically completed and stored, awaiting printout. Harper was working on actual homework, typing in the essay-style answers needed to indicate he understood the course material at hand. Except he seemed to be taking a break. Stretching a second time, he scratched his stomach, then tilted his head back and over the edge of his chair so that he could glance her way.

"Ten weeks of this, and I *think* I'm getting used to the pace . . . except they keep increasing it incrementally. If I didn't have an eidetic memory for visual information, I don't know how I'd be able to keep up. Hell, I don't know how anyone who *doesn't* have a picture-perfect memory can keep up—and just because I can remember it doesn't mean I can automatically *comprehend* it."

"Wait until Hell Week," Ia quipped back. "It won't be quite as physically demanding in the Navy as it was in the Marine Corps—and only five days instead of seven—but everything I've heard about the Academy version says it'll still be a brutal slice of mental hell."

He gave her a lopsided, sardonic smile. "That's what I like about you, Ia. You're always so *cheerful* and uplifting!" Scrubbing his face, he sighed. "*Ehhh* . . . enough of this. I need to get my brain off of insystem thrusters, or it'll explode."

Closing the lid of his writing station, he scrubbed his hands through his collar-length hair, then stood and stretched a third time. This time, his shirt rode well above his navel. Ia found her gaze drawn to the exposed skin for a few fascinated seconds before she caught herself and dragged it firmly back down to the screen of her writing pad.

"So. What made you think of bleaching your hair white?" he asked her. Meyun grabbed the back of his chair and pulled it farther back from his desk, straddling it so that he faced her.

"I didn't. I was born this way. Light brown eyebrows, light brown lashes, light brown body hair . . . and a scalp full of old woman white." Saving the work on her pad, she rested it against her uplifted knees. Apparently he was in the mood for another getting-to-know-you chat. Ia shrugged. "Of course, my lashes and brows were so thin and fine, the doctors took one look at my pale hair and blue eyes, and promptly pronounced me an albino . . . even though I had this slight Asiatic tan to my skin from birth." She extended an arm in indication, then rested it on her blue-clad knee. "They thought maybe it was a touch of V'Dan in my father's background."

"When did they figure out you weren't an albino?" Meyun asked her, crossing his wrists on the back of the chair. He rested his chin on his forearms, slouching a bit.

"I think my biomom said my eyes changed color at about three months of age. It was a bit early, but not unheard-of," she added. "Then again, being heavyworlders, we do age a little faster."

"*Mm*, true. Mine started out dark blue, and didn't change for a good eight months, according to my mother. She was hoping they'd stay blue, or turn green, since there's a recessive gene for that somewhere in the family line," Meyun told her. "On the Irish Harper side of the family, naturally, not the Hwang. Green eyes are supposed to be lucky."

"I kind of like your eyes being that shade of dark brown," Ia offered. She felt an urge to blush as she said it, but fought it down.

He smiled. "I like yours, all honey brown. Or maybe amber brown. Baltic amber. Like a contradiction, hard and lightweight, warm and unyielding, yet very lovely."

The blush won. Ia looked down at her pad, waiting quietly in standby mode. Harper cleared his throat.

"Not that I'm particularly good at forming compliments," he muttered. "Plus there's that whole fraternization rule, making things awkward if I witlessly babbled anything more . . ."

The blush deepened, heating her cheeks further. Ia felt her heart skip a beat and struggled against the urge to both grin and scowl. *Do* not *feel such things,* she admonished herself. She couldn't let his comment pass unanswered, though. "Then I'll take it exactly as it's no doubt meant: a simple, poetic compliment. Thank you."

"You're welcome." Straightening, he swung his arms, flexing his shoulders, then rested his elbows on the back of the chair. "It's almost nine thirty . . . twenty-one thirty, rather. I'm still getting used to converting everything into military time.

Anyway, they were talking about that new Gatsugi comedy show coming on about now, *Red Is Green*. Did you want to head to the common room and watch it with everyone? It's supposed to be really good."

Ia shook her head. "You go on. I'm still working on my essay questions."

Rising, he leaned over the back of the chair for a moment, giving her a mock-chiding look. "All homework and no play makes Cadet Ia a dull little girl. You really should try to socialize more, you know."

"I will. Later," she promised. "Gatsugi humor is pleasantly translatable for Humans, but I'm not in the mood for eye-blaring colors right now. Trying to come up with my 'own interpretation' of 'the thermal efficiency of the Stirling engine design as incorporated by the modern military into shipboard hydrogenerators' is giving me an engine-sized headache. There's really only so many ways you can describe a heat transference regenerator before you run out of words that haven't been said over and over, before."

"Well, I suppose adding alien fashion-emotion color sense on top of a headache isn't a good idea." Shifting free of the chair, he pushed it back into his desk. "I'll see you in about half an hour, then."

Nodding, she picked up her writing station and made a pretense of reactivating the pad. Covertly, she watched him tug his T-shirt back into place, smooth his hair with his fingers, and head for the door. Only when the door had slid shut behind him did she move, setting the pad aside and rising from the bed.

Might as well get my nightly blood draw out of the way. Fetching the kit box from her bureau, she moved into the bathroom. She had the box halfway open when she heard the dorm room door slide open, and quickly fumbled the plain plexi box shut again. It was a good thing, too, for the next thing she knew, Meyun had hooked his arm around her elbow and was pulling her out of the smaller room.

"I've changed my mind. You *need* some serious fun and socialization, Cadet," he mock-chided her.

"Harper!" Ia protested. She didn't want to hurt him, which his implacable hugging of her right arm would risk if she tried to free herself. Awkwardly tossing the box into the bathroom sink, she let him draw her out of their shared quarters. *Stupid of me not to close the bathroom door, first . . .* "Harper, honestly, I *don't* need socialization."

"*Ah*, but you *do* need fun. You can't quite bring yourself to deny that, can you?" he teased. Grinning, he tugged her down the hall. Ia rolled her eyes, doing her best to match his stride.

"They're just going to bother me again about being Bloody Mary," she muttered, wondering what this was going to do to her scheduled plans. Or worse, the perceptions and reactions of the other cadets, and their impact on the future. She didn't think Meyun was psychically sensitive, but she couldn't risk dipping even lightly into the timestreams while anyone was so physically close.

"So what if they do? Just redirect their attention to *Red Is Green* or something," he told her. "Or better yet, we can don the virtual gear and play a shoot'em game on one of the spare vid consoles."

"Lovely, a shooter game," she muttered. "Let's dredge up memories of my days in the Corps, oh, yes, *that'll* relax me."

Meyun switched his arm from her elbow to her shoulders, giving her a sideways squeeze. "Hey, it's for that very same reason that I can't think of anyone else I'd want firing away at my side during the zombie apocalypse."

"Try Cadet Djalu," Ia quipped back, her freed arm treacherously slipping around his waist. "She has better aim than I do."

"Nah, I figure she'll be somewhere near ground zero when the invasion comes," Meyun dismissed, guiding her down the hall toward the common room at the center of the dorm building.

"Nonsense," Ia scoffed. "She'd be holed up at the secure fortress, up in a guard tower position with a sniper rifle and the paranoid fear that someone with an infected scratch might make it through the gate."

"Which would probably be Cadet Bruer," Meyun joked as they entered the common room.

"Do I hear my name in vain?" the brown-haired cadet asked, looking up from his hand. He and three others were playing some sort of V'Dan card game, based on the triangular cards.

Meyun released Ia's shoulders. That forced her to release his waist. Hands dropping to his hips, he shrugged lightly. "Oh, we were just figuring who'd be the sap who tried to smuggle an infected scratch in through the fortress gates during the inevitable zombie apocalypse."

"Bruer," three of their classmates immediately agreed in near-perfect unison.

"Hey!" Bruer protested. "I'll have you know that I'd be too damned cowardly to even *leave* the fortress in the first place. No, I'll be the guy in the back of the bunker, hogging all of the *good* supplies for myself." He scooped up a handful of snack nuts from the bowl and munched on a few, gesturing at Ia with the rest. "Besides, it'd be our resident spacegrunt, here, who'd charge into the zombies, slaughter the masses, then come limping back to a hero's welcome, desperately trying to hide her infected wounds."

Now that Meyun wasn't touching her, Ia could safely tap into the timestreams. Bruer's comment gave her an opening, a small shortcut in establishing the reputation she would one day need. Sauntering up to the table, she rested her hands on her hips, subconsciously imitating her roommate. "Now that's where you're wrong, Bruer."

He raised his brows at that, munching on a few more nuts. "What, you think you'd be cowering in the back with me? If you're *nice*, I might let you have some of the bourbon . . . but only *some* of it."

"No, I meant I wouldn't get scratched," she corrected.

"*Pff* yeah, right," he scoffed. The other cadets playing the card game with him smirked as well, not believing her.

Picking up the bowl of nuts, Ia smiled at him—and sharply flicked her wrist, tossing the contents straight up, some of them by over a meter. Eyes and hands working in coordination, she guided the falling peanuts, almonds, pecans, and hazelnuts with her left hand, guiding them back into the bowl held in the right. Catching the last nut just before it reached table height, she slid the wooden bowl back onto the card-scattered surface. She had only tossed twenty or so nuts from the nearly empty bowl, an easy catch for her reflexes, if a little difficult for a light-worlder.

"As I said, I wouldn't get scratched," she murmured, smiling at him and his impressed classmates. Her smile deepened into a grin. "*Mainly* because I'd run farther and faster than the rest of you, grab the nearest fighter ship, and bombard the zombies from a nice, safe distance."

"Dibs on being your copilot!" one of the other female cadets quipped from her spot on one of the sofas. The brightly hued opening credits for the *Red Is Green* show were starting to roll, so Ia didn't quite look that way, but she lifted her chin in acknowledgment.

Bruer lifted his own chin sagely. "*Ahhh*, yes, the old 'Nuke them from orbit, it's the only way to be sure' gambit. An oldie, but a goodie . . . unless you're one of the saps still stuck out in the open, and not safely tucked away with me in my bunker."

"Tucked away with all the good bourbon, too, you lousy bastich," the cadet to his right muttered. "Just don't hog all the scotch." He tossed down one of his triangular cards, aligning it with the other cards on the playing mat. "Three of Crystals, to the Red Keeper of the Dawn. Your move, Bruer."

Ia turned away from the card game. Meyun had moved over to the vid consoles and was skimming through the titles. He beckoned her over. Resigning herself to losing an hour or so of sleep later in order to make up for the loss of prophecy-writing time now, she joined him. It wouldn't hurt the future too much if she socialized, and maybe even help her cause a little. She just couldn't afford to make a habit of it, that was all.

CHAPTER 9

There is no school for prophets. No academy, no course credits, no instructors, no textbooks. Nothing but what our common sense, our ethics, and our best intentions can offer in the way of guidance and direction. Of course, there are scam artists who claim to be prophets, those whose moral compasses have gone astray, or never existed in the first place. Thankfully the law has a system of retrospective indemnities to penalize those charlatans who try to fake precognitive powers, particularly if they try to use them for garnering fame and fortune. You can usually tell a false prophet by how often they push their supposed "powers" in your face without actually using them, and by how much they promote themselves . . . and by their eventual failure at prognostication.

For myself, it wasn't a case of not wanting to be accused of chicanery and con artist games. Anyone who ever questioned my abilities to see clearly into the past and future needed only to spend a single day in my presence to have their doubts erased. Unfortunately, the sheer scope of people who needed to have confidence and faith in my predictive abilities made that an impractical, if not impossible, course of action.

So, instead, I spent my early years in the military building up my reputation as a reliable, knowledgeable,

*competent soldier, and slipped in the occasional piece of
prophecy. Sometimes it was little, temporally localized
things. Other times, it was the things that my classmates
and shipmates wouldn't think much of at first, but which
they would remember years later. Only then, when the truth
finally became known, would the impact of such simple
things be heightened in their minds . . . because by then,
they would already be living proof of my prophetic powers.*

~Ia

JANUARY 30, 2493 T.S.
TUPSF *VASCO DA GAMA*
ACADEMIA DE MARINHA ESTRELAS

The ship jolted and shuddered around them to the left, rocking
with the simulated impact of projectile missiles. Cadet Bruer,
seated in the captain's chair, grunted as the restraint straps
bit into his shoulders when his body slammed to the left from
inertia. The black projection nodes squeezed them into place in
short pulses that dampened some of the kinetic energy jolting
through the ship, but couldn't stop it all. With the ship already
damaged from the start of the scenario, they had limited options
left. That, of course, was the point of this exercise.

Bruer wasn't the only one to grunt; even Ia winced at the
strength of the blows from the enemy's cannon fire.

"Engineering reports they have just enough power for either
the insystem thrusters or the gunnery pods, but not both, Captain," Cadet Dostoyevska called out from her position at the
monitoring station for that department.

"*Ah . . . ah . . .*" Bruer grunted as the ship rocked again.
"Options, quick!"

"Hit 'em back, Captain!" Ia called out from her position at
the communications panel. "Take out their weapons, now!"

"This isn't the Marine Corps, Cadet! We're carrying vital
intelligence that *must* arrive safely," Cadet Jinja-Marsuu argued
back, quoting the scenario. "With communications knocked out,
we *have* to deliver it in person. Use the engines, Captain!"

"We don't knock out those guns, we're *dead* in twenty seconds!" Ia retorted.

"All engines ahead full!" Bruer commanded. "Head for the ice rings, for cover!"

"Engines ahead, aye, sir!" Dostoyevska repeated, relaying the command. The ship "lurched" forward, some of the vidscreens showing views of the Dlmvla warship at their aft, firing once more upon them. Others showed a view of the nearby gas giant and the rings Bruer wanted to use for shelter. The rest, secondary and tertiary and lesser screens, were filled with scrolling ship's data, missile trajectories, and so forth.

The projectile missiles were abruptly outpaced by the bright searing lines of laser cannonry. Lists of ship systems started flashing in bands of yellow and red on the screens; the simulated lasers had scored direct hits on the shield panels protecting the gunnery pods from incoming missiles. They were followed seconds later by explosions which shook the *da Gama* like a rat in a dog's mouth, shuddering everything around them to the right. The *da Gama* jolted abruptly to the left again . . . and klaxons blared, sharp and sudden, making every cadet wince. The main lighting on the bridge flashed triple time in red, and the ship slowed its shaking, coming to a gentle, upright rest.

"Congratulations, 'Captain' Bruer and the rest of Class 1252," Lieutenant Commander Spada's voice stated over the intercom systems. "The enemy successfully triggered chain reaction explosions in the gunnery pod ammunition bays. You have just successfully slaughtered your crewmates."

"Shakk," Bruer muttered, slumping back in his seat. He scrubbed his hands over his face. "Sorry, meioas. I just can't get the hang of quick command decisions when I'm in a panic. With my luck, it'll take ten years."

"I predict you'll only have three, maybe three and a half," Ia told him. Behind everyone, the door to the bridge slid open. She ignored it in favor of giving him a piece of advice. "You'll be in this exact same position, Bruer, only it'll be against the Salik, not the Dlmvla, and you will need to tell *your* CO engines or guns. Go for the guns, but tell your gunners to pick their targets as carefully as the Dlmvla picked ours. Don't just fire in a rush. In a situation like this, they'll only get one, maybe two shots before the enemy shoots back. Those shots have to count."

Bruer snorted. "Yeah, right, like when am *I* ever going to be on a Blockade Patrol? God . . . you'd *think* I'd think of using the guns, with my background. I just got too focused on completing the mission."

"Your assessment of the problem is accurate, Cadet Bruer," Spada stated. His image flashed across every primary screen on the bridge. It was also being broadcast to every other cadet's station, letting them know what was happening on the bridge.

"Lieutenant Commander on deck!" Ia called out. Everyone sat up a little straighter in their seats, but since they hadn't been told the simulation was over, no one unstrapped. The lecture their trainers had given them on that little *faux pas* had been lengthy and involved the assignment of more punishment details than the lifesupport filters alone could cover.

"At ease, bridge crew, but remain strapped in," Spada told them. "Lieutenant Commander Spada to all cadets, remain at your posts. We will be rerunning the simulation in just a few minutes from time index five minutes thirty seconds. Alright, Cadet Ia. You'll get your chance. Swap places with Cadet Bruer and take command of the *da Gama*. The simulation will start at the exact same point as the last three tries. Let's see if *your* choice was the better one . . . *or* if it was the wrong one as well. Lives are in the balance," he ordered. "The clock is ticking, and the DoI is watching."

Unbuckling her straps, Ia immediately complied. "Aye, sir."

"Aye, sir," Bruer added, releasing his own restraints. "Transferring command to Cadet Ia, sir."

Spada nodded and strode back out, not bothering to stay and watch the two cadets swap places. Then again, he had a perfectly good view of everything back in the observation cabin, along with his fellow instructors.

Hooking the straps into place on the captain's chair, Ia punched a few buttons on her console, changing the priority of the displays to suit her own preferences and needs a little better. "Okay, bridge crew, I want a slightly different set of priorities. The moment that ship pops up on the screens, I want a fast tactical analysis of its hull. Every single weak point, starting with shield nodes, gun pods by category, engines, and sensory equipment, in that order, but *not* the comm dishes. Relay exact coordinates of priority listed targets to all gunnery pods on whatever flank any enemy ship appears."

"On whatever flank it appears?" Bruer asked. "It'll appear

on the starboard side, like it has for the last four simulation tries!"

"I don't care if it's appeared on the starboard for the last fifty-*six* simulation tries," Ia countered briskly. "If it appears on the starboard or the port side, fore or aft, dorsal or ventral, I want this crew ready to act." A touch of her station controls connected her headset to the rest of the ship. *"This is Acting Captain Ia. Prepare for resumption of simulation at time index five minutes thirty seconds, by order of Lieutenant Commander Spada. Repair teams, if you can get me a short-range communication bandwidth operational without sacrificing energy to engines or guns as needed, I'll give the first one to pull it off my next Leave voucher. All hands, this is a ready check, greenlight for go."*

Her fifth tertiary screen—the farthest right in the row of smaller screens lining the bottom of her primary and two flanking secondary screens—started lighting up a large list of names, first in speckles, then in broader swaths, most of them green. A few stayed neutral yellow for several long seconds before they, too, turned green.

"Acting Captain Ia to Lieutenant Commander Spada, we are greenlit for go," she stated.

Spada's voice came back across the ship intercoms, though not on their screens. *"All hands, brace for simulation. Resuming scenario in ten . . . nine . . . eight . . ."*

The ship thrummed and rocked hard at *zero*, struck by both the bright red bolts of laser cannonry and the thumping of simulated munitions attempting to slam their way through the *da Gama*'s shields. Braced for it, Ia rolled with the impact, then danced her hands over the keys at her control station, setting up her counterattack.

"Ship's on the *starboard*, Ca—aaahptain!" Cadet Jinja-Marsuu told her. Her voice jostled into a yelp at the end as they were struck by another attack. Now that the simulation had begun, she had dropped the "Acting" part of Ia's title, and was treating the scenario as if it were real, as all of them had been instructed to do. "It's on the starboard, just like it was *last* time."

"The last of the external comm systems are down, Captain!" Bruer told her. "They took out the fore and aft insystem dishes."

Ia flicked on her headset with a tap of her finger. *"Starboard*

L-pods, target and destroy all shield nodes, and only the shield nodes, fire at will! Engines full forward, get us the maximum insystem speed." Switching it off with a second tap, she called out, "Cadet Jimenez, on my mark, I want you to crack to five percent width the doors on the airlock list I'm sending to your station. Blow them, but only on my mark."

"Sir?" she questioned Ia. Jimenez had to raise her voice over the distant, thrumming pulses of their own laser cannons firing back. "I don't understand . . ."

"Careful observation brings comprehension— *Ungh!*" Ia grunted as the ship rocked under another hard blow, hand going back to her broadcast controls. *"Ventral P-pods, prepare to target enemy engines and laser gunnery pods. Do not, I repeat, do not target enemy P-pods until ordered to do so. Target only the L-pods!"*

"They're digging a hole through to Engineering, just like last time!" Jinja-Marsuu warned Ia.

"Lieutenant Harper, get those repair teams on the communications arrays, bounce it triple time!" Ia ordered. *"Get me anything, so long as it broadcasts past our hull."*

"I'm on it personally, Captain!"

"Good meioa," she muttered under her breath, off-mike.

"Captain!" Cadet Ng called out from his position overseeing the gunnery teams. "We've destroyed their forward shields. I'm ordering the P-pods to fire at will."

"Belay that!" Ia snapped, toggling on the intercom. *"Starboard P-pods, hold your fire. I repeat, hold your fire! L-pods, concentrate your fire on their aft shields and take them down."*

They rocked hard to the left. Jinja-Marsuu cursed. *"Shova v'shhh*—aft shields are gone; we've lost engines, Captain! Power dropping rapidly. We're deadheaded on course, no maneuvering capacity."

"Midsection shields dropping," Cadet Smith warned everyone. "A few more hits on the starboard and we're done for!"

"Jimenez, blow it!" Ia ordered.

"Ahh—aye, sir!" she replied, jabbing at her own controls. The ship jolted and rotated, rolling under the force of the escaping gasses from the upper starboard and lower port airlocks. "That . . . that's doing it, sir. We're rolling!"

"You're presenting fresh shields to the enemy? It's brilliant!"

Bruer praised. Then grunted as the ship rocked again. "Unfortunately, they're still killing us, just a little slower."

"Captain, I have EM radio online. Sending it to tertiary two."

"Good meioa," Ia praised, this time into her headset. She dragged the packet she had prearranged from her middle tertiary screen to the second screen from the left on the bottom of her bank of monitors. The look Bruer shot her through the transparent display told her she was usurping his duties as comm officer, but Ia didn't care. "Cadet Bruer, prepare to fire off that comm packet on all available bandwidths on my mark, and ping me an open broadband cast to the enemy. Tell me the moment you get any return response. Cadet Ng, tell the portside L-pods to prepare to continue firing on the targeted enemy. Starboard P-pods are to target sector zero by two seventy and prepare to rapid fire three volleys each, five degree spread, odds on the long, evens on the lat, on my mark."

"Sir?" Cadet Ng asked, confused. The ship shook again, but not quite as hard this time; the enemy weapons were having to contend with undamaged shielding, which meant it would take more time to hammer through and cause damage.

"Careful observation leads to comprehension, Cadet," Ia repeated tersely. "Do as you are ordered. Relay those commands!"

Ng turned back to her console, fingers flying over the keys and jabbing at the screens.

Bruer looked back at Ia. "Captain, sir, broadband channel is open, tertiary one. We have received a ping from the enemy; they are listening."

Ia activated her headset again, this time broadcasting to the alien ship, ring finger hovering over the switch before cutting it off between sentences. *"Behold, the doors of the Room have opened wide, and the dead were embarrassed with shame, for the living had none!* Cadet Bruer, fire off that data packet lightspeed only, all bandwidths!"

"Aye, sir," he confirmed. "Data packet awa—*Shova v'shakk!* Captain Ia, *that's* the information we stole!"

"Careful observation brings comprehension—lock and web it, Cadets," she ordered, cutting off not only his protests, but any attempts from the others. "Cadet Ng, *fire!*"

"Firing now, sir." The ship *thu-thu-thumped*, jolting to the right as the projectile guns fired, following her orders. Some spread up and down relative to the ship, others spread fore and aft, following the longitude and latitude of the *da Gama*.

"Holy *shakk*—there's a second ship out there!" Jimenez exclaimed. "I'm getting missiles impacting on *their* incoming missiles and shields!"

Ia flipped open the external comm again. *"Greetings to the new Dlmvla warship. Welcome is your presence. Target your sister ship and attack, if you please."*

The Dlmvla responded, their words filling the bridge. *"Poetic is your illogic, yet requires explanation still."*

Ia smiled. She loved the Dlmvla mind-set, because they loved illogic. They *used* logic, harnessed it for their science as any other sentient species needed to do in order to attain the stars, but they *loved* illogic. It was poetry to whatever passed for their souls. So in answer, she replied by referencing a bit of actual poetry. Dlmvlan poetry, to be precise.

" 'The doors of the Room have opened wide.' The crew of your sister ship are following orders from a faction whose acts are in violation of the Alliance Treaty. Compliance in their designs will bring shame to all your nests. The confirmation you need is in the information we have broadcast—to our attackers, I say: 'Shame be upon the living, and your nests shall burn. With you in them, if cease you do not your attack on our sovereign nest.' "

"Thieves! Dwell in your nests of egg-suckers!" The words came from the vessel that had started this scenario. *"Enter the Room ovulations first!"*

Ia bit her lip to keep from laughing. Terranglo might be the interspecies trade tongue, and there were xenotelepaths capable of implanting most of the necessary language skills out there, or at least augmenting the lesson-learned skills, but that did not guarantee mastery.

"Captain, weapons fire from the first ship!" Jimenez warned her.

"Oh, it's far too late for that," Ia warned the unseen enemy, still amused.

The *da Gama* rocked. Jinja-Marsuu cursed. "Dammit—we're about to lose portside shields! What the *hell* are you up to, Ia?"

A feral grin curved her mouth. She ignored her fellow cadet, focusing instead on broadcasting her message. *"You can't stop the signal once it's been sent . . . and you have passed that threshold by one limb yourself. Stand down, or enter fully the Room for the Dead!"*

"Weapons fire from the second ship!" Jimenez squeaked. "It . . . Captain, the trajectories are *missing* us! They're firing on the *other* ship, sir!"

"And lo, I followed the words of the Prophet, for the Prophet was never wrong," Ia stated on the comm link to the second ship. *"Honor be upon your hides and your hands; let your nests stand strong with the wisdom displayed this day. We will continue on our way and convey this information to the Alliance Council, so that they can back up your saner decisions. Let all sentient acts be against these insurrectionists; let there be no path for them but a swift surrender, or the Door to the Room. This is a Dlmvla internal matter, we do concede. For your hands, we leave them."*

Closing the channel, she gave her last set of orders for the exercise.

"Cadet Ng, order the gunners to switch to Standby. Keep an eye on both Dlmvla, but do not order any weapons fire unless we ourselves are directly attacked," Ia stated, addressing her bridge crew. "Bridge crew, tend to your stations. Repair teams are to focus on getting the FTL panels functional, and getting at least one hyperrelay back online as soon as possible. Divert all spare power to insystem thrusters, and get us the hell out of here before they change their minds. You have your orders: Execute."

A ragged chorus of "Aye, sir!" met her commands.

Bruer shook his head slightly. "I don't get it . . . *How* did you know there was another ship out there?"

"Careful observation leads to comprehension," Ia repeated. "Look, can you remember that last run? We made it farther than we had in the previous three; you did a good job of navigating the initial hazards. But right before the last blow that destroyed us from the starboard, we were attacked from the *port*. You could feel it through the way the ship jolted around us from the *other* side."

The overhead lights flashed in rapid-fire green. The bridge

door slid open, once again admitting their chief instructor. The primary screen at every station lit up, projecting his crisply dressed image across every duty station's primary screen, both here and across the rest of the mock starship.

"Lieutenant Commander on deck!" Ng called out, announcing Spada's approach.

"An excellent observation, Cadet Ia," Spada said. He lifted his wrist and keyed in a few more commands on his arm unit. "However, I am curious about your choice of attack commands. Explain your reasons to your instructors and your crew."

"It's basic xenopsychology, sir," Ia stated, lifting her chin. She knew her words were being projected around the ship, just as other Acting Captains had explained their own actions in earlier scenarios. "We could disable part of the first ship's functionality, which is a defensive course of action, but if we actually damaged it to the point of endangering their crew, the second ship would be obligated by Dlmvlan honor-against-outsiders to take *their* side and destroy us, whatever information we might have carried. Using only the lasers on the first ship to disable some of their systems slowed down their attack on us, threatening them with the vulnerability of losing their shields, without threatening the integrity of their hull nearly as much as projectiles could.

"Using only the *projectiles* on the second ship couldn't have harmed them beyond a little shake-up, since their own shields were still intact, but it also gave us the opportunity to force their weapons and ours to lock on to each other as the nearest, greatest threats, preventing all but a handful of missiles from actually making it through on either side." She shrugged. "Once we had their attention without having to badly damage either ship, broadcasting the mission information on an EM bandwidth made the most sense for the next step. If it's truly that politically sensitive, it won't reach anybody's satellite scanners for several more years, long past the point where it could cause us problems. *But* the information would be out there, and it could cause the threat of political repercussions.

"If we didn't report in on time, ships would be sent to our last known coordinates," Ia reminded the others, glancing their way. "Their sensors would pick up that broadcast as the Space Force scouted the system's farthest edges, looking for lightspeed records of what happened to us. It might be several days after the fact, or even several weeks, but they would pick it up relatively soon, and they would still have the information to bludgeon the rebel faction among the Dlmvla into complying with Alliance law. You can't stop the signal once it's been broadcast at light."

"But that information was rated as Classified," Jinja-Marsuu protested. "By broadcasting it, you violated the security protocols governing our mission, Cadet!"

"The *mission* was to get that information back to the Alliance by any means necessary," Ia countered. "Look, it's all well and good to hold an ace up your sleeve in a poker game where the stakes are life and death, like this situation was. But if it *remains* up your sleeve just because you're holding out for a royal flush when you've already got the makings for a full house of aces and threes, you'll lose the hand, lose the pot, and lose everyone else's life right along with your own."

Catching Spada's wryly amused look, Jinja-Marsuu subsided.

"Besides," Ia said, "since we haven't gone missing and are still potentially capable of getting out of the system under our own efforts, that means we will report back in time. If no one has to come looking for us, then no one will go looking for any lightspeed signs of what happened to us, and *that* means no one but those Dlmvla will find that short-range broadcast, because they won't need to know what happened to us. At least, they won't find it until it's several years down the road. By then, the whole matter will no longer be important, and thus no longer an interspecies embarrassment. So, yes, it was a calculated risk."

"Cadet, is that the reasoning you'd give to a Board of Inquiry convened over your violation of security protocols?" Spada asked Ia.

"Aye, sir. Technically at the moment, this is still an internal matter for the Dlmvla to handle," Ia offered. "The moment this information hits the Alliance Council hands, it becomes an interspecies incident, *if* the Dlmvla government in general doesn't yet know about it. By offering the truth to the second ship, I am giving their command structure a chance to spread the information of the impending rebellion to their own people, which gives them a chance to contain it before the Alliance has to step in. By giving the Dlmvla a chance to save face by handling the matter themselves, and not seriously damaging either vessel, they will look more favorably upon the Terran Empire in future interactions with our Space Force.

"My methods may not have been *orthodox* . . . but orthodox wasn't getting us out of this situation alive. I may have bent a few military protocols of the Space Force, Commander, but I definitely followed the political policies of the Terran United Planets, sir. We are still in the process of achieving our mission objective, because we're still alive enough to try."

Spada studied her for a long moment, then dipped his head. "Well defended, Cadet. And technically just within the parameters of your mission. Not orthodox, as you said, but within the parameters nonetheless. Alright, Cadets," he acknowledged, switching his gaze to the viewscreen pickups. "All of you have performed well in these simulations, and you have earned a break. Fill out your practice reports on all five runs, and have them turned in by twenty hundred hours tonight.

"Once again, Class 1252, there are five vouchers scattered throughout the ship. The clues to their whereabouts are being sent to your right secondary screens," Spada informed his cadets, both in the bridge and across the ship. "When you have finished tidying your workstations, you will report to the nearest petty officer for an inspection of your stations. If everything comes back greenlit, you will be given permission to disembark. Don't forget to come find me in the observation cabin behind the bridge if you find a Leave voucher. Spada out."

Ia sighed and dug into her shirt pocket, pulling out a folded, tissue-thin square of paper. She held it up. "Here's one of them, sir. Make sure this gets to Cadet Harper. He'll know which member of his repair teams got that EM relay back online, allowing us to communicate with the enemy ships."

Lieutenant Commander Spada raised his brows. "Now, how did you get that, Cadet? And why would you give it up?"

"I promised the repair team a voucher if they did as I asked. When I make a promise, sir, I carry it through," Ia told the baffled officer, answering the second question first. "As for how I found it, I had a runny nose when we came on board, and went looking in the supply closet behind the bridge head for a fresh box of tissues. The voucher was tucked in one of the

storage bins. Since it's now a Friday, we're the last class on
the ship before supper, and you didn't offer any vouchers to
Class 1252 earlier in the week, I figured this one was meant
for us."

"Give it to Cadet Harper and his team members yourself,"
Spada directed her. He toggled his arm unit. *"All hands, stand
down. This simulation is officially over. Cadets, you are free
to search for the remaining four vouchers, but report in to the
nearest petty officer to request permission to disembark by no
later than seventeen hundred. I will be collecting all intact
vouchers at the Deck 8 Juliett gantry. Spada out."* Shutting
off the link, Spada studied Ia, who was unbuckling her restraint
harness. "I look forward to reading your incident reports, Cadet.
Try to fill in a little more detail, this time?"

He left without waiting for her reply. The moment the bridge
door slid shut behind the lieutenant commander, Bruer whistled
under his breath. "You're in for it now. That had better be a
helluva strong, airtight incident report, 'Acting Captain.'"

"Don't I know it," Ia muttered. She tucked the voucher back
into her shirt pocket and stood up, extricating herself from the
captain's station. "If you'll excuse me, I have a Leave pass to
deliver."

"One thing," Bruer stated, stalling her. He lifted his chin.
"You said I'd be in the same situation, only with the Salik, but
you also said your choices were based on xenopsychology. The
Salik are *nothing* like the Dlmvla."

"True, and in that case, I'd advise you to shoot to cripple
and kill. But make sure you don't rush your shots," Ia told him.
"You'll have just enough time, I think, to get it right. The rebellious Dlmvla in this scenario wanted to kill us outright. The
Salik would want to cripple your ship, board it forcefully, and
have you and your crew for lunch. I'd suggest faking a greater
level of incapacity than you actually possess, taking the time
to aim manually so their sensors don't pick up a targeting lock,
and destroying their guns just after their boarding pods are
launched. But then, that's what *I'd* do, were I in your shoes in
that situation. Trying to run would only have them leaping on
you from behind."

"Maybe. But that's presuming I ever end up in a situation
like that," he countered lightly. "God willing, the Blockade

will continue to hold. It has for two hundred years, after all. And it's not like you're a precog or anything."

"God willing, yes," Ia muttered dryly. She turned her attention to the others. "Good job under both Bruer and me, all of you."

"Yes, good job," Bruer added.

He joined Ia in waiting for the bridge petty officer to finish inspecting Jimenez's station so that their own could be checked off as well. They exchanged a few murmurs, small talk about the day's exercise, but otherwise waited quietly. It didn't take long for Ia's station to be cleared, nor for her to make her way down to where she knew Harper was located.

The ship was designed to simulate damage in the interior as well as the exterior, and she did pass a few "damaged" sectors. The Navy personnel who did the actual maintenance on the ship, playing the part of the enlisted crewmembers whom the cadets were supposed to order around, were checking over some of the "hardest hit" spots, but otherwise the ship was restoring itself to its proper shape. By the time she reached the heavily battered Engineering section, most of the various mechanisms had pulled themselves back together and petty officers were busy checking off each cadet's duty station.

She found Cadet Harper going over some questions with a couple of his repair team members. As soon as he finished, Ia addressed him. "Thank you all for getting that comm relay set up in the last scenario, Cadet Harper." She fished the voucher out of her pocket once more, holding it up. "So, who does this go to?"

Harper grinned and held out his hand. "Me. I told you I'd see to it personally."

"It was *brilliant*," one of the other cadets gushed. She grinned at Harper. "He wired the *handrail* on the upper engine deck for an antenna, and tuned it with a jury-rigged comm board. The whole *deck* became the transceiver!"

"And he did it in a matter of minutes, too," the other female added, also smiling at him.

Blushing a little, Harper shrugged. "My mother works in R&D in the Special Forces on Dabin. She taught me a few tricks. I've had a lot of practice at improvising. I see you're rather good at it, too, 'Acting Captain' Ia. One of the petty officers down here in Engineering said that was the fastest escape a class has ever pulled on this particular scenario. At least, in the six years he's been assigned here."

She found herself smiling at the praise. His praise. Shaking it off with a blink, Ia held out the voucher. "Here you go, then. One Leave voucher, as promised."

"Yeah, well, that's the ironic thing," Harper told her, mouth twitching up on one side. "When I went digging for the spare comm boards . . . I found *this*."

Digging a matching tissue-thin sheet of paper out of his own shirt pocket, he held it up and shrugged. Caught off guard, Ia laughed. She wiggled the one caught between her fingers. "Okay, that *is* ironic. So. Who should *this* one go to?"

"Me, of course. You wouldn't want to be accused of going back on your word, would you?" Harper asked, giving her a pointed look.

"No, Cadet, I would not," she agreed, holding out the folded ticket. He accepted it with his left hand, and held out the one in his right. Ia looked between it and him. "What's that for?"

"We're only allowed to have one per week," Harper reminded her, smiling ruefully. "If we find two, then it is our responsibility to find someone we believe worked hard enough to deserve an extra couple of hours of Leave. You pulled our fat out of the fire on that last run. I say that deserves a reward." He glanced at the other two cadets. "Wouldn't you agree?"

Both young women nodded. Harper pushed the paper at Ia, poking her hand with it. Since refusing to accept it would risk getting it torn and rendered useless for anyone else, Ia took it from him. "Alright, then. Enjoy your Leave, Cadet."

Harper wasn't the only one to give her a bemused look. Nodding politely to the other two, who were eyeing Ia askance, he hooked his arm around her elbow, drawing her toward the section exit. "Actually, it occurred to me that if you'll be having a three-hour Leave and I'll be having a three-hour Leave, we should combine said Leave and hit the town together. Between your tactical skills and my technical savvy, I figure we could divide and conquer the whole place in fifteen, twenty minutes, tops, and have plenty of time for dinner and a show. Teatro Timpani will be in town, and I think I can get us tickets to the performance. If I spring for those, will you spring for dinner?"

She had originally planned on spending her time writing contingency prophecies. Ia knew she should pass, so that she could go into town merely to print out said prophesies at the copy shop in town. They were growing used to seeing her every few weeks, requesting archival quality paper and printers for the stacks of prophetic missives that, for whatever reason, couldn't just be shipped home or to the Afaso headquarters on a data crystal. But Meyun's offer was undeniably appealing.

He grinned at her, handsome and charming and determined to get her to agree. "Well?"

Under the weight of that grin, Ia found herself caving. She smiled back at him. "Okay."

JANUARY 31, 2493 T.S.
DOWNTOWN SINES, PORTUGAL, WESTERN EUROPROVINCE
EARTH

Meyun Harper raised his wineglass, saluting her with it. "Thank you for coming. And I'm glad you agreed to the early show. This gives us more time for dinner."

"That kind of time is an illusion," Ia murmured, sipping at her iced tea. "If we don't pay attention to it, we'll still risk being late."

"Spoilsport," he muttered back, sipping. "You know, I don't think I've ever seen you drinking alcohol."

"Alcoholism in the family," she half lied. "I don't want to risk it."

He raised one of his brows skeptically. "Shouldn't that be, you're secretly a self-control freak and you don't want to lose command of your faculties? I *have* been getting to know you in the last few months."

Ia stilled, glass still pressed to her lips. She hadn't expected such perception from him. Feeling uncomfortably vulnerable, she managed a careless shrug and set her drink back down. "There's nothing wrong with wanting to be in control of one's self."

"Up to a point. But as they say, everything in moderation, even moderation," he countered. "I think I wouldn't mind seeing you cut loose."

She gave him a sardonic look. "When I cut loose, Harper, people tend to die. I'd rather save that for the battlefield—and even then, I'd rather limit how many deaths I make."

"Maybe you just need to learn how to create a new kind of death." He smirked a little as he said it. At her confused look, he held up thumb and forefinger a tiny space apart. "As in, a little death? Oh, come on . . . Sex? Lovemaking? Orgasmic release?"

Ia blushed, but shrugged. "I don't do that. *Ah* . . . I mean, with others," she amended, blushing harder. "With myself, sure; everybody does *that*. It's healthy. I just . . . don't date."

That made him frown. Their server appeared with their plates of *bacalhau com natas*, however, so he had to hold off asking her any questions until the waiter had gone away again. Picking up his fork, Meyun poked briefly at the layers of cod, onion, potato, and cream sauce, then set it down again. He leaned forward, frowning again in confusion at her.

"What do you mean, you don't date? Everyone dates. Terrans date, V'Dan date, the Gatsugi date . . . hell, even the Salik date. They have to switch genders to date, but they *do* date . . . I think. It's part of growing up, the whole socialization and selection of a suitable mate process."

"Well, I don't." She ate a mouthful of her own meal, then sighed, swallowed, and set down her fork. "Look, I tried dating a little bit when I was fourteen. After I turned fifteen, I figured out what I wanted to do with my life, which was serve in the military. But military life and family life don't always mesh so well . . . so I just gave up on dating. Not to mention, they don't allow any fraternization in Basic Training. Then, when I got out of Basic and was assigned to Ferrar's Company on the *Liu Ji*, I was promoted up the ranks. I was a noncom within months, and that was that. Everyone I met after that point was either a superior or a subordinate."

"Yeah, but surely you found *someone* you could date?" he challenged her. "What about the Navy crew?"

"Fatality Forty-Nine, Fraternization, prohibits any conduct that would weaken the chain of command *or* impose undue influence upon a fellow soldier serving within the same command structure in the areas of personal or business life. You don't date anyone in your own Company, and you don't date anyone on your own ship. Unless your CO permits it, and mine didn't," she told him. "Just as you don't make or take loans with anyone below or above you in rank, you don't enter into business partnerships while you're still enrolled in the Service, and you *definitely* don't copulate with anyone above or below you . . . and I honestly didn't have that many who were my equal in rank. Not to mention, Ferrar believed in promotions based on merit, and those could come at any time, after any engagement."

"But you *could* have dated someone you saw regularly whenever your patrol wound up on a Battle Platform or a space station," he said. "Didn't *anyone* make a pass at you?"

He had her there. She smiled wryly. "If you don't count the ones made over a drink . . . Yeah, there was one civilian. A merchanter captain and businessmeioa."

"And?" Harper prompted her.

"It didn't go anywhere. I only ever had a couple of free hours here and there, and he wasn't always in the same vicinity when I did. When we did meet up . . . it was usually just for drinks or a meal, and a bit of conversation. 'Dating-Lite' as it were. I didn't have time for anything more," she dismissed.

"Why not?" Meyun asked her. "We've been learning in our classes on scheduling that most patrol ships dock for a full twenty-four hours Standard, and most people get a full eight hours of Leave."

"Not if you take the accumulated Leave option—Meyun, my family is on the backside of Terran space," Ia reminded him, addressing his skeptical look. "By cutting my weekend Leaves down to the absolute minimum, I was able to build up enough accumulated hours and days to go visit them. It's just a matter of being willing to go without in the short term in order to benefit in the long term."

He pointed at her with his fork. "You are *too* self-controlled, meioa-e. We'll have to do something about that."

That made her laugh. Grinning, she dug into her meal. "Good luck. I'm very stubborn, and very goal-oriented. Nothing is going to stand in the way of me passing through this Academy with flying colors. Literally, since my next stop will be piloting school—and I would've gone to piloting school first, but the classes I wanted were booked."

They ate in companionable silence for a few minutes, then Meyun looked up at her again. "So . . . in all two years you served on the *Liu Ji* . . . only *one* meioa, male or female, ever made a pass at you?"

She quickly cleared her mouth with a sip of tea. "Well, I didn't count the ones made by fellow Service personnel," Ia told him. "But then most of those were made in a bar, where anyone could make a pass at anyone else, and most were made casually, just for the fun of it. I didn't take them seriously."

"Except for this one fellow, the civilian," Meyun reminded her. "Apparently he was the only one you did. Why him, and what happened to him? Or . . . is he still lurking out there among the stars as a potential date?"

"He's not lurking anymore, trust me. His crew kidnapped, drugged, and sold me to the same crime organization that had stolen away the rest of my Company's cadre. We're not on speaking terms anymore." Ia smirked when he gaped at her. She lifted another forkful of cream-covered cod. "There's a lot more to it than that, but most of it's Classified. So how about you? How many men or women have you dated?"

He shook his head, answering as she ate. "I don't know, eighteen or so? If you count the casual dates, that is. The serious ones, only three girls stand out, but none of them were ultra-serious. None of them were the love of my life."

Ia found herself feeling relieved at that confession, and annoyed at her relief. *I have no say in who he dates, so long as the act of dating doesn't disrupt the Future,* she reminded herself. She shrugged, picking up her iced tea again. "Well, good luck mixing your military career with a personal one—seriously, I hope you do have good luck. And I do hope you get to find and keep the woman of your dreams. Just about everyone deserves happiness. We don't always get it, but we should."

"Speaking of which, what are you doing after graduation?" he asked her as she sipped.

She choked on her drink. Coughing, Ia quickly wiped her mouth and hand with her napkin. She aimed a dirty look at the grinning man seated across from her. Voice harsh, she rasped, "That was *not* funny, Harper."

"Oh, yes it was!" he countered, chuckling. Picking up his own napkin, he dabbed some of the spluttered tea from the tablecloth. "It was completely worth it, just to see your face. You are normally so unflappable . . . I am going to enjoy this mental image of you for *years* to come." Lifting his free hand to his head, he tapped his temple. "Photographic memory, remember?"

"Well, the actual situation you implied won't ever happen, Harper, so enjoy your one precious memory while it lasts," she warned him, tidying the rim of her glass. That thought disappointed and depressed her. Breathing deep, Ia forced herself to let it go, as she had let go of so many other things in her life. "I don't have time to date. That's all there is to it."

The happiness of a single individual is nothing, compared to the survival and prosperity of so many others. Even if that individual is me. A depressing thought, but there it was.

CHAPTER 10

There are certain positions in the Terran military which require special levels of service. Anyone wishing to attain the rank of Lieutenant General or Vice Admiral has to have served in at least two Branches, and anyone wishing to become a General or an Admiral has to serve in at least three of them. Others require even more, such as the Council General, who is the military officer serving as liaison between the Space Force and the governing body of the Terran Empire . . . or even the position of Admiral-General, the highest-ranked military officer in charge of all four Branches, who must have served in all four.

In order to fill these vital positions, the candidate must fulfill the following conditions: They must have served at least one year each in the Army, Navy, Marine Corps, and/or Special Forces. They must be a duly Academy-trained officer of at least one of those Branches. They must have proven their command abilities in a combat tour of duty for at least one Standard year, such as a Border or Blockade position, and they must have proven their command abilities in a training capacity for at least one year, serving at a Camp or an Academy.

Additionally, to be qualified for the position of Admiral-General, the soldier in question must have spent at least one full year as an enlisted soldier in a combat zone, and *have earned a Field Commission—this ruling guarantees that our topmost brass understands what the common soldier is being asked to do by his or her superiors. We don't ever want to make the mistake of those in charge being so far removed from the realities of war that the orders being given are utterly inappropriate for the situations at hand.*

Despite the fact that there are literally billions of soldiers serving in the Space Force at any given point in time, there aren't more than maybe ten or fifteen thousand soldiers who qualify on all of these counts, such as having served in all four Branches, and only a few hundred thousand that qualify for three Branches of service, et cetera. If a soldier is particularly good, the officers within that Service Branch aren't going to want to give them up to another Branch. But for those they feel have a solid chance at improving the leadership of the Space Force as a whole, the DoI will watch them very closely, and even aid that particular soldier . . . in their own, sometimes convoluted way.

~Ia

APRIL 3, 2493 T.S.

The beep was hard to hear, but at least she knew when it was coming. Closing her writing station, Ia got up from her bed and crossed to the front door. The noise of the shower pounding away through the closed bathroom door drowned out the faint sound of the panel sliding open. On the other side, waiting for her, the grey-clad, red-haired older woman smiled warmly at Ia.

"Hello, Ia."

Ia rolled her eyes and saluted. "Commander."

Commander Christine Benjamin, chaplain and psychologist, saluted her back. "Cadet. So, how have you been?"

"I've been just fine, thank you." Softening her expression into a smile—since she was glad to see the other woman—Ia leaned her shoulder on the doorjamb. "You could even say I've been taking it easy. Mind you, the workload is heavy, but at least no one's trying to kill me, here at the Academy. So, what brings you all the way to Portugal, Bennie? Did you have a good flight?"

"As good as could be expected. In their infinite wisdom, my superiors figured I could use at least one tour of duty planetside at this point in time," she explained. She gestured at the room, and Ia obediently stepped back, letting her enter. Once inside, Bennie looked around, nodded in satisfaction at the neatly organized quarters, and borrowed the chair from Ia's desk. Unbuttoning the jacket of her Dress Greys, she seated herself and propped her feet up on the foot of Ia's bed. "Your bed's a mess. You should neaten that up before Inspection."

"For one, it's Sunday, and that means there's no inspection until tomorrow morning. For another, I was sitting on it just now. Do you want anything to drink?" Ia offered, gesturing at the caf' dispenser above her desk.

Bennie shook her head. Ia smiled ruefully and returned to her place at the head of the bed. She knew the outcome of this conversation—mostly, save for whatever input her temporally mysterious roommate might add—but she still had to make a show of ignorance. Pushing aside her writing pad, she settled against the pillows.

"Let me guess," Ia murmured. "Since you were in the vicinity, you decided to drop in and check up on an old friend while en route to your new station, right?"

"This *is* my new station," Bennie corrected her. "And you're not that old—by the way, happy birthday in advance. It's tomorrow, isn't it?"

"You're a month late. My birthday's March 4th, not April 4th," Ia told her.

"*Ah.* Well, happy birthday anyway," Bennie amended. "The Chaplaincy Division figures someone with my experience at counseling active-duty soldiers will 'hopefully be able to prepare these up-and-coming young officers for the rigors, trials, and tribulations of real-world command.' Presuming, of course, that I turn out to be well-suited to dealing with a bunch of cadets. I've been told it requires a somewhat different skill set than tending to the religious and mental needs of a Border ship—I trust having me back in your life for a little while isn't going to drive you mad?"

Ia snorted. Leaning forward, she wrapped her arms around

her knees and gave the older woman a wry, borderline sardonic look. "Not at all. I like you. But I do have the sudden impression of a dozen sticky DoI fingerprints all over this situation, and *that* might drive me mad."

Bennie laughed at that. She slouched a little bit more in the chair, lacing her fingers across her silver grey dress shirt. "You always did have a keen, quick grasp of a situation. *Yes*, they want me to keep an eye on you in specific while I'm here. I am to gauge your 'suitability for continued service in stressful situations' or some such rot."

Ia sighed and sat back with a faint smile, satisfied. "Blockade Patrol." She broadened her smile at the chaplain's surprised look. "As you yourself said, Bennie, I have a keen grasp of the situation. I am provably stable in moderate combat zones. The Space Force is desperate for soldiers who can withstand the rigors of a truly heavy combat zone. If I can handle Blockade duty as well as I handled the Border, then they'll *want* me to handle it."

"And you don't mind?" Bennie asked her. The sound of the shower cut off in the bathroom.

"I can probably do a lot of good on a Blockade post," Ia admitted. "I'm looking forward to it."

"It's good to hear your confidence in your own abilities. But do you really think you can handle the stress? Even in a hot spot Border zone like the *Liu Ji* traveled, the potential for combat is only once or twice a week," Bennie said. "Blockade, it's once and twice and even more, each and every day. However much the politicians may try to whitewash it, the Blockade Zone *is* a war zone."

Ia smiled wryly. "Well, I guess it looks like I'll find out. Think they'll drag you along with me?"

It was Bennie's turn to smile wryly. "Now that, I don't know. I guess we'll see—oh, that reminds me, Sergeant Spyder says hello. Or rather, he says . . . let me see if I can get this right . . . 'Why doncha say 'ello t' the li'l white dove fer me, eh? Tell 'er we're missin' our bloody-winged cardinal a' doom, an' if she ever gets reassigned t' the *Liu Ji*—though she's a right bloody traitor, skippin' out onna Marines like that—tell 'er she's gotta blow us grunts a liddle kiss fer good luck, eh?' "

With just the first sentence, Bennie's rather mangled version of her old Company mate's accent reduced Ia to giggles. The bathroom door slid open, and her roommate poked his damp head through the opening. The rest of him followed, equally bare and damp, save for the white towel wrapped haphazardly around his hips. Ia, still guffawing, choked on her own spit at his appearance.

"My god, Ia, you're actually *laughing*?" he exclaimed, staring at Ia. It took him a few steps forward to realize there was another woman in the room, and a stumbled half step after that to realize she was an officer. "Wha— Oh, my g—Sir!"

Snapping to Attention, he saluted—and broke the salute awkwardly, grabbing at the hem of the towel. Cheeks pink, he straightened and resumed the salute, free hand clutching his only covering carefully in place.

He also wasn't the only one who blushed. Bennie did a double-take, looking back at his state of undress, then glanced back at Ia, who was wide-eyed and red-faced. At the speculative lift of the chaplain's brows, Ia groaned and hid her face in her hands. Chuckling, Bennie addressed Harper.

"At Ease, Cadet. This is just an informal visit. Feel free to, *ah*, go about your business or whatever."

Ia peeked between her fingers, mortified at the amusement coloring Bennie's tone. The older woman was smiling at her roommate. Still flushed, he edged over to his wardrobe drawers and quickly grabbed a set of clothes, then retreated back to the bathroom for the privacy to change. She couldn't blame him. Under normal circumstances, neither of them had been very body-conscious. They didn't exactly lounge around naked, but neither had hesitated to strip or dress in front of the other. This, however, was not exactly a normal circumstance.

The moment the bathroom door shut, Bennie let out a rush of breath. "*V'dayamn*—and I'll say penance for swearing later—but that cadet has some rather nice muscles on him. What does he do, lift weights in his spare time?"

Face still a bit warm, Ia slid her hands from her face, crossing her arms. "More like a weight suit. He's a heavyworlder. Dabin, 1.85Gs. His mother's been stationed there with the Joint Human Research & Development Corps from before he was conceived. He said her superiors were glad she got pregnant on a heavyworld, since that gave them that much more excuse to keep her working on various R&D collaborations with the

V'Dan military. Apparently she's some sort of mechanical genius, and it looks like her son's taking after her."

"Oh? How so?" Bennie asked.

Ia nodded at the closed door. "He's managed some rather amazing off-the-cuff repairs on board the *da Gama*, our simulation ship. I'd suggest to the DoI the idea of sending him out either to a deep space survey ship or to a Border Patrol. Anywhere that needs a competent officer in charge of quick and dirty repairs."

"Border, but not a Blockade Patrol?" Bennie asked, glancing over her shoulder at the door. She looked back at Ia. "Wouldn't you want him on your own ship, if he's that good at making things work?"

Unbidden, another blush warmed her face. "I really don't think that would be necessary . . ."

The chaplain scooted up a little in her seat, green eyes narrowing. "Ia . . . are you *attracted* to him?"

Her cheeks burned. Bennie widened her eyes, then started to snicker. Ia glared. The other woman's mirth morphed quickly into outright giggles, including a few undignified snorts.

"It is *not* that funny, Bennie," Ia hissed under her breath, embarrassed further by the thought that Harper might be listening to the two of them through the bathroom door.

"Oh, yes it is!" Bennie squeaked, bright red from her half-suppressed laughter.

Oddly enough, that killed her urge to blush. Sobering, Ia settled a stern look on her friend. "No, it isn't. *Nothing* will happen between us. We are fellow cadets and roommates. Nothing more."

Settling down a little, Bennie wiped at the corners of her eyes with the edge of her hand. "Pity. But that situation can change. After you graduate . . . Wait, is he on a fast-track program like you? Or . . . ?"

"He's fast-track like me, but as soon as I get out of here, I go off to my pilot certification classes, and he goes off to wherever the military sends him." Sobered—even slightly depressed—Ia sighed. "Bennie, he's a good friend. I do like him. But that's all it's going to be. Now, can we change the subject? In case he feels trapped in there, wondering what we're talking about behind his back?"

"Oh, fine. Spoil my good mood," Bennie teased. She quickly lifted a hand at Ia's pointed look. "Okay, okay . . . Tell me what life is like, here at the Academy."

Glad for the change in topic, Ia obeyed. A few seconds later, a remarkably calm-looking Meyun emerged from the bathroom, neatly dressed in his cadet blues. She broke off long enough to formally introduce the two, then went back to telling Bennie about life at the Academia de Marinha Estrelas. Apparently deciding the previous incident was being politely forgotten, he grabbed the chair from his desk, straddled the back of it, and joined the conversation.

It did not escape Ia's notice that Chaplain Benjamin subtly interrogated Cadet Harper about himself and his opinions of Ia. It also did not escape her notice that Harper interrogated Bennie just as subtly about her opinions of Ia, and Bennie's memories of her days on board the *Liu Ji*.

They were in the middle of discussing one of the *Liu Ji*'s many escapades when the doorbell buzzed again. Sighing, Ia rose from the bed, gesturing for Harper to sit back down. "Keep talking, I've got this."

Crossing to the door, she palmed it open. And stared. Stared, and glanced sharply over her shoulder before looking back at the short, brown-uniformed man waiting in the hallway. This, she had *not* foreseen.

"What the slagging hell *is* this?" Ia finally demanded, eyeing the man in front of her. "Old home week?—Please, Sergeant, come in and be welcome. I'm just going to bang my head against the wall here for a few minutes while the three of you make the necessary introductions . . ."

"What the hell are you going on about, Cadet Ia?" Sergeant Tae ordered.

"Uncle!" Bounding up from his chair, Meyun hurried to greet the shorter man. Ia flattened herself against the bathroom door, astonished to see her former chief drill instructor grinning and embracing her roommate. Harper even picked up the stout Marine a few inches as they hugged, then set him back on his feet. "You said you weren't sure if you'd be able to drop by on your way to London!"

"Well, here I am. Now what the hell are you doing with *this* pain in the asteroid in your quarters?" Tae asked, poking his thumb at Ia.

"I told you, she's my roommate," Meyun said.

"No, you told me she was your *classmate*," Tae countered.

"Well, I'm sorry the exact terminology slipped my mind, Uncle." Meyun paused and looked between the two of them. "How about you telling me how *you* know her? Or rather, how she knows you?"

Ia recovered her voice, glancing at Harper. "*This* is your uncle?"

"*Yes*, this is my uncle," her roommate confirmed. "Uncle, this is Cadet Ia. Ia, this is Master Sergeant Ulliong Tae, TUPSF-Marine Corps," he stated, gesturing between the two of them.

Squaring her shoulders, Ia nodded politely at her former drill sergeant. "Congratulations on your promotion, Master Sergeant."

"Thank you, Cadet," Tae replied just as politely. "Congratulations on your Field Commission."

"Thank you, Sergeant." She fell silent, feeling a bit awkward at having been caught unawares. *Not that it's been the first time. And I should've realized why; anything to do with Meyun, here, has a bad habit of not showing up on my precognitive radar . . .*

A throat cleared itself from further in the room. Ia quickly mended the breach, gesturing for both males to finish entering the room.

"Ah, Sergeant, this is Commander Christine Benjamin, Special Forces Chaplaincy Division, formerly assigned to the same ship and Border Patrol as myself. Bennie, this is Master Sergeant Ulliong Tae, my former drill instructor from Marines Basic . . . and apparently my roommate's uncle."

The pair saluted politely, Bennie sitting up a bit straighter in her chair. Meyun offered his chair to his uncle, dropping onto his bed for a seat. Ia resettled onto hers. She felt a little awkward in doing so, given the surprise of her old drill instructor's visit and his connection to her blank spot of a roommate. Glancing from face to face, Bennie cleared her throat.

"I have a suggestion. Why don't Ia and I take a tour of the Academy grounds while the two of you catch up? I'm going to be stationed here, so I can always chat with you later, Cadet Harper," she offered politely.

Tae glanced between her and Ia. "Actually, sir, I wouldn't mind hearing about Ia's time in the Corps, and your impressions of her. It's not often a drill instructor gets to hear firsthand accounts of how his charges fare long after they leave Basic. Particularly in a military the size of the Space Force."

Ia rolled her eyes. "Honestly, you don't *have* to dissect every little thing I have done. Particularly not in front of me. I'm not that special."

"You may be a cadet when you're on the clock, and thus an officer in training," Tae told her, "but a drill instructor *always* outranks a former recruit *off* the clock. And I really do want to know. I always imagined you'd do me proud . . . *if* you ever learned your own limitations."

Bennie glanced at Tae, then looked at Ia. "Wait—you said Sergeant Spyder went through Basic with you. Would that mean Sergeant Tae knows him?"

"You're telling me that Recruit *Spyder* made it all the way up to Sergeant?" Tae asked, raising his brows in surprise. "That green-haired, tangle-tongued . . . ?"

"Sergeant, yes, Sergeant. He even led Ferrar's Fighters in the rescue invasion at Zubeneschamali, with their full confidence in him," Ia bragged, grateful for the excuse of being able to talk about someone else for a change. "He was the senior-most of the few sergeants who hadn't been kidnapped, and the one with the most boarding party experience, both with Ferrar's Fighters and his previous Company. I gave him the layout of the place, discussed several options, and put him in charge of carrying it out—and I'll tell you, he saved our hides in record time. We got pinned down in this big room with no way out, until Spyder and the rest broke through the enemy's forces."

"Yes, he has handled himself very admirably, Sergeant," Bennie added. "If he'd had a full year of noncomm experience under his belt, *I'd* have nominated him for a Field Commission, and I'm outside the normal chain of command."

Ia nodded in agreement, glad her friend was getting the recognition he was due. "That's pretty much all he was missing. Here—there's even a song in the Corps about him."

"A song?" Tae asked, lifting one brow. "Recruit Spyder ranks a Marines song? This, I gotta hear."

"A song?" Meyun repeated, giving the trio a bemused look.

"It's a Marines thing," Ia reassured him. "Marines sing, and make up songs about each other."

"It's to the tune of the Itsy Bitsy Spider," Bennie warned him, grinning. "It's not *much* of a song, but he did get one, and it has circulated all over the *Liu Ji*'s patrol route."

She gestured at Ia, who launched into the tune, replete with Spyder's mining colony accent.

Th' itsy bitsy Spyder, 'e climbed into th' ship,
'E knew it was the Salik from how th' ceilin' dripped!
'E loaded up 'is weapons an' leaped into th' fray,
An' th' itsy bitsy Spyder, 'e blew their brains away!

Tae blinked, winced, and started laughing. "That's too funny! If your voice were just a little deeper, you'd even sound like him, Rec . . . *Cadet.*"

Harper grinned as well. "So what other stories have you got for us?"

Ia and Bennie smirked at each other and started compiling a verbal list for both men.

MAY 27, 2493 T.S.

The steady *thoom thoom thoom* of rapidly running mechsuit legs echoed across the confidence course. Her inner thighs always chafed a little bit when she did this, but that was as much the fault of the body-hugging pressure suit she wore beneath the ceristeel plates as the need for the slightly waddling movements required by the bulk of the machinery itself. Ia was used to it, though, and ran with almost the same ease she would have used without her burden.

Leaping for the cover afforded by a low bluff, she tumbled over one round-planted shoulder, spun, and aimed the black-painted rifle in her grip at the target, just barely visible through the trees. The beam of light was difficult to see in the bright light of day, since the e-clip powering the laser had been fitted with a calorie restrictor chip, but the heads-up display flickering across the inner curve of her faceplate let her know she had scored an accurate enough hit. The holographic, vaguely humanoid-shaped target darkened on the left arm. Not a vital hit, but enough to temporarily incapacitate it.

She could have aimed a little better, but not today. Today, Ia was holding back on the confidence course. Launching herself away from the berm of grass and earth, she sprinted for the next obstacle, shooting on the run at the other targets. She clipped two more enough to incapacitate, and scored killing blows on the last three.

Dodging through the maze of wooden logs, she used their scant cover at the end to crouch low and take potshots at the hologram of an enemy vehicle. Two, three shots scored deeply enough into one wheel well to sever a lubricant pipe. The rest knocked out the illusionary enemies scrambling to organize themselves in a semblance of counterattack and defense. After the eighth volley, she leaped forward, firing one more shot to knock down the last simulation. Hooking a servo-hand around another log at the end of the course, she used it to swing herself around and sprint back down toward the finish zone.

The confidence course and its obstacles were squeezed into a crowded, back-and-forth pattern between two long, high walls on which some of the holographic scenery for the current training simulation was being projected. Ignoring the rope swing— the weight of her and her suit, hitting the rope at that speed, would have ripped it from its frame—she leaped over the mud pit, clearing it by a meter and a half from sheer power-assisted momentum. Ia dodged a fake hand grenade and sprinted over the last dozen meters of trampled dirt, until she dropped back into the bunker where everything had begun.

Thud.

Panting inside her suit, Ia took the time to power down her mechsuit-sized rifle, stripped the energy clip from the butt of it, and returned both to their storage lockers. Only when the lockers, one for rifles and one for calorie-restricted e-clips, were sealed tight did she turn around and slap the red button on the bunker wall, ending the simulation run. Lights on the course outside flashed amber for ten seconds, then glowed green for five more and shut off, removing all the holograms.

The display board totaled the number of obstacles successfully navigated, enemies killed, incapacitated, or still capable
of combat, objectives achieved and objectives missed, ending
with a number that wasn't quite 85 percent of her best run to
date. *Solidly in the mediocre, for me.* Satisfied, Ia relaxed.

With the course both cleared and shut down, Ia unsealed
her faceplate, sucking in the warm, pre-summer air. Unlocking
the exit door of the bunker, she eased her bulky, mechsuited
body up the stairs, emerging in the sunlight to an audience of
observers. A few clapped in applause, but the rest gave her
performance wry looks at best. Several of the other cadets
formed up and jogged down the stairs, taking her place in the
bunker for their own run.

Others at the Academy might choose to run the obstacle
course as a part of their daily exercise regimen, but at the
moment, Ia was the only one who ran it in a mechsuit. That
meant she had to run it alone to avoid accidentally injuring a
fellow cadet. She didn't mind, though; the lack of others on the
course meant that she could split her attention between carrying
out the familiar tasks of mock-combat and skimming the timelines, practicing her battlecognition.

Two people hung back in the viewing stands. One was Chaplain Benjamin; the other was a commodore, the one-star equivalent of a brigadier general. The commodore moved to intercept
Ia. Bennie followed, her expression sober.

Since he was wearing his Dress Blues cap, Ia saluted him,
servo-arm whining faintly as she lifted its mechanical fingers
to her helm-bubbled brow. "Commodore, sir."

"Cadet Ia, this is Commodore Hadrabas," Bennie introduced
quickly. "Commodore, this is Cadet Ia."

He saluted her back, then dropped his hands to his blue-clad
hips. "So, you're the infamous Cadet Ia. I didn't know you could
run the confidence course so . . . quickly."

Considering it wasn't her speed she had slacked on, Ia
shrugged inside her suit. The joints and servos hummed quietly,
copying the action externally. "I've had better days, sir. And
worse days. Can I help you, sir?"

"Yes, actually. The Command Staff is thinking of fielding
a number of Service personnel for the 2494 Alliance Winter
Olympics. Can you ski?" he asked bluntly.

"No, sir . . . and if you are thinking of suggesting I learn in order to compete in the biathlon, sir, I would like to point out there are many, many more personnel in the Space Force who shoot far better than I can, *and* already know how to ski," she countered firmly. *This is indeed what I thought it was going to be. Time to nip this firmly in the bud.* "Not to mention it would become a public relations disaster if you attempted to order me to learn and participate anyway, sir."

"Excuse me?" he asked, lifting his hand to his cap so he could tip it back and look up at her. Wearing her mechsuit as she was, Ia stood taller than the commodore by almost half a meter.

"Commodore, I would have to refuse to perform any task that could be considered a dereliction of my duty, sir," she stated crisply, ignoring the sweat beading on her skin under the heat of the late spring sun. "My *duty* as a Field Commissioned officer is to return to an active combat post once I have graduated from this Academy, sir. I am not the best marksmeioa in the Service, I am not qualified to ski in a biathlon, I *cannot* learn either skill well enough to improve them in time to compete at the regional level, never mind qualify nationally in time to register for the 2494 Olympics . . . and it is *illegal* for anyone to be coerced into cooperating in the Games, sir," Ia told him.

Commodore Hadrabas frowned up at her, clearly not happy at being thwarted.

She lifted her chin half a centimeter and smiled ever so slightly. "It is also my duty to point out these facts to you, sir, in order to ensure that *you* take no action which would be detrimental to the Space Force. Now, is there anything that *is* within the proper course of my duties as a cadet and future officer that I can do for you at this time, sir?"

He frowned, scowled, quirked a brow, and sighed roughly. Folding his arms across his chest, Hadrabas lifted his own chin. "Are you always this stubborn and intent on having your own way, meioa?"

The corner of her mouth curled up further. "Commodore, at this time, I would like to 'plead the Fifth,' sir, as, one way or another, my answer would probably incriminate me."

He chuckled for a moment, then raised his brows. "Are you *sure* you wouldn't like to learn how to ski, Cadet? It would be a cushy reassignment."

Ia dropped her smile, giving him a cold, sober stare. "I was very serious in my reply, sir. I would consider it an order to commit Fatality Number Four, Dereliction of Duty . . . and under the Terran United Planet's duly registered Alliance Charter of Rights, I would have to register a formal protest as a conscientious objector to any such 'cushy' reassignment. Sir."

Bennie spluttered at that, apparently choking on her own spit. She coughed hoarsely a few times, cleared her throat, and visibly bit her lower lip in the effort to contain her amusement. Ia didn't show any such signs of mirth, herself.

Staring at her, Hadrabas shook his head slowly. "I'd been told about you . . . but I'll confess I didn't believe it until now. Mind you, Cadet, I'm disappointed you won't even try. It's been a sting in the Terran pride that the damned Solaricans have won nearly every single biathlon event, particularly in the heavyworld categories, since the inception of the Alliance Summer and Winter Olympics not quite two hundred years ago. You're from the heaviest inhabited planet we have, yet no one on Sanctuary wants to learn how to ski. Hell, no one on Parker's World wants to learn, either."

"The concept of willingly hurtling oneself down a hill at speeds in excess of one hundred kilometers per hour, on a planet where just *tripping* can kill you, is not one easily grasped by my colonymates, Commodore," Ia muttered, softening her expression with a touch of humor. "Let alone one that they'd willingly embrace. We don't even have skating rinks . . . and I'd imagine the people of Parker's World would be just as reluctant."

"I'll pass that information along, Cadet. What about the Summer Olympics?" he asked her, tilting his head slightly in speculation.

"That would still be a dereliction of duty, sir," she countered bluntly. "I'm not the fastest, I'm not the strongest, and I'm not the best. If I may be excused, Commodore, I need to get my mechsuit powered down and cleaned up for the day. That takes a minimum of half an hour after rolling all over the obstacle course, and I have . . . forty-seven minutes before the supper hour," she explained, glancing at the subtle numbers of the chrono built into her left forearm plate. "It's also Wednesday, sir. All Cadets are required to attend supper in Dress Blues on Wednesdays at the Academia. I'd really rather not be late."

He flipped a hand at her. "Dismissed. I guess I'll just go watch the other cadets as they perform on the course, then."

"Sir, if you're looking for a good marksmeioa among the cadets," Ia offered, "I suggest watching Cadet Djalu. I don't know if she skis or not, but she's leading all the scores from the targeting range, right now."

Hadrabas nodded to her. "I'll keep that in mind, Cadet."

"Mind if I accompany you, Cadet?" Bennie asked, trotting to catch up with Ia as she turned and strode away.

Ia slowed her steps, since her mechsuit legs were longer and covered more ground than the other woman could comfortably walk. "Not at all, Commander." She shared a brief smile with Bennie at the long-standing joke between them from their time on the *Liu Ji*, addressing each other by titles instead of names, despite their long friendship. Sighing, Ia wriggled her nose. "The worst part about being in a mechsuit is either I have to disengage my gauntlet just to scratch my nose, or risk putting out my eye. Or endure the itch endlessly."

"Here," Bennie ordered, lifting her fingers.

Ia obligingly stopped, and with a few muttered directions, got the spot just below the bridge of her nose satisfactorily scratched. "Thank you, Bennie."

"Not a problem. Now, if you could scratch an itch of *mine*," she replied, "I'd appreciate it. But it can wait until you're out of that tin can of yours. We can talk while you clean up."

Sighing, Ia led the way to the building housing the mechsuit pool. "Aye, sir."

Most of the mechsuits used by the Academy were more like stevedore suits, designed for hauling and manipulating heavy loads, or for construction purposes. There were only a dozen or so combat-grade suits like hers, most of which were reserved for training purposes. The TUPSF-Navy had less use for such things, particularly its officers, than either the Army or the Marine Corps. Their "mechsuits" were usually their ships, after all, and those few times when they needed such things, it was usually supplied by the Army and Marine Companies most ships carried.

Being fully mechsuit-trained was one of the things that would make her all the more suited for Blockade work, literally. Some Naval Academies specialized in mechsuit work, but not the Academia in Sines, which leaned more toward ship-to-ship combat in its training style. Reaching the combat mechsuit bays, Ia sealed her helmet and stepped into the cleaning alcove. It didn't take long to spray-wash the suit, nor for the scrubbers to go to work. In fact, it was sort of like being in an automatic car wash; kind of fun, if a little hard to balance at times.

As soon as the buffers retracted and the protective force field vanished from the entrance, Ia moved to her suit's designated storage alcove. Backing up into the alcove, she rocked it back onto its chargers and powered down the suit, cracking it open so she could step out.

Bennie eyed the tight-fitted, silvery grey p-suit Ia wore, and the pressure-squashed muscles and curves it displayed. "Have you lost weight? I think this is the first time I've seen you without loose-fitting clothes."

She shrugged and reached for the diagnostic kits, needing to check the suit's levels of hydraulic fluids. The arms had felt a little weak during today's run. "I've lost four kilos of muscle mass since I got here. I do what I can in the gym, but it's only for an hour a day, not three or four. And without the pull of my home gravity to fight, I can't stay in top shape. I also gained half a kilo of body fat. The food here is better than back on the *Liu Ji*."

Bennie chuckled. "On that point, I'll agree. Okay, time to get down to brass tacks. Cadet Harper tells me you're barely talking to him anymore. What's up?"

Ia ducked her head to hide her blush, crouching to give the leg pistons a quick pressure check. "Nothing's up. And I talk to him all the time."

"Bull *shakk*. The two of you get along fine in the classroom, but he says once you're alone in your dorm room, you clamp up tighter than an airlock," Bennie countered. "He also says you barely look at him. Treating your roommate like he doesn't exist is rude, unhealthy, and a sign that something is seriously wrong."

Slag, she's not going to give up on this, is she? Sinking to the floor with a sigh, Ia rested her diagnostic kit on her knees. She stared at her mechsuit, cheeks warm, and did not look at the chaplain. "It's under control, sir."

"Bull *shakk*," Bennie repeated. Crouching, she settled onto the edge of the alcove dais, squeezing in next to Ia. Off in the distance, someone was stomping around in a stevedore suit, but the two of them were alone in this corner of the building. "What's wrong, Ia?"

Her blush deepened. "I'm . . . abiding by regulations as best I can."

Bennie leaned over, interposing her freckled face between Ia and her suit. "And what does *that* mean, *hmm*?"

Rolling her eyes, Ia tipped her head back with another sigh. "It means I'm *attracted* to him, alright? But I don't dare ask for a room transfer, because if I cannot 'handle' being in the same quarters as him in a professional manner, it'll *shova v'shakk* my career chances." She eyed Bennie, whose green eyes had widened. "Fatality Forty-Nine, Bennie. No Fraternization."

The chaplain sat back with a smirk. "Now *that*, I can believe. I've seen that man almost naked, after all."

Ia gave her a disgusted look. The edge of her mouth couldn't stop quirking up, though. "Be that as it may, I'm stuck with it, Bennie. If I ask for a transfer, the DoI will black-mark me for a high command. If I did get to know him any better . . . I *know* he'll distract me from everything I need to do . . . and I'll run up against Fatality Forty-Nine. And that's not a black mark; that's an outright career bombing."

She didn't have to be precognitive to know that. Not that she could, precognitively—Mcyun Harper was still as much of a blank as ever, save for the concrete moments of the past she herself had spent with him—but instincts older than Time were screaming that warning at her. Feminine instincts, the kind someone in her particular position could not permit to take control.

Shaking it off, she leaned forward and restarted her postworkout diagnostics. Bennie stayed silent for several minutes while Ia worked, occasionally leaning out of the younger woman's way. Finally, the chaplain sighed and stood.

"Right, then. Report to my office tonight at nineteen thirty sharp, Cadet," Bennie ordered.

Ia blinked and looked over her shoulder. "Sir?"

"Nineteen thirty hours, Cadet," Bennie repeated, holding Ia's gaze.

"Sir, I don't understand." This wasn't in any future she had foreseen. "Are you writing me up for this?"

Bennie smirked. "Well, now that depends on you. If you *don't* show up, it's guaranteed that I'd have to, now wouldn't I?"

"V'tekh na n'kah!" The insult escaped her before she could stop it. At least it wasn't in Terranglo, but from the arch of one auburn brow, Bennie understood the V'Dan version. Flushing, Ia ducked her head. "Sorry, sir."

"Under the circumstances, it's understandable. And in the name of our friendship, I'll let it pass. But do try to avoid calling me that a second time, Cadet," Bennie warned her quietly.

"Yes, sir. No, I won't, sir . . . Thank you," she added quietly.

"Nineteen thirty. Don't be late." Brushing off her trousers, Bennie left the mechsuit pool.

Resisting the urge to throw the diagnostic kit across the room, Ia instead closed her eyes and leaned her forehead on the elbow joint of her suit. The mirror-polished plates of the special alloy of ceramics and metal rapidly dissipated the heat of her skin, just as it would the heat of laser fire or the radiation of outer space.

It could not, however, dissipate the sick fear gathering in her stomach. She had no clue what Bennie wanted from her . . . which meant it clearly had something to do with Meyun bloody Harper. Bane of her precognitive skills.

The one man who could undo everything she was striving to save, simply by *existing*.

CHAPTER 11

Hell Week in the Marines was physically difficult. Surviving all seven days of it remains the single toughest thing I have ever done with my body outside of actual combat. And in the end, Hell Week didn't break me. I broke myself. But Hell Week in the Navy . . . that was different.

Hell Week for cadets, officers-to-be, is quite different from Hell Week for raw recruits. The common soldier has to be physically tough, because much of their work is physical. Their duty is to carry out the orders they are given. Officers, on the other hand, need to be mentally tough. Their duty is to plan those orders, and oversee their execution. So the Academy instructors and the Department of Innovations, or rather, their psychology sub-division, work together in the months before the five day trial-by-fire of Hell Week to find and pick apart each cadet's weakest points. To hammer home that weakness and force the cadet to confront it, over and over, until that particular cadet acknowledges that flaw at the very least, and hopefully figures out how to work around it.

Alas, they never did figure out what my greatest mental weakness at that point was. Or rather, who. The one person who did figure it out in time . . . well, let's just say they put me through a version of Hell Week that was compressed down into a handful of minutes.

~Ia

Back on the TUPSF *Liu Ji*, Chaplain Benjamin had possessed a cramped little office, a somewhat larger counseling room that doubled as her living room, a cramped bedroom cabin, and a head, the starship nickname for a bathroom. Here at the Academia, her office was completely separate from her apartment. That office was in the administration hall, at the far end of the wing opposite the admissions desk. In fact, the easiest way to get to Bennie's office was to use a side door near the wastebins holding those rare few things which couldn't be recycled on the Academy's grounds in some form or another.

Which is appropriate, Ia thought, her rare morbid sense of humor surfacing briefly, *because I certainly feel like I'm about to be tossed into the rubbish bin like useless slag.*

She did not like this amorphous, shapeless, senseless feeling of dread. Not since she turned fifteen and had her precognitive epiphany had Ia suffered from such sourceless fears. No, since that pivotal morning, her fears had taken on all too solid identities. Not now, however. Stepping into the shadow-darkened hallway didn't help. It reminded her too much of old monster-in-the-closet fears, the kind where she didn't know what lurked behind that closet door.

Ia hated—feared—the unknown.

Wiping her face with the back of her hand, and her palm on the back of her thigh, Ia squared her shoulders and touched the door buzzer. She was a full minute early, she had made sure of that much. When the door opened, she braced herself for the unknown. *Show no fear. Know no fear. Confidence, calmness, these things will sustain, whereas fear will only drain . . .*

"Come in, Cadet," Bennie told her. "I'm glad to see you're on time."

"I strive to be, sir," she muttered, following the chaplain inside. The front room of the suite served as the general office for all the Academy's chaplains and psychologists. The rest of the rooms in this sub-wing were either designated office space or counseling space. They bypassed the door with "Cmdr. Christine Benjamin, Chaplain" on its nameplate and entered the room two doors down.

Meyun Harper rose from one of the padded chairs at the far end of the modest-sized room. He glanced between Bennie's face and Ia's, his expression as confused-looking as Ia felt. "Sir?"

The chaplain edged in behind Ia and poked at the door controls. The panel slid shut and clicked. "There. We are now locked in, only I have the access key, and this room is sound-proofed. It's also after hours, I have turned off the recording equipment, and the two of you *will* discuss your problems under the privacy code of the confessional."

She prodded Ia on the back, and when that didn't move the stunned woman, pushed her forward a few stumbling steps. Comprehension dawning, Ia turned and narrowed her eyes. Bennie leaned back against the door, arms crossed over her chest.

"Meyun, the real reason why Ia, here, won't talk to you when you're alone together, or even look at you . . ."

"Oh, no you don't," Ia whispered, rage heating her cheeks.

"Is because she's falling in love with you," Bennie finished.

Embarrassed, furious, Ia clenched her hands into fists. Not from the urge to hit Bennie, but from the need to keep her gifts locked down. Glaring at the chaplain, she growled, "You know what? I take it back. You *are* a two-fisting bitch!"

"Ia!" Meyun snapped, striding forward. "You do *not* say things like that to a superior officer!"

He caught her shoulder. Overwrought by Bennie's betrayal, Ia didn't dare risk prolonged physical contact. Shrugging him off roughly, she backed up a couple of meters. "Don't touch me! And *she is* one." She pointed at the redheaded woman. "What I told her was said in the confidence of a soldier to her chaplain—in the confidence of the *confessional*! And that . . . *skut* just *violated* that!"

"Loving someone is *not* an unforgivable sin, you know," Bennie snapped back.

"No, but violating military code *is*," Ia retorted. "He *didn't* need to know! Everything was under control before *you* stepped in."

"You had *nothing* under control," Bennie scoffed, giving Ia a disgusted look. "You were running away from the problem, *not* controlling it!"

Ia bristled at that. She wanted to protest it wasn't true. If she *did* run from her problems, what the hell was she doing in the military? But . . . *Damn her, she's right. But that doesn't make* this *right.* "So?" she asked, arms folded tightly across her chest. "Lots of people do that. It's a valid reaction."

Bennie pushed away from the door, swaying forward with a glare of her own. "If you expect to become a *successful* officer, that means you *cannot hide* from your own emotions!" She pointed at Harper, who swayed back from her jabbing finger. "If you want to get out of here without this session being recorded and going on your permanent record, you will *look* at Cadet Harper and tell him *exactly* how you feel about him!"

"Excuse me," Meyun interjected, "but can I join this conversation, or should I just pretend that I'm not actually a part of this?"

"Stand down and wait your turn, Harper," Bennie ordered, pointing her finger at him. "Ia has the bigger problem at the moment."

Ia closed her eyes, struggling for self-control . . . and the strength do it. She *knew* Bennie wasn't bluffing. With Harper standing next to her, there was nothing she could to but comply, in order to navigate the invisible rocks that threatened to overturn all her work. But it wasn't that simple. It could have been so easy, to just tell him—and Bennie—the truth of her work. Tell them both about her gifts, and the future she was driven to save.

But Meyun Harper was the Great Grey Mist in her mind, his actions obscured, his motives unsure. She had no way to foretell *what* he would do with that information. That meant she could not risk telling him any of it . . . and by extension, that meant keeping her friend and chaplain in the dark as well. Letting it all go, Ia breathed deep and opened her eyes again. She glanced at him. He was busy giving the chaplain a dark look; somehow, that made it easier to confess what she had to say.

"Meyun Harper . . . you scare the *shova* out of me." That shifted his gaze from Bennie's face to hers. She looked into his dark brown eyes and continued. "I find you brilliant, funny, handsome, sexy, companionable . . . I stand in awe of your technical genius, and since you're a heavyworlder, I don't quite feel like I'm going to break you in half if I so much as sneeze on you. I *can't* predict what you'll do or say, and that scares me, yet it fascinates me at the same time, since I never know what you'll do next. *But*."

"But?" he repeated, folding his own arms defensively over his chest. "But, what?"

"*But*, I am going into pilot training after the Academy. Every sign indicates I will be posted to a Blockade Patrol, where I know I can do some real good in the Service . . . and I *cannot* be assigned to the same ship as you. Not on Blockade. *Everything* about you is a distraction to me." She glanced at the chaplain waiting patiently by the door, then back to Meyun. "Don't mistake my meaning. I *do* want to get to know you better . . . on several levels . . . but I cannot afford it. *You* cannot afford it. Between the rules against fraternization between cadets, and the fact our career tracks are taking us off in two different directions, we have no viable future together.

"So I was *ignoring* it," she groused, shooting Bennie another dark look. "*Not* running away, just ignoring it. I apologize if that spilled over into ignoring you. I'll try to be less of an asteroid in our quarters from now on. That is, presuming all of these 'confessions' don't disgust you."

"Oh, they don't disgust him," Bennie interjected, earning another glare from Harper. "He's already confessed to me that he's fallen in love with you."

The blood left Ia's face. In fact, it looked like it went straight to Meyun's. Tan cheeks reddening, he sputtered a moment, glanced between the two women, then growled at Benjamin, "Ia's right. You *are* a two-fisting—!"

Ia's rare sense of humor surfaced, at that. Smirking, she met Bennie's scowl. "As you said when you arrived here, Bennie, I have a quick, keen grasp of most situations. Pain in the asteroid, isn't it?"

Bennie scoffed. "Except when it comes to your own heart, you don't. Meyun, look Ia in the eye and tell her how *you* feel."

Like Ia, it took him a few seconds to gather himself before he could look her way. She held herself still, waiting to hear what he had to say. Wanting to hear it, and dreading it.

"*Exactly* how you feel," he murmured. "I feel it, too. I like you, I'm surprised by you, and you make me laugh. I enjoy just sitting in the same room with you, both of us working on whatever . . . but I don't like being ignored. That hurt."

Ia nodded slightly to acknowledge his pain. She looked down, only to glance up sharply again as he continued.

"I *want* your eyes on me. I want your mind on me, your hands on me. I've probably spent three out of every seven showers playing with myself, thinking about you—"

Oh, dear god . . . She blushed so hard at his confession, it felt like her feet were going to faint.

"—and the other four banging my head against the wall of the stall. I *know* you're headed for a Blockade Patrol, whereas I'll get whatever duty post the system throws at me," Meyun admitted, his own face red. "I admire your devotion to duty at the same time that I hate it, because I *want* to keep you to myself, yet I couldn't keep you here and keep you the woman that . . . the woman that I'm falling in love with."

Taking a step closer, Meyun caught one of her hands, sending a thrill of excitement and fear up her nerves from the warmth of his fingers cupping hers.

"You're absolutely right, this could torpedo our advancement possibilities if it gets out of hand . . . but the bitch of it is, Chaplain Bennie is *also* right. If we don't confront this, get it out in the open and *deal* with it, we won't stand a chance at effectively leading anyone under our command." Holding her hand a moment longer, he squeezed her fingers and released it, stepping back. Tucking his hands into his trouser pockets, Meyun shrugged. "So. The question is, where do we go from here, and how do we handle this . . . attraction . . . between us?"

"I don't know. I've never had to deal with this situation before," Ia admitted honestly. "I'll try not to ignore you in our quarters, but . . . I *won't* compromise the rules."

"If I may make a suggestion—and no, you may not say I've already suggested enough," Bennie interjected, "I'd like to point out that there is a narrow window of opportunity that both of you are overlooking."

Both Ia and Meyun gave her bemused looks.

"Just because your careers are headed in different directions doesn't mean you can't have a little fun before parting company," Chaplain Benjamin pointed out. "After all, most cadets are given a week of Leave after graduation before being shipped out."

"I was planning on saving that week for later, so I could

have more time to get back home again in a few years," Ia pointed out.

"I've done the calculations. The next round of the flight school you've picked doesn't start until five days after you're scheduled to graduate, or twenty-five days after, and I know you'll be aiming for the earlier session," Bennie said. "Factor in a day for travel to the Academy Saturnia, and that gives you four whole days with nothing to do. It's not like you can offer to do guard duty around here in the interim, like you did back on the ship," she added pointedly. "Take the vacation, take each other off somewhere, and take some of the edge off your sexual tension—if nothing else, it'll be a good test of your characters, holding off when you know you *do* have something to look forward to," she finished.

Twisting his mouth, Meyun pulled his hands out of his pockets. Eyeing Ia, he fisted his fingers, gesturing forward and down with both arms in silent insult. Ia snorted and nodded in equally silent agreement. Watching them both, Bennie tightened her mouth for a moment, then flipped her hands at the seats in the room.

"Sit down and talk it out. Whatever you decide to do is whatever you decide, but ignoring it *won't* make it go away."

Meyun eyed Ia, lifting his brows. She smiled mock-politely at him and gestured toward the seats. He mock-bowed in return and took himself back to the chair he had been occupying upon her entrance. Following suit, Ia dropped into one of the thickly cushioned chairs across from his and curled up her leg, tucking her ankle behind the other knee. Both of them ignored Bennie, who remained leaning against the counseling room door.

"Alright. Fine. How do we go about resolving this?" Ia asked him. "It's not like we *can* do anything about it while we're still both cadets, roommates or otherwise."

"Well, it *is* the elephant in the corner of our dorm room," Meyun agreed. "I like having you as a friend. I enjoy talking with you. But we can't go any farther than that. So . . . let's just keep a watch on each other's conduct. I want to talk with you, but if we start straying into the wrong topic, or look too long, we just say . . . 'elephant' I guess."

"A code word?" Ia asked. He nodded, and she nodded as well. "Yes . . . that could work. I do miss talking with you. It was just easier to do it when other people were around. I was always aware about not going beyond the bounds of propriety with them there."

"I can understand that," he acknowledged. "It was a pain in the asteroid, because I didn't know why you were being so friendly in public and so . . . not . . . in private, but it makes sense. So. The rest of the term is covered. What about Bennie's suggestion for the days immediately after? Would you care to get a hotel room somewhere nearby and go at it like a pair of rabid rabbits for a few days? Get it out of our systems?"

Ia blushed at the suggestion.

"It'd be something to look forward to," Harper offered lightly. "A way to deal with the elephant in the room, even if it's a delayed one."

"Harper . . . I haven't *ever* 'gone at it like rabid rabbits,' " she warned him. "I'll probably be lousy at 'it.' "

"Nonsense, you'll do fine," he dismissed, flicking his fingers. "Everything else I've seen you try, you've picked up quickly and competently."

Yeah, but that was with the forewarning of precognition guiding me, she thought. Sighing, Ia rubbed her forehead with one hand. The idea of finally getting her hands and other things all over him was too appealing to resist. *I'll have to contact the priests back home, see what tips they can give me for locking down my gifts during intimacy so they hopefully won't trigger. Or rather, find something in the Nets that'll give me a clue, since my calls are probably all monitored as a "cadet of interest" to the DoI, and a conversation* that *blatant would give everything away. My gifts, our attraction to each other . . .*

"Besides, I could always try teaching you. Not that I'm the best myself, but practice does make perfect," Meyun joked.

That coaxed a rueful smile out of her. "Only a few days' worth . . . I don't know. I'll have to think about it."

A snort from the far side of the room drew their attention back to the other elephant on hand. Bennie pushed away from the door, approaching the two of them. She rolled her green eyes at Ia. "If you give yourself enough time to talk yourself out of a solution as simple and elegant as this, Ia, you *will* regret it. Your restraint while in the Academy is both admirable and necessary. But once you've graduated, so long as one of you isn't placed in the chain of command over the other, such restraint will no longer be necessary. If you talk yourself out of this and turn him down, so help me . . ."

"Excuse me, but my sex life is *my* own business," Ia reminded the older woman. "*Or* the lack thereof."

"But don't you want to know?" Meyun asked her. Ia looked back at him. "Don't you want to know what it's like to make love with someone who cares about you? I don't know about you, but if I don't take the chance, I *know* I will regret it for the rest of my life."

Ia flushed, unsure what to say. Duty demanded she ignore her desire and focus on the future. Desire demanded she take that handful of days for herself, as compensation for everything else both her conscience and Time itself were forcing her to give up.

"What was it you said in our Ethics course two months ago?" Meyun muttered. He lifted his chin after a moment. "That you'd rather be damned for something you *did*, than something you *didn't* do?"

Ia winced inside. *Everything* she was doing, she was doing because of exactly that: She knew she'd be damned, one way or the other, but it was far better to be damned for what she had to do, than to do nothing at all and be damned by the consequences of her failure to act. To hear him using her own words against her like this was a lower blow than he could possibly imagine.

A resolve-shattering blow. Giving in, Ia sighed roughly. "You're right. And I probably *will* be damned for this, since we do have to part company afterward . . . but you're right."

He frowned at her. "Oh, gee, thanks for making lovemaking with me sound like a trip to the guillotine!"

She made a face at him, sticking out her tongue a little. "I'm not talking about the act itself. I'm talking about the possibility that either of us could end up wanting a lot more than our career tracks would permit. Just . . . I don't want to hurt you, Meyun. Ever. If nothing else, please believe that. Whether it's out of friendship, or love, or whatever, I don't want to hurt you if we try hopping on the back of this particular elephant together."

"And I don't want to hurt you," he returned, tapping the table between them. "But I'd rather be damned for giving it a try—in the right time and the right place, obeying the letter of the regs—than be damned for turning my back on this chance and walking away."

Silence fell between them. At least it wasn't as strained as before. Shifting her hands to her hips, Bennie nodded. "Well, then. That's better. A lot better. The two of you are finally working through your differences, confronting your feelings and figuring out how to handle them in a responsible and mature manner."

Meyun dropped his head onto the padded back of the chair, while Ia rolled her eyes at her chaplain friend.

"I'm a psychologist as well as a priestess. Deal with it," Bennie ordered both of them. "Speaking of which, I'm going to want weekly evaluation sessions with each of you, separately and together. Just in case the 'elephant in the room' starts getting out of hand. You both have promising military careers ahead of you. Let's not shoot it all into the nearest star, shall we?"

"Aye, aye, sir," Ia muttered. Meyun grunted and lifted a hand in acknowledgment.

"Good." Folding her arms across her chest, Bennie studied both cadets. "Now, as for calling me what you did, regarding the . . . ?" She freed her arms long enough to show two fists, then tucked them back together again. "I'll admit my method of forcing this confrontation was a bit blunt, but I wouldn't say it was *that* blunt. Apologize, both of you, and I'll let the matter drop."

"Sorry, sir," Meyun apologized promptly. "It won't happen again."

"Yes, I'm sorry, too, sir," Ia added. "You know I do respect you."

"I know it won't, and I know you do. Apologies accepted. One more thing, before I kick you out and send you back for the rest of your study hour," Bennie said. "Ia . . . what exactly is a '*skut*'?"

"You know, I'm not entirely sure?" Ia quipped, looking up at her friend. "It was a new form of insult being tossed around on my homeworld, back when I was on extended Leave, but nobody ever actually explained it to me. Using it just seemed to fit the moment."

Bennie chuckled. "Next time, Cadet, if you're going to insult an officer? Be *damned* sure you know what that insult means. Particularly if you really mean it."

"Oh, I meant it," Ia quipped. "I don't know what it means, but in that moment, you *were* one. And a total, complete one at that, I'm sure of it."

Glancing between the two women, who were now smiling at each other, Meyun flopped his hands in a shrug. "Now I *know* the two of you are best friends."

As much as Ia wanted to protest otherwise, she kept her mouth shut. In her mind, best friends didn't keep major secrets from each other. Her best friends were her brothers, her family. But if it was possible to call someone a close friend who didn't know the most important parts of one's life, then Bennie would be at the top of that list. And, scary as it was to include her Invisible Rock in the Timestream, Meyun Harper was high on that list, too.

I am so shakked . . .

"Go on, get out," Bennie ordered, moving back to the door to unlock and open it. "I'm sure you both have homework to do. I'll set up weekly appointments for each of you—I'm supposed to be setting up counseling appointments with most of your class anyway, to make sure none of you are getting close to cracking from the strain of the fast-track pace. I'll just schedule yours back-to-back, so we can have a few minutes of mutual elephant-discussion time."

Ia pushed to her feet. "Understood, Commander."

"Thank you, sir." Rising as well, Meyun followed Ia out. He waited until they were outside, walking through the golden light angling in from the west, where the sun was getting close to the horizon. Glancing around to make sure they were alone, he asked, "So . . . *will* you plan on spending some of your postgraduation Leave days with me? You never did say an outright yes."

She sighed, gaze more on the path they were taking back to the dormitory building than on him. "Yes. I *will* go with you to a hotel after we've graduated, and try all the things we cannot do while we are still enrolled in this Academy. But between then and now, it is the elephant in the corner, and we must ignore it so that it *stays* in the corner."

He nodded, but said nothing more. Tucking his hands behind

his back, he strolled along beside her. Halfway to the dorm rooms, Meyun finally spoke.

"I think it has roller skates."

Thrown off by the non sequitur, Ia blinked at him. "What?"

"The elephant, in the corner of the room," he stated, shrugging. "I think it has roller skates. What do you think?"

"Ahh." Caught off guard by the quip, she scrambled to think of a suitable reply. "I . . . think it's . . . black with gold polka dots?"

That made him laugh, while Ia chuckled. It also released some of the tension still lingering between them. Some, but not all. There was still an elephant between them, after all.

JULY 25, 2493 T.S.
HELL WEEK, TUPSF *VASCO DA GAMA*

They tried everything to break her. They tried demoting Ia to the lowest ranks, where she simply performed to her best ability, earning praise from the crew and the other cadets. They tried assigning her to the wrong departments for her skill sets. She asked questions, picked the right people for the job, and let *them* handle the crises afflicting the ship, giving praise when they handled it. The testing staff moved her quarters on board the *da Gama* seventeen times; she just packed and unpacked each time with heavyworlder speed and Marine Corps efficiency.

Sleep deprivation was nothing new for her, though it did cause several of the others to stumble. They were given slightly more sleep than the recruits back in Basic had been allotted, but never quite enough. On the last day, with everyone—even Ia—numb-tired from constant alerts, battle scenarios, engine breakdowns, stellar anomalies, pressure-suit drills, and more, the orders Ia had anticipated finally echoed through the ship's intercom system.

"Cadet Ia, report to de bridge on de double. Acting Keptin Wong, prepare to transfer command of de da Gama *to Cadet Ia."*

Pausing just long enough to lock and web her cleaning equipment so it wouldn't go flying about in sudden maneuvers, Ia left the upper lifesupport cabin at a fast jog. Her uniform was damp and dirty in several places from mopping up spilled tank contents, she hadn't had time for a shower in three days, and she hadn't dared eat a heavy meal the last time one had been served.

A deck and three bulkhead seals later, she had reached the brain of the ship, the bridge. Unlike the old seafaring ships, the bridge on a Space Force starship was buried deep in its interior, behind layers of extra plating and redundant circuit relays. This one was located slightly above the middeck, and on the Frigate Class slightly to the aft as well, but otherwise more or less centered.

Cadet Wong unstrapped himself from the captain's console. Saluting Ia, he stated crisply, "Acting Captain Ia, you have the bridge."

She saluted back. "Thank you, Cadet Wong. Report to Acting Lieutenant Jinja-Marsuu in lifesupport, on the double." Dropping into the seat, its cushions still warm from his body heat, she strapped herself in and entered her command passcode, then toggled the intercom system on. *"All hands, this is Acting Captain Ia. I believe we have only a matter of hours left before the end of Hell Week, so prepare for the absolute worst they can throw at us. But don't worry. Obey my orders, put your trust in me, and I'll do my best to see that we make it through."*

She didn't bother to request a greenlight from all stations. They had been at this for a solid week, with the non-cadet crewmember swapping out every eight hours in different duty shifts, the same as their evaluators. But not the cadets being tested. In space, there would be no chance for a greenlight ready-check. Whatever happened, whenever it happened, they would have to be ready for it as they were.

Right now, Ia was tired enough that skimming the time-streams took more energy than she wanted to spare, because right now, the probabilities were just about dead even that any single one of a dozen different scenarios would be played upon them. The level of confusion was not quite to the point of forming a grey mist over the streams, but it was close.

Swapping channels, she contacted the Special Forces captain she had met on her first full day at the Academy, the chief officer of the DoI oversight team assigned to evaluate each and every cadet in Class 1252. *"Acting Captain Ia to Captain Rzhikly, the* Vasco da Gama *is ready for orders."*

"Your orderz are to rendezvous vit Battle Platform Freeman. *Coordinates are being zent to your left secondary—"*

"Query, sir," Ia interjected before he could order the start of the simulation. *"Is the location of Battle Platform* Freeman *at the rendezvous point widely known, or a military secret?"*

"Vhy do you need to know dat?" Captain Rzhikly asked, his confusion conveyed in his tone.

"It might have a bearing on my command decisions, sir. As the captain, I'd know in advance if its location was public knowledge, or if it had been secretly moved to this location for whatever reason."

"Ehhh . . . fleep a coin!" he ordered over the comm.

A couple of mouths twitched upward on the cadets around her. Ia quickly patted down the front of her shirt, squirmed in her seat, and dug a handful of brown tenth-credit chits out of her trouser pocket. *"Right. Heads, it's a secret rendezvous; tails, it's a widely known location."*

Flicking the quasimetallic coin with her thumb, she tumbled it up, down, and deftly caught it in her left hand, slapping it onto the right one. Lifting her hand away, she displayed the "heads" side of the iridescent chit balancing on the back of her hand toward the observation pickups in the ceiling.

"Heads, sir. The rendezvous coordinates are a military secret. I will keep them us a secret for my eyes only, and relay only directional instructions to the crew."

Dropping the coin in her shirt pocket, Ia studied the coordinates on her left secondary screen, then closed the file, locking it to her command passcode. She tapped in a quick query to identify their ship's location in the simulation, and noted that they were just a single star system away. That suggested they were going to be hit hard and fast before they could even leave this system. Another touch of the controls pulled up information on both systems, this time on her right secondary screen.

"Right. Anything else we should know about this simulation, Captain?"

"Just get your ship and her crew bekk to de Platform, Cadet. Scenario beginz in five . . . four . . . tree . . ."

"All hands, brace for *anything*," Cadet Bruer muttered. A

couple of the others laughed mirthlessly at that. The green lights indicating the pause between simulations faded out, leaving the normal white-spectrum lights glowing softly overhead. Ia was the last cadet to be given the captain's position. Their last test had begun. From this point forward until the end of the exercise, they were to treat everything as if it were real, from actions to reactions, ranks to regulations, essentials to emergencies. Just like they had all week long, whenever they were freed from the verdant glare of the green overhead lights, this was all presumed to be real.

Nothing happened.

In fact, nothing happened for several minutes. Ia didn't trust it. There were still too many choices for the testers to pull on them. She spent those minutes checking the database records on the local system, and the system where they were to rendezvous with the Battle Platform. Tired as she was, reaching deep enough into the timestreams to gauge the probability of which scenario would actually be picked would be too exhausting. There were too many choices, and she had to stay too close to the real world to be able to react in time.

It was better to stay loose and flexible right now, and that meant having plenty of information at her fingertips. They were on the fringe of Terran space, not far from the Tlassians and the Choya. Neither system was inhabited, which would cut down on the potential for civilian casualties—crossing off at least three possible scenarios on her precognitive list—but then neither was fully mapped, either. That added at least two more possibilities. Ones which, at FTL speed, made her nervous.

"Helm, slow to one-quarter Cee. Shields up and sensors on full. Navigation, get us the system buoy pings, on the double."

"Aye, sir."

"Aye, Captain."

The ship lurched as it slowed across the lightspeed barrier. Centuries ago, either Einstein or the people who followed him had made a major mathematical mistake. Faster-than-light travel was quite possible, but the Terrans had reached for the stars believing it was impossible, developing other-than-light technology instead. It took the other races of the Alliance to introduce them to the gentler, healthier, if slower FTL method of interstellar travel.

"Sir?" Bruer asked from his position at the gunnery system. "Insystem speeds? You only want to go a quarter the speed of light?"

"This system is only partially surveyed. I don't want—"

CLANNNGG!

The ship rocked, jolting everyone in their seats. The interior force fields snapped on, cutting down on the bad bruising the restraint straps would have delivered. They cut off a second later, just as loud klaxons blared in the eerie up-and-down stuttering wail of a hull breach.

"*That* to happen," Ia finished, teeth clenched. "All stop! Report!"

"All stop, Aye, sir!" Cadet, or rather, Commander Vizzini called back, hands working the helm controls.

"Captain, hull breach on Decks 2 and 3, starboard bow," Abbendris reported from her position at the ship systems station. The decks rumbled with the application of the thruster fields, and everything swayed forward. "We've lost L-pod 1 and P-pod 1, sir."

"Do we have casualties?" Ia asked.

"No one was in those pods, sir," Bruer reminded her. "The last scen—*Ah*, the last duty watch didn't need them to be manned."

"*All hands report for greenlight,*" Lieutenant Abbendris ordered over the ship comms. "*Repair teams suit up and report to Decks 2 and 3, Section 1 interior airlocks.*"

"Captain." That came from Cadet, or rather, Lieutenant Shinowa, stationed at the navigation post. "System buoys are silent. I've tried pinging them, but I'm getting nothing. We're flying blind on lightspeed wavefronts only."

"I'm not getting a ping on any of the system hyperrelays, either," the communications officer, T'siel, warned her.

"Either they've been destroyed by an enemy, sir, or there's one hell of an ion storm coming our way," Lieutenant Chen stated from his seat at the engineering workstation. "System buoys and hyperrelay stations are over-engineered to prevent casual failures."

Both, her precognitive instincts warned her. But there were still too many possibilities. "Until we find out otherwise, we will presume we have lost the buoys to *both* solar storms and enemy ships, and act accordingly," Ia ordered. "Engineering, standby on external repairs."

"Sir?"

"Repair teams are to use remote drones to survey the damage, first. If the drones can't manage the repairs, the teams will have to suit up in ceristeel, in case it's an ion storm," she ordered. "Helm, roll the ship to put the system sun on our portside. Gunnery, crew the aft Sections 3 and 4 P-pods and launch seven scanner probes, six in the cube and the extra sunward, staggered, so we can get realtime estimates if there *is* an ion storm out there."

"Rolling the portside to sunward, Captain," Vizzini stated, complying with a touch of the controls. The ship swayed slightly under them, but the hint of a tilt was subtle at best.

"Seven scanner probes launched in the cube, two to the sun staggered, aye, sir," Bruer agreed, repeating her orders. That meant launching one probe in each direction, to the fore, aft, dorsal, ventral, starboard, and two to the port, the second one several seconds behind the other. He relayed them on his comm headset directly to his gunnery teams, not over the intercom like Abbendris's orders had been sent.

"Captain! We're in the yellow for three enlisted personnel," Abbendris told her. "They're trapped in a maintenance locker on Deck 3, Section 1. All the others managed to evacuate."

"Are the door seals holding? Do they have p-suits and oxygen in there?" Ia asked.

Abbendris relayed the query, reporting within moments the results. "Captain, they say the door seals are leaking very slowly, but they're suited up, with two-hour standard emergency oxypacks each. However . . . they'll freeze within the hour, with the starboard side now in the shade. The damage interrupted most of the power to that area. They have some gravity, but zero heat, sir."

"Captain, scanner pods away," Bruer told her. "They'll be up to full insystem speed in twenty seconds, deadheading away from us in the cube."

"Noted. Lieutenant Abbendris, send the Section 1 schematic to my primary screen," she stated, addressing the cadet by her scenario simulation rank. "I want to know exactly where our three trapped crewmates are located, and what's around them."

"Aye, sir. The damage alterations will be incomplete until we get pingback from the repair drones," Abbendris warned her. "Most of this will be an intact schematic."

"Understood, Abbendris," Ia told the other woman.

"Repair drones are now launching, sirs," Bruer stated. That was his duty as the gunnery officer, though it was up to Abbendris to make sense of the readings, just as it was up to astronavigation officer Shinowa to make sense of the data the launched sensor pods were collecting and sending back. Each one was equipped with insystem thruster fields, minimum shields, enough ceristeel plating to protect the delicate instrumentation in most conditions, and more.

The repair drones had a variety of flexible servo-arms to make repairs, while the sensor drones bore miniature hyperrelay units to boost the data streams above the speed of light. Both kinds were expensive, if necessary, and it would be a mark against her if Ia didn't make sure each one came back intact.

Within moments, her largest, central screen brightened with the three-dimensional wire sketch framing the decks of the *da Gama*'s foremost section. Three yellow humanoid shapes lit up one of the cube-chambers. Frowning in thought, Ia tapped the screen, rotating the image, zooming in and out. She touched keys on her console, adjusting the opacity of walls, highlighting power conduits and other ship systems, coaxing her tired mind into thinking.

"Lovely . . ." Abbendris murmured. "Captain, we're beginning an exterior survey of the damage."

"Noted. Send a couple remote 'bots through the section airlocks, too, to examine the damage from the inside."

"Aye, sir." The cadet overseeing ship systems relayed the orders, then hesitated. "Captain? Aren't we going to send in a rescue team to pick up the yellowlights?"

"Not until we get a system report. We are still lightspeed blind, Lieutenant," Ia reminded her. "We have three problems that are slightly more urgent at the moment. We don't even know yet what we hit, if it was an isolated asteroid or a chunk of ship. There might be other debris out there. If we get overtaken by a solar storm and the radiation gets in through the cracks in the hull during a rescue operation, it'll kill those three faster than if they stayed locked up for half an hour while we wait to find out. And if there are enemies lurking somewhere nearby, taking out those system buoys, better for our crewmates to be in an intact cabin with functional interior fields to help cushion them from sudden maneuvers, if we have to bolt and run."

"Careful observation leads to comprehension," Bruer murmured.

Ia smiled wryly. "Exactly. Right now, our biggest need is information."

Shinowa spoke up. "We're getting initial system telemetry from the probes, Captain. We struck one of . . . what looks like seven asteroids within twenty lightseconds of our position. Comparison with known system data suggests these are unregistered bodies, possibly rogues. There's also some strange radiation in the system. Some of it's leaking from the damaged ship section, I think. I'll have a better analysis of it in a few moments . . ."

"If we hadn't slowed down, the FTL field should have pushed them aside," Chen groused. "Slowing down *caused* the collision."

Shinowa shook her head, her gaze dancing between her primary, two secondary, and bank of tertiary screens. "Incorrect, Lieutenant Commander. If we hadn't slowed when we did, we would have plowed into the largest of them, which is now dead ahead by five thousand klicks. We are damned lucky we stopped when we did. FTL can't push aside a rock that's 2.3 kilometers long. Instead of being banged up by a rock two hundred meters across—which I'll admit *would* have been pushed aside by the warp panels—we'd have been dead. Very dead."

"This system is only partially surveyed," Ia reminded the others, backing up her navigation officer's assessment, and explaining her own reasoning. "Prudence demanded that we drop to sub-light speeds and ping the buoys for the latest system updates. With those buoys dead, it's even more imperative we hold position until we know what's out there. That's why I ordered the scanner drones deployed."

"Those are rather large for rogue asteroids. They should've been on the system charts at that size, rogue or otherwise," Bruer muttered, staring at his screens.

"We deal with what is, not with what we want it to be, Lieutenant Bruer," Ia reminded him.

"Scanner probes edgeward are picking up traces of massive ion trails, Captain," Shinowa reported. "Looks like this system's been hit with a really big solar flare in the last week—*ah*—!" She slapped the intercom. *"All hands, brace for an ion storm!* It's a big one, Captain, coming up fast. We have maybe twenty minutes at lightspeed before the worst of the radiation hits. We're going to have to seal as many sunward ports and panels as we can. It's either shut it all down for the duration, or be rendered sensor-blind on that side."

"Right." Tapping her screen and her console, Ia sent the sketch she made to the ship systems station. "Lieutenant Abbendris, to your primary. Use this plan to get those crewmates out of that locker."

"Sir?" Abbendris asked, looking up from her screen to Ia. *"This* plan?"

Ia met her gaze impatiently. "You heard Lieutenant Shinowa. You have less than twenty minutes. Execute it."

"Aye, sir." Turning back to her station, Abbendris started relaying them, directing the repair crews to power up a welding drone, empty out a storage crate, and have two team members don stevedore mechsuits. The plan was to use the welding drone to cut through the back wall of the supplies locker from another room deeper inside the ship, and bring up the two-meter-square storage chest for the three pressure-suited crewmembers to crawl into, so they could be carried out of the damaged sector.

P-suits were silvery grey to help retain body heat and ward off some forms of stellar radiation, but an ion storm would pass its energy right through the relatively thin material. The ceristeel chest wasn't very dense either, but then neither were the stevedore suits; their only advantage was that they would be more protection than the p-suits alone. All five crewmembers would be at risk until they reached the safety of the unbroken ship sections, where layers of ceristeel would absorb and diffuse the energies hurtling toward them from a mass ejection of the local sun's corona.

Connecting her headset to the infirmary, Ia contacted the head of the medical cadets undergoing their own version of Hell Week along with SF-Navy Class 1252. *"Captain Ia to Doctor Underhill. Prepare to receive five patients. Three will have decompression sickness and all five will probably have ion radiation burns."*

"Understood, Captain."

Tense, quiet minutes passed on the bridge. Abbendris reported the extent of the damage to the starboard hull, in between reporting the progress of the welders. Shinowa reported increasing levels of ionized gasses expelled from the system's star. T'siel warned Ia that the ion storm was now so intense, their connection to outsystem hyperrelays were failing. More than one tertiary screen at the various bridge workstations included shots from the cameras on the welder drone and the stevedore-suited crewmembers hauling the oversized ceristeel crate.

A subdued cheer broke out among the cadets on the bridge when the oval slice of metal was extracted from the wall. Another muffled cheer accompanied the sight of the crewmembers climbing into the crate, piling one on top of another, and the lid being fastened.

"Eyes to those boards, sailors, and keep your minds on your jobs," Ia ordered the others. "We're still running lightspeed blind."

"Here comes the radiation crest!" Shinowa warned everyone.

"Repair Team Sierra, the ion storm is cresting. Get everyone back through the section lock, bounce it on the double," Abbendris ordered the men and women listening on her headset. *"Don't make any careless mistakes."*

"Lieutenant Shinowa, what's the estimated density of the storm?" Ia asked.

The other cadet shrugged. Navigation was not her track specialty. "It's a big one, Captain. Big enough, the crest is starting to push *us*, sir. If there were other, relatively recent storms the size of this one, they could have altered the orbits of those asteroids, turning them rogue."

"Rogue asteroids and ion storms, just our luck," Vizzini muttered. "Captain, do you want me to use the thrusters to maintain our position? We're starting to tumble from the stellar winds."

"Maintain portside sunward, Commander Vizzini," Ia instructed him. "Protect that broken hull section. But the moment those crewmembers are safely in Section 2, I want you to swap ship ends."

"Sir?" he asked, giving her a puzzled look.

"Point the bow back the way we came, maintaining portside to sunward," Ia clarified crisply. Unclipping the stylus from the edge of her workstation, she lifted it in her fingers and twisted her wrist, using it to demonstrate how she wanted the ship ends swapped.

"Sir?" Vizzini repeated. "I don't understand, sir. Wasn't the direction we were originally headed the correct one, Captain? Why would we go back?"

"Repair Team Sierra has reached the airlock, Captain," Abbendris reported quietly. "They're cycling through, sir."

"Commander Vizzini, you are to swap the ship ends, keeping the portside sunward and the damaged hull to the edgeward side of the system, in the lee of the ship. You have your orders. If you are too tired to carry them out, let me know and I will relieve you of the burden of commanding the helm so you can get some rest. *Are* you tired, Commander?" Ia asked her second-in-command softly.

"Sir, no, sir," he responded, turning back to his controls. "Helm is now swapping the ship ends, keeping the portside sunward, sir." Left hand in the thruster glove, right hand dancing over the buttons on his console, he slowly rotated the ship. Half under his breath, he muttered, "I just don't understand *why* . . ."

Ia didn't explain. Instead, she worked on building a new set of orders. Her right secondary screen flashed with an incoming comm message. Linking to it, she listened to the report from the infirmary, and nodded.

"Thank god . . . The infirmary reports they have received all five crewmates and are treating them for very minor ion storm burns," she told the rest of the crew. The others cheered. Ia allowed herself a small smile, until her right secondary screen flashed again, this time with a text message from a different part of the ship. "Well. It looks like supper for the cadre has now been prepared."

"Rapture," Bruer quipped. "Redlight or greenlight, routine or emergency, the cooks keep on cooking. Pass along my compliments to . . . uh . . . Lieutenant Harper? It's his duty shift, isn't it?"

"Yes, he took over from Lieutenant Jinja-Marsuu three hours ago. She swapped back to lifesupport for the second half of her duty shift," Ia said, calling up and checking the duty roster. "Given our delicate situation, and the general exhaustion of the crew—meaning we don't have a lot of choices for relief watch officers—I am going to authorize permission to the bridge crew for us to go eat one at a time."

They looked at each other. The order wasn't usual, though it wasn't unheard-of. Chen shrugged. "Who goes first, Captain? By rank, or . . . ?"

"All bridge stations, ping me a standard RNG to my tertiary three. Highest random number goes first, lowest goes next to last. I'll take the absolute last supper in the rotation, and handle each of your stations in the meantime." Waiting for the numbers to scroll up the center of her five bottom screens, Ia touched the monitor as soon as all of them had reported in. A swirl of her finger on the screen and a tap of the other hand on the keyboard reorganized the numbers in descending order. "Congratulations, Lieutenant Commander Chen; you rolled a ninety-seven, which means you get to be the first victim of tonight's version of a culinary masterpiece."

"My stomach thanks you from the bottom of its random number generator, Captain," the man at the engineering console quipped. "Transferring engineering command to your station, Captain."

"Transfer received, thank you," Ia murmured a few seconds later. "You are free to leave the bridge, Lieutenant Chen. Don't eat so fast that you choke, but don't dawdle, either. Commander Vizzini will be next."

Unbuckling himself from his seat, he hurried to leave. She envied him; she hadn't eaten a lot at their last meal, for fear some of the scenario options selected would be too rough a ride to keep the food down. But the job of being the ship's captain—of being an officer, period—meant asking nothing of her crew that she wouldn't ask of herself. That meant waiting until last.

"Commander Vizzini . . . I am having the engineering department reverse the directional pulse pattern of the insystem thrusters. Upon my command, you will put this ship in reverse, quarter speed," Ia commanded. "Lieutenant Shinowa, alter course of the sensor drones. Keep them in the cube, but match course and pace to our own. Heading is one eighty-three by one seventy-two. Maintain portside to sunward at all times."

"Uhh . . . *reverse*, sir?" Vizzini asked. "You want me to back up the ship?"

"We *cannot* go forward into a solar storm as dense as this one, Commander," Ia said. "The holes in our bow would act like a scoop, gathering up far too many ionized particles for our safety. We will therefore, as you put it so succinctly, back up the ship. We cannot afford to waste time sitting out a storm this bad. It's either move to get out of the storm and stay on course, or move to find a planet to hide behind, and we're in the wrong quadrant for that this year."

"Aye, sir," he agreed, shrugging and returning to his controls. *"Ahe . . . er, reverse engines, one-quarter speed, heading one eighty-three by one seventy-two."*

Satisfied he would comply, Ia relaxed a little. Her screen flashed again, this time a request for a private commlink. Ia linked into it. *"Captain Ia here."*

"Captain, this is Lieutenant Commander Jinja-Marsuu, down here in lifesupport," the other woman spoke, voice projecting solely into Ia's left ear. *"I trust this is a private channel? It's not something that needs be broadcast to the crew."*

"Go ahead, Commander," Ia replied, adjusting her headset a little more comfortably in her ear. *"You're in the clear."*

"Captain, your, ah, replacement, Lieutenant Wong, has taken his sweet time getting down here to lifesupport. In fact, I was told by Lieutenant Harper that he swung by the officer's galley and chatted up some of the crew, cadging a snack before making his way down here. And when he did finally show up, he broke one of the drinking water pipelines, and made a mess of repairing it. I would like to request permission to replace him . . . and to ask if you think I should write him up for a Fatality Four, Dereliction of Duty."

That was a fairly serious charge for a cadet to accrue during Hell Week. It was something that would go on his permanent record, in fact. For a moment, Ia wondered why Wong—who had looked reasonably alert when she had reached the bridge and was relatively competent in his lifesupport classes—would have been so tardy. Curious, she dipped into the timestreams, looking into the past, not the future, for a glimpse of what had delayed him.

What she saw widened her eyes. Blinking as she came back

to herself, Ia quickly smoothed out her expression and silently weighed the best options based on the variables she could foresee. *"Replace him, but order him confined to his quarters for the next eight hours. Make a note of the incident, but do not put any charges into his record at this time. We're all exhausted by now, Commander. Hopefully with a bit of sleep, he won't be so slow to report next time."*

"Understood, sir. Jinja-Marsuu out."

CHAPTER 12

Mind you, they did try . . . but once again, they didn't break me.
I broke myself. Painfully.

~Ia

The first wave of vomiting swept through the crew roughly an hour later, while they were still trying to out-crawl the ion storm. The first one on the bridge to succumb, naturally, was the first one to have eaten. Lieutenant Commander Chen cast up the contents of his stomach on his workstation console. Thankfully, the keys were sealed against all manner of spills, but the sound and the mess were disturbing.

Ia quickly transferred the engineering controls back to her own station, adding them to the gunnery controls. Excusing himself, Chen rose and wobbled out of the bridge, heading for the cleaning supplies. They heard him retching again just beyond the door, before he managed to slap the controls, shutting the panel.

Shinowa let out a soft whistle. *"That* was unpleasant."

"Please," Vizzini muttered. "I'm trying not to think about the sound or the smell . . . and I don't feel so good myself."

Ia's right secondary screen lit up. She opened the commlink to the whole bridge. *"Lieutenant Harper, I was just about to call you. Commander Chen just cast up his stomach all over my bridge."*

"Uhhh . . . *sorry, Captain. I don't know how, but . . ."* He sounded horrible. *"Captain, I think some sort of contaminant got into the cadre galley. I've just sent five crewmembers to the infirmary, and I need to report in, myself. I'm taking samples of food, drink, and water down there for . . . uhhh, god . . ."*

"Get everything examined, Lieutenant," she said. Then had to wait as he retched. She thumbed down the volume while she waited, then dialed it back up again. *"Report to the infirmary with samples of everything, Lieutenant Harper. Make sure the unaffected members of your crew suit up before they assist, to ensure nothing is cross-contaminated."* Ending the connection, she addressed her bridge crew. "Lieutenant Abbendris, wake up the first watch officers and have them report to the bridge on the double. Make absolutely sure they have eaten and drunk nothing in the last three hours before you permit them to come onto this bridge."

"Aye, sir." The other woman bent to her task . . . and flinched as Vizzini groaned and struggled out of his restraints.

He managed to lurch halfway to the bridge door before retching right next to Ia. Nose wrinkling, she struggled not to breathe too deeply. She hadn't consumed anything beyond the bottled water available to the bridge crew in the last few hours, but the smell was enough to make her feel nauseated, too.

Thumbing open the ship intercom, Ia announced, *"Attention all hands, this is the Captain. Attention. We are experiencing some sort of shipwide illness. It looks like it's going to get at least half of the officers. Either this is biological, or it's sabotage. I am therefore or—"*

"Holy shakk!" Shinowa swore. "Captain! Ships emerging from FTL to our af . . . er, bow—behind us! Three . . . five . . . oh, holy ancestors—Captain, they're *Salik* vessels! *Twelve* vessels, Captain!"

"Shakk," Bruer swore. "We can't run with the front half of our warp panels powerless, and we can't fight back against that many. And if they board us, they'll *eat* us! They've given us a goddamn *Kobayashi Maru*, on top of everything else!"

"The *Kobayashi Maru* scenario should be *illegal* in these tests," someone else muttered.

"Not to mention clichéd," one of the other cadets agreed.

Ia jabbed her controls, bypassing T'siel's communications station. Fingers stuttering as fast as she could go, she linked into the ship's broadcast relays, and into all seven drones. Two final taps opened up a recording unit, and the broadband broadcast command. Her words echoed through space as well as through the ship, since the ship's internal comm systems were still active at her station.

"This is Captain Ia of the TUPSF Vasco da Gama with a Quarantine Extreme warning. I transmit this in the broadband lightspeed; I transmit this on rotating hyperrelays. By the rules of Sentientarian Spacefaring Aid, this vessel is sealed under the rules of Quarantine Extreme. All ships, do not attempt contact with the TUPSF Vasco da Gama. All ships, do not attempt to load any water from the ice rings of the fifth planet in star system Ceti Ceti Delta 175 until further notice.

"We are under biological attack from an unknown contaminant traced to the hydrosupplies we collected from the ice rings of the fifth planet at Ceti Ceti Delta 175. This biological agent is jumping species. I repeat, it is jumping species. Any attempt to contact the atmosphere, fuel, or life-forms aboard the TUPSF Vasco da Gama will risk your own biological contamination. This is a Quarantine Extreme warning."

Ending the recording and the external broadcast, she patched it into a loop, letting the ship's automated systems repeat her message. Turning to the ship's internal comms, she addressed the crew.

"Attention, all hands, this is the Captain. We have twelve Salik warships within three million kilometers of our position. We have one shot at getting out of this mess. Listen closely to the following orders: If you are sick, I want you to vomit on whatever nonvital surfaces are within range of the interior pickups. Do not hit anything sensitive," Ia stated dryly, *"but the floor and the furniture are all fair game. I want* evidence *that we are sick, and I want it all over this ship. Infirmary, grab a list of everyone who hasn't eaten anything in the last six hours, and dispense oral emetics for the unaffected crew to carry at all times; bounce it on the triple time. Lifesupport, get ready to screw up the numbers three and four fish tanks in Bay 1, and kill at least a dozen hens. Do your best to make them all look*

like a bacterial or viral death, not *a physical one, and send some of the fish and hens to the infirmary for examination."*

"Captain, we're getting pingback from the Salik vessels," Lieutenant T'siel told her, craning his neck to look past the edge of his monitor banks.

"I repeat, this is Captain Ia," Ia stated, finishing her instructions to her own ship. *"If you are sick, retch it up for the shipboard cameras. Infirmary, dispense emetics to the off-duty crew, and get some up to the bridge. Lifesupport, make it look like whatever we've got is hitting the other species on board. These are your orders for now; more will be coming shortly."* Cutting off the interior comms, Ia lifted her chin at T'siel. "Put them through on audio, Lieutenant, and make it bridgewide incoming, but only my headset outgoing."

"Hhewman vessel Vasco da Gammma,*"* the bridge comms relayed. *"Your desssception will not save hyew. We outnumber you. Open hhyour airlocksss or be destroyed."*

"This is Captain Ia of the Vasco da Gama *to the Salik vessels. This is not a deception. We have dead V'Dan gamehens and dead Solarican carp on board. Whatever is in our water, it is jumping interplanetary species and killing the lesser lifeforms. We are under Quarantine Extreme. Any attempt to board this . . . You know what?"* she asked, switching tone and topic abruptly. *"I would love to see you board this ship. I would love to open my airlocks to all of you, just to see if this whatever-it-is affects* your *biology, too.*

"Unfortunately, by the conventions of Sentientarian Spacefaring Aid, I am obligated to warn you that my ship is under Quarantine Extreme. Of course, by those same rules of Quarantine Extreme, you are *permitted to transfer a maximum of two duly informed medical personnel to this vessel, with the understanding that they will also potentially be at risk for lethal interspecies contamination,"* Ia stated. *"You think this is a bluff? Well, I'm calling that bluff. If you wish to board this ship, you will select two duly informed medical personnel and transport them, and only them, in a boarding pod to our midships sunward airlock at the end of this ion storm."*

"And hhavve hhyew kill them? Or try to essscape while we wait for the pod to connnehhct?" The sibilant reply came from whoever was broadcasting on behalf of the twelve alien ships.

"Captain, they're altering course, heading our way," Shinowa warned her.

Bruer breathed hard, groaned, and unstrapped his restraints, lurching out of his seat. Unlike Vizzini, he made it to the door. They could hear him casting the contents of his stomach on the corridor floor outside, before the panel slid shut again.

"By the rules of Sentientarian Spacefaring Aid, any medical personnel who volunteer to go to the aid of other starships are to be considered inviolate and unattackable so long as they conduct themselves in a manner befitting sentientarian aid, and do not engage in any acts of injury, damage, terrorism, espionage, or warfare. By my word of honor as a Captain of the Terran Space Force, I and my crew will abide by these rules of conduct so long as your observers abide by them.

"If you choose to send them," Ia bartered, *"your two volunteers will be treated as noncombatants for as long as they remain neutral and render nothing but observation and sentientarian aid. Furthermore, I will personally guarantee that, if this illness is discerned as curable for your species and they are given quarantine clearance, they will be returned to either your vessels, to Sallha, or to one of its outlying colonies unharmed, whichever is nearest, in strict accordance with the conventions of the code. However, until this illness is resolved and cured, they will be locked into this ship under Quarantine Extreme, the same as the rest of my crew."*

Seconds stretched into minutes as they considered her offer. However, none of the Salik vessels fired on the *da Gama*, though they did spread out and turn to follow her backwards-sailing course. The bridge door slid open and a cadet in the grey-striped blues of an infirmary medic hurried inside, a bottle of pills in his hand. Ia accepted two from the man, tucking them into her shirt pocket. As he left, the Salik pinged them again.

"The lengthhh of Quarantine Extreme is unknown. Will hhyew provide sssssussstenance for our volunnnteers?"

The query was followed by the *pop-pop-pop* of the speaker smacking his lips. The insult, Salik-style, was one delivered to their enemies just before the amphibious race tried to eat their sentient prey. The few cadets remaining on the bridge shuddered, save for their acting captain.

Ia smiled. If they had been communicating via the

vidscreens instead of merely via audio, she would have bared her teeth, too. *"Most cheerfully, I am required to inform you that feeding potentially contaminated food sources to sentientarian aid-givers is against the rules. Whoever you send will have to bring sufficient supplies of non-sentient foods from their own stores, or chew on the standard Terran ration packets like everyone else . . . and I'll remind you that this disease is hopping between species, so even your non-sentient live food sources will be at risk for contamination."*

Behind her, the door opened, admitting the duly assigned third-watch bridge crew. Most of them had bleary eyes from lack of sleep. A few swallowed quickly, grimacing at the smells left by the missing cadets. With quiet murmurs coordinating everything, they swapped places one at a time with the remaining bridge crew, or left to grab cleaning equipment to sterilize the hastily emptied stations.

"Captain," T'siel warned her, not yet giving up his seat. "The Salik are pinging us again."

Nodding, Ia let him put it on bridgewide broadcast once more. *"This is Captain Ia. You have something to say?"*

"Bring your ssship to a sstop, Hhewmans," the Salik speaker ordered. *"We will sssend over two obserhhvers."*

"Lieutenant Shinowa—*ah,* sorry, Lieutenant Pushnatta, what's the status of the ion storms?" Ia asked, adjusting to the change in bridge crew.

"Still going strong, Captain," he replied, checking his screens.

Shinowa patted him on one restraint-strapped shoulder and picked her way out of the bridge. She, too, had eaten the food from the galley. "I'll report to the infirmary to get my digestive tract pumped, Captain—I'm sure that sounds much more pleasant than it actually will be, but I was the last one to eat and get back, so I'm bound to be contaminated."

"Good idea. Dismissed, Lieutenant." Flicking open the channel once more, Ia addressed the aliens. *"Negative, Salik vessels. The ion storm is still too strong to launch a boarding pod at this time. Accompany us to system's edge, on our current heading and speed. When we're . . . four hours lightspeed ahead of the solar storm front, we'll come to a stop, effect repairs from the asteroid we hit, and board your volunteers."*

"*Negative, Hhhumans. Hhyew will sstop now and outwait the sstorms,*" her counterpart argued.

"*Negative, Salik,*" she replied. "*If we really did pick up this bug from the ice rings in the Ceti Ceti Delta System, we have to proceed there with all speed. There is a risk that other ships might pass through that system, and a risk that they might stop by the rings of the fifth planet to refuel like we did, rather than pick up hydrofuel somewhere in the Oort zone. Sentientarian Spacefaring laws require that we track down the source of the biological contaminant as quickly as possible and either eradicate it, develop and distribute a counteragent, or place Quarantine buoys around the materials in question.*

"*As we're the only ship currently infected, we're the only one worth risking a second wave of contaminants. I repeat, this contaminant is jumping species; your own race is potentially at risk. Those ice rings must be examined for the source-point as soon as possible.*" She paused a beat, waiting for a reply. When none came, Ia added, "*At most, you waste nothing but a day or two: a few hours to get to system edge, a few hours for repairs, a few more hours to get to Ceti Ceti Delta 175 once we have full FTL capacity, and hopefully just a few hours past that to find where we picked up the fuel and discern the extent of the contaminant. You can accompany us all the way to the fifth planet, if you like.*"

"*Hhhyew do not sssound like you are in disstress, Captain,*" the Salik speaker pointed out.

"*That's because I myself haven't eaten anything since before we processed part of the ice into our drinking water. I only drink bottled water while on duty, and don't snack. Naturally, this means I'm rather hungry, but Terran ration packets aren't exactly known for their appetizing qualities. Of course, if you'd like to volunteer, I'd be happy to have one of* you *for lunch, for once.*"

The wheezing-whistling and *smack-smack-smack* of the alien's lips that came over the ship-to-ship channel let her know that her rather morbid, disgusting joke had struck the equivalent of the Salik funny bone.

"*Prosssceed to system's edge on your heading, Hhewman. We will accompany hyew, all of our ships. If you lhhied to usss, I will personally eat your sssoft meats.*"

"*My spleen quivers in anticipation,*" Ia drawled. "*Captain*

Ia out." Shutting off the link, Ia sighed and sagged into her seat cushions. "Well. Now we head for system's edge, and hunt down the *real* source of the contaminant. Lieutenant Commander Zagrieve, pass the word through the ship for crew and cadre to rely only on bottled water and ration packs for sustenance until further notice."

"Aye, sir," the cadet now in charge of ship systems agreed.

The relief watch cadets finished cleaning up the mess left by Chen, Vizzini, and the rest, and took their posts. Ia's right secondary screen lit up again, indicating another direct comm call. Once again, it came from lifesupport.

"This is the Captain, go," she ordered.

"This is Lieutenant Jinja-Marsuu again, Captain. After reviewing the security logs of Lieutenant Wong's actions, both here when he was 'repairing' the water pipe, and back up in the cadre galley . . . the evidence points very strongly to sabotage, sir. You can review it if you want, Captain." Jinja-Marsuu added, *"But the evidence is there. He deliberately poisoned this crew."*

"Lieutenant Broxt, call up your security teams," Ia ordered, covering her headset pickups with one hand as she addressed the new gunnery officer, who doubled as the *da Gama*'s security officer. "Find Lieutenant Wong and throw him in the brig. He was supposed to go to his quarters, but he could be anywhere. The charge is Fatality Thirty-Five, Sabotage."

"Sabotage, sir?" Broxt asked, eyes widening.

"Lieutenant Jinja-Marsuu in lifesupport says she has evidence. *Find* him," Ia stressed, "strip and zip him, and throw him in the brig bare-asteroid naked. If he resists or fights back, tell him that should a trial of his superior officers find him guilty, I will *personally* feed him to the Salik medical observers that are coming on board if he doesn't surrender immediately. And do remind him, in case he has forgotten my Service record, that Marines *don't* bluff. I see no reason why I shouldn't continue that tradition, now that I'm a member of the TUPSF-Navy. Let's hope he doesn't resist, however."

"Understood, sir," her new gunnery officer stated. He readjusted the headset tucked around his ear, moving to comply with her orders.

Lieutenant Commander Zagrieve, scenario-senior-most of

the third-watch cadets, finished relaying orders and checking over his system controls. Turning to face her, he asked, "Captain, are we really going to board Salik *observers* onto this ship?"

"Yes, Commander, we really are," she told him. Not that Ia thought the testers would actually go that far, but she knew they were listening and wanted them to hear the confident determination in her voice. "We are also going to do our damnedest to get the *da Gama*'s starboard bow warp panels repaired, repowered, and the section secured for FTL speeds. Once we do, we are going to head straight for the fifth planet of the Ceti Ceti Delta 175 star system . . . which is more or less in the very same direction we're headed right now.

"The only thing is, that same course will take us right over the top of Battle Platform *Freeman*, which is due to arrive at the rendezvous point around the *ninth* planet at Ceti Ceti Delta, which is on the *near* side of its system relative to us . . . and they will arrive about five hours before we're due to hit the system's edge," she stated. Her mouth quirked up on one side. "We'll drop out early without warning our friendly little escort, and ping the Battle Platform to scramble all ships and fighters. Even if it's undermanned due to an abrupt relocation, the defensive and offensive capabilities of a Battle Platform is easily a match for *twenty* warships, never mind twelve.

"Lieutenant Bruer thought the latest of our problems was a *Kobayashi Maru*," Ia told her fellow cadets. "Under normal circumstances, I'd have to agree with him. Had we been at full health, our choices would have been to fight and die, or be boarded, eaten, and die. But in a strange way, we owe Lieutenant Wong our lives. Unless of course, I'd been quick-witted enough to think of faking an Extreme Quarantine lockdown, and ordered the infirmary to distribute medicines capable of faking a suitable level of illness among the crew." Smirking, she patted her shirt pocket, with its two capsules of emetic medicine. "As it stands, I believe we should all remember this little maneuver for the future."

"Captain . . . you said Marines don't bluff," Broxt stated warily. "Yet isn't *this* a big bluff, what you're having us do? Pretending to be sick from some sort of spaceborne contaminant?"

"It isn't a bluff. If any of this were true, Lieutenant, I'd carry it out in a heartbeat," Ia promised him. "Marines don't bluff. We make promises, and we keep them. We *do*, however, lie to our enemies . . . but only when it's absolutely necessary. Now, eyes back to your boards, gentlemeioas. We have a long way to go to finish pulling this off, and hours of constant vigilance to ensure we *do* pull it off—and not a word about any of this to our 'observers' once they're on board."

He nodded and returned his attention to his workstation. The ventilation system was finally getting the stench of sickness out of the air. Ia debated getting up to fetch a ration packet. Dabbling a mental toe into the nearest timestreams, she decided to refrain.

Four minutes later, the white overhead lights flashed yellow and turned green, and they heard the Eastern European Province accent of their chief tester once more.

"All hands, stand down," Captain Rzhikly announced, voice echoing through the mock starship. *"Congratulazhuns, Class 1252, you heff successfully survived your Hell Veek. Howeffer, you vill clean op each of your messes before you vill be allowed to disembark de ship."*

Ia opened the shipwide comms. *"Acknowledged, Captain Rzhikly. All hands, this is Acting Captain Ia. You are under orders to scrub-and-shine from stem to stern. Consider this your last task of the simulation. Captain Rzhikly, for the sake of quelling false rumors among those who were on the bridge or in the infirmary, I respectfully request that you please explain to everyone on board exactly how we ended up sick, and why."*

"Reqvest granted. All hands, Cadet Wong vas asked to join de testers for a moment vhen he left de bridge at de end of de last scenario. He vas instructed by us to simulate sabotage via biological contamination. De illness you are suffering is nothing more dan a time-released liqvid emetic, very much similar to de version Acting Captain Ia ordered distributed in order to fake further illnezzes. You vill, of course, be reqvired to hand back in each and every distributed emetic pill before you vill be allowed to leave de ship," he finished. *"Now attend to your cleanup detail. Captain Rzhikly out."*

"You heard the Captain," Ia sighed, unbuckling her safety harness. "Let's grab some gloves, buckets, and cleaner bottles, meioas. Don't think for a moment the enlisted sailors will do it all for us."

"Let me guess: The best leaders lead by example, and all that rot," one of the other cadets muttered. "I just thank god we weren't slipped a diarrhetic on top of the emetic."

Disgust warred with amusement across the bridge, finally settling into a collection of wry chuckles from most of them, Ia included. She lost her humor as she exited the bridge, erased by a stray thought.

A pity this was only a simulation. I can warn, and warn, and warn . . . but to some beings in this galaxy, I'm nothing more than an ancient Cassandra, whose prophetic warnings went utterly unheeded, however true they turned out to be. But I will be believed by everyone else before all of this is through. Everything depends on it.

At least the rest of my time here will be easy to endure. We don't have that much longer before Class 1252 graduates . . . and then . . . Right. Don't think about any elephants just yet, Ia, she ordered herself, taking a pair of gloves from the box being passed back to her by two cadets who had gotten into the supply closet ahead of her. *You have other problems to pursue.*

SEPTEMBER 1, 2493 T.S.
SOUTHEAST OF SINES, PORTUGAL, WESTERN EUROPROVINCE
EARTH

"I don't believe you," Meyun dismissed. Head propped up on one palm, the other covering the muscles of her stomach, he shook his head slightly. "An entire planet of colonists experiences massive, widespread, spontaneous bouts of precognition? Even the non-gifted members of sentiency?"

"It's true. The Gatsugi, the K'katta, the Solaricans, and the Tlassians have all experienced it, the same as the Humans," Ia told him, shrugging. "The Chinsoiy don't like the electrosphere's energies, the Dlmvla can't tolerate the atmosphere, and the Salik have been Blockaded all this time, so we don't have any information on them, of course."

"What about the Choya?" he asked.

She rested her head back against the pillows of their shared bed and sighed. "Of all the sentient species, the Choya—and the Salik—are *truly* mind-blind. Zero psychic sensitivities, and zero abilities whatsoever. I think it's something biological, some neural wiring or protein combination they're missing . . . Anyway, the few rare Choya to risk the high gravity didn't sense a thing. Not during *any* visits, not that we know about. The Fire Girl Prophecies are truly the single weirdest thing about my homeworld."

"Well, how do they *know* these prophecies are truly prophetic?" Meyun pressed.

"When the Elders of the Church of the One True God arrived on Sanctuary, they had already designed plans for the Great Cathedral. The holopics of the mock-up matched *exactly* to the visions everyone was having, of a great cathedral catching on fire. Only they hadn't *shown* everyone the final draft of the models before that point, just the few on the Church Council," Ia told him. "When they discovered people who didn't even know what the cathedral would look like were having visions of it being built, and then possibly destroyed—the images aren't entirely clear as to which will actually happen, which is the usual nature of precognition—well, they realized these were true psychic visions."

Meyun shook his head, frowning slightly. "How is it a whole planet of colonists can experience these visions? Is it something in the water? In the air? In the food? If even the tourists get it, it's obviously not a genetic mutation."

Ia shrugged eloquently. "No one can say. And you can experience it the moment you come into the troposphere, never mind actually land on the planet, breathe the air, drink the water, or eat the food. In fact, it could even be a side effect of the planet's electrosphere meddling with our brains. So. Your turn. What is the single weirdest thing about Dabin, in your opinion?"

"I'll have to think about that one. My home's not nearly as strange as yours," he demurred.

Ia nodded, letting him think. This cottage, tucked into the hills overlooking some of the villages south of Sines, was quiet, peaceful, and secluded. Perfect for a four-day tryst. It had taken her most of a day to quell the guilt over taking this time for herself, but Meyun had proven to be quite distracting when he put his mind to it.

In fact, his hand on her stomach, thumb subtly caressing her bare skin, was still quite distracting. It reminded her of all the other things his hands had done with her in the last two days, as well as other body parts. The things he had showed her . . .

"Passion moss," he stated out of the blue.

"Hmm?" She looked at his face.

"Passion moss," Meyun repeated. "It grows on the northwest continent, and comes in shades of yellow and orange and red, and even hints of purple, and the oil it secretes when it's in bloom—if a moss-like plant could be said to bloom—enhances the fertility cycles of all the native animals around it. In fact, biologists have even been able to artificially induce fertility by coaxing the moss to bloom and ooze its oil. But only in the native animals. It doesn't do anything for the imported livestock."

"How does it smell to nonnatives?" she asked, curious.

He wrinkled his nose. "Like oily, burnt plexi with hints of sugar. Some people like it, but most can't stand it. There are rumors that some of the newest generations are starting to be affected by it," he added, subtly rubbing her stomach, "but it's such a subjective thing, the scientists aren't yet convinced it's a planetary adaptation. It's probably just a placebo effect."

Ia chuckled. "If they ever do adapt, your homeworld will have a major population explosion."

"Well, it's rare for a genetic mutation to crop up so quickly, so I think it's just psychosomatic at best, like most so-called aphrodisiacs," he dismissed. Then grinned and slid his hand upward, exploring a different part of her skin. "I suppose we'll just have to rely on the old-fashioned methods of rousing passion."

Smirking back at him, she slid a hand down his chest, doing some exploring of her own. Her smile turned wry, wistful. "I am going to miss you, you know. Not just this," she added, tickling his bare stomach, making him squirm and grin, "but everything else. Talking with you, laughing with you, getting to know you . . . and even being surprised by you. Meyun . . . You have *no* idea just how rare that is."

"Maybe I can convince you to save up some of your Leave time for me." He leaned forward and kissed the corner of her mouth. "In the meantime, let me surprise you some more . . . unless you can guess what's on my mind?"

She grinned and pulled him closer. "I don't have to be a telepath to guess *that*."

SEPTEMBER 3, 2493 T.S.

Bliss. Sweet, aching bliss. For the first time in a very, very long time, nothing existed for Ia but this: The moment of *now*. No past, no future, just right *now*.

Rational thought had been replaced by pure feeling. This close to him, this intimate, she could sense his every thought, his every emotion. Yet never had she felt so safe, so free. Euphoria filled her with soul-deep longing. *Ohhh . . . if only I could stay here forever . . .*

Meyun groaned and kissed her throat. "I don't want you to leave."

"I don't *want* to leave." The confession escaped her in a whisper, bittersweet bliss. So many possibilities hovered on the edge of her consciousness, the timeplains so close, so many potentialities almost within her grasp. No thought existed of caution, nor of control, only of wistful wishes. Such closeness bred a level of comfort and trust Ia hadn't expected.

Clinging to him, she let the bliss carry her forward, deep into herself. Deep into him. Like her limbs, her mind entwined itself around him, cradling him in this precious moment. *If only we had more Time . . .*

A unity of thought, as much his own as hers. Shuddering, he whispered fervently, "If only we had more *time* together . . ."

Time.

Time. Word and thought, sense and psyche. They dragged her—both of them—onto the timeplains. Ruthless, remorseless Time.

Meyun gasped, eyes wide. A golden explosion of amber-hued water enveloped them, a tsunami of possibilities. Caught off guard, too closely entwined, it was all Ia could do to cling to him, to try and keep him from drowning. It didn't work. Flailing for purchase, for understanding, for anything, Meyun dragged both of them under.

Them. *That was the key word. Images flashed through the waves crashing through their senses. Scenes of him, of her. Intimate moments, public moments, laughing with friends, weeping over deaths, scenes of battle, scenes of domestic bliss. Children—the children they could have, should have, would have. Enemies—tearing them apart, carving them up, scorching the universe*

*and stealing their last breath. Pride in accomplishments . . .
and regret. Regret for the deaths of innocents . . . and the madness that surged up because of it.*

Regret. *That wasn't the word for it.*

*Madness, death, despair, destruction. The golden light with-
ered and turned an arid, lifeless, fiery brown. The water chilled
and froze, filled with the bodies of untold lives, slaughtered and
wasted. They pressed in, ice-cold and clammy, bumping closer
and closer in the sloshing waters of Time with inexorable horror. Their arms, their legs, their corpses pushes against the
two lovers. Pushed them apart, though Meyun screamed in
wordless bubbles and tried to cling to her.*

*The galaxy burned, the dead froze, her lover lived and died,
lived and died, lived and died . . . all because she wanted to
reshape Time for herself.*

*Climbing onto the banks, saving a future for her and Meyun,
that would only be met by the fires of her conscience. The
flames of destruction would burn away her sanity. If she stayed
in the water, the ice of her duty would freeze everything else
she wanted right out of her life. If she stayed immersed in the
waters, she would drown from the effort of trying to push everyone else out. If she climbed onto the bank . . . every world
would burn, and the stars would be snuffed out.*

Everything would die, because she wanted things for
herself.

"NO!"

Desperation thrust them out of the timeplains. Thrust them
out of the water. Thrust him physically and mentally away from
her, off of the bed. He hit the wall with an *oof* and thumped to
the carpeted floor.

Once again, she had chosen the ice over the fire. To drown,
rather than let everything burn. And it *hurt*. It hurt because this
time, she had *seen* the personal cost to her . . . and to the one
she loved. Now Ia *knew* why she hadn't been able to see him
in Time. Not because he somehow didn't exist, but because he
was the single greatest threat to her plans. Her gifts had pro-
tected her by sheer instinct, until now.

Love was the one thing that *could* sway her from her path,
as well as keep her on her self-imposed course. Love for this
wonderful man, a very concrete, tangible, and real love that

would be returned wholeheartedly . . . versus love for the untouchable, unknowing, uncaring, unrequiting universe.

Love that could save her sanity, or love that would steal it away.

Tears welled up and spilled over in a silent rain of regret. On the floor at the foot of the bed, Meyun groaned, recovering from his stupor of too many visions, too much information. "Oh, god . . . oh, god . . . what . . . what am I seeing? Ia, what am I *seeing*?"

Concerned by his dazed demand, she scrambled to the end of the bed, scrubbing at her tears. He had pushed himself onto all fours, but his dark brown eyes gazed through the foot of the bed. He wasn't seeing anything in *this* world. Warily, she extended a hand. Her fingertips brushed against the locks of his hair, connected with his brow.

He was still on the timeplains, immersed in the waters of his own multiple lifestreams. Of *their* multiple lifestreams . . .

Shock snatched her hand back from his brow. Panic sent her mind racing. This was nothing she had experienced before—none of her brothers, none of her followers, no one she had touched had ever been trapped on the timeplains once she withdrew her touch.

"Ia?" he asked, pushing up onto his knees, only to sag to one side, visibly disoriented. "*Ia?* Why can't I see you anymore?"

"It . . . it's going to be alright—I can fix this," she muttered, mind racing in frantic circles. "I *can* fix it . . . I think . . ." She castigated herself a moment later. *Stupid stupid stupid!*

Closing her eyes, Ia blocked out his sightless gaze, his groping hand. The first step was to fix *herself*, to stop the useless, energy-draining panic. Reaching for the old centering exercises, she breathed in deep, gathering in her scattered sense of self. Exhaling, she reabsorbed her fragmented thoughts, her faceted personalities, and pushed out the negativity and fear. In again to blend, out again to cleanse. By the third breath, her thoughts were stabilized. By the fourth, she was calm.

Or at least calm enough to act. Slipping off the end of the bed, Ia caught his hand. He clutched at her, mind still racing too fast, too full. Cupping the side of his face, she insinuated her thoughts into his. Dove gently back into the waters, rather than plunging without control as before.

. . . He was swimming. Stormy waters crashed and sloshed, and he was barely afloat, but he was somehow swimming. Ia swam as well, used to the waters. Getting close to him, she reached for Meyun's hand as lightning flashed, bringing with it another stream of possibilities.

"I can help you out!" she shouted, trying to catch his attention as well as his hand. "Meyun, I can get you out of the water! But you have to trust me!"

That focused him on her, not on the visions swirling in the waters around them. "You? Trust you?" he shouted back. "You're going to leave me in here!—You're going to leave me to die!"

"*Shakk* that, I love you too much to *let* you die!"

Grabbing his hand, Ia pulled them out of the raging lake the timestreams had become. By sheer force of will, she separated each potential-probable-possible future back into its own unique, disparate streambed. Holding on to him grimly, she reorganized Time itself, water and wind whipping around them, grass and storm and streaks of light forced into separation until the amber-drenched grasslands unrolled around them, resettling into an orderly network of life and light.

"What . . . what *is* this place?" Meyun asked her, peering at the rolling fields and interweaving waters.

"Time." The word echoed as it always did, like thunder, though this time it darkened the skies in memory of the storm that had swept him up and held him prisoner. Ia forced the skies to stay clear and free of dusk's gloom, to brighten in the golden light of afternoon. "I'm never quite sure if it's all in my head . . . or if I've somehow tapped into the actual dimension . . . I never told you what I am, nor what I can do. I couldn't risk it. I didn't . . .

"Meyun, I couldn't *see* you," Ia confessed awkwardly, looking at him warily. "Of all the lives and life-choices around me, of all the possible, potential, probable paths in the future, I couldn't see *you*." She looked down at the waters beyond their feet, orderly streams of images like liquefied vids. Rippling snapshots of existence, they surfaced and sunk almost randomly. "Any grey spot, any blank, any anomaly, was and is a danger to my task."

"What task is *that*?" he challenged her, gaze fixed on her face. "I saw horrible things. Destruction, death . . ."

It was the same conversation she'd replayed hundreds of times with others here on the timeplains. She looked away from him, off to the future and the desert in the distance. "As melodramatic as it sounds, I'm trying to stop the galaxy from being destroyed. I'm setting up a path of dominoes, each to be knocked down at the right time and place, to prevent an extragalactic invasion centuries from now. I am . . . I *was* supposed to be ignoring the side possibilities that would otherwise lead away from that path. Including things like dating."

He looked at her. "But I know we could have a good life . . . good lives . . ."

Ia shook her head slowly, still not quite looking at him. "I told you I never wanted to hurt you, Meyun. I knew when I was fifteen that I'd have to give up quite a lot. But I never foresaw you. And . . . I would beg your forgiveness, but I suspect you aren't in a mood to forgive me for what I have and will have done."

"Get me out of here," he growled. "Return both of us to sanity—to reality!"

Sighing, Ia complied. Grasping his hand, she flipped both of them inside and up again, pulling them out of the golden light of the timeplains, and back into the half-shadowed light of their rented cottage bedroom.

Meyun shuddered as he came back to himself. A moment later, he flinched away from her fingertips. Away from her. Ia let him move away. While he sagged back against the base of the wall, slumped and struggling to deal with whatever he had seen in Time, she rose and padded over to the closet.

Shrugging into one of the complimentary robes that came with the use of the rental house, Ia brought the other one back to him. When he didn't reach for it, she dropped it onto his lap, letting the nubbly white fabric pool over his knees. It did seem to give him something to focus on. His hand shifted to touch the material, fingers first resting, then clenching. A frown of confusion creased his brow.

"You're going to Antarctica."

"What?" Ia asked him, confused. The statement had come out of nowhere, a non sequitur in an already unstable moment.

He looked up at her. "It was one of the things I saw. I had a . . . a vision of you, an older you, and you—*we*—were in Antarctica."

"That's impossible," Ia said flatly.

"No, it felt *real*," he argued. "I *was* there, at your side. Or will be."

She shook her head. "No, I mean that's impossible, because I'm going to walk away from you."

He pushed to his feet. He fumbled and clutched at the robe, shrugging into it, and faced her. "I *know* what I saw. You were a ship's captain, I was a commander, and we were going to . . . to steal schematics for something from a . . . a place you called the Vault of Time—*why* would you walk away from me? Away from *us*?"

Ia shifted back a step, putting distance between them; his demand had made her flinch, and she didn't like what his vision implied. He stepped forward, closing the gap between them. His hands caught at the sleeves of her robe, holding her in place.

"Ia . . . why can't I see you?" Meyun asked her, staring into her eyes. "Why can't we be together?"

She could see him now, in the timestreams. Not always clearly, but she could finally see the consequences of allowing him to stay with her. *This is going to hurt* . . . "Because you'll distract me. You will distract me so *much* that I will fail. And failure is *not* an option."

"*Shova v'shakk!*" he swore. "You may only *think* you know—"

"I have known for five *years*!" she snapped back. "I can see *every* possibility, and I have searched every corner of Time itself for some *other* way to get through to what must be done. Do you honestly think I would be in the military if I had any other choice? I grew up wanting to be a singer. A *singer*, Harper! Innocent. A civilian. With *un*stained hands."

She lifted her hands, fingers curled into claws at the memory of all the blood she had spilled so far, and in warning of all the lives she had yet to take. His hands slipped from her sleeves at the movement, letting her clutch the air between them.

"I dropped out of school and spent half a *year* of my life trying to find *any* sane path that would stop the coming invasion and save our galaxy—you spent a *minute* in the timestreams!" she scorned. "What do *you* know about the path I need to take? Or sacrifices I'll have to make? Or the ones I've *already* made? *Yes*, I will walk away from you. For *two* reasons. One . . . because the feelings I have for you are a distraction and a liability. Because my *sanity* is on the line. I cannot, *dare not* fail because I'll have a trillion screaming lives echoing in my brain until the day I die!

"And for the other . . . I *promised* I wouldn't hurt you." She held his gaze fiercely, willing him to understand. "If I tried to divert the future so we *could* stay together, I'd hurt you a lot more than I already have. A *lot* more."

He started to argue the point. His breath caught in his throat, his eyes unfocusing for a moment. "Suicide . . ."

"I'll be driven mad. Literally mad. And worse," she agreed quietly. "Meyun . . . I may not have *wanted* to go into the military, but when I realized what course the future would have to take, I made a pledge to *myself*. As long and as strong a vow as that which *any* soldier makes to defend their country, their people, and their beloved homes. I swore a solemn oath that I would do *anything* to save the future of our beloved homes. It's the only way I *can* retain my sanity."

"Such as it is," Meyun shot back, though without much heat. He stared at her for several seconds, then flipped his hands helplessly, taking a step back. "So you'd just walk away? No second thoughts, no looking back, no hesitations, or even a single regret?"

"I didn't say *that*," Ia retorted, folding her arms over her robe-draped chest. They glared at each other for a moment, then Meyun lowered his gaze. Ia let out a shaky breath, looking away. "All I wanted . . . was one moment of peace. A moment to call my own. Some . . . some *semblance* of everything I must otherwise give up—the same things I'm fighting a race against Time itself to give to everyone *else*.

"Something to warm my heart when the days ahead grow long and cold . . . but that one *golden* moment has turned to useless dross and slag. Regrets? Oh, *yes*, I have regrets. But no matter how much I love you, I will *not* be distracted from my task," she stated roughly, slashing a hand between them. "If you cannot understand just how important this is, or at least how important it is to *me* . . . then we have nothing more to say."

He wrapped his arms tight across his chest. "It's not like you're giving us—*me*—that much of a say, anyway."

"I wish I could, Meyun," she confessed softly. "But you've only had a small taste of what it's like to be me. A single bitter drop from my ocean of misery."

"An ocean of misery?" Meyun challenged. "Well, you *seem* to be fully capable of enjoying life."

"Well, maybe I'm just a good actress. Or maybe I'm just a masochist," she offered.

Meyun snorted at that. It wasn't entirely mirthful, though her quip did feel like it had softened some of the sharper edges buried in the mood between them.

Shaking her head, she gazed at her former roommate and brief lover. "I'm *sorry* I hurt you, Meyun. I truly am. I'd give up a lot to be able to go back in time and *not* hurt you. I just . . . I cannot give up the universe. I cannot give up my conscience, and I cannot give up my duty, and I *cannot* give up the future. I'd gladly give you my heart," Ia offered, "but my life is no longer my own. I've already traded that."

Meyun gave her a sarcastic look. "Trade it for *what*? Your sanity?"

"That, and saving the lives of everyone else." She gave him a lopsided smile. "You could say I got a real bargain."

"You're going to throw away *your* life for people you don't . . . even . . ." Faltering at his own words, he hung his head. "You're doing what *I'm* doing. What any soldier would do."

"Just on a larger, far more complex scale." She started to say more, but a horrified look widened his eyes.

"You . . . you're going to have your *ovaries* removed?" Meyun stared at her as if she had grown a second set of arms, Gatsugi-like. "Why would you do *that*?"

She didn't realize that was one of the visions he had seen in the timestream flood. Uncomfortable, she tightened the arms folded across her chest and gave him the truth. A modified piece of the truth. "One set will be donated to my homeworld, the other to the heavyworld genetics repository, to be distributed to worlds like Eiaven and Parker's, and other 2G-plus planets. Since I don't plan on having any children myself, it makes sense to send them where they'll be of use."

Shaking his head slowly, he leaned back against the wall behind him. "How can you . . . how can you just *give up* something like that?"

She wasn't about to tell him how much her younger self had agonized over this choice as a teen. "Some people are born to be mothers. Others aren't. I've never been maternal, but there are women out there who would literally do anything to be fertile. Why should I hog all my eggs to myself, when they actually want them?"

It seemed to take him a few moments to absorb that idea. Ia gave him the time to think about it. Finally, Meyun shook his head. "That is just . . . *not* the choice I would have made. I, *ah*, can respect your reasons, but . . ."

"It's the best choice, really." She didn't know if she was trying to convince him, or reconvince herself. Ia shrugged. "I'm career military, heading into an unofficial war zone. They'll be removed between flight school and shipping out to the Salik Interdicted Zone—thank you for respecting my right to choose what to do with them."

Meyun shrugged, then raked his hands through his hair. "What else could I do? It's your body, not mine. Though a part of me . . ."

He didn't finish that thought out loud, just shrugged and folded his arms across his chest again. Moving to the bed, Ia sat on its edge. She tucked the edges of her robe over her legs. "So . . . What do we do now?"

"What do we do? What do you mean, what do we do?" he retorted. "Can't you already tell?"

She gave him a chiding look. "Meyun, I above all others know that the future is *fluid*. And I told you, I cannot see *you* clearly. Or I couldn't. Now I can *sort of* see you in the future. Some of the potential possibilities, but not all of them. I think it's my mind trying to protect me from myself . . ."

That earned her a confused look. "What do you mean, protecting you from yourself?"

Ia shrugged, tightening her arms protectively under her breasts. "If anything happened to you, I'd . . . want to prevent it, whatever it was. Which could upset the delicate flow of events that *must* progress, if I am to achieve my goals. Which means if we stay away from each other, there's less of a chance I'd be tempted to veer off course."

"Is that what you want?" he asked tersely.

"*No.* But it's what I *need* to do." Sighing, she ran a hand over her short locks. "I should pack and go to the Afaso Headquarters . . ."

His eyes widened at that. "No . . . *no*, if you go there, you'll

die! I've seen it, in one of the visions. A hovertaxi accident."
Dropping to one knee, Meyun caught her hands. "*Don't* go to
Madagascar."

Even knowing it was really the wrong response, given the
intensity of his reaction, Ia couldn't stop the laugh that escaped
her. She squeezed his fingers. "Meyun, *don't worry*. What you
saw was just one of the *many* possibilities that could happen if
I ever go there. Trust me, I'd see it coming, and take a completely different cab. I have no intention of dying anytime soon."

He squeezed her fingers in his, holding her gaze intensely.
"Don't you *ever* die, you hear me?"

That made her roll her eyes. "Meyun, *everybody* dies. Even
the Feyori, though it takes them a few thousand years." She
started to say more, but honesty prompted her to tilt her head
and amend, "Well, everyone except for the Immortal, but technically she *can* be killed. She just keeps popping back to life
afterward. Which is why the Feyori think she's so dangerous,
and why they want her destroyed somehow."

Brow creasing, Meyun gave her a confused frown. "You . . .
We've had this conversation before. Or . . . will have had it . . . ?
In the Vault of Time—Ia, what *is* the Vault of Time? And what
is it doing here on Earth, if it's the creation of . . . of some sort
of Feyori?"

"Don't ask—*don't*," she asserted. "Don't go there, don't try
to get inside, don't even think about it. Just put it from your
mind. As much as having you around would be a severe distraction and a danger to my goals, having the Vault's owner take
an interest in anyone even remotely connected to me would be
an outright disaster."

"Why? Would she try to stop you?"

Ia shook her head. "Worse. She'd try to help."

He started to speak, then sighed. "Right . . . because some
kinds of help end up being far worse than the problem at hand,
don't they? Is that why you don't want me at your side? You
think I'd mess things up for you?"

Instinct warned her this was one of *those* questions. One
she had to answer carefully. Ia opted for honesty, because that
was the one course least likely to stab her in the back, later. "I
think . . . I *know* you'd want to help me. I think you could actually *be* helpful. But . . ."

"But?" he prodded her.

"There is no way that our paths will cross in the next few years," Ia told him bluntly. "Even if you weren't such a huge distraction, our orders will keep us apart. You're headed to the Terran–Tlassian Border for the next six months, whereas I'm headed off to flight school for the next three, then being shipped out to the Blockade. We won't get within four hundred lightyears of each other, Meyun," she told him. "Not unless the probabilities shift you to that seventeen percent chance that you'll wind up on Blockade for your second tour of duty. But even then, we won't be on the same patrol routes. Trying to keep something going between us would be an exercise in futility and frustration. A distraction for *both* of us."

He looked down and away at that. With her fingers tucked into his, she could sense the press of the thoughts racing silently through his head. She did not pry, though she could sense him coming to some sort of conclusion, and the resolve backing it. When he lifted his head again, she met his gaze steadily, gripping his hands.

"Fine. We'll part ways, as we originally planned. But not without a cost," he warned her. Dropping her hands as he rose from his knees, he pushed her back onto the bed. "I've never considered myself as a bastard type before now, but I plan on making *damn* sure you will regret walking away from me."

Trust me, I already do, Ia promised him silently, arms already lifting to help bring him back down to her.

CHAPTER 13

The stress and performance pressure required of Service personnel serving on the Blockade were such that, per capita, it had the highest ratio of psychologists, psychiatrists, and parapsychologists to soldiers in the Terran Space Force. I suppose it was similarly high in any of the Alliance races serving to keep the Salik confined to their worlds, but I can only speak from the Terran Human perspective with the greatest certainty. Blockade Patrol personnel cycled through much more rapidly than in any other position, with roughly half serving two duty posts in a row, and less than 20 percent serving for a full year.

I've been asked many times through the years, how could I remain stable, constantly exposed to danger, violence, death? I am stable because I not only know I can do something about it, I am doing something about it. My code of conduct will allow nothing less. My duty and my conscience will permit nothing less.

That, and I had my own personal chaplain-counselor officially assigned to me by the DoI by the time I left flight school. They wanted to make absolutely sure I remained stable, in the hopes I could prove to be all that they wanted me to be. Luckily for them, I've always tried to be all that they've needed me to be.

~Ia

JANUARY 1, 2494 T.S.
BATTLE PLATFORM *MAD JACK*
SS'NUK NEH 2238 SYSTEM

"Happy New Year, everyone!" The cheerful call came from a woman clad in Army greens. She was carrying a bin of supplies and peered around the large package as she maneuvered her way through the lobby of the transient soldiers' hotel on Battle Platform *Mad Jack*. The woman received several callbacks.

"Happy New Year!" "Happy New Year!" "Enjoy the last holiday for a while!"

"*Happy* New Year? Why in the name of mutant squirrel nuts are we even *celebrating* that?" someone else catcalled back. The young soldier, one green-clad leg over the arm of his chair, his head resting on the padded back, flicked his hand. "It's not even relevant, anymore. Earth isn't the only world we're occupying, and it certainly doesn't share the same solar rotation as any other planet we've colonized. Certainly it isn't on the same cycle that this miserable, slime-covered rock uses."

Done with checking out of her room, Ia grabbed the handles of her weight suit case and kitbag. Bennie, at her side, looked like she was going to speak. Ia answered the Army private first.

"Time is relative, meioa-o; that's a given. But the Command Staff says we have to use Terran Standard time, so we have to use Terran Standard time. So Happy New Year, for what it's worth." She started to move toward the lobby doors, then checked herself. "And if that doesn't suit you, then have a Happy Mutant Squirrel Nut Day."

Rather than sulking and arguing further, the young man burst into laughter. "I'll do that, thank you!"

Bennie snickered. Strolling beside Ia, she accompanied the younger woman out onto the promenade overlooking the atrium. It was part and parcel of the Battle Platform's lifesupport systems, though it was designed to look more like a pleasure garden, with its fruit trees and berry bushes, its carp ponds with waterfalls and scattering of tables and chairs. It smelled as fresh and green and sweet as the biotechnicians and botanists could make it. Ia still thought it needed the spark-smell of ozone to be complete, but instead, there was a faint, persistent odor of cleaning products.

She sneezed.

"Bless you," Bennie murmured. "Need a tissue?"

Ia sniffed experimentally, then shook her head. "No, I'm fine. And you don't have to walk me all the way to the *Audie-Murphy*. I'm a big girl, I can find my way."

"Hey, I told you, the brass on both sides want me to keep an eye on you," the redhead warned her. "Just because you've survived a tough Border Patrol doesn't mean you'll be just as fine on Blockade duty. So I'm supposed to mother-hen you until the last minute or whatever."

"How does one mother-hen a fellow adult, anyway?" Ia quipped. "For that matter, how does one mammal mother-hen another mammal?"

"Oh, *now* you show off your sense of humor?" Bennie mocked, and nudged Ia in the side with her elbow.

Ia winced and subtly covered her abdomen with the arm carrying her kitbag. Modern medicine and biokinetic abilities were fine for the physical aches, but mentally, she still missed her reproductive organs. A pair of hormone-releasing spheres in their place took care of the chemical needs of her body, but not the needs of her mind. *For which, I blame Meyun, for making me think about what I was giving up . . . and for the implication that he* wanted *to have children with me.*

Mindful of the woman at her side, Ia shoved away her darker thoughts. The regret-filled ones. "If you don't like it, I can always pack it away again."

"No, no, you'll need it," Bennie dismissed. "Just don't go so far into a sense of humor that you start laughing as you lop off heads out there. You might start lopping off the wrong heads, and that would be bad."

"Not in this lifetime, I promise you that," Ia murmured. The corner of her mouth quirked up. "I'll save that for my next life."

"You're a reincarnationist?" the chaplain at her side asked, reaching for the lift buttons as they reached a bank of elevators. "I know you said you were Unigalactan, branch Witan, and your personnel file says sect Zenobian . . . but there isn't much in the records on *what* the Zenobian Sect believes."

"I have encountered some compelling reasons for believing in reincarnation," Ia admitted lightly, ignoring the other half of Bennie's comment. The lift arrived, and they stepped inside, joining a group of blue-clad soldiers on their way somewhere. A touch of the buttons lifted them up a few floors.

Bennie didn't say anything, waiting as they rode the lift, exited, and crossed to the tram that would carry them sideways through the massive battle station. When the car they entered proved to be empty, the chaplain asked, "So . . . care to talk about these encountered reasons? Or what these Zenobians believe in?"

"Nope. They don't really matter," Ia said. The tram swayed, and both women grasped one of the poles inside, swerving with the subtle curve of the tram's circular track through the station. Catching the chaplain's wrinkled nose, she shook her head. "Bennie, while I am a card-carrying priestess of one of the local branches of the Witan Order on my homeworld, and am thus qualified to philosophize with the best of theologians, to try and debate the theological implications of a belief or disbelief in reincarnation when I am very much interested in focusing on *this* life would be a futile exercise in sophistry at best, and an annoyance at worst. Now, do you really want me annoyed?"

That made the older woman chuckle. "If you had said, 'do you really want to annoy me,' I might have said yes, since that can be fun. But no, I don't actually want you to *be* annoyed. And I'd ask you why you didn't ask for a cushy chaplain's job if you really are an ordained clergywoman, except after following your career for the last two and a half years, I know better. Have you talked with your family recently?"

Ia took the change in topic in stride. "No, but my plan is to shamelessly abuse my officer's privileges and call home from the ship on the military's tenth chit."

That made her friend chuckle. "Just make sure you do that *before* leaving the Battle Platform. No extraneous—"

"Yes, yes, no extraneous calls are to be made while on patrol, because they'd be a distraction and a potential security risk," Ia dismissed. "I did pay attention to the Standard Operational Procedures lecture when I got here. The same as you did. At least, you didn't *seem* to be falling asleep next to me."

"I hid it very well," Bennie quipped. "All those years of seminary school were good for something, you know."

The tram came to a stop and they disembarked into a small crowd of Navy personnel. The two waded through the mostly enlisted group. Bennie's chaplain pins, larger than her rank insignia, earned her polite nods and friendly smiles. Ia's single brass bar on each blue collar point and shoulder board earned her polite nods and a slightly wider berth than Chaplain Benjamin, despite the older woman's much higher-ranking silver oak leaves.

If she had been a normal graduate of a naval academy, Ia should have had only a small brass square as the mark of an ensign, not the longer bar of a lieutenant. Being a Field Commissioned officer with more than a month of leadership in the field and good marks from her superiors let her skip the tedious "learn how to be an ensign-ranked officer in the field" stage of her post-academy military career. Of course, no enlisted soldier ever earned a Field Commission without first learning how to lead as a noncommissioned officer, whether that was as a sergeant or a petty officer, but there were instances where a prematurely advanced rank had been rescinded. The chance that she would be busted back down to ensign was slim, though.

Flipping up the screen of her arm unit as they walked, Bennie consulted the station's schematic. "Not much farther. Good. This station has a different configuration than I'm used to. It doesn't help that it's so huge."

"It's not that much different. You're just used to accessing a ship like the *Liu Ji* via the docking gantries. The Delta-VX Harrier Class ships use docking bays," Ia pointed out. "Repair work goes much faster if you can do it in an atmosphere, even if most of it's modular."

"You don't like the convenience of modular ships?" Bennie asked.

Ia wrinkled her nose. "I'm not sure I like everything being so uniform; once the enemy analyzes a component, they know the configuration, strengths, and weaknesses for that part on just about any other ship."

"Well, we kind of *had* to jump-start our starship assembly system with modular units," Bennie pointed out. "Joining the Salik War with just a handful of spaceships capable of interstellar travel made it vital to mass-manufacture the things. The only things that got manufactured even faster were the hyperrelay communication satellites that turned the tide of the war for the Alliance. Since the whole chain assembly thing worked out so well, why complain?"

"God bless Henry Ford, *eyah*?" Ia quipped.

"Hoo-rah," Bennie quipped, echoing the Marines rallying cry. The upraised fist she made drew a chuckle out of Ia.

"Nice to see the Corps is rubbing off on you. Here we are; this is the right bay." Ia nodded at the large, thick, half-silvered plexglass window next to the airlock doors. The view allowed them to see the usual suspects in a maintenance hangar, masses of robotic equipment, engineering mechsuits, testing equipment, and the impression of a pair of oversized courier ships mating back-to-back, one resting upside down over the other.

Bennie peered through the window. "So that's what a VX looks like? But . . . wouldn't it be rather awkward to be upside down that close to a second set of gravity plating?"

"The upper half isn't actually upside down, on the inside," Ia said. She tapped the window, tracing on it with her finger to separate each section as she explained. "When one ship proved to be taking too much of a pounding on its own, but constantly running two ships that close together in FTL proved too risky, someone got the brilliant idea to invert the shells to each other, connect them via the fore and aft airlocks on the dorsal sides, and arrange plug-in ports for everything from data streams to lifesupport."

Ia inverted one hand over the back of the other, echoing the look of the two butterfly-like sections, then parted them as she continued, swerving her hands in imitation of combat.

"They can separate in combat to have twice the maneuverability and a little extra firepower, and if one gets damaged, the other can swoop in and pick it back up. The ventral airlocks are in the same place as the dorsal ones, so they can be matched up the other way around if need be, in case one or both sets of dorsal connections are damaged too much to connect. All in all, it's a good design," Ia praised. She outlined the swept-back, triangular wings, tracing them on the window. "Both halves are fully functional as tri-state ships, too. They can fly in an atmosphere, maneuver with insystem thrusters, and each half can spark a hyperrift for OTL between star systems."

A wistful smile curved up the corner of her mouth. Bennie caught sight of it and arched a brow. "You really like these ships?"

"My brothers hung up models of them, or rather of ships like them, growing up. This newer model came out about . . . five years ago?" She shrugged, dismissing the exact date as irrelevant. Pulling back from the window, Ia studied the sign-board next to the airlock door.

The signboard read, "TUPSF *Audie-Murphy*," followed by the jumble of letters and numbers that were its registry code, the name of its commanding officer and Navy organization numbers, the timestamp for when it had docked, the timestamp for when it was due to depart, and a scrolling checklist of redlit, yellowlit, and greenlit repairs in various stages of high priority, low priority, and completed status respectively.

"Of course, I never dreamed I'd wind up on one of these ships myself, as a little girl." Resting the weight suit case on its wheels, she dug into her kitbag and fished out her Dress Blues jacket and cap. Shrugging into the former and donning the latter, she checked the faint image of her reflection in the docking bay window, buttoning and adjusting her uniform. When she was done, she faced her friend. "How do I look?"

"Officer-ish," Bennie promised. "Wait a moment. One of your piloting pins is crooked." Stepping close, the redhead adjusted one of the pins on Ia's shoulder boards, three pairs of wings forming a triangle shape around the partitioned letters *O/F*.

The pin identified her as having been certified for atmo-spheric, orbital, and insystem maneuvers, plus capable of manning the helm for both other-than-light and faster-than-light interstellar travel. If it had been just the one set of wings, she would have been planet-bound, or just the three, restricted to sub-light speeds. With either an O or an F alone, it would have meant she was qualified to use one or the other, but with the slash, it meant she had passed the exams for both. Doing so had meant spending eight and ten hours a day in flight simu-lators for weeks on end, on top of additional hours of theory and instruction in class each day, but she had passed with rat-ings high enough in OTL for this assignment, and sufficient enough in FTL for future ship assignments.

"There. I kind of feel like a proud mother, sending her little girl off to her first day of school. Except you're not my little girl, and you're fully capable of tearing a K'katta limb from limb," Bennie quipped drolly.

Ia groaned and rolled her eyes. "Not you, too? For the record—yet again—I did *not* actually rip off that K'katta's leg and beat him to death with it!"

The airlock door cycled open just as she got to the "rip off" part of her complaint. From the wide-eyed looks of the petty officer and her three coverall-clad teammates, none of them had heard the "did *not*" disclaimer. A quick probe of the timestreams convinced Ia it wasn't worth pursuing a correction in their minds.

Still, the petty officer was made of stern stuff. Lifting her chin, the shorter woman stepped up to Ia and saluted her, a requirement since Ia was wearing her cap. Belatedly, the three maintenance crewmeioas saluted as well. "Lieutenant, Commander. Chief Petty Officer Browne, Bay 16 Security. Is there something I can do for you, sirs?"

Ia returned the salute. "I'm Lieutenant Second Grade Ia. I'm here with orders to board the TUPSF *Audie-Murphy* under Commander Salish."

"*Ah*, aye, sir. Welcome aboard the *Mad Jack*, Lieutenant," the petty officer added, smiling. "We were told to expect you. The Delta-VXs jump around from bay to bay, depending on which bay is open, but the moment the *Audie-Murphy* came in early, they routed your clearance for this bay, today."

"Thank you. Is the Commander here?" Ia asked her.

"One moment, sir, I'll check," Browne promised.

Since she had a few moments, Ia turned to face Bennie. She held out her hand to the chaplain, but the older woman didn't bother with it. Instead, Bennie embraced Ia and pressed a kiss to her cheek. The move didn't quite twinge Ia's psychic sensitivities awake, but then the chaplain kept her touches brief.

Pulling back, the older woman gripped Ia's blue-sleeved arms lightly. "Since your mothers can't be here, let me give you a blessing in their stead. Or rather, a blessing and a nag. May the Universe protect you and keep you in the warmth of the Light, no matter how deep into the shadows your paths may take you . . . and if you come home with more of your own blood on you than the enemies', I am *never* going to let you live it down. You have a Marine Corps nickname to live up to, sailor."

"Aye, aye, sir," Ia agreed. "I won't disappoint you, sir. I promise."

"Just make sure it's not *gratuitous* amounts of enemy blood," the chaplain warned her, waggling a finger at the younger woman.

"I'll try my best to spill only whatever blood is absolutely necessary, and not one drop more," Ia promised, mock-solemn. Sincere, but mock-solemn.

Bennie rolled her eyes, gave her one last hug, and stepped back. "Just make sure you come back sane and whole, okay? I'll be worrying about you."

"I'll try not to give you anything to worry about, Commander." Saluting, Ia held the pose until Bennie returned it. Grabbing the handle of her weight suit case, she turned back to the petty officer, who stood ready at the airlock door.

"Ident scan, sir?" Chief Petty Browne asked, nodding at the reader by the door controls. "All hangar bays are restricted areas, sir."

Nodding, she held her arm under the projection for a moment. The lights turned green, and the petty officer nodded, unlocking the airlock with her own passcode. Ia followed her through the double doors, hauling her belongings in her wake.

"Once you've been logged into your new duty post, sir, you'll be able to enter and leave at your discretion," Browne told her as the airlock pressurized. "We do run repeated security checks on everyone posted to the Blockade at multiple checkpoints, but it's still possible for smugglers and terrorists to infiltrate personnel into the Service. Speaking of which, once you're logged in as your ship's cadre, you'll need to scan your hand in order to open the airlock from the inside. It's required from all personnel for going either way, unless you're accompanied by security personnel like myself."

Ia waited for the petty officer to cycle them through, then stepped into the large but crowded bay. Here lay the smell of sparks, the ozone she had been missing elsewhere on the Battle Platform, mainly from the use of arc welders. Safety stripes marked a path through the pallets of damaged and pristine components, the stacks of ceristeel hull segments, the crates of delicate instrumentation wrapped in recyclable plexi, items meant to be installed deep within the thick layers of the ship's carefully fitted hull.

Commander Salish was waiting for them at the gantry attached to the lower airlock. She had rolled up the sleeves of her blue dress shirt at some point. She also wore only the bare minimum of pins at her collar points, shirt pocket, and shoulder boards, but she did have her Dress cap perched on her thick, dark hair. One of her cheeks gleamed with the blue sheen of regeneration goo over a pinkish scar, giving her mouth a twisted, sardonic look. But she did smile, and returned the salute Ia gave her.

"Lieutenant Second Grade Ia, reporting as ordered, sir. Here is my transfer chip with the orders on it," Ia added, handing over the small disc. "I request permission to come aboard, sir."

Salish nodded, opened her arm unit, and slapped the disc inside for an immediate review. "Good, good. Everything's in order. Permission granted, and welcome aboard, Lieutenant Ia. We'll be in dock for two days, but there's still plenty for you to do, as they've just started repairs. Lieutenant Piezzan is still in the process of removing his personal effects. For now, you can stow your . . . wait, what's in that case, Lieutenant?"

"My weight suit, sir. I'm a heavyworlder," Ia explained, glancing in the direction Salish pointed.

"I *know* you're a heavyworlder. Master Chief!" Salish called out. One of the noncoms chatting nearby with some of the workers broke off and headed their way. "You'll be on the *Audie*, which is top-deck. You can set the gym closet to whatever gravity setting you like, provided it doesn't imbalance the ship or stress the hull. Just don't do it while anyone else is in there. Master Chief Rutgers, please issue a storage ticket for this weight suit to Lieutenant Ia. She won't be needing it—do you need anything else out of the case, Lieutenant?"

"No, sir," Ia said. "Just the things in my kitbag."

Salish nodded. "Good. Take the weight suit case, Master Chief. We run a tight ship, Lieutenant. Excess weight is reserved for more important things, not for useless clutter. This way."

Pausing just long enough to accept the receipt chip from the petty officer, Ia shrugged her bulky kitbag higher on her shoulder and hurried after her commanding officer.

The exterior of the ship was the same silvery hematite grey of any ceristeel hull. Most of it near the airlock was polished enough that she could see a shadowy reflection of everything in the curves of the composite material. Some sections were pitted and scorched, others crumpled, mainly along the leading edge of the V-swept wings below the boarding gantry. Technicians were removing the damaged pieces with the help of servo-bots and construction cranes. The majority moved with the practiced, swift pace of long experience with such maneuvers.

"As you can see, we take a lot of damage. Our hull plates

are extra thick for extra heat dispersion and impact resistance. If they're not too deeply scored, they'll be taken elsewhere, ground down to a polished shine, and used on other ships," Salish pointed out with one hand while placing her other palm on the scanner of the door lock. "A lot of the OTL supply couriers follow a similar hull configuration, so they're able to adapt most of the panels easily. Of course, on this run, we lost a bit more than hull components. The starboard bow wing tanks on both the *Murphy* and the *Audie* took a beating, along with some of our thruster panels. We're actually in port a couple days early because of it, but it's an easy enough set of repairs.

"As soon as they extract the twisted bits, they'll take up the wing panels that are good enough for an inspection, yank out and replace the tank, and rewire new parts into place. Plus the food stores and the reoxygenators will be replenished, the recyclers and waste compartments emptied, the lifesupport filters replaced—we don't usually scrub them ourselves; we rarely have the time—various missiles and scanner probes will be reloaded, and the hydrotanks topped up. Oh, your file said you come with your own mechsuit. Halfmech, right?" Commander Salish asked her, leading her into the ship. "Marine Corps?"

"Yes, sir," Ia confirmed. "It arrived intact five days ahead of me. I ran the assembly diagnostic yesterday, packed it back up, then signed it off to be brought into the *Audie-Murphy*'s docking bay. It should be out there."

"Good. Leave the packing case here on the *Mad Jack*, but suit up and march it on board. You'll be our designated boarding officer. I'm *counting* on you to be able to handle that, Lieutenant," Salish added, giving Ia a pointed look. "We won't have time to coddle you through combat."

"I have been a boarding officer before, Commander, searching ships for contraband and engaging in combat with smugglers and pirates," Ia told Salish, following the older woman to an airlock-style lift. "Including nine separate engagements against the Salik, sir."

"So your file says, but not quite like this, Lieutenant. We run into the Salik every damned week." Salish gestured at the ship around them. "The two ships forming the *Audie-Murphy* are identical in facilities, but are mirrored to each other vertically. It starts with what we call the Numbers up in the *Audie*, which will

be your half, with Deck 1. Deck 1 corresponds to the bottommost
deck of the *Murphy*, Deck C. The *Murphy* runs the Letters."

"Deck 2 would then correspond with Deck B, and Deck 3
with A, correct, sir?" Ia asked.

"Correct," Salish agreed, programming the controls. "Please
note that accessing various rooms requires sticking your fingers
in various openings. Do also note, Lieutenant, that it is inappropriate to make jokes or innuendos about such things . . . but that
sometimes, for crew morale, I sometimes ignore certain quips."

They were, Ia noted, located in recessed little holes, and
required a downward curl of the finger to activate. This, she
knew, was the equivalent of Salik buttons which had to be lifted
away from their panels by the aliens' suckered pseudo-fingers.
Salik had no bones in their lower arms; the manual pressure
required to insert a tentacle-tip and press down would not be
easy for them to manage.

Salish headed out of the lift without looking back, trusting
Ia to follow her. "Decks 2-B contain Lifesupport, the bridge,
Engineering, that sort of thing. The other four decks have living
quarters, gunnery pods, and so forth. Decks 1-C, being the two
broadest sections, have the most room, so they have the most
living quarters, the gym closets—you can really only fit maybe
four people inside at most, hence the nickname—and of course
the common rooms. I do not restrict access to either ship, but
for the sake of ensuring each ship is properly crewed in the
event of an emergency, I prefer the two sides to keep to their
own vessel, or at least keep things even.

"In particular, if you have a need to come to the *Murphy*
side for anything that will take longer than five minutes, you
will arrange to swap ships with me," Salish stated briskly.
"Otherwise, it's not a good idea."

"That makes sense, sir," Ia said. "Does each crewmate also
have a corresponding swap partner?"

"Yes. Your quarters will be in front of the bridge, once Lieutenant Piezzan clears them out. I do encourage hobbies, but they
have to be something that's quick and easy to pack away. His
is painting watercolors, and he has a lot of them pinned to the
walls with magnets. Do you have any hobbies, Lieutenant?"

"Yes, sir. I make beads." At the quirk of Salish's brow, Ia
elaborated a little. "I make them from a special material crafted

on my homeworld. I receive shipments of them, boxes at a time, from my family, tint and reshape them in my spare time, and ship them back home. It's a way to keep in touch with my people, and a way to contribute to the family income."

"Considering the shipping costs, these beads must be astronomically priced," Salish murmured, unlocking the bridge with a wriggle of her fingertips. "I read that your homeworld is on the backside of Terran space."

"It is, sir. But they're special beads. There's a bit of a . . . religious offshoot, I suppose you could say, back home. It's a harmless religion, but the beads are considered holy symbols," Ia hedged, lying smoothly. "That they're made by my hands, a soldier serving in the military so far from home, makes them all the more special to my people. So I agreed to do it, the last time I was home. Do you have any objections, sir? I do follow the Lock and Web Law very closely while I'm working with them."

Salish settled herself into the command chair of the bridge. She transferred the datachip to the workstation and tapped in a few commands while she gave Ia's question some thought. "No, I don't think I'll have any problems with that. Provided of course that I see the beads in question, as I am responsible for anything that gets brought on board this ship. And provided that you do make damn sure you obey the Lock and Web Law at all times, even while we're at dock."

"Aye, sir. I'd be happy to show you the beads as soon as I have the chance . . . but I do ask that you respect their sanctity as holy symbols, sir, and not mess with them," Ia bartered. "Other than that, I always follow the Lock and Web, sir. You don't serve for a year and a half in space without seeing the reason why at least once."

"Good meioa," Salish murmured, praising Ia. "Okay, I'm ready for your biometric scan."

Ia obligingly leaned forward, placing first her left hand on the scanner pad, then her right.

"Once you're logged in, you'll be able to come and go as you please. More to the point, you'll be able to log others in and out, though for the first five base touches, I'll be overseeing your half of the crew," the commander told her. She pressed a few more keys, then nodded, giving Ia permission to straighten up again. "On board the *Audie-Murphy*, we run a double crew of twenty-eight: fourteen on your side, fourteen on mine. One com, one noncom, one yeoman to back us up—since you and I are both pilots—and the rest are enlisted.

"On board the *Mad Jack*, our immediate superior, Captain Yacob, oversees the off-rotation crews for not only the *Audie-Murphy*, but the *Kublai-Khan*, the *Ed-Freeman*, and the *Yzing-Chow*, our sister ships. We have our own particular off-rotation pool under him, but we can and do draw from the others if one particular ship gets heavily hit," Salish told her.

"Off-rotation crews," Ia murmured. "That means the ones who are on medical rest, right?"

"Yes, and a few spares. Plus we cycle them out, wounded or whole, for the span of a full patrol every fifth cycle. Those who have healed up get put on the repair crews for the other ships that call Bay 16 home. We fly patrols for six days at a stretch, and come back here for two, unless we're badly damaged and have to come into port early, like we did this last time," Salish told her. "It'll be your job as pilot to avoid as much damage as possible.

"The same goes for boarding enemy ships—and out here on Blockade, if it isn't an Alliance military ship, isn't a duly assigned and previously known mining or transport vessel, or isn't being escorted by at least three patrollers from at least two different governments, it's presumed to be, and almost always is, an enemy ship," Salish warned her. The console beeped, and Ia's ident flashed on the screen, updated with her new duty posting information. "*Ah*, here we go. You're now registered as the second-in-command. Welcome aboard, Lieutenant."

"Thank you, sir," Ia murmured. "So . . . since I'll be in charge of boarding parties, what are my standing orders?"

"Our priority is, if it's an unauthorized ship and it shoots at us, we disable it if we can, kill it if we must, and blare its location and identification to the rest of the fleet the entire time we're fighting it. If it runs from us, we disable and board it; if the crew fires on us during the boarding, we shoot to kill unless our orders are to take prisoners for interrogation, rather than the other way around," Commander Salish stated. "If it stops and submits to being boarded, we board with extreme caution and search it stem to stern.

"Finding contraband means disabling the ship—you'll want to go over the ship's manual with the list of what qualifies as

Alliance contraband, versus what is considered an internal matter, something for a particular government. Then, for all instances, we bind the crew if there are any survivors, and call for a tow so a larger ship can handle the matter. We don't usually take on prisoners, since we only have room for a maximum of four prisoners, and that's only if we cram them two at a time into each ship-half's brig. Mostly, we just shoot at things that run, and board things that don't.

"We also occasionally cut deals with our fellow Delta-VXs, swapping patrol segments at random. It's to try and shake things up, keep the frogtopi from figuring out our patrols," Salish told her. "And we can vary things up within our own routes. Usually it's only by a system or two, but three or more will get you hauled in front of a board of inquiry—at which point, you'd better have found and shot down an enemy ship, if you expect to get off scot-free. I've only heard of it happening half a dozen times, and two of those, the officer who made that decision got a couple strokes of the cane for it."

"You said at least three military ships, from two governments. Any particular reason?" Ia asked her.

Salish nodded. "Two or three decades back, they got hold of a couple of derelict Solarican military vessels and patched them up enough to be spaceworthy, then started 'escorting' ships through the Blockade. They succeeded twice before the Solarican contingent realized they were using defunct call signs and alerted the rest. These days, you have to get an escort from at least two Alliance governments if you're not a duly authorized work vessel posted to the Interdicted Zone. One of our jobs is to check and double-check with each Blockade member's registry if we see ships being escorted. Even then, most of the intermittent visitors are well-known. I'll get you a list to memorize, the same with the list of names and faces from our off-cycle crew."

"I'll have it done by the time we launch," Ia promised. At the older woman's questioning look, she shrugged. "I noticed the departure time listed at the hangar entrance. It won't be any worse than cramming for my piloting lessons. What's your policy on calling home?"

"Never while we're on patrol, and mandatory once per base touch—yes, it's mandatory," Salish told her as Ia raised her brows politely. "Morale is the single most important factor on

Blockade. You call someone you like and you talk to them for up to half an hour, that's the rule. You can call out more than once, but only the first one is on the Navy's tenth chit. Or the Marines' tenth, depending on which Branch is footing the bill."

"Good thing Blockade pay is above average, then," Ia quipped, smiling.

Salish didn't quite return it. Her mouth twisted up, but that was about it. "Yeah, well, you'll earn it. We have only two duty shifts, which means we're on alert twelve hours at a stretch— when you're on and we're not at alert, you'll be overseeing four crew on my side of things, while four of yours will be off-shift and resting or asleep, waiting to be up and awake when it's my side's shift. We also rotate duty watches every two hours, and all of us are trained for multiple positions.

"So that's two gunnery posts running at all times, at least one of them installed in the bridge, plus a ship's systems post usually run from the engine room, and a spare on the offside ship, with a full crew running on yours," the commander summed up. "The spare is usually the one who ends up cooking for everyone on both sides."

"How many in a boarding party?" Ia asked her.

"With a known ship we're set to inspect, just four. With an enemy ship, eight—that's including you, by the way. That's why our standing order in hand-to-hand combat is shoot to kill. This isn't *Space Patrol*, Lieutenant," Salish warned her. "There are no closing credits, and unless we get the whole crew back to base alive and unharmed, there are no happy endings. If we're *lucky*, our problems wrap up at the end of each bad encounter when the tow ship arrives. But unless it's time to head back to base, the very next episode begins without any pauses or commercial breaks."

"Trust me, sir. Even as a child, I knew that the real military was nothing like the way it's portrayed in the entertainment business," Ia promised.

"I hope so. Let's get you settled in and familiar with the controls," Salish offered, shifting out of the seat. Somewhere beyond the bridge, a heavy *clunk* rattled through the ship. The commander winced and cursed. "Goddamn techs . . . If they put an extra dent in my hull and we fall behind schedule, I *swear* heads will roll."

"You did say a number of them were off-rotation soldiers," Ia pointed out, settling into the chair. Out of habit, she fastened the restraints, even though the ship technically wasn't going anywhere for two more days.

Salish sighed. "Yes, and while some of the techs are Navy, which makes me feel slightly better in regards to their technical competency, some of them are Marines—the ratio will vary, patrol to patrol, depending on who's healed up and ready to ship out the next time their ship's in port. We get rotated out once every five patrols ourselves, for four patrol sets, then on the fifth one we switch to being backups for everyone else.

"Speaking of which, you'll need to meet Commander Jeston and the other lieutenants. They're our backups, this set. The COs of each ship rarely get hit as much as the boarding officers, so there are more lieutenants than commanders running around, taking their turns at getting healed up. But we do get rest weeks, same as the crew—they're mandatory for anyone on ships as small as ours," Salish told her, "and they thankfully don't count as Leave time.

"My first rotation offside will be on your third patrol. Commander Jeston will take over for that week, and then on your fifth patrol, we'll see who's free among the junior officers to spell you—that's another reason why we're expected to pack light. We'll get you assigned a set of relief quarters on the *Mad Jack* by the end of the day. You'll need to swap out with other lieutenants, and it'll feel more like a hotel than a home, but at least you'll be able to take a much-needed break," Salish promised. "They don't expect officers to work on the ships, so you will get some actual rest between patrols."

Ia smiled wryly. "Unless the Battle Platform falls under attack."

Salish chuckled. "Well, aren't *you* a ray of sunshine? Let's hope it doesn't come to that. The space lanes get awfully cluttered with debris whenever someone goes up against one of these things. A pity they're so expensive to build and maintain, compared to building and repairing a bunch of Delta-VXs . . ."

CHAPTER 14

*My first day of Blockade service pretty much set the tone
for the majority of my time out there. Moments of tedium
and camaraderie crowded into the minimum of allotted
space, interspersed with moments of intense tension and
frenetic activity. It was very much like the day-to-day life
of soldiers patrolling in a war.*

*Then again, it was a war. The politicians just thought
that calling it a Blockade would sound more reassuring to
the folks back home.*

~Ia

JANUARY 4, 2494 T.S.
SS'NUK NEH 1334 SYSTEM

Ia stayed in her bunk for a few minutes past the end-lurch that
was the emergence from the hyperspace tunnel. Her stomach
insisted on it, churning unhappily at having been woken by the
OTL klaxons. Worming a hand free of the covers she slapped
the button that locked the narrow, cradle-like bed in a stable
position and released the webwork of restraints holding her in
place. Everyone strapped in for OTL; going without restraints
and cushioning of some sort meant the risk of being pasted

against a rearward bulkhead by the abrupt acceleration forces sucking a hypership into its wormhole.

The one drawback the restraints couldn't help with was the exhaustion of having lived too fast. The side effects for everyone, Ia included, were shaking muscles, dry mouth, nausea, and hunger. The last three did not mix particularly well. Once she was sure she could stand, Ia climbed out of her bunk, then straightened it and restored the webbing. The comm by the door came to life as she padded toward the closet-sized room that served as her private bathroom.

"Commander Salish to Lieutenant Ia, rise and shine. This is your wake-up call. You have one hour before your duty shift begins."

Swerving by the doorframe, Ia touched the private return-call button. *"Gee, and here I thought the OTL warning was supposed to be my adrenaline-based wake-up call."*

"I like to do both. Private Ryker says breakfast will be ready for the Audie's crew in ten minutes. He likes to cook extra spicy, just to warn you."

"Acknowledged." Ending the call, Ia padded into the head. From the storage cupboard over the toilet—which came with its own set of acceleration restraints, just in case—she pulled the locking boxes that held her "holy beads." She had already showed the untainted ones to Salish. Now, she pricked one of the veins on the back of her hand, extracting the day's allotted dose of blood with the Triple-S she had washed and passed under the sterilizer last night.

Sticking her hand into the box of beads, she extracted energy from the mass, molding and shaping roughly a quarter of it into a single large glob with a shot-glass-sized hollow. Injecting the hollow with the blood, she mashed and melded the two with mind and hands, then divided them into beads telekinetically before rehardening them and dropping them back into the padded box in a trickling clatter of crystal on crystal. It took up most of her allotted ten minutes, but breakfast would be kept hot and ready for her in its own warming tray.

Securing the box, she quickly scrubbed and sterilized the extractor and put it away, then used the facilities, scrubbing hands and face and giving a sketchy wash of the other areas.

She also dampened her sleep-rumpled hair, allowing her to comb the white locks straight. Once that was done and everything stowed, with even the rag she had used tucked into the sonic cleaner, she exited and dressed quickly in black ship boots with their steady, deck-gripping soles, dark blue trousers, and a light blue shirt.

Her arm unit, Ia clasped over her left sleeve; jacket sleeves had snaps so the units could be discreetly covered or easily accessed, but shirt sleeves were often tucked under the bracer-like devices. Before retiring to sleep, she had pinned her bars and wings on the collar points and boards with the wings centered inside the stripe loop that designated her part of a ship's bridge crew. On the left breast pocket, she added a flat triangle pin with the middle point carefully aimed downward, mark of the upper crew for a Delta-VX patrol ship. Once the tails of her shirt were smoothed into her trousers and a stray fold of sleeve fabric tugged straight under her command unit, she was ready to go.

Ia didn't have far to go, to get to breakfast; her tiny cabin was attached to the equally small captain's office, with both squeezed between the bridge at the heart of the ship and the galley. Orienting herself more from precognitive familiarity than from the colors banding the placards holding every door and cupboard sign lining the portside corridor, she headed toward the bow and entered the dining half of the galley.

Most of her crew were there. They had departed from the *Mad Jack* at the start of the *Murphy*'s watch, which had given Ia's half the chance to rest. Eight soldiers, five in the blue of the Navy and three in the brown of the Marines, occupied the space. All of them wore a shallow triangular pin on their shirt pockets with the middle point turned down, indicating they crewed the upper of the two ships.

Private Ryker entered behind Ia, dangling a carrying case from one hand. The pin on his shirt had its middle point facing up. He nodded to her. "Sir. Breakfast has been delivered to the *Audie* four still on watch. Shall I fetch your breakfast now, sir?"

Ia nodded and took her place at the head of the long metal table. At the far end sat First Petty Officer Michaelson, the *Audie*'s noncommissioned officer. Down each side sat most of her crew, save for the four manning the *Audie*'s systems during the off-watch, and one missing soldier. The absent, brown-clad woman came hurrying in a moment later, still tucking her shirt into her pants.

"Morning," she murmured, nodding to the others. She lifted her chin at the *Murphy* crewman working in the actual cooking space at the far end of the galley. "Hey, Jack, I'll take a caf', hot 'n black. None of that creamy-sweet *v'zuei* the officers drink."

"Private Knorssen, your language is highly inappropriate," Petty Michaelson snapped. "Your disrespect will not—"

"*Will* be tolerated, Petty, before the first cup of the day," Ia interrupted, holding up her hand. She met Knorssen's slightly pink-cheeked glance with a wry smile, knowing the woman had planned to test her new commanding officer this way. "But be advised, Private, *only* before the first cup of the day. Also understand that I will give as good as I get." Lifting her chin and her voice, she, too, addressed the man in the galley. "*I'll* take the Marine's choice of breakfast drink, Private Ryker."

"Sir?" he asked, ducking his head enough to look out through the pass-through between the two spaces.

"Milk," she told him, and slipped a wink to the nearest enlisted Marine on her right, who choked on his caf'. "Cold. Straight. You got a problem with that?"

"No, sir." Pulling back, he finished gathering her meal together.

A couple of the crew were whispering and snickering softly among themselves, casting her amused looks. One of them whispered a little too loudly, "Maybe Jack should make that a *chocolate* milk."

Her petty officer gave her a disgruntled look. Bracing her elbows on the table, Ia loosely clasped her hands together and addressed the men and women around her.

"Over the last two days, we were briefly but formally introduced to each other. Myself as your new lieutenant, and you as the various members of my half of our joint crew. But we were pressed for time in getting the *Audie-Murphy* turned around, and did not have the opportunity to go into background details," she explained, pitching her voice just loud enough for Ryker to hear. Ia knew he would carry this information to his own crewmates on the *Murphy* side of things. "Allow me to enlighten you with a few of those details.

"I started in the Service as a grunt in the Marines. I bear more decorations from my two years of service than anyone else outside of a Blockade Patrol. *Most* of my career in the Corps, I served as a noncom officer. I earned my Field Commission at the battle of Zubeneschamali . . . and I earned my military nickname from my very first combat three and a half years ago. My CO looked at me standing there before him, covered multiple times from head to toe in Choya blood and Salik *guts*, and dubbed me 'Bloody Mary.' I have *kept* that nickname throughout my career to date, and kept it *fresh*.

"Call me whatever you want before my first cup of the day, *whatever* I may choose to drink . . . but you will learn to call me it with *respect* the moment we go on duty."

She paused a beat as Ryker came out, bearing one of the multilidded trays the others were eating from. He clipped it onto the table in front of her and tucked a lidded mug of milk into its holder at her side. Opening the compartment with her silverware, she plucked out the fork and snapped that lid shut before opening the next, following the Lock and Web Law of shipboard life even as she dug into her pepper-fried potatoes.

"For those of you who doubt my nickname, and doubt my abilities as either a combatant or a commander, you will have ample opportunity to see both in action firsthand. This is the Blockade, after all." Popping the forkful into her mouth, she chewed and swallowed, then unclipped her mug. "In the meantime, while I may take combat very seriously, I see no reason why our breakfast should be considered a mirth-free zone. Or a conversation-free one. Private Tamaganej, tell me something about your home. Your file says you're from North Mumbai? How long have you lived there?"

"*Ah* . . . yes, sir," he said, glancing briefly at the others. Shrugging, he dug into his salsa-slathered eggs. "My family's lived on Earth, in one part or another of India, for . . . for as long as the Ganges has flowed, I suppose. My family line has been traced all the way back to before the Persian Empire. Or so I've been told."

"You're tryin' to tell me that your family line goes back three thousand years?" one of the brown-clad crewmen across from him asked. "I can barely trace my family line back three hundred, when we moved into Lower New York."

"You lived in Lower New York, Kipple?" Private Nguyen asked, lifting his head from his meal. "I have family in Lower New York, too. I used to spend every summer there, with my cousins."

"You did?" Private Kipple asked him. "Well, hell, I've served with you for a tour and a half, and I never knew that. I grew up in Jersey Province, but I used to visit Saint Vinnie's Deli every time I was in town. You ever eat there?"

Nguyen snorted. "Who didn't? Mind you, they couldn't cook *pho* worth a *shakk*, but the *matzo ball* soup was pretty good."

Private Kipple leaned over and nudged Ia's elbow. "How 'bout you, sir? Ever been to Lower New York? Or even the Upper side?"

"Can't say I have. Most of the time I visited Earth, it was either to Australia for Basic, Portugal for the Academy, or Madagascar to visit friends." She unsnapped the lid over her toast and discovered Ryker had dusted it with pepper as well as butter. Plucking one of the triangles from the tray, she gave the man cleaning up in the galley a wry look. "Pepper even on the *toast*, Private Ryker? This is like eating my brother's cooking! Are you sure you're not a long-lost relative?"

The others chuckled among themselves. She bit off a corner of the bread before the others could try and tease her directly, enduring the tingling burn of the little flakes without any change of expression. This was the real reason why she had requested the milk, to kill the fire of the capsaicin seasoning her meal.

The rest of it was equally spicy, from the cold salad of steamed vegetables in a vinaigrette to the pepper-smoked bacon. Even the cheese had pepper dusted on it. She would suspect a deliberate trick played on her, if it hadn't been for Salish's warning that this was indeed how Private Ryker cooked all the time. At least it was reasonably well-cooked beneath all that fire. Private Kipple, she precognitively knew, could barely slap together edible sandwiches whenever it was his turn in the galley. *Which is hardly any better than what I can do . . .*

"Think we'll find anything today, Petty?" one of the Navy privates asked the noncom at the far end of the table.

"Three mining ships and a petrotanker, all FTL, plus twelve mining skiffs, insystem speed only. That's on the docket for 1334. We board the petrotanker, two of the mining ships, and a minimum of four of the skiffs, chosen at random by the Lieutenant," First Petty Michaelson stated, nodding at Ia before looking back at the private. "Anything else, we shoot it down, and if there's anything left, ask a lot of questions. The exact same as always."

"Well, sir?" the private asked her next, turning to look at Ia. "Any guesses?"

"The three mining ships are Tlassian-run, under contract with the Alliance to supply the Salik back on the domeworld of Ss'nuk with basic metals and petroleums in carefully controlled amounts. If the profits weren't so good, between what they mine for themselves, what the Blockade pays, and the premium the Salik are forced to pay, they wouldn't bother. As it is, the Tlassian hate the Salik—they share the common insult of 'egg-suckers,' except that for the Tlassians, it was a very real tragedy of the war. One which the crewmembers of this particular mining consortium have neither forgiven nor forgotten, despite the intervening centuries. I doubt many of them would collaborate with the enemy."

"And that means we search . . . ?" he asked, shrugging. "Which ships?"

Ia shrugged back. "I'll flip a coin." Checking her chrono, she dug into her eggs. "Eat up and tidy up; our shift is in forty minutes."

They dug in. The Marine woman, Private Knorssen, leaned closer to Ia and frowned at the heaped contents of her tray. "Hey! How come you get more food than I do? Food is supposed to be strictly weighed and rationed."

"I'm a heavyworlder. We have more muscle mass, so we burn more calories." Opening one of the untouched lids on her compartmented tray, she eyed the cinnamon roll warily. No pepper flakes, but he had dusted the premade roll with extra cinnamon. "For future reference, Private Ryker, try not to *waste* excessive amounts of spice. Since I know you are capable of cooking otherwise edible food, I would like you to try following the preparation instructions a bit more closely than this.

"I do expect all of you to toe the line and give your absolute best while you are members of this crew, and on duty," she added, looking around the table. "I *know* you can do it, therefore you *will* do it . . . and it is easier to live up to these expectations than you'd think. All you have to do is put your mind to it, and it'll get done."

"Easier said than done, sir," Private Kipple muttered.

"Not in my experience, Private," Ia corrected him, opening up the compartment that held her eggs. Overspiced or not, she needed to eat. "It's often easier done than said. Just make up your mind to do it, and you'll get it done."

Left hand swooping and flexing subtly, wrapped in the sensor glove that controlled the direction of the twinned starship, Ia played with the controls. Her right hand tapped and stroked the piloting controls, adding and subtracting the power of thrust from the panels dotting the hull. She didn't pull any high-speed maneuvers, no tight turns or sudden reversals, just moved it enough to get herself used to piloting the ship. With her seat centered in the bridge, which was centered on the middle deck in the upper ship, everything was almost perfectly balanced around her, maneuvering-wise.

Salish put up with it for a few minutes before her voice crossed Ia's headset. The commander's tone was light, though, when she asked, *"Are you done playing with the controls, Lieutenant?"*

Ia grinned and swooped the ship a little harder, just a quick back and forth, then steadied their course. *"Now I'm done, sir. I believe I can handle her."*

"Good. I am transferring the off-watch command to you, Lieutenant Ia. Logging the time and control of the Audie-Murphy *to you . . . now."*

"Thank you, sir. Have a good night, sir." Closing her end of the link, but keeping the incoming channel open in case the four off-watch crewmembers on the *Murphy* side needed to talk to her, Ia shifted the current sensor readings to her left secondary screen. She adjusted their heading and read the new results. "ETA to pinging range of the Tlassian mining ship *Red Iron Tail* . . . seven minutes insystem. Any sign of unusual activity on the lightspeed, Private Kipple?"

"No, sir," he replied from his position as combined navigator and scanner tech. "They are still in a standard mining orbit around asteroid 75,331, exactly where they said they'd be. Skiffs are still displaying standard mining activities." He shrugged, restraint straps creaking slightly against the pull of his shoulders. "Which means either they're doing exactly what they should be doing, or they're very cleverly concealing their true activities."

"Nice to see you have the proper mind-set for Blockade work, Private," Ia quipped.

"I have been out here for a tour and a half, sir," he reminded her.

"Sir," Private Knorssen asked from her position at the combined engineering and ship's systems post. "Do you want me to give the orders to start warming up the mechsuits for the boarding party?"

"They're apparently law-abiding under the conventions of their Blockade mining contract. I want Private Higatsu to suit up in halfmech. He'll be the only one; Privates Tamaganej and Nguyen will don close-quarters armor," Ia instructed.

"Sir?" Knorssen questioned. "That's not standard procedure."

"Dealing with aliens is a tricky business, Private. Did you read the crew manifest for the *Red Iron Tail*?" Ia asked in turn. "Almost eighty percent of the crew are warrior caste."

"Yes, I know, Lieutenant, and that's why I'm concerned about your orders, sir," Knorssen told her. "I don't feel comfortable with you going into a ship filled with venom-spitters, sir."

"Well, that's where you and I differ, Private," Ia stated. "I feel very comfortable going among them unarmored."

Out of the corner of her eye, Ia could see Knorssen open her mouth, close it, open it again, and again hesitate.

"Whatever it is, Private, go ahead and say it. Just say it respectfully," Ia told the other woman.

"Then, said with respect, sir . . . you're *crazy*." She shot Ia a sideways look of her own before returning her hazel green eyes back to her screens.

"More like well-versed in alien psychology, particularly that of the Tlassian warrior caste," Ia explained. "That, and almost half the crew comes from Glau. Two hundred years ago, that colonyworld was so hard-hit by the Salik during the war, less than fifteen percent of the adults and less than five percent of the children survived. If the non-Glau crewmembers tried anything vaguely resembling cooperation with the Salik, the Glau colonists among them would tear them to shreds. Instruct Private Higatsu to suit up in halfmech, and Privates Tamaganej and Nguyen to don light armor," Ia ordered.

"Aye, sir." Turning back to her workstation, Knorssen did as ordered.

Ia watched the distance count down on her tertiary screen, numbers for both distance and magnification scrolling rapidly as the scanners constantly readjusted the displayed size of their target. They could have used the hyperrelay comms to contact the *Red Iron Tail* sooner than this. Or they could have short-hopped to a point much closer to the alien vessels and caught them by surprise. The point of gliding in at sub-light insystem speeds was to take advantage of lightspeed wave fronts, matching what they saw with their own sensors against the hyperrelay pings from the system buoys, in case of sabotage or ambush.

There were times when it would be more prudent to sneak up with a short-hop and surprise the ship in question, but Ia knew this wasn't one of them. As soon as they were in range, she sent out the signal requesting communications with the Tlassian ship. Within moments, she received a pingback, and an open transmission.

"Thiss is the Red Iron Tail, *of the Rurrulda Minnning Compannny to the* Audie-Murffphy. *We are ssstanding down operationsss to comply with boarding prosssceduresss."*

"Acknowledged, Red Iron Tail," Ia returned. *"Your prompt diligence honors your employers. Estimated boarding time, seventeen* ziknnah *Tlassian Standard."*

A pause, then the comm tech on the other end hissed, *"Who do I have the pleasssurrre of ssspeaking with?"*

"Lieutenant Second Grade Ia. Mok'kathh ssuweh neh khunnsssswerreah Ssarra L'kuhl Kunhienn," she added in Tlassian. *"And yes, I do know my accent is atrocious."*

A staccato hiss of laughter echoed back along the link. *"Wissse is shhhe who confrontsss her own ffflawsss."*

"Alas, it is a form of combat only a seasoned diplomat could win. I am but a soldier. Who do I have the pleasure of speaking with?" Ia asked in turn.

"Thhird Chief Watcherr Ffred, captain of the Rrred Ironnn Tail. *My kinssship affiliationss are not quite ssso essteemmed."*

"I am sure you bring honor to your kin with each sun's rising. I will see you shortly, Third Chief Watcher," Ia promised.

"It will be a pleasssurre to be insspected by you. May all otherrrs be ssso polite. Rrred Iron Tail *ending call."*

"Acknowledged."

"Okay, now I *know* I'm missing something. Sir," Knorssen added politely. She craned her neck, looking at Ia over her shoulder. "Kinship affiliations?"

"When I was still a young teenager, I sent a letter to the brand-new Grandmaster of the Afaso, a Tlassian named Ssarra. I managed to impress him enough that he not only corresponded back, we stayed in contact through the years," Ia explained. "Just before I joined the Marines, he adopted me as a sort of clan-cousin-sister-thing. Terran cultures have no exact equivalent for it, though the closest are a combination of . . . sister-in-arms and honorary extended family member. Though more of the sister-in-arms thing, as it's a warrior caste thing, but a closer kinship than just a strict military affinity would be. That's why I know it'll be more impressive to the warrior caste if most of us board their ship in light armor, rather than in mech. I've had the opportunity to get to know how they think."

"If you say so, sir. I was more into the Gatsugi in my Alien Culture classes," Private Knorssen dismissed.

Kipple, watching the scanner boards as they approached the mining ship, snorted audibly. "Well, that certainly explains your choice in civilian clothes . . ."

"Stuff it, Kipple," Knorssen muttered.

He shook his head. "I'm just saying it's a good thing you aren't working the scanners, because with your color sense—"

"Stuff it, Kipple," Ia echoed, keeping her tone mild. "Eyes to the boards, thoughts on your tasks. We'll be docking with the *Red Iron Tail* in twenty minutes."

Ia wiped another trickle of sweat from her brow with the back of her hand, then stroked her finger up the writing pad's screen, scrolling through the last of the supply logs. The dry heat of the ship was a bit more than the standardized temperature Terran military vessels used, but it was tolerable enough, if warm. She nodded and handed it back to the captain of the *Red Iron Tail*.

"Everything appears to be in order, Captain. Thank you for your cooperation. *Sschah nakh*."

"*Ssthienn nakh*," the saurian replied, bowing at the hips. "Sssuch courtessy iss appreciated. As iss your effficiensscy."

"You have money to make, the same as any other business-meioa," Ia told him, shrugging. "These delays are an unfortunate but necessary evil. You have a solid record of complying with Blockade laws and procedures. To approach you without courtesy or efficiency would dishonor your efforts—oh, you might want to change out your power relays in the forward cargo hold. I could smell the ozone from sparks near the starboard-side junction," she added. "The minerals you're mining aren't particularly volatile, but it would be prudent to replace them."

"We will lllook into that," Third Chief Ffred promised. He curled one of his scaled arms upward, gesturing for her to precede him out of the bridge.

Ia tapped her arm unit, activating her headset. *"Alpha team to Beta, we're done here. Everything is in the clear. Pack it up and move it out."*

Private Nguyen, clad in the same navy blue and ceristeel grey body armor as Ia but cradling his laser rifle against his chest rather than down his back, nodded politely to the captain of the mining ship. Ffred was staring at him with wide eyes and a cocked head, a species-similar show of curiosity. Nguyen acknowledged him politely. "Third Chief, you are, ah, curious about something?"

"I would lllike to offffer you a drrrinnk, warrior," the alien murmured, eyeing the private.

"*Ah*, thank you, sir, but no, thank you. I'm not allowed to drink while on duty, sir," Nguyen replied, glancing briefly at Ia.

Ia bit her lip for a moment, quelling the urge to laugh. An invitation to share a drink among the Tlassians wasn't quite the same as an invitation to share a drink among the Terrans. Or rather, it was, only *more* so. Facing the Tlassian captain when she was sure her face wasn't a Gatsugi-like shade of red, she gestured at Nguyen. "*He* is male, Captain. Meioa-o, not meioa-e."

Ffred flicked his tail. "Sssorry, it iss not alwayss easy to tell ssubspesscies apart. I . . . apolllogize if my prropossition offended you."

"No, no offense taken," Nguyen agreed, eyes widening slightly with comprehension. "The armor does conceal a lot, I'll admit. I'll, *ah*, take it as a compliment. But gender aside, I *am* on duty, Captain. Have a good day-cycle."

Neither of them said anything about the incident until they had reached the airlock. Beta team had already cycled through, having come from a spot in the ship closer to the connection point between the two vessels. Nguyen glanced at her several times as they cycled through the *Red Iron Tail*'s airlock, the boarding tube, and the *Audie-Murphy*'s aft airlock.

Only when they were in the actual corridors of their own ship, where their presence wasn't being monitored, did he finally speak. "*Um* . . . sir? You're not going to tell the others I was, *ah*, propositioned by a Tlassian, are you?"

"What, and have you end up with the nickname of 'Pretty-boy' Nguyen?" Ia quipped. She shook her head. "No, I won't say anything, I promise. Stow your weapons but stay in your armor and strap in to your prep alcove, Private. We'll be short-jumping to the next ship in fifteen minutes, and I'll want you ready to go."

"Understood, sir."

———

The crew of the *Six Claws of Dirt* were not thrilled to have the *Audie-Murphy* emerge from hyperspace less than two hundred kilometers away. That gave them just one minute to receive the ping and its command for them to stand down and prepare to be boarded while the Terran vessel braked hard. Ia flipped over the conjoined ships even as the message went out, preparing to dock the alien vessel's aft airlock to their starboard side. It wasn't unusual for a patrol ship to sneak up on a vessel this way, but that didn't mean they had to be happy about it.

"Yeoman Bashramahtra, take over the helm," Ia announced as they stopped just within grappling distance. "Extend the airlock gantry and match locks with the *Six Claws*."

"Aye, sir. I have the helm," Bashramahtra agreed, his hand

already strapped into the attitude control glove. "Sir . . . that was some rather nice flying. What was your final flight score?"

"It was 97.3. Not quite high enough to qualify for the Shikoku Yama Academy." Unstrapping herself from her seat, Ia tapped in a final command and left her post. "You have the bridge, Yeoman."

"Aye, sir, I have the bridge," the yeoman confirmed.

Exiting the bridge, she climbed one of the ladderways rather than wait for the lift and emerged at the weapons locker. As he had earlier, First Petty Michaelson issued her a laser rifle and matching pistol, scanning her wrist unit and the ident chip embedded in each weapon. One went over her back, the other into the holster at her hip. Reaching the aft, she found the other three waiting, Higatsu in halfmech armor taking up slightly more than the space occupied by Tamaganej and Nguyen in their nonmechanized body armor.

"Unlike the members of the last ship," Ia warned the three men waiting for her, "most of the crew of the *Six Claws of Dirt* do not have a personal, familial, or social grudge against the Salik. They're here almost strictly for profit. But, like the last ship, most of them are warrior caste. So they may try to test our boundaries. If any of them do try to test you, be rude to you, push you, or act slow in carrying out your inspection orders, you will inform them that they are not permitted to insult you or refuse you the right to carry out your orders, but must instead come to *me* as your warchief."

Nguyen flicked up his inner faceplate, addressing her directly rather than through his halfmech suit speakers. "Warchief, sir?"

She tapped the side of her brow. "Xenopsychology, Private. They are our allies, but they are aliens, and they don't always see things quite the same way as we do. We're lucky there are enough common threads of wisdom, morals, and ethics from sentient species to sentient species that we can get the Alliance to work, most of the time. The Salik being the current notable exception."

"There's always an exception, sir," Tamaganej muttered.

"Just about always. Let's move," Ia ordered. She entered the airlock with Nguyen at her back. The gantry tube was cold, the gravity supplied by the weave under the fold-out decking nothing more than a weak tug. The airlock on the far side opened promptly at their arrival. Cycling through, Ia and Nguyen found themselves facing the captain of the *Six Claws*, a particularly tall Tlassian female. Ia bowed slightly to her. "Second Chief Watcher Nnlill."

"Lllieutennant," she returned. The alien studied Ia for a long moment before finally moving back, giving room for the two to enter the access corridor. "You may sssearch my sship."

"Sschah nakh," Ia thanked her. A huff of breath was the Tlassian's only reply. Ia waited until Tamaganej and Higatsu had cycled through, then gave them their orders. "Search the lower deck cargo holds. Match them to the manifest, which the captain will provide to you. Captain, we will need to see the crew quarters. The records list that they have not been searched in a while. This needs to be done, to comply with the law."

Nnlill rumbled and bared her teeth a little, but activated her wrist unit. She snapped a set of orders, then gestured with a curl of her arm. "I willl be presssent for the crew cabin inssspectionns."

"Of course," Ia agreed, fishing a pair of exam gloves from one of her black and grey vest pockets. "Private Higatsu, Private Tamaganej, be respectful as well as watchful."

"Aye, sir."

Like the previous ship, the temperature in this one was on the warm side. By the third crew cabin, Ia and Nguyen were sweating again. This one, unlike the previous two, was occupied. Rather than doing it herself, the Tlassian ship captain hissed something at the crewman, who grunted, climbed down from his sleeping alcove, and started opening cupboards.

Instead of pulling out the garments and belongings, however, the kilt-wrapped saurian just sort of shoved things around before moving to shut the panel again. Ignoring the sweat threatening her eyes, Ia stared at him. "You will need to pull it out, meioa-o. *All* of it."

Nnlill hissed an order and cuffed her crewmate on the shoulder, claws scraping across his scaled hide. He grumbled and pulled out the collection of boots, sandals, the odd trousers that looked like they had three legs, though technically one was meant for his tail . . . and a collection of plexi packets containing . . .

stuff. Herbal-looking stuff. The enraged roar that escaped his captain's throat made both Ia and Nguyen wince and sway back.

She lit into him in their native tongue so hard and fast, even Ia couldn't make much sense of it. Not that Ia was exceptionally fluent in Tlassian without dipping into the timestreams, though she was good enough for casual conversation. Second Chief Nnlill growled, babbled, hissed, and claw-cuffed him again, this time visibly scratching his hide. Tail lashing, she turned to face Ia, but from the flaring of her neck-flaps, the "hood" that marked her as warrior caste, she looked like she was still too enraged to remember how to speak Terranglo.

Ia held up her hand, palm toward herself in nonthreatening Tlassian fashion. "Calm yourself, meioa. Whatever his personal choice of plant-based suicide may be, I am *not* here to enforce the Tlassian drug laws. I am here to check for a different source of contraband. Ship schematics, hyperrelay manuals, and other engineering specifications. Weapons, both designs and actual armaments. Schedules indicating patrol ship routes and times, past, present, and future. The truly dangerous stuff, not this *shova*."

"You willl do nnothing?" Nnlill managed to hiss, neck hood still flared slightly.

She shook her head. "The incident will be filed in my report, of course, but I'm not going to draw special attention to it. Provided you take disciplinary actions and report the matter to your government before mine passes along this incident, there shouldn't be any problem. Drug violations are technically an internal matter for the Tlassian government to handle," Ia pointed out. "They are not a Blockade matter.

"However . . . the fact that he has them at all *is* a potential security risk. His suppliers could blackmail him into providing contraband information to the black market community. I suggest you contact your government immediately, and have him removed," Ia told the other female.

"It willl be donnne," she growled. Jabbing at her wrist unit, the Tlassian snapped several orders to what sounded like her bridge crew.

The male widened his eyes. His own neck flared, and he scrambled to his feet with a *hrrnk* deep in his throat. Ia snapped her sidearm out of its holster, pointing it at his chin even as

Second Chief Nnlill caught and dug her claws into his shoulder in warning. He froze in place.

"Swallow it." Ia ordered, glaring at him. She flicked the safety off, letting the faint whine of the weapon warm up to an audible pitch. "You have insulted me, meioa-o. You. Will. *Swallow* it."

"Vhok na-ashh!" Nnlill repeated in their own tongue.

The crewmember blinked and gulped. Then coughed, gagging a little. Touching her headband with her free hand, the Tlassian mining captain lifted her chin. "Messsage is ssent."

Ia's headset beeped, a channel opening from the *Audie*'s crew.

"Lieutenant, we just received a split-bandwidth transmission from the Six Claws. They're reporting to us the presence of illegal drugs on board, with a copy sent to the Tlassian War Command," she heard Kipple state. *"Is everything alright, sir?"*

Lowering her gun, she flicked it off and tapped her arm unit. *"The Second Chief is complying with Blockade procedures, Private. Ia out."*

The crewmember grimaced and rubbed his abdomen. He hissed something, but found himself shaken by the shoulder instead. Nnlill still had her neck-skin flared. "You will *nnnnnot* get your ssstomach cleannsed jussst yet. Show all sstorage contentsss, ffirst!"

Cowed, the male Tlassian crouched and began digging through the rest of his storage lockers. Ia holstered her weapon and watched. He grunted after a few seconds, hunching over more and more as those seconds turned into minutes.

"Uh . . . sirs?" Nguyen asked hesitantly after a louder groan from the alien. "If he just swallowed his own venom, shouldn't he get medical help? Doesn't that stuff corrode flesh?"

"It willl nnnot killl him," Nnlill hissed. "Jusst make him *wishh* he werrre dead."

"Their digestive tracts have a lining vaguely like our own stomachs, Private. One which resists and neutralizes the proteinic acids in their venom," Ia explained absently, her attention more on the items being revealed than anything else. "They're designed to handle it in small amounts. Swallowing enough to spit will simply give him a very bad stomachache, followed by a case of the *shilva v'shakk*, if it isn't expurged in the next twenty minutes."

Nguyen mulled that over for a moment, then offered, "So . . . it's sort of like eating Private Ryker's cooking, sir?"

Ia bit her lip again to control the urge to smile. She didn't want to bare her teeth in front of the Tlassians, since that meant something completely different. "From what I've heard, it's worse. Not by much, but still worse." Nguyen grinned at her quip, forcing her to snap, "*Teeth*, Private!"

That sobered him. Quickly pulling his lips back into place, he sketched a bow to the Tlassians, armor creaking faintly with the move. "Sorry, meioas. My apologies."

"Acsscepted," Nnlill muttered. Stooping, she snatched a flat, vaguely rectangular device from the floor where her crewmate had pushed it, emptying out his cupboards. "Book rrreaderr. You will wannt to ssscann thiss fffor conntraband."

Nodding, Ia unsnapped one of her thigh pockets. Fishing out her translator interface, she sorted through the connectors tucked into the back and hooked the right one into the reader's socket, checking both screens as soon as they lit up. "Thank you for your cooperation, Captain. *Sschah nakh.*"

Nnlill bowed and gave Ia the equivalent of "you're welcome" in her native tongue, as she had not done when Ia and the others had first boarded. "*Ssthienn nakh.* Let usss hope thiss is the onnly violationn on board. I would nnot carrre to have my sssship dissabled."

"Neither would I, meioa," Ia agreed.

CHAPTER 15

Space is huge. I mean really, really huge. You may think
it's a long way down to the ... Okay, alright, that shtick
has been done before, and done by someone a lot more
amusing than me. But Mr. Adams was right. Space is almost
unimaginably vast. Even in our own little corner of it, here
in the Orion Arm and parts of the Sagittarius and Perseus
Arms, there are hundreds of thousands of star systems, if
not millions. Not all of them are inhabited, but many of
them have resources, usually minerals and ice water, which
can be mined.

Keeping the Salik confined on their homeworld and
eight colony planets is therefore a galactic-sized headache.
Any direction, right or left, front or back, up or down, can
be a direction in which secretly built Salik ships can flee.
Thousands of star systems are technically within their
reach ... but that's not counting the interstellar void
between systems, and the vast volume of space itself, which
is really, really, really huge.

We therefore took great pains to destroy their fleets at
the end of the war two centuries ago, and even greater
pains to monitor their colonial and homeworld star systems
in great depth. Instead of trying to monitor the vast depths
of the interstellar void, we took to monitoring the resources
that they would need to rebuild. We knew some ships would

slip through the tiny cracks around their worlds, and sail merrily through the vast cracks away from their home systems, but we did our absolute best to monitor for any signs of enemy activity and brutally destroy all such vessels when we found them.

Our standing orders were also to bring back any evidence of secret Salik bases located far outsystem. Evidence was to be found, and the bases destroyed with extreme prejudice by a massive coalition of Alliance forces. Which meant it was standard operating procedure to board enemy vessels wherever and whenever possible, once they were disabled. Even for a crew as small as the Audie-Murphy's.

~Ia

JANUARY 7, 2494 T.S.
NUK NUKLIEL 83 SYSTEM

The *Audie-Murphy* had two small boarding pods. Technically, they also doubled as the ship's escape pods. That meant, when they were launched, they immediately broadcast a broadband distress beacon, both on several lightspeed wavelengths and on at least three hyperrelay bands. It guaranteed that someone would be coming by in a few hours to see why the pods had been launched, a necessary precaution when space was so vast.

It was also the most dangerous thing Ia and her crew could do, since launching the pods meant risking being shot at by the supposedly disabled Salik vessel ahead of them. Only when a commanding officer was certain the ship was disabled did they risk launching the pods. Sometimes they were right and landed safely. Sometimes they were wrong. The casualty rate was 80 percent for a reason, though this time Ia and the others were fully suited and sealed, just in case something cracked open the small boarding vessel.

This time, they were crammed four to a pod, with Ia, Tamaganej, Higatsu, and Nguyen in one pod, and Chief Petty Officer Kendric with Privates Doolittle, Quangyan, and de la Soleza in the other pod, all members of the *Murphy* half of the crew. This time, Ia was the only one who was relaxed inside her suit. She knew—she had *made sure*—that all of the alien ship's weapons systems had been disabled, plus she had directed the gunners to hit the ship hard enough in the right spots to disable their self-destruct capacity.

Instead of fretting, she reviewed known ship schematics for this general configuration, and for known Salik databank units, using her heads-up display to pretend like she was studying for the coming encounter. Swaying against her restraint sockets, Ia listened to the *thump* and buzzing *hiss* of the pod sealing onto the ship's hull, and then cutting into it. Like so many other things, modern ceristeel technology had been denied to the Salik, but their own version of hull armor was still quite tough.

Giving the others the thumbs-up with one servo-glove, Ia moved to the airlock door and slipped through, with Nguyen right behind her. A twist of the controls activated the cutters, the heavy, mining-quality laser drills that sliced into the ship's hull. With their bodies wrapped in p-suits inside their jointed armor, the eight members of the boarding team would be fine if the Salik ship depressurized. The Salik might or might not be alright, depending on whether or not they had donned their own suits in the aftermath of the battle.

Nguyen passed her the buzzbomb cannon. Fitting it to the port in the center of the door, Ia hooked her helmet's HUD to the pod's external cameras. The lasers were still drilling, circling around and around on their oval track. Finally, a faint *clannng* rippled into the pod from the other ship as the pistons pushing on the hull shoved the layers of armor plating and bulkhead into the depths of the Salik vessel.

Ia pulled the trigger on the cannon, pulsing it four times. Four orbs spat down into the alien vessel. The first one exploded in a *pzzzt* of sound and light, a stunner grenade that flashed its electrosonic pulse through the cabin beyond the opening she had made. The second through fourth flew down, bounced, and rolled off under self-control, automatically seeking out live bodies to pulse a second wave of sonic shocks.

Unhooking the cannon let in a hiss of steam. The heated vapor didn't do anything to her mechsuit, so Ia ignored it. She passed the launcher back to Nguyen with a murmur through her external speakers. "We could've seriously used these on board the *Liu Ji*, back in my old Marines Company. They would've made boarding pirate ships a lot easier."

"Let's trade places, sir," he offered, lifting his chin behind the half-silvered curve of his inner faceplate.

"Why?" she asked. She turned her attention to the controls for the airlock door.

"Sir, you shouldn't go in first. Leave that job to a Marine," he stated.

"I *am* a Marine. Even if I wear Blues these days," she amended. "Either way, I am the boarding officer for this little party."

The door hissed open, swinging and pivoting almost like a rolltop door in order to give them the clearance to enter. More steamy air billowed their way, though not as saturated as before. Nguyen touched Ia, the rubberized tips of his servo-fingers gripping her arm plates.

"Then let an enlisted meioa go first, sir. It isn't right our leader should risk herself as the first one into the enemy's ship," he argued.

"Duly noted, Private, but denied. I lead from the front," Ia told him. Ducking into the opening, she climbed over the still-hot edges of the oval. The sensors on her mechsuit boot soles flared their temperature warnings at the edges of the heads-up display shining off the inner curve of her faceplate. A blink-code slid her thick-silvered blast plate into place, and a shift of her servo-arms pulled her HK-114 mechsuit-sized laser rifle to the front of her armored body.

Static swept across her faceplate display, pulsed from the stunner grenade on the floor inside the cabin. By the time it cleared, she was inside. From the trio of lidded tanks lining three of the walls—or rather, two and the remains of the middle third, which had been crushed by the falling chunks of hull and overhead storage lockers—this was some sort of crew quarters.

Ignoring the debris, Ia stepped over it and slapped the sucker hand over the controls for the cabin door, lifting on the buttons to open the panel. Rolling through as soon as it hissed wide, she pointed her rifle both ways down the corridor outside. Nothing and no one. The stunner bombs bounced out the door and rolled down the hall, occasionally flashing electrosonic shockwaves, which, like stunner rifles, would disrupt the neural networks of just about any form of life that used electrical signals. Ceristeel absorbed most of the shockwave, but the sensors built into her mechsuit fuzzed a second time with another brief moment of static before they cleared.

Still, her suit's scanners, upgraded for Blockade work, showed no other life-forms nearby. No stray sounds, no Salik-shaped heat signatures, with their distinctive, ostrich-backwards knees and rear-facing flipper-feet, nor their pseudo-tentacle arms with the four, supple, sucker-covered ends. She flicked on her comm with another blink, triggered by the sensors picking up the focal point of her gaze flicking over the command options hovering around the edges of her faceplate display.

"This is too quiet. They'd know where we latched on. We should be facing resistance. Heads up, people. *Petty Kendric, report.*"

"*It's too quiet here, sir,*" the noncom replied over her headset. "*We emerged in a storage locker just off the hangar deck, but there's no sign any of them tried to get to the courier to flee.*"

"*Did you say courier?*" That question came from Salish, back on board the *Audie-Murphy.*

Ia knew what was coming. She let First Petty Kendric reply, since he was the one who "knew" for sure.

"*I'm staring at what looks like a hyperspace nosecone on the pointy end of a Salik—*"

"*Shakk!*" Ia swore into her headset mike. "*All units, get to the bridge! I repeat,* get to the bridge!*"

She took off at a sprint, startling Nguyen and the other two. They lumbered after her, rattling the deckplates with the weight of their halfmech. Snatching up the nearest stunner ball without crushing it as she ran—no mean feat in the bulk of a mechsuit—she confirmed her course from a light skimming of the time-streams.

"*Lieutenant, report!*" Salish snapped.

"*It's a suicide ship, sir,*" she stated, skidding around a corner and slapping the sucker hand over the controls for one of the ship's emergency stairwells. "*They* must *have been carrying navigation data on either the location of a secret base or the coordinates for a rendezvous. That's why there's no resistance;*

they're holed up somewhere, either dead or killing themselves off to ensure they can't be interrogated. Our best chance is to hope they haven't completely slagged the relevant data consoles."

As soon as she got the door open, she pulled off the device and clanged down the steps. The Salik version of feet— backwards-pointing flippers on ostrich-like legs—weren't exactly adapted for using ladder rungs, which meant there was plenty of room for her halfmech suit to charge down two levels. By the time she reached the right door, Private de la Soleza's voice rang over the comm channels.

"I think I found the bridge, sir! Something just shot at me!"

"All units, converge on de la Soleza," Ia ordered, more of her attention on getting the stairwell door open than on either her scanners or the timestreams of who or what was attacking the private. The ball in her grip *pzzzzted* with another wave of stunner energy, but the brief fuzzing of her sensors didn't matter. The who or what wasn't far away; within moments, they reached the right cross-corridor, one with a pair of gun turrets mounted on the ceiling outside two sets of mirror-image doors.

Swinging her gun up into position, Ia fired, slicing through the power conduits feeding both lasers. One of them managed to swivel around in time to take a potshot at her, but the blood orange bolt merely scuffed her armor. Without missing a beat, she turned to her left and started lasering through the seam sealing the double doors together. Nguyen joined her, while de la Soleza and her partner Doolittle used their own HK-114s on the double doors opposite.

One set of the mirror-image doors would lead to a shallow storage locker; the other would lead onto the real bridge. Ia knew which set were the real doors. Tamaganej from her left and Higatsu from her right pulled out pocket crowbars from storage compartments on their thighs. Jamming them into the glowing-hot crack she and Nguyen had made, they flexed their synthetic muscles, prying the doors apart. On the other side, Quangyan and Kendric started to do the same.

The moment the opening was barely big enough, Ia tossed the stunner grenade through. Just in time, too; it went off on the other side of the glowing door edges. A smattering of static sparkled across her heads-up display. It didn't stop her from bringing her rifle back up into position . . . nor did it stop the deadman switch from triggering on the grenade in the limp grip of one of the stunned Salik inside.

Ignoring the bloody, smoldering pieces smacking into the doors, the bits that spattered down her armor, Ia crouched a little, aimed carefully below the Salik-style overhead screens dotting each workstation, and fired. The acid poured over the data cubes beneath the navigation console ignited in a rush of light and heat. The flames burned swiftly, extinguishing themselves as they used up the available oxygen in their vicinity.

"Whoa," Nguyen muttered over the open comms. "What'd you do *that* for, sir?"

"They use a corrosive acid to destroy their memory banks, but the acid is highly flammable," Ia stated. She waited while another stunner-pulse from the grenade rolling around on the floor fuzzed her heads-up view, then stepped onto the bridge. "I tend to play the *Audie-Murphy*'s logs for past encounters before falling asleep. With luck, I've saved enough of the units that the higher-ups can extract something useful. *Commander Salish, I don't know how many of the Salik are still alive elsewhere, but I think we have four prisoners here. Um . . . maybe three. I think one of them is bleeding to death.*"

"*I've already received a pingback on the hyperrelays,*" Salish promised her. "*The TUPSF* Kaiwinoka *is on her way to give the enemy a tow back to base. They've also promised to bring a spare set of starboard insystem thrusters for the* Murphy. *Thank our lucky stars, that's the worst of the damage we sustained. Stay on board the enemy ship, Lieutenant, and do your best to finish securing it. Don't hesitate to make a run for the pods if it looks like things are going southward. I'll be keeping the* Audie *and the* Murphy *separate until the* Kaiwinoka *arrives, just in case they have a few crewmembers stashed away, waiting for a chance of sabotage.*"

"Understood, sir," Ia agreed. "You heard our fearless leader, meioas. Strip and zip the prisoners, and haul them out of here. I want them duct-taped to a bulkhead outside and unable to do anything but hang there and breathe in ten minutes flat—and yes, I do mean that literally. Strip 'n zip, and strap 'em flat!"

A ragged chorus of "*Aye, sir*" answered her command, both locally and over her headset.

"Be careful and scan each one before you move them," First Petty Officer Kendric ordered. "Some of these sons of squids have a bad habit of lying down on a deadman's switch, particularly if they think they'll be stunned. The moment you turn them over—boom!"

"Don't count on your armor protecting you, either, if you're close enough to turn 'em over," Ia added in warning, backing up the noncom. "No one buys a star out of carelessness, today."

JANUARY 9, 2494 T.S.
BATTLE PLATFORM *MAD JACK*
SIC TRANSIT

"So, how was your first week?" Bennie asked as she came back from the caf' dispenser. Once more, she was stuck in a small office attached to her quarters, though at least they were larger than the ones back on the *Liu Ji*.

Accepting the mug of hot liquid, Ia shrugged. "Not bad. I'm getting some respect from the crews of the authorized ships we've boarded, and we've caught three that weren't authorized. Well, exploded, disabled, and boarded."

The redheaded chaplain curled one leg under the other as she settled in her cushioned chair. A wry smirk curved the corner of her mouth. "The way I hear it, you earned your nickname again."

Ia shook her head, sipping at the slightly bitter beverage. "Not really. It was just a small amount of spatter, this time. Mostly down the midline. The bridge doors weren't open very wide when the grenade went off."

Blowing on her own mug, Bennie shrugged. "Any nightmares from it?"

"Not as far as I know. Besides, everyone on my side lived," Ia pointed out. "That's the best nightmare deterrent I can have. The techs might be able to get useful navigation data out of the banks we salvaged. I won't hold my breath, but even if they just have a series of slightly more detailed starcharts for several systems, that'd give them a place to start looking. The really disturbing thing, though, is that someone gave them OTL technology."

Bennie nodded. "Oddly enough, I'm not surprised. If they dug a giant tunnel under the surface of their worlds, sealed it and removed the atmosphere, they could launch ships into hyperspace that way. It would make the most sense as to how they could come and go without being seen."

"The stress of a wormhole tunneling through a planet could show itself as a series of microfaults and microquakes, giving them a possible way to locate it . . ." Ia gave up and shook her head. "Eh. That's speculation better left for better heads in the military to mull over."

"How are your crew doing? Are they giving you respect, yet?" Bennie asked next. "Or are they giving you a hard time?"

Ia blew out a breath. "I find myself wanting to be short with them sometimes. I try to hold it back, though; it's not their fault."

"Oh?"

The single word held a wealth of inquiry. Not once did Ia forget that the woman across from her, friend or not, was a trained psychologist as well as a spiritual advisor, and a Department of Innovations–assigned watchdog. Slouching a little, Ia rested her head on the high, padded back of her own chair. "I served with Ferrar's Fighters for several tours of duty. Some of them came and went, but . . . we *knew* each other by the time I was put into a position of great authority—being a corporal-ranked Squad leader doesn't count. I'm talking non-com, real authority.

"I just have to remind myself, I've only served with these soldiers a week or so," she finished, shrugging.

What she really meant was, *I precognitively remember serving with them already, but I have to remember that I haven't actually done so in reality, yet.* But Ia didn't *say* that to Bennie. As much as she liked the older woman, as much as they were friends and Bennie was her confidante, there were certain things she couldn't yet say.

"So long as you realize this, rein in your temper—what little temper you have," the chaplain teased dryly, "and treat them fairly, they'll come to respect and follow you." She sipped at her mug of caf' for a few moments, then frowned softly. "I don't know if you've noticed, but you have an . . . air of command about you. No, not command . . ."

She fell silent for several seconds, thinking it over. Ia gave her the peace to do so. Finally, Bennie shrugged.

"The only words I can think of are *purpose* and *drive*. Or maybe *destiny* . . . whatever it is, it puts me in mind of the story of Joan of Arc." Bennie shook her head, her thick braid sliding across her shoulders. "Not exactly the most pleasant of comparisons, sorry."

Ia chuckled softly. "Here's hoping I don't get burned at the stake. Though my enemy right now are the Salik, and that means they'd rather eat me alive than cook me, first."

"And how do you feel about *that*, as a possibility?" Bennie asked her. "You *are* working the Blockade, and it has been known to happen."

Ia lifted her mug in mock-salute. "I hope they consider me eminently worthy of being eaten."

The look Bennie gave her, taken aback to the point of dismay, tickled Ia's sometimes strange sense of humor.

"Oh, don't give me that look," she chided the chaplain, chuckling under her breath. "The only way they'd find me 'eminently worthy' of being devoured alive is if they thought I was a major war-prize. *That* means I'd have given them so much grief and hell, destroying ships and capturing Blockade-runners, there'd be fewer of the frogtopus bastards around to give *other* soldiers hell. *That* kind of reputation, the one that puts me at the top of their To Be Eaten list? I can live with that, Bennie."

"You *want* to get eaten?" Bennie asked her, still dubious.

That made Ia burst out with laughter. "*God*, no! What kind of masochist do you take me for? *Ahahaha! Ha! Heheheh . . . heh . . .* Oh, stars. I haven't laughed like *that* in a long while . . ."

Bennie smiled over the rim of her mug. "Well, at least I've finally tickled your funny bone. You don't laugh a lot, do you? Chuckle, yes, and other restrained forms of mirth, but laugh outright? Nooo, our Ia is *far* too sober and serious to guffaw."

That made her snort with laughter. Blushing, Ia covered her nose, reducing her "guffaws" to a mere chuckle once more. Bennie grinned and lifted her mug in salute.

"Gotcha."

Ia stuck out her tongue, then buried her fading smile in her mug. There were reasons why she rarely laughed. It was hard to be that carefree with the fate of the future looming constantly throughout her thoughts.

FEBRUARY 5, 2494 T.S.

Her older brother peered into the pickups on his end of the vidlink and frowned. "You look like hell, Sis. What've you been up to? That isn't a sunburn, is it?"

Ia shook her head. "Decompression sickness. It was a sneak attack by ore smugglers. They blew a hole in my half of the ship. Everyone got into their p-suits okay, but *okay* doesn't cover how the damned pressure foam expands and makes it that much harder to climb into them. We're confined to the Battle Platform on Sick Leave while they put the *Audie* back together. By the time she's flightworthy again, the docs tell me the broken capillaries will have healed. The daily goo baths don't hurt, either."

Despite the speed of the micro-sized hyperrifts used in interstellar communications, traveling hundreds of lightyears to the second, it still took several seconds for him to hear her side of the conversation and respond.

"Lucky you, you *get* regeneration goo," he muttered. "There's been a media storm locally on certain doctors at the hospital refusing to use the stuff on patients who 'aren't that badly injured' according to said doctors," Thorne warned her. "More specifically, on patients who are known to be particularly anti-Church."

"And?" Ia asked, waiting to hear the most likely probabilities confirmed. She had already foreseen something like this, but the variables had created several minor possibilities. None of it would seriously change the near-future timelines, but it would be a point to be dredged back up again when it came time to sway the undecided members of Sanctuary's population.

"They've stirred up a board of inquiry, and the victims are now suing in court," Thorne told her. His mouth pressed into a grim line. "Regeneration biogels are disgustingly expensive to acquire on Sanctuary, so the doctors are arguing that it's being saved for cases that truly need it. Except three of the victims were badly burned in a chemical fire and could've used doses of the goo to prevent severe scarring. They're suing the physicians on grounds of religious discrimination and the violation of their Hippocratic Oaths. The results are . . . unpleasant . . . to look at, so the consensus is that they'll win the sympathy vote from the jury.

"As it is, if they want the scars gone, they'll have to have their skin peeled away from the affected areas before the biogel can be applied—the more liberal of the media services have been romping and rolling all over that part of the news."

"How charming. I hope those so-called doctors get what they deserve. On a more cheerful topic, did you get the gift I sent for Little Brother?" she asked.

It took him a moment to catch her meaning. Raising his brows, he nodded slowly. "Yeah, I got it, along with your latest shipment of holy beads. But he's off camping in the mountains with some friends this week. I should be able to give it to him next Tuesday."

Camping in the mountains was a prearranged euphemism for working down in the lava tunnels. "Just so long as he's careful. How are Mom and Ma doing?"

"Pretty good. They found a new harpist for the restaurant. Not quite as good as the last one, or the dulcimer player, but then he's still learning how to control the picks. Their anniversary is coming up. Did you remember to ship a gift?"

Ia winced. This time, the reaction wasn't feigned. "No, I honestly forgot. Extend my apologies and get them something nice in my name. I'll wire some credits to your account to cover it."

He lifted his hand into view, warding off the suggestion. "I'll pay for it myself. What they'd really like is a chance to talk to you themselves. *Uh* . . ." Thorne looked away from the vid pickups for a moment, frowning slightly, then nodded. "In nineteen hours Terran Standard, they'll just be waking up, locally. That's the best time to catch them. Right now, they're busy with the restaurant."

She nodded. "I'll be up at that time anyway. It's the Opening Ceremonies for the Winter Olympics, and everyone in the Blockade Fleet is looking forward to seeing the displays the Gatsugi have planned for their show. I don't know what news-Net channel you're watching, but the ones piped out here have said they'll be posting a chromatic scale with colormood translations to help the non-Gatsugi understand what they're seeing."

"Alien cultures," Thorne quipped. "Gotta love 'em. Well, everyone but the Church."

"How are your classes going?" she asked her brother.

"I'm just about finished with my midterm project in Integrated Delivery Systems, and I'm halfway through my graduate paper on Satellite Spaceport Systems Design. Since Sanctuary doesn't have any moons or habitable rocks worth speaking of, I'm pretty much the only one at the college studying domeworld structures and building logistics," he told her. "I'd tell you all about it, but I wouldn't want to bore you. Or take up too much time on this call."

"I wish I had time to *be* bored, because I'd love to hear it," Ia confessed. "Unfortunately, you're right, my free calling time is almost up. Pass my love to Fyfer, Mom, and Ma, will you? And keep a share for yourself?"

"Always," he promised. *"Mizzu."*

"Mizzu, tu," she returned. *"Ghin t'Fyfer sa numcha, eyah?"*

"Eyah," he agreed, giving her a pointed look, before affecting a look of remembrance. "Take care, Ia—oh, I don't know if you heard, but the Power Pick numbers just leaped to the astronomical level. The multipliers are pushing the winnings into the trillions of credits. I think I'll try buying a ticket myself, even if gambling's not normally my thing. It's always been more Fyfer's thing."

"Well, you know me," Ia quipped dryly. "I don't like to gamble. Not to mention, the odds are too high for my taste, especially with the Power Pick tickets limited to one per sentient, once it shot past the ten billion mark."

He grinned, enjoying the secret joke embedded beneath her words. "Still, you have to admit, that's a lot of cold, hard creds. It's very tempting, even for us straight-laced types. Good luck, and keep your head down, Sis."

"Always," she promised. "Love you. Tell Mom and Ma I'll call them in nineteen hours Terran Standard."

She watched him reach for the controls and shut off his image, leaving her with a blank blue holding screen. Sighing, she gathered her thoughts and tapped in her account number, preparing to pay for the next call. *So much for the free call. Now*

I need to put one through to the Grandmaster. That'll cost a pretty tenth chit . . . as will wishing my mothers happy anniversary.

Her arm unit beeped, startling her. Flicking open the lid, she saw she had a vidletter waiting for her. Downloading it to the commscreen, she opened it with a tap of her finger. Meyun Harper filled the screen. The one Human she still had trouble predicting.

"*Umm . . . hello, Ia,*" the prerecorded image stated. "I miss you, and I was thinking about you . . . and they want me to call someone every week, something about improving morale. I've already contacted my parents, that was last week. This week, I thought of you. Oh, the Navy wound up stuffing me into Blockade duty midtour. Seventeen percent, I believe it was. Anyway, that's why it's mandatory to call someone."

Ia quickly paused the letter. Pressing into the timestreams, she searched for signs of his presence. It took her several minutes of effort, but she located shadows of him about a third of the way around the edge of the ragged bubble outlining the Salik Interdicted Zone. Relief staged a bittersweet, ambivalent war with regret inside of her.

Don't even pretend the two of you can do otherwise, she admonished herself. *You know you're better off staying far away from this man . . .*

Tapping the screen, she restarted it. Better off or not, she would listen to what he had to say, because she still wanted to hear it. She just couldn't do anything about it without risking the timestreams.

"It's gotten a bit chaotic here from time to time, but I'm already getting recognition for my talents—look, see?" he offered, picking up an awards box, tilting it so the silver and brass flower inside flashed and glittered. "Not two weeks in, and they've already given me the Compass Rose for extraordinary acts of engineering. I'd tell you what it was for, but . . . well, you know, it's the Blockade. Everything's been classified down to the last millimeter out here. Or it seems like it.

"Anyway . . . I just thought I'd drop you a vid, let you know I'm alright. I, *um* . . . can't stop thinking about you," he added carefully, staring into the pickups as if he could see her eyes.

"It's not getting in the way of my work or anything, but . . . Yeah. Take care of yourself, alright? Remember to duck when going through airlocks, and stuff. Meyun Harper out."

Duck when going through airlocks? Ia repeated to herself. His image gave her a hesitant smile, then the recording ended. She probed the timestreams. Ahhh . . . *right. Duck when going through smuggler ship airlocks, got it. Not bad, Harper, not bad,* she silently praised. *You're already getting the hang of this covert message stuff. Luckily for you, I already knew about the potshot in question. I promise you, I'll duck in plenty of time.*

She did not, however, compose an actual response. Ia didn't have to be a precog to know that it would tempt her into communicating with him on a greater basis. That ran the risk of letting feelings—hers or his, it didn't really matter—sway her from her task.

Bennie's going to give me hell for this, she realized, wincing. *The moment she finds out he called me, and learns I didn't respond . . .* Compared to everything else, it was a relatively small price to pay. Of course, that didn't mean it would be comfortable to endure, not when Chaplain Benjamin enjoyed teasing her so much.

FEBRUARY 10, 2494 T.S.
ATTENBOROUGH EPSILON 14 SYSTEM

It was difficult to focus on her meal. It was a good meal, too, roasted chicken, garlic potatoes, fresh V'Dan vegetables acquired from the *Mad Jack*'s multiple hydroponics bays, and greens from their own smaller pair of lifesupport gardens. The problem was that others had the Winter Olympics playing on both of the big primary screens lining either side of the room. Between the roar of the crowd, the action calls of the commentators, and the cheers or boos of her crewmates, it was hard for Ia to think.

"Turn the channel! Turn it!" Knorssen urged after looking at the chrono on her military wrist unit. She was almost dancing in her seat. "Turn it to the Nebula Network, channel 2! It's almost time!"

"*Shakk* that, Knorssen," Kipple joked. "You'd think *you* had a shot at winning the Power Pick. Besides, the rest of us are still watching the hockey game."

"Oh, right, like your home team has any more shot at winning the gold than she has at winning two and a half trillion creds," Yeoman Weavers called out from her position inside the galley kitchen. "I vote for the Power Pick. I bought a ticket, too."

Several of the others broke into argument. Two were with Kipple in keeping the North American Terrans versus the Southstream Solaricans hockey game going; the rest were with Weavers and Knorssen, wanting to see the Power Pick drawing. Someone turned and jabbed at the controls on their screen, someone else tried turning it back, the volume for the hockey game was turned up, the news network was turned up, and a small scuffle broke out.

Giving up, Ia picked up her mug and *cracked* the heavy ceramic onto the metal dining table. Not hard enough to break it by any means, but loudly enough to cut through their fighting. *"Enough."*

They sobered and quelled, returning to their seats. Flipping open her arm unit, Ia typed in the command that linked her to the Nets . . . and used her authority override to shut them off.

"You will stop acting like squabbling little children, and start behaving with the decorum expected of Space Force personnel. Is that clear?" she asked them in the sudden quiet filling the galley cabins.

"Commander Salish to Lieutenant Ia," the ship's intercom stated. *"Is there a particular reason why you cut off the news Nets? I was about to watch the Power Pick Lottery drawing."*

Ia's level glare kept anything greater than the slightest twitch of their mouths from quirking up. She activated her arm unit in reply. *"Just enacting a temporary point of discipline, sir."* Closing the line, she reprogrammed the monitors and removed the block. The news Nets blossomed on both screens, albeit with the sound muted. "In honor of our Commanding Officer, we will now watch the Power Pick Lottery. The hockey game is being stored in the Net archives. You can watch the play-by-play later, Private Kipple."

"Aye, sir," he mumbled.

Tapping her unit, she cycled up the sound to a decorous, tolerable level, and returned to eating her dinner.

". . . ion storms continue to rage in these sectors. Please consult your travel agency or local System Control Center for more details on any stellar-based delays," the announcer stated. Briefly, the vid pickups displayed him giving his viewers a species-neutral, closed-mouth smile. Sergei Hasmapana was a familiar face for most of the Terran news-Net viewers, having held his job for the last nine years. "For your local weather, should your homeworld have any, please consult your local planetary news; just touch one of our affiliate channels listed at the bottom of your screen for more details."

He turned his attention to the woman at his side. Unlike the male Human, who had tanned skin and dark hair reminiscent of Tamaganej, the woman had golden blonde hair, pale golden skin, and bluish-green stripes angling down over her face and the visible portions of her hands and forearms. Not many of the V'Dan still bore the old *jungen* marks; Kellena Var-D'junn, news anchor for Nebula News, was one of those that still did, playing on her visual distinctiveness to make a name and a face—pun freely admitted—for herself. Ia preferred the previous coanchor, but that woman had finally retired two years before.

"Coming up next," Kellena stated, "the results and highlights from the Meioa-o's Short Program, Freestyle Figure Skating."

"Don't tease them, Kellena," Sergei joked. He turned serious once again "Yes, meioas, it's the moment you've all been waiting for. This is an unprecedented benchmark in the history of the Alliance Lottery, which was instigated one hundred seventy-six years ago last month. This month, the Power Pick Lottery has broken records left and right, with an unprecedented jackpot. We've had an unfortunate string of winner tragedies, compounded by a surprising number of non-winning tickets even among the Standard Draw, which is any ticket with the correct numbers for the lottery, but not selected in the correct order. These events have multiplied the jackpot winnings to an astounding 2.3 *trillion* credits."

"As you know," Kellena continued, picking up the story from her coanchor, "in order to quell ticket riots, false claims, and even murder, the Alliance Lottery Commission has instigated a 'one sentient, one ticket' policy for all jackpots exceeding ten billion credits. If you are not the genetically and legally provable purchaser of the winning ticket, you will not be able to claim your prize."

"Even worse, as a reminder to everyone out there, not even a deceased person's heirs can inherit a winning ticket, nor can they be transferred to an inheritor for a minimum of ten Alliance Standard years, or approximately eight Terran Standard years. That is, if there *is* a winning ticket," Sergei warned her. "There might not be."

Kellena mock-touched her chest, clad in a grey suit that didn't go badly with her *jungen* marks. "Oh, please, Sergei, don't even suggest that. My nerves wouldn't be able to handle it a fourth time. I don't think anyone could. Again, our condolences to the relatives of Trrrgul the White Tail of the Family Hwarrenn, L'Oolou of Green-Happy-Green Clan, and Mrs. Nettie Attewell. If you have a health condition that could be triggered by sudden shock or stress, the Alliance Health Organization strongly suggests that you refrain from playing the Power Pick at times like this."

"For the rest of us with good hearts and other circulatory organs," Sergei told his viewers, "let's just hope someone gets the numbers right. The Alliance Lottery Commission has declared a temporary cap of 2.5 trillion credits to comply with the Lottery's current maximum cap of eighty percent of lottery income, and will be reworking the jackpot progression levels to comply with the new, upcoming cap of fifty percent," he reported. "Please remember that non-distributed Lottery earnings are used to help fund infrastructure and education systems for new colonyworlds across all the member governments of the Alliance for their first one hundred Standard years. What you don't win does go to support a very good cause—know your limits, and contact the Alliance Gambling Helpnet if you think you may have a problem."

"Enough with the suspense, Sergei. Tonight's numbers will be drawn and verified by the certified examiners of the D'marid-Hastings Investment Group, as overseen by His Eternal Majesty's Royal Guard," Kellena stated. "We go now, live, to the Alliance Lottery Headquarters at K'Seddua, Summer Capital of the V'Dan Empire."

The image shifted, revealing the brightly lit, tastefully

appointed lottery drawing chamber. The opening speech was interrupted by Commander Salish's voice. *"This is Commander Salish. All stop for the Lottery numbers. Keep your eyes to the boards, but you can keep your ears open for this. Good luck, meioas."*

"And the first number is . . . 13!" the unseen announcer stated as the V'Dan lottery workers fetched the first number from the tumbling balls in the archaic machine, drawn physically rather than electronically so that no accusations of code-fixing could be made.

Eight of the ten bodies in the galley groaned, though three of them looked vaguely hopeful. Knorssen shouted in glee, rising from her seat so fast, she thumped the edge of the table with her thighs. Given it was solid metal and firmly welded to the floor, she dropped back down with a grunt.

"Ow, dammit!"

"Shhh!" The mass of hushing didn't quite cover up the next number.

"The second number is . . . 74."

"WOOOO!" Again, Knorssen leaped up—and again whacked her thighs. She dropped back with a twisted expression that was half grimace, half grin. Higatsu and Schumacher, seated on either side of her, quickly grabbed her by the arms and shoulders, pinning her in her seat.

The third number was announced. Tensed to cheer, Knorssen let out a wail instead. *"Noooo! Noooooooo!* Dammit, that was my *fifth* numberrrrr!"

"SHHH!"

As the others hissed, Schumacher clapped his hand over her mouth, careful not to cover her nose so that Knorssen could still breathe. Higatsu gave her shoulder a consoling squeeze. One by one, the ten numbers were drawn from the pool of one hundred possible. When the last one came up, Knorssen had only the three numbers, which wasn't enough to qualify for even the minimum winnings. From the mutterings of the others, three numbers were the most that they had, too.

"This is the Commander to all awake hands. Do we have any Power Pick or Standard Draw winners on board? And no, I do not want to hear from those who did not win. We can hold

a little pity party later. For now, I just want to know if anybody actually won anything."

"Captain, this is Corporal Benaroya, down in Engineering. I, ah, just won four thousand credits. Or I will have won, once we get back to the *Mad Jack.*"

"Congratulations, Corporal. It's not the grand jackpot, but it is still significant. Alright, meioas. Let's make sure he gets back in one piece, so he can collect his winnings. Resuming course. Commander Salish out."

"Oh, god," Knorssen muttered, rubbing at her thighs. "I have deep bruises on my legs, and *nothing* to show for—"

"Shhh!" Kipple hushed her as the vid view switched back to the Nebula Newsroom. "They're going to announce if anyone won!"

Higatsu rubbed his hands together, grinning. "With any luck, it'll be someone who owes me money, and I'll get to charge them interest for not having paid it off right away!"

Another *shhh* hushed him. On the monitor screens, Kellena Var-D'junn blinked, nodded at the teleprompter screen beyond the pickup cameras, and stated, "Yes . . . yes, we do have a Power Pick winner. I repeat, we *have* a Power Pick winner!"

Sergei squinted a little. "The winning ticket was registered on the Independent Colonyworld of . . . Sanctuary?"

Ia buried her smirk in her mug of milk, then dug into the last of her roasted chicken.

"—Which I believe lies approximately seven hundred light-years from Earth," Kellena quickly filled in, covering for him. "If I remember correctly, it is the heaviest inhabited M-class heavyworld, though the exact gravity escapes me at the moment. Rest assured, we'll be running a special series of info-news programs on the winner's homeworld later on this week."

"Yes. The winning ticket was purchased in the city of . . . Our Blessed Mother? Is that right?" he asked, glancing first at his coanchor, who shrugged, then off camera for a brief moment. He gave his audience another close-mouthed smile, this time an apologetic one. "With so many worlds to keep track of in the known galaxy, please forgive us if we get any of this information wrong."

Kellena lifted her hand. "Remember, viewers: The winning

numbers will have to be verified by examinations conducted by the Royal Guard of the V'Dan Emperor and by the D'marid-Hastings Investment Group, but . . . yes . . . we *do* have a confirmation on the identity of the winning Power Pick Lottery ticket holder."

"But first, the Standard Draw winners," Sergei stated, drawing out the suspense. "Sharing the Standard Draw jackpot of twenty-three billion credits are the following five meioas—"

"Oh, for star's sake! Get to the Power Pick winner's *name* already!" Petty Officer Michaelson growled, his voice drowning out the start of the five winners' names. Knorssen was the first one to crumple up her napkin and toss it at him. Kipple, Schumacher, and two others followed suit.

"Meioas," Ia stated crisply, cutting through their assault. "However much he *does* deserve that, I do have to agree with him. Now let us . . . *Shhh!"* She cut herself off, since the female news anchor was speaking again.

"Our deepest congratulations, and our sincerest wishes of continuing good health, go out to the Human winner of the Power Pick grand jackpot, Meioa-o Fyfer Quentin-Jones of Our Blessed Mother, which is apparently the capital city of I. C. Sanctuary. May you spend it wisely . . . and may you share some of your newfound, astronomical wealth with your fellow sentients out there," the news anchor stated wryly. "Because I certainly didn't win any of it."

"Yes, good luck, Meioa Quentin-Jones, and congratulations," Sergei stated. "I'm told it will take six days at the bare minimum to get the nearest branch of the Alliance Lottery Commission's Power Pick Prize Team all the way out to Sanctuary, due to the great distance that must be traveled and the inherent risks of stringing that many OTL jumps in a row. Nebula News and others from among our fellow news agencies across the Nets will be accompanying them to bring you the action live . . . or as live as anything streaming from the far edge of the known galaxy can get."

"Off," Knorssen muttered, rubbing her face. Her palms half muffled her words. "Turn it *off.* Put it back to hockey, or whatever. I can't stand to hear anything more about a meioa I have no hope in hell of getting to know."

Leaning over, Kipple jabbed the controls, programming it

back to the Terran/Solarican game. On the other side of the table, Nguyen did the same. The excitement of the Winter Olympics had paled a little, however.

"Wait a second," Nguyen muttered, swiveling in his seat. He frowned at Ia. "Lieutenant, aren't *you* from Sanctuary? Heaviest heavyworld in the known galaxy?"

Ah, damn. I lost that gamble. The odds hadn't been more than 20 percent that one of them would've remembered that much of her background. Opening the compartment that held her dessert, a whipped pudding, Ia picked up her spoon. "That would be correct."

"Oh, c'mon, Mike," Kipple admonished Nguyen. "There's bound to be a million people on her homeworld."

"There's barely even a couple hundred thousand, yet," Ia corrected mildly, dipping her spoon slowly, carefully into her dessert. "It was settled less than sixty years ago, and even though the wombpods have been popping babies like mad, we don't have that many people there, yet. We're only just now starting on our third native-born generation—I don't know the population numbers anymore. I didn't exactly stop to count heads, the last time I was there."

"But, with only a couple hundred thousand, that means there's a chance you actually *know* the guy!" Knorssen crowed. "Or at least know someone who knows him!"

The hard look Ia shot Knorssen silenced the other woman. "If I say I know him, you will press and press and press in the hopes that I'll somehow connect you to the lucky meioa, and get you a handout, Private. If I say I do *not* know him, you will think me a liar, and *still* you will press, and press, and press. Telling the truth, or telling a lie, it *does not matter.* My answer will be the same: silence. This subject is closed, because it has *nothing* to do with our mission, here on Blockade Patrol . . . not to mention, it could be considered a potential violation of Fatality Forty-Nine.

"The *only* gambling I am interested in is the gamble that I can lead the lot of you effectively enough that all of us get back home alive. But in order to *do* that," Ia warned the men and women seated around her at the table, "I need you to put your minds back onto our job. Is that clear? Because if it isn't, you need to get your heads out of your daydream-stuffed asteroids."

Her crude statement made them blink, but Ia figured it was more from the tone of her delivery than its actually content. "You cannot spend money you will not have, if you get shipped back home in a coffin."

She swept her gaze around the table, pinning each soldier with a stern look. Half of them looked down or away just before she got to them, and the rest lowered their gazes within a second or two. Lifting her spoonful of pudding, Ia mock-saluted them with it.

"Now that we have that settled, I suggest you remind your crewmates on both sides of the *Audie-Murphy* that this is not only a closed subject, it is also not one I'd care to have discussed outside of our ships. I'll remind you that the Salik get some of the same news Nets that we do, and they'll be looking for *any* signs of distraction among the crews serving on the Blockade. Eyes to the boards, thoughts on your tasks, and diligence in your vigilance . . . though I'll grant you that since our duty shift is over, the *Audie* half doesn't have to look at the boards for the next . . . eleven hours, unless and until we get called to action. But the moment we do, Commander Salish and I need you to be at your best.

"In the meantime," Ia finished briskly, "I have pudding to eat, Kipple has a hockey game to watch, and *all* of you will need your rest."

Popping the spoon into her mouth, she took her time savoring the treat, deliberately showing by actions as well as lack of words that the subject was indeed firmly closed. Sighing, the others turned away, either murmuring among themselves their mutual condolences, wistfully suggesting what they would've done with all that money, or speculating idly on the outcome of the now closely matched hockey game.

A couple of her crew snuck glances Ia's way, but she pointedly ignored them, calmly scraping up every last scrap of her dessert. No one was going to weasel one scrap of information out of her, particularly not regarding one Meioa-o Fyfer Quentin-Jones.

CHAPTER 16

Did I lie about not knowing Meioa Quentin-Jones, the biggest Power Pick winner in Alliance history? Of course I lied. Wouldn't you? Ah—let me rephrase that. Knowing that if you admitted it, you'd be pestered to death, literally to the point where it would interfere with everything you were trying to do and thus risk the safety of your crew and your missions . . . wouldn't you lie, too? No, I had far bigger problems to deal with than dwelling on the fact I was related to someone who was now suddenly and rather astronomically wealthy.

The Salik did try to push through the Blockade. I'm not sure just how many slipped through the Lottery-distracted cracks, but I don't think it was all that many. Luckily for us, it was a hastily planned event. Luckily for us, the Salik weren't quite ready for the Big Push that would break the Blockade. And most crews pulled it back together fast enough to survive.

Eyes to the boards, thoughts on your tasks. That was the Navy's motto on Blockade Patrol. Wise words for any situation, if you ask me.

~Ia

FEBRUARY 13, 2494 T.S.
BATTLE PLATFORM *MAD JACK*
SS'NUK LULK 46 SYSTEM

"So how *do* you feel about your brother winning the Power Pick?"

Ia groaned and dropped into one of the two easy chairs in Bennie's office. "Not you, *too . . .*"

The chaplain worked on pouring the caf'. "Don't worry, I'm not interested in a handout. And the only reason why I asked is that it's pretty easy to figure out 'Fyfer' your brother back on Sanctuary is 'Fyfer Quentin-Jones' from the news Nets. Fyfer isn't a common name."

"I'm glad you're not interested, Bennie, because I've figured out that *asking* me for a handout is a potential violation of Fatality Forty-Nine, Fraternization. On the business side of things, not the intimate version," Ia added in clarification. "Thou shalt not mix personal business and any situation in the military wherein a superior/inferior situation exists—actually, if you could do me a *huge* favor?"

"What's that?" Bennie asked, coming over to the chairs with the usual two mugs. She handed one to Ia before settling into her own chair.

"Flag my file," Ia said. "Flag it so that if anyone probes deep enough to discover Fyfer's my brother, *also* make sure the warning pops up that anyone who asks me about him and the Power Pick winnings automatically risks Fatality Forty-Nine . . . because if anyone *does*, I'm going to ram that down their throats until they choke on it and shut up."

"Jealous of his good luck?" Bennie asked, lifting her auburn brows.

Ia chuckled and flicked the fingers not holding her caf' mug. "Oh, hell, no. Actually, I'm extremely proud of him. Pleased for him. Whatever you want to call it. Of course, when I finally do make it back home, I shall have to do my best to pop his ego, since it'll undoubtedly get rather overinflated over this. But no, I'm honestly happy for him. And *no*, I don't want the money for myself. I don't need it."

"Is that so?" Bennie challenged lightly.

Sipping from her mug, Ia shrugged. "Okay, so I *will* insist that he pay for my next ticket home. But otherwise, most of my personal needs are covered by the stipend I get as an officer. And I didn't grow up in a materialistic family, so I've never *needed* possessions. Not that I *could* haul around all that much these days, living the itinerant military life."

"So why don't you want anyone to know that Fyfer's your brother?" Bennie asked.

"Because Blockade Patrol is too serious and too dangerous to permit even moderate distractions," Ia said, shrugging. "Being pestered to death by requests for handouts and introductions would severely weaken our defenses. I need my attention on the task at hand, and I need the attention of everyone around me on the task at hand."

"Okay . . . different question," Bennie allowed. "Why did you declare emancipation from your family at the age of sixteen?"

That was an uncomfortable question. Mindful of Fatality Forty-Three, Perjury, Ia glossed over the subject with the mildest version of the truth she could give. "Because I came to realize that the direction my family wanted and expected my life to go in was not the direction *I* wanted it to go in."

"Oh?"

The single word held a wealth of interrogation. Sighing, Ia slouched in her chair, trying to figure out something to get the chaplain's curiosity satisfied. "I . . . differ from my parents on the standpoint of children. Very strongly. I don't want any. Yet as a second-gen first-worlder, and living on a world with a high mortality rate, it's almost obligatory to have multiple progeny." She circled one hand vaguely. "The wombpods can produce children, yes, and Population Expansion can provide crèche-mothers and crèche-fathers . . . but children need real parents. And I do *not* want to raise any kids. Even knowing that, my mothers still made the 'so when are we getting grandkids' speech, last year. It's a classic case of *I love them, but . . .*"

"Fair enough," Bennie agreed. "Not everyone wants children. Not everyone *should* have children. Domestic abuse, bad parenting skills, neglect . . ."

"I wouldn't neglect, abuse, or whatever a child," Ia dismissed. "I just don't want that kind of responsibility in my life."

"What about the responsibility of a relationship?" Bennie asked, slanting a look at Ia over her mug.

Ia wrinkled her nose. "Don't get started, Bennie. We agreed to part company. We're stationed nowhere near each other. Yadda yadda—how about I ask *you* a few questions this time?"

Bennie chuckled. "That's what I'm here for. Though I'm more skilled in philosophical debates than in questions about, oh . . . say, particle physics."

Smirking, Ia asked, "So, how 'bout them strange quarks?"

The redhead mock-frowned and shook her head. "I don't think they have a chance at the gold. It'll be the charmed quarks at the top of the podium, this Olympics."

Ia chuckled. Then sat up. "Oh—I wanted to watch the Biathlon Mass Open. We have two soldiers competing on the Terran team . . . uhh . . . Jana Bagha, and I forget the other fellow's name. They're both Sharpshooters in the Special Forces. I think it's supposed to be starting soon . . . *ah*, slag," Ia muttered, checking her chrono. "It's *already* started. I didn't realize it was so late. You want to watch it with me? Catch the end of it, at least?"

"Sure." Twisting, Bennie tapped the wall monitor, turning it on. "It doesn't help that the host-world, Brown-Valley-Green, has a day-cycle that's rather difficult to convert into Terran Standard." She consulted the programming list and changed channels to the right one. "Yep, already in action. Six klicks into the race, too. Care to wager who buys dinner on the outcome?"

"Sure," Ia agreed, stretching out her legs as the screen started blaring the noise of the crowd as they watched the racers alternating between skiing and shooting at targets. "And just because I like rooting for the underdog, I'll pick the Terrans to place at least one medal on the platform."

Bennie snorted, curling up with one ankle under the other knee. "Terrans haven't placed in any medals on the platform for the last five Olympics—not in the Biathlon, at least. It'll be Solaricans all the way. Fast, furry, and native heavyworlders. Triple sweep."

Ia hid her smirk behind the rim of her cup, already knowing the outcome. "You're on. And since the bet is a lobster dinner, I'll raise the dessert stakes to one of those medalists on the podium being a soldier—Terran, Solarican, or whatever, we'll have a soldier on the stands."

"Oh, you are *so* on. I heard Samdie's Restaurant up on Deck 14 just got a shipment of live lobsters and Belgian chocolates. Prepare to lose *two* weeks' salary, meioa," Bennie quipped. She paused and eyed Ia. "You *do* have enough money to cover the bet, right?"

"I do, if you do," Ia shot back, draining her mug.

FEBRUARY 16, 2494 T.S.
SS'NUK NEH 1334 SYSTEM

Ia was alone in the gym cabin, watching the last event of the Olympics as she exercised in extra gravity, when Commander Salish apparently decided to switch the main channel feeds to the Nebula News network. The *Audie-Murphy* was sitting on the system's edge, doing nothing more strenuous than monitoring lightwave readings. They were permitted only six hyper-relay channels when out on patrol, one for the news Nets, another for communication with their Battle Platform base, one for communicating with any ships they encountered, and the remaining three reserved for coordinating lightwave data with insystem buoys and any scanner probes they might launch.

Instead of catching the end of the icefalls speed climbing event—one of the few winter sports events the K'katta could participate in, since their legs weren't built for skating or skiing—Ia found herself being given a hovercamera's-eye view of the main docking promenade on the space station orbiting her homeworld, Gateway Station.

". . . just told that the winning ticket owner has agreed to come up to this station, so that we do not need to go through the inconvenience and potential health risks of donning gravity weave suits," the correspondent selected for this mission informed his audience. The redheaded man frowned in confusion, staring ahead of him. "*Huh.* It seems we have another checkpoint set up just ahead."

"Stars," one of his companions muttered, "where did they find the uniform to fit *that* overgrown ape?"

Ia almost missed a step on the treadmill when she realized the "overgrown ape" in question was her older brother. Smirking, she watched as the camerawoman, reporter, and trio of representatives from the Alliance Lottery Commission reached the row of barriers blocking off their docking port from the rest of the station. The other news network representatives moved up behind them.

"Identification, please," she watched Thorne order gruffly, holding out an ident scanner wand. Beside him, clad in the same plain beige coveralls as his brother, stood a dozen other, shorter natives. Including Fyfer, who had a palm scanner ready for a biometric reading. All of them wore caps with brims and sunglasses. Only her familiarity with this moment in time allowed Ia to identify each of them.

"We've had five shiploads of con-meioas arriving in the last twenty hours," Fyfer told them gruffly. "All claiming to be ALC members. I'm afraid you'll have to stand back there, off to your right, meioa."

The head spokesmeioa for the Alliance Lottery Commission, a slender female Gatsugi, blinked her mouse-black eyes. She lifted her two right hands in a gesture of bemusement, skin mottling in shades of tan and green in visible show of her confusion. "I do not/not understand/comprehend. I am/exist as myself/Meioa Sliin Mpau Djuu/Meioa Green Waters Falling On Meadows. I cannot/cannot act/lie very well/sufficiently in person/face-to-face."

"Please step to the right, meioa, until I have processed your companions," Fyfer ordered, pointing to the side. "Please/Please move/step to your/the right," he added when she hesitated, using her own species' emphasis patterns. Gesturing compliance, she moved. He scanned the hand—some would say paw—of the Solarican next in line, measuring the male's biometrics. "Thank you. Please step to the right, meioa, until I have processed your companions."

The correspondent, whose name flashed across the bottom of the screen as Mark Optermitter, looked up at the nearest hovercamera. "It seems we have yet another delay on arrival. First the standard docking customs to get off our ship, and now this. I don't . . . wait . . . Georg, get a close-up of the meioa with the palm scanner. He looks familiar."

Just as one of the three cameras zoomed in, Fyfer also stepped to the right in the wake of the V'Dan Lottery Commission member, forcing the hovering vidunit to sway and follow him. He smiled at the trio, closed-mouthed and polite.

"I apologize for the inconvenience, but there really have been far too many con-meioas attempting to deceive the true winner," Fyfer stated. "Not to mention at least six false ticket winners trying to get onto the station from planet-side. Please get out your own biometric and ident scanners now."

"*You're* him!" Mark the reporter exclaimed. He pointed at Fyfer. "Or at least, you *look* like Meioa Quentin-Jones . . ."

"Which is why these gentlemeioas need to get out their scanners *now*, so we can get this over with. Because *your* antics are going to draw far too much attention," the beige-clad young man added sternly, looking straight at the reporters.

Not just Mark and his camera operator, but the three other reporters and their crew who were now pressing forward. Except that half a dozen more beige-clad bodies stepped between them and Fyfer, who turned back to the Commission members and began submitting to their identity verification requests.

One of them, the youth Leuron, spoke up. "Please hold your questions until after the verification process is complete. Anyone who starts shouting, yelling, or otherwise making a spectacle of themselves will be removed."

Mark challenged him. "You're just a kid. Whose authority says you can remove us?"

Leuron ignored the question. "Anyone who violates common sense, common decency, and discretion will be denied the right to interview Mcioa Quentin-Jones."

One of the other reporters, a Solarican, tried to push past the youths in beige coveralls. An *oof* and a *thud* found her tossed to the floor face-first. The young man who had tossed her down picked her up again. He did so by using just one arm, hooking his fingers under the belt of her suit. Her tail lashed as she regained her feet, but she wisely did not challenge him a second time.

Leuron smirked and folded his arms across his chest. "We are the heaviest of heavyworlders, and we are Afaso trained," he told the reporters. "Do not start anything, and we will not harm you. Start something . . . and we *will* finish it. We are the meioa's security team. I suggest you cooperate."

Ia shut off the treadmill and moved over to the resistance weights. Just as she settled onto the bench, the Solarican gestured to someone beyond the range of the cameras. With a *thunk thunk thunk thunk*, two assistants, both Human, rolled a giant mock-up of an oversized, ten-sided credit chit into view. The Nebula News cameras zoomed in on Fyfer, who finished shaking hands with the V'Dan presenter.

Removing his cap and his sunglasses, he glanced their way and smiled, all pleasantness and charm now that business had been handled. In fact, he unsealed his coveralls and stepped out of them, shaking off the oversized legs. What lay underneath made Ia groan and stop pulling on the levers, just so she could bury her face in her hands.

"Oh, *Brother*," she muttered. A peek through her fingers showed the results were still the same. Tight black pants and a tight black and gold shirt showed off his heavyworlder muscles. Black knee-high boots and a gold-studded belt completed the outfit. Fyfer swept his hand through his hair, loosening the curls squashed by the cap. He even winked at the camera.

Ia rolled her eyes. She didn't have to be precognitive to know her brother was going for Heartthrob of the Century. Millions of young females and males would be plastering their walls with pictures culled from this one newscast, and her younger brother had clearly prepared for it. Sighing heavily, she went back to pulling on the overhead levers, needing to get her workout done before the crew finished scanning and analyzing the local lightwave readings.

"Alright, meioas, *now* I'll talk to you. Yes, I'm the real Fyfer Quentin-Jones . . . and this is the *only* interview you are going to get out of me," her brother stated, voice carrying over the hiss of the hydraulics in the small cabin. Out of the corner of her eye, Ia could see him smiling closed-mouth at the cameras. "Allow me to get the most pressing questions out of the way.

"First of all, a message for anyone attempting to hack into my bank accounts: Good luck. Alliance Lottery Commission policy is to divide up the actual funds into thousands of sleeper accounts tucked away behind various different kinds of security, and all of it safely obscured by registry numbers only, no names. Second, should I die before the first ten years Alliance Standard are up, that's it. No more money for anyone. And if I should die *after* the next ten years, my heir has already been designated. Trust me when I say there is no way in hell *any* of you will be able to get your hands on the inheritor in question.

"Thirdly," he continued as Ia picked up the pace, grunting with effort as the machinery hissed. Hydraulic resistance was one of the few methods of weight training that could both withstand the rigors of her strength and maintain her muscle mass. Fyfer again smiled for the cameras, charming but implacable. "I refuse, categorically and permanently, to listen to *any* requests for money. Loans, gifts, charities, threats, demands, or whatever, I will ignore it. I'll also remind everyone that I live on Sanctuary. The local gravity is 3.21Gs Standard. I suppose you *could* try to use gravity weaves to get to me in person, but I would still turn you away.

"Fourthly, as for any attempt to kidnap me, or any of my family members, or anyone else I may even so much as remotely care about, and hold any of us ransom? It will *fail*. I have already made arrangements to make sure that anyone attempting such a thing—and everyone *they* care about—will regret it. What that *means*, I shall leave up to your imaginations. Remember," Fyfer warned, "I now have the wealth equivalent to an entire interstellar nation at my fingertips . . . and like most nations, I *refuse* to bargain with kidnappers and terrorists. You have been warned.

"Fifth on the list . . . yes, you have a question, meioa-e?" Fyfer asked the reporter from the Solarican empire.

"Yes. If you'rrre not even going to lllisten to philllan-thrrropic rrequests, what *arre* you going to do with allll that money?" the woman asked. "You can't just hoarrrd it all to yourrrsellf."

"Oh, I suppose I could," the young man in black and gold drawled. Ia snorted and reconfigured the machine so she could work on her legs for a bit.

"But will you?" the Tlassian representative asked. "Or do you hhhave sssomething innn mind?"

"Well, Sanctuary *is* a new colonyworld. My hope is to . . ." Fyfer broke off as a scuffle formed at the barrier. Thorne was leaning to one side, then the other at the gateway of the temporary barrier. Being taller and broader than the neatly suited gentlemen trying to get close, he didn't have to move far to

intimidate them into failing. Like Fyfer, he had taken the time
to remove his beige coveralls, revealing black and silver clothes
that fit almost as tightly as Fyfer's did, though unlike Fyfer,
his were made from local leathers.

Flustered at being so effectively blocked, the lead male
pointed his finger at Thorne. "You had better move, young
meioa, or I will have you *arrested* for interfering in government
business!"

"Considering that Gateway Station is officially independent and separate from the government of Sanctuary, President
Moller," Thorne rumbled, his face coming into view as some
of the hovercameras shifted his way, "that would be rather
difficult. You are *outside* your jurisdiction."

"We'll see about that. All I have to do is contact the
Stationmaster—" the president of Sanctuary began.

Thorne smiled. "This entire station has been *hired* by Meioa
Quentin-Jones. Whatever my little brother wants, my little
brother gets."

*And in doing so, you have just doomed the entire station to
being obliterated when the civil war begins, in a petty act of
revenge,* Ia thought. She smiled as she worked her lower muscles. *Pity for Moller and the Church, they'll have had plenty
of advanced warning to strip the station of everything potentially valuable and evacuate all but the most skeleton of crews
just before that happens . . .*

"*Ah,* President Moller," Fyfer drawled. "How extraordinary
to see you here."

Thorne looked over his shoulder, nodded at his brother, and
stood aside. The politician, who was also one of the chief
Church Elders, stepped through the gap. Thorne immediately
moved back into place, cutting off the president's bodyguards.
A flex of Thorne's muscles made the leather of his shirt *creeeaak*
audibly, even with the hovercameras several meters away. It
was enough to make the guards hesitate. The open-air nature
of the promenade and the presence of so many hovercameras
kept them from pressing the matter, since it was obvious no
one *could* do anything to Sanctuary's president without it being
broadcast all over the known galaxy.

Smiling, Moller approached Fyfer with outspread arms.
Leuron stepped between them. He had not removed his

coveralls, but adopted the same arms-folded stance as Thorne, presenting another barrier between the politician and the young trillionaire.

Giving the younger man a dirty look, Moller managed to keep his smile. "There you are, Meioa! Our most important citizen—congratulations on your most fortuitous win! Naturally, I'm here to discuss with you all the wonderful contributions you can make toward making your home the most amazing colony in the known galaxy. Think of the hospitals, the universities, the construction of the Holy Cathedral and the glory of—"

"No." The refusal, plain and flat, set Moller back on his heels. Fyfer smiled tightly. "*You* personally assured the voters that you would see that funds were channeled toward greater medical facilities and education. The money *is* there in the budget, Mcioa President. Particularly if you stop shoveling extra money into the *non*essential fund for the Cathedral of Truth, and put it back into the *essential* needs of the colony, which you have consistently short-funded during your terms in office."

"Careful, Fyfer . . ." Ia admonished her brother. Not that he could hear her, but she didn't want him to overplay his hand.

"You would *deny* giving your fellow colonists the *essential* services you yourself insist are so important?" Moller countered, his voice edged with a hint of triumph for his counterargument.

"I don't/cannot understand/comprehend," the Gatsugi reporter interjected, curling the four fingers of her upper left hand in a touch of confusion. "Wouldn't/Shouldn't the taxes/collections on/regarding the lottery earnings/winnings pay for/fund such/these things/needs?"

"Yes! They indeed should. I almost completely forgot," Moller stated, his smile not quite a smirk. "Why, the taxes on 2.3 trillion credits alone would pay—"

"For *nothing*," Fyfer stated coldly, cutting him off again. He gave the president a tight smile. "Or have you indeed forgotten the fine print of the Sanctuarian Charter, as ratified by the Alliance? Allow me to *remind* you, Meioa President: The Alliance Lottery *funded* half of the settling of Sanctuary. In fact, thirty percent of all local ticket sales are reserved *for*

Sanctuary's personal use, given it is still within our first hundred years of settlement."

"That is correct," the V'Dan representative of the ALC stated, shifting a meter or so closer to Fyfer. "In exchange, all Alliance Lottery winnings are to be considered tax-free for the first one hundred years of a new colony's settlement. After that, the winnings drop to fifteen percent for local use, five percent for interstellar use, and the remainder—under the current cap—goes into the jackpot. Any violation of your planet's Charter agreement by a particular planetary government will force a rollover of that government."

Thorne, who had turned to watch the tableau, grinned. His voice rumbled through the monitor's speakers. "That means the *minority* government, the Free World Colony party, will take over. The Truth Party will then be banned from holding a majority of offices for . . . what is it, eight years?"

"Ten years Alliance Standard, or eight years, four months, three weeks, Terran Standard," the V'Dan commissioner confirmed. "You will forgive me if I cannot convert that into Sanctuarian Standard just yet. Not off the top of my head."

Fyfer gave her a little bow in acknowledgment and thanks before turning back to the flush-cheeked Moller. "As opposite as we may be in political views, Meioa President . . . I find that I cannot in good conscience allow you to torpedo your party's access to your full political and citizenship rights. That would *also* go against the Sanctuarian Charter.

"Unfortunately, this means that the *only* money you can tax off of me are my wages for the year. Given that I quit my job as a waiter at my parents' restaurant the moment I found out I won, you will be able to collect on just over six weeks' worth of wages, Terran Standard. That's seven weeks, local," Fyfer added, smiling briefly at the V'Dan Lottery agent. "By *any* measure, seven weeks' worth of taxes on wages at the minimum pay a waiter gets is hardly enough to buy a case of medicine, never mind an entire hospital!"

"But that stilll begs the questionnn, what arre you going to *do* with alll that monney?" the Solarican reporter asked him.

Fyfer smiled softly. "I am a good son, meioa. My family has never had much, but my parents gave their children, my brother, sister, and myself, as much love and care as they could.

They raised us to know what is right, and to do what is right. My first task, therefore, will be to build my parents a home they can be proud of. One where they can retire in great comfort."

Ohhh, Fyfer, why'd you have to mention you have a sister? Ia mentally groaned. Sighing heavily, she moved to the next machine position as her brother continued.

"After that . . . well, for all that President Moller and I have numerous *political* differences, we are both men of faith, and men who are capable of planning for the future. I shall attend to the long-term needs of my people." He flicked a glance at Moller, or maybe at Thorne behind him; the camera angle made it difficult to tell. "Specifically, I shall attend to them in the order of priorities which *I* feel must be addressed, and in the manners I and my closest advisors choose. Yes, I *do* have plans for all that money. But those plans are my own business, not yours.

"Now, back to my list. Fifth, and final, I *am* single at the moment," Fyfer confessed, looking into the hovercameras once more. "But I am also in love, and the person whom I love returns my affections. This being has returned them from *before* the time when I first purchased that winning ticket, so I know these feelings are not being faked simply because I am now wealthy. As a result, any and all offers of marriage, sex, procreation, and so forth are futile. I am not interested, and I never will be . . . and I will not reveal the identity of the person I care about.

"I will not have the meioa's life put in danger by the stupid and the forgetful—please review my previous comment on how I will *not* negotiate with kidnappers, terrorists, or tormentors of any kind," Fyfer repeated, "and in fact will react in a most unpleasant and polar-opposite manner to the one such tactics would try to demand. This interview is now over, meioas," Fyfer finished politely. "I have nothing more to say, beyond that I am going to go back to my li—"

A woman screamed in the distance. Cameras jiggled and swooped, focusing in that direction. One of the real dockworkers, wearing stained beige coveralls, collapsed to her knees. Her yells echoed badly off the hard angles of the promenade's bulkheads, distorting her words, but the words *fire* and *birds* and *arise* could be heard. The Nebula News camera operator recovered quickly, switching views back to one of the cameras still pointed at Fyfer.

Except Fyfer wasn't there anymore. The entire group with him had taken advantage of the distraction to hustle away. Two youths had hoisted the giant novelty chit between them, painted opalescent and inlaid in gold numbers with the exact amount Fyfer had won. They carried it with great ease despite its obvious bulk, moving quickly across the docking ring.

In fact, the group moved so quickly, the camera had barely focused for more than a few seconds when they vanished through a door marked Authorized Personnel Only. Proof that their presence was indeed sanctioned by the station's governor.

A bit over the top at points, Ia decided, pausing in her exercises to check the timestreams. *But otherwise more or less on target. You shouldn't have mentioned that you have a sister, Little Brother . . . but good job all the same.*

The cameras for Nebula News swerved back to the reporter. Finally, the show had a view of the crowd of sentients behind him, almost two dozen bodies who had won the chance to travel with the Lottery members directly. Others no doubt were arriving on the station elsewhere, hoping to get an interview, but it was too late.

The correspondent for Nebula News was willing to acknowledge that much. ". . . Well. There you have it. One of the richest, and quite possibly one of the most headstrong, meioas in the known galaxy. Given the speed of our arrival via OTL, we have a mandatory two-day waiting period before we can safely turn around and head back home. I shall be bringing updates on Meioa Quentin-Jones's background, education, and other news from interviews with those locals who may know him in the meantime . . . since the meioa-o does not seem inclined to grant further interviews at this time.

"Hopefully in the future, that will change. But for now, that seems to be all. I'm Mark Optermitter, reporting live for Nebula News, currently in orbit around Independent Colonyworld Sanctuary," he concluded.

A brief holding message covered up the handful of seconds it took for the main anchors at Nebula News to come back on screen. Just as they reappeared, the channel switched back to the Olympics. Ia smiled wryly and switched positions again on the hydraulics machine, this time working her abdominal muscles.

Apparently Commander Salish doesn't want to hear the "post aftermath wrap-up" speeches. As far as I'm concerned, that's great, because neither do I—ah, even better! she thought, peering at the mid-race scores posted in the corner of the screen. *L'k'tikkitt is in second place in freestyle ice climbing. There's a 58 to 42 percent chance he'll win. I bet Bennie another lobster dinner on this one. The probabilities were stronger on the biathlon, but this one is a much more honest wager, since ice climbing is so difficult to master. Or so I've heard, offworld. Anything to do with moving on ice or snow is far too potentially deadly, back home . . .*

Back home. But it wasn't home, anymore.

With all that money, my brothers are going to change, well, not the face *of Sanctuary, but they'll definitely change its future . . . and what a relief to know they've pulled it off. One less worry on my mind.*

Resting back on the bench, Ia stared up at the pale grey ceiling and smiled. She even closed her eyes for a moment. The deep pleasure of having surmounted this major hurdle—funding the survival of her homeworld—unfortunately didn't last very long. Once again, she was running out of time. She would have to finish exercising soon, prepare for hyperjump, and then try to get at least three hours of sleep before the *Audie-Murphy* would run up against a trio of pirates.

They would be caught skimming rare isotope vapors from one of the gas giants in the next system, and do their best to outflank and outfight the *Audie* and the *Murphy*. Which meant it would take all of Ia's concentration to make sure she navigated the fight to a Navy-favorable outcome, but still allow one particular pirate vessel to escape. *Which goes against my orders, and will count as a black mark on my record. A very black mark, if I don't position things just right and they figure out it was deliberately let go, on my part.*

Unfortunately, I need that particular ship to still be out there, and to have a very good, repeated reason to hate Bloody Mary in the coming year, in preparation for three years down

the road. Which means at least three more black marks on my
record in the near future. Then again, having perfect records
would start making the DoI suspicious of my success rate.

APRIL 28, 2494 T.S.
BATTLE PLATFORM *MAD JACK*
SIC TRANSIT

Arms tucked behind her back in Parade Rest, Dress Blues cap
squarely leveled on her brow, Ia tried to flex her knees subtly.
Light gravity or not, standing in one position for a long time
was tiresome. Her efforts to shake the numbness from her
muscles did not pass unnoticed, however. Commodore Deng
looked up from the desk-level screens and printouts he was
reviewing.

"Feet getting sore, Lieutenant?" the commanding officer of
Battle Platform *Mad Jack* asked.

"Sir, no, sir. Just making sure the blood is still flowing, sir,"
she explained.

"Bored, Lieutenant?" Captain Yacob asked next. He was
seated next to the commodore, reviewing the same files with
his superior. On Deng's far side was one of the other officers
in charge of Delta-VX patrols, Captain Harrison.

That question was low on the list of probabilities. Ia consulted the timestreams briefly, lightly. She shook her head
slowly to stall for time. "No, Captain. Just . . . concerned about
time, that's all."

"Oh? What sort of time, Lieutenant?" Commodore Deng
asked, glancing up at her.

"Well, sirs, if you deem me still psychologically adjusted
and fit for continued duty on Blockade Patrol, I should be
returned to duty. The *Audie-Murphy* is scheduled to drop and
depart for her next patrol as soon as we hit the Annabelle 27
System, which is in about one hour. If I'm fit to continue, I
should be on board and ready to go when that happens," Ia
stated. "And if you judge me *not* fit for continued Blockade
duty, sirs, I need to be dismissed equally soon so I can go pack
up and remove my things from the *Audie-Murphy*."

Commodore Deng shook his head. "We already knew the

answer to that particular question before you even came in here, Lieutenant."

"Sir?" Ia questioned. She wasn't questioning the outcome; she knew—all three of them knew—that she was as stable as anyone could hope to be in a high-stress zone like the Blockade. More stable than most, really. Instead, she was questioning why she had been kept here.

Captain Yacob answered her one-word query. "We're debating whether or not to promote you."

"Do you have an opinion on the matter, Lieutenant?" Captain Harrison asked Ia. She lifted her chin as she did so, no doubt waiting for Ia to eagerly promote herself. Ia wasn't about to play that game. That was the wrong way to advance. But neither would false modesty help her cause.

"It would depend on what a promotion meant, sirs," she said instead. "I feel I've managed to strike up the right level of camaraderie and leadership within the rotating crews of the *Audie-Murphy*. They've come to trust my judgment. I also feel there is still much I could learn under Commander Salish. Her battle instincts are more finely tuned to the needs of Blockade work than most. I've missed some calls that she's made, much to the detriment of our work.

"If you feel I'm ready for a promotion, then I would do my best to live up to your expectations of me. Perhaps I simply am in need of cross-training under another commanding officer, to get more seasoning under my cap—if the lattermost is the case, and you're moving me from the *Audie-Murphy* to another Delta-VX, then I'll still need time to pack and board the next ship, depending upon its own patrol schedule."

"And if we feel you have peaked in your promotable career track?" Commodore Deng asked her. "If we choose to mark your file as unpromotable?"

"If my superiors and the Department of Innovations feel, in your best judgment, that I have peaked in my capacity for leadership, then that would be your prerogative, sirs," Ia admitted. "I will continue as I have done, trying my best to lead by good example, and doing my best to figure out what a good example actually is." She smiled slightly, wryly. "After that, the only objection I could possibly have is if I served for several more years but never got another pay raise, sirs."

Captain Harrison leaned her forearms on the edge of the table, her face twisting with sarcasm. "Wow, Lieutenant. You have *every* possible answer oh so neatly covered in your reply. Did you practice that little speech in your cabin before coming to this performance review?"

"No, sir." She couldn't dip into the timestreams deeply enough to read the other woman's motivations, since Ia needed to be *here*, aware of what was happening in the real world. But she could sense the possibilities branching out immediately before her.

"Somehow, I don't believe you, Lieutenant." Sitting back, Captain Harrison spread her hands. "In fact, I think you're grandstanding. Manipulating the system, so we'll be *convinced* . . . or rather, *conned* . . . into giving you greater responsibility."

"Commodore Deng, permission to speak freely?" Ia asked, shifting her gaze to the older of the two men.

He studied her for a moment, then nodded. "Permission granted."

Ia looked back at Harrison. "Either stuff your attitude up your recharge socket, *Captain*, or you can kiss my asteroid."

Captain Harrison widened her eyes, affronted by the insult. Captain Yacob frowned at Ia. "Lieutenant!"

"Sorry, sir, but it goes against *my* nature to tolerate the grandstanding of a *hypocrite*," Ia growled. Externally, she glared at Harrison. Internally, she was enjoying the ride. There were ways, and then there were ways, to advance her career. This was—at least to her warped sense of humor—one of the more enjoyable routes she could take. "I have *never* asked for a promotion. I have *never* asked for any of my medals. I have *never once* filed an incident report glorifying or exalting my actions. I have simply stated the *facts* of each matter, and moved on to the next task.

"I'm sorry if you think my standards are so low as to *fake* my devotion to service . . . and you may have the right to bust me all the way back down to Private for saying all of this . . . but I *refuse* to do less than my best just because *you* want to call it 'grandstanding.' So. If you have a problem with me, Captain Harrison, then I suggest you get over it. You can demote me, or promote me, or put me in charge of a garbage scow, it will *not* change my efforts, sir. You can slur my reputation all you like, even to the point of casting lies, but *don't* expect me to just stand here and take it."

"You're not in this to make friends, are you, Lieutenant?" Captain Yacob asked dryly, sitting back in his seat.

Ia relaxed her hard stance, shrugging slightly. "I'd say I'm quite capable of making friends in the Service, Captain. In fact, I *have* made several friends. I just refuse to lick asteroid while doing it. Sycophancy will only weaken and destroy the effectiveness of the Terran military. That's why we have the Department of Innovations, to make sure that nepotism and backroom deals don't ruin the quality of our leadership."

Commodore Deng raised one brow at that. "Is *that* what this is all about? Are you aiming for an eventual transfer into the DoI?"

Ia blinked, her surprise genuine. She hadn't expected him to draw that conclusion, and shook her head. "*Ah* . . . no, sir. To be honest, the thought hadn't even crossed my mind. I'm *good* at combat, and I always figured I'd *be* in combat. The DoI strikes me as too much of a desk job for my particular skill set."

Harrison studied her for a long moment, then tapped something into her workstation. Yacob blinked, glanced at her, and tapped something into his own. Between them, the commodore nodded slowly.

"Are you going to apologize to Captain Harrison, Lieutenant?" Commodore Deng asked her.

"If I am ordered to, sir, I will, since I do still respect each of you . . . but I should point out that you *did* give me permission to speak freely," Ia reminded them. "Apologizing for free speech when given permission to use it seems a bit contradictory to me."

Captain Harrison chuckled at that. The other two glanced at her. From their puzzled looks, neither man could figure out what she found so funny. Lifting her palms, she shook her head.

"No apologies are necessary, Lieutenant. You *did* have permission. For the record, I was playing Devil's Advocate. You do have a track record of . . . *mm* . . . bluntness about your devotion to duty, and I wanted to test it. By that, I mean more in your deeds than in your words, but I won't fault you for turning around and matching words to deeds, this time."

"In that case, I *do* apologize for any offense given, sir," Ia stated.

Harrison snorted, mouth twisting wryly, then turned to look at her companions. "Are we ready, then, Commodore, Captain?"

"Quite ready, Captain." Commodore Deng neatened the stack of printouts in front of him, then clasped his hands together, regarding Ia steadily. "It is the judgment of this review board that you are indeed stable enough to continue serving in a Blockade Patrol combat position. You will retain your current rank of Lieutenant Second Grade, and your current rate of pay. As you yourself have pointed out, you are best placed continuing to serve on board the TUPSF *Audie-Murphy* as its second-in-command. You will therefore do so."

"Thank you, Commodore. I shall do my best, sir," Ia promised, not at all disappointed at retaining her exact same rank for the next little while. It would give her a chance to prove her words were true . . . which ironically would help convince her superiors the next time her rank was up for review.

"You'd better. Dismissed, Lieutenant," Deng told her.

Nodding, Ia saluted the three of them. They saluted her back, and she turned to go. Palming open the door to the review room—used by officers for evaluating fellow officers; enlisted went through a different, less face-to-face process—she stepped into the corridor beyond. That had gone well. Her little display of rebellion and disrespect had proven to her superiors that she wasn't an entirely "perfect" soldier; that she had an all-too-Human side. Being *too* perfect would've been detrimental to her goals. It didn't hurt that her little tirade was the honest truth about how she felt.

Just before the door slid shut, she heard Harrison's voice. "Hey, Jake? If you ever don't want her, I'll take 'er."

"Oh, hell, no. I'm—" The door sealed, cutting off the rest of his response.

Ia permitted herself a tiny smile.

CHAPTER 17

My time on Blockade Patrol was fairly predictable—yes,
I know that's an ironic choice of words for someone like
me. But it was. Scout star systems, match lightwave information with system buoy data, check for any ships and
either inspect or fight them. One four-month tour of duty
became two, and two became three.

Commander Salish retired from the Blockade to go
serve a normal six-month tour on Mars. I was eventually
promoted to Lieutenant First Grade, and given command
of the Audie-Murphy. Yeoman Weavers stayed on as
co-pilot, and Kipple and Sikmah stayed as well. Others
came and went, some due to injuries, some due to stress.
A lot of them cycled through the Interdicted Zone, though
at least I was able to cut down on the number of unnecessary deaths. And I was finally free to alter our routes within
our patrol zone as I saw fit.

They actually encouraged us to do that in Blockade
Patrol, since being unpredictable meant increasing the
odds of catching the enemy by surprise. But most of what
we did was routine, for the Blockade. Dangerous and messy,
but routine. I will admit a few incidents do stand out in my
mind, though.

~Ia

OCTOBER 3, 2494 T.S.
NUK NUK 1338 SYSTEM

"C'mon, stay with me, stay with me," Ia murmured, hands working swiftly as she mopped up Private Dixon's wound. "Don't you go anywhere, Helia, that's an order! You are *not* following Private Kings into the afterlife, you hear me?"

Engineering rocked with the force of another explosion. She swayed with the quake. Private Natmah was less skilled; his fingers slipped off the grey material cupping Dixon's inner thigh, allowing blood to spurt through what used to be her knee.

"Tighter!" Ia snapped. Dixon grunted as Natmah regained his pressure on her femoral artery. There was also a tourniquet around her lower thigh, but it couldn't be applied for very long. The other woman grunted again as Ia rubbed across the torn flesh with the scrap of cloth she had found. It was dirty with petrochemicals, but that didn't matter; water-based moisture was Ia's enemy right now, moisture which would make cauterizing this wound rather difficult.

The hissing sound of welders stopped. "Sir!" one of the other members of the boarding party shouted. "The last hatchway to Engineering is sealed. I don't know how long it'll be until they bring up cutters of their own, though!"

"Understood!" Ia called back. Shifting back, she picked up her mechsuit rifle. It really wasn't designed to be fired by someone outside of their suit, but she'd had no choice. Fixing the biggest problem on their hands meant ditching both her and Dixon's armor. A crude cauterizing had cut down most of the bleeding from the other woman's maiming, but the future needed Helia Dixon to survive. Ia needed her to survive. Dixon's leg from the knee down could be regenerated, given enough time. Her whole life couldn't be restored if it was wasted.

"Brace yourself, Dixon; this is going to hurt like *v'shova sh'naan . . .*"

Aiming carefully, arms stretched to their fullest to clutch both the oversized trigger and the matching e-clip brace, Ia pulled the trigger. Deep red light seared slowly across the edge of Dixon's flesh. Dixon screamed and slumped, passing out.

Steam and smoke boiled up from the wound. She cut off the beam two-thirds of the way through, rocked with another deck-shaking explosion, and finished searing the last few centimeters of the stump. Stripping the e-clip from the rifle in a swift, subtle move, she tossed the bulky weapon aside and leaned forward over the comatose private, fluttering her hand to signal Natmah to let go of the comatose woman's artery and strip off the tourniquet.

Nothing leaked. The cauterization was solid.

"Stay with me . . . Stay with me . . ." Energy crackled into the fingers of her left hand, jammed as they were against the power points at the top of the energy magazine. Her right hand pressed over Dixon's throat, ostensibly to feel for a pulse. Instead, Ia spun the electrical energy from the clip into her biokinetic gift, and poured that into the unconscious young woman.

Nothing seemed to happen. Then again, only another psychic, one trained to sense the subtle flow of kinetic inergy, would have noticed anything. Beneath her fingertips, Ia could feel the private's faltering heartbeat strengthen. She couldn't forge miracles in flesh, unlike her father's kin, but she could give the other woman enough biokinetic energy to survive. As soon as her instincts told her Dixon would survive within a comfortable probabilities margin, Ia slumped back, exhausted but relieved.

"She'll live."

Private Culpepper turned to face her, his fear visible since he had raised up both his outer and inner faceplates. "She'll *live*? The hell with that, sir! *Nobody's* gonna live! Kings is dead, Dixon's down—they've got us *trapped* in here. We're helpless!"

The sheer absurdity in his claim pricked Ia's rare sense of humor. Sagging back onto her p-suited hip, she laughed. Culpepper did not take that well.

"You're *laughing*?" he demanded. He pointed one servo-hand back at the main doors, almost smacking it into Corporal Kipple, who was obeying the spacer's law of Lock and Web by carefully returning the welding gear back to its storage locker, even though it was Salik gear on a badly damaged Salik ship drifting dead through space without any functional engines. "Any minute now, the goddamn *frogtopuses* are gonna cut through those seals, and have us for dinner, and you're *laughing*?!"

Corporal Kipple grinned through his faceplate. "*Eyah*. You haven't served with the Lieutenant very long, have you, Culpepper? What, two patrols, now? Not quite two and a half?"

"What has *that* got to do with anything?" Culpepper snapped.

"*Everything*, Private," Ia stated, drawing in a deep breath. "Kipple knows I don't believe in the 'no-win' scenario. We have *plenty* of options, if we just open our eyes."

Pushing to her feet, she swayed a little, exhausted, but made it over to her mechsuit, open and waiting in standby mode. She didn't climb back into it, however. Instead, she dug out her holdout knife from one of the thigh compartments, then crossed to the pile of dead Salik which Privates Bissel and Lee had dragged into a corner. Bracing herself for the disgusting task, she sorted out one of the tentacle arms, and started sawing through the flesh just above the macrojuncture, where the bone ended and the lithe muscles began.

Culpepper gasped, then gagged. "Sir!"

"If you are having problems with the sometimes extreme requirements of Blockade duty, Private, I'd quite understand," Ia told him, most of her attention on her task. "But I'd prefer you to wait until we have escaped this situation before voicing them. In the meantime, please remain calm. What I am doing does not violate the protocols of Blockade Service. He's already dead, so this isn't torture."

She severed the four-limbed "hand" from the rest of the dead alien, then cut through the joint of the macrojuncture, ignoring the blood seeping from the limb. From the elbow at the end of the arm-bone to about where the midforearm would be on a Human, the Salik version of an arm split into two suckered tentacles. Below the macrojuncture lay the microjunctures, where each tentacle again split in two, forming four longish, tapered digits lined with yet more suckers.

Carrying the severed pair of limbs over to one of the consoles, Ia studied the controls for a long moment, long enough to rock through another explosion. Then, with great care to match up what she saw in the timestream possibilities, she draped the tentacles just so over the pressure-sensitive controls. Prodding into the flesh with the flat of her knife, she gently squeezed air out of key suckers, working more patiently than quickly.

"Anything I can do, sir?" Kipple asked her.

"Yes, actually." Gently prying up a misplaced sucker, she tugged the tentacle into better position and carefully pressed the segment of flesh back into place. "Okay, I'm going to need some help on this. Private Natmah, you're already out of your suit. Get over here. Kipple, get out of your suit and join us. We'll need at least five hands to pull this off, if I remember right."

"Aye, sir." Moving over to join her, Natmah wrinkled his nose at the dead pair of limbs sprawled over the otherwise smooth-surfaced console. "Uhh . . . what sort of help, sir?"

Ia winced as something *banged* into the sealed doors protecting them from invasion by the rest of the ship's very much alive crew. "We're going to save ourselves, that's what."

"How?" Culpepper demanded over the whines and hisses of Kipple powering down and opening up his mechsuit. "Our ship had to *flee* to draw off that second cruiser while we were still in the act of boarding *this* one. The rest of the *shakking* frogs out there could blow us up at any moment, or burn through and *eat* us! *How* are we going to save ourselves?"

"We're in the *engineering* section, Private," Ia reminded him. "With the bridge destroyed and voided to space, *we* control what's left of this ship. Natmah, pay attention. When I tell you to, on count one, I need you to press down right here, and pull up over here. Then on count two, you'll press down on *these* two spots, and on count three, end with pulling up on these two, and stretching your pinky finger over to press down *here*."

Kipple, free of his armor, joined her. "Lemme guess, we're playing with the controls, sir? Gonna muck up lifesupport for 'em?"

She shook her head. "By now, lifesupport is on independent systems in the intact parts of the ship. No, we're going to mess with the one thing we *can* affect. As for you, Kipple, on count one, I need you to pull up here, and here. On count two . . ."

"Wait, sir. I have a highlighter in my thigh pocket," Kipple told her. Retreating to his armor, he opened up the compartment. Grabbing the oversized pen, he brought it back and uncapped it. "Here, mark all the spots, so we know exactly where to touch, sir."

"Good idea, Corporal," Ia praised, pleased by his creativeness.

Natmah grimaced. "It won't be easy to see, given this meioa was chartreuse and the pen is yellow, but I suppose it's better than getting the wrong spot . . ."

Nodding, Ia took the pen and carefully marked with tiny numbers and up or down arrows. She didn't dare press hard, but she did ink over everything a few times to intensify the color. When she was through, she tucked the pen over her ear, under the band of her headset, and grabbed her own spots on the carefully draped limbs. "Places, everyone . . ."

Another explosion shuddered through the hull, making Natmah's fingers pull up unexpectedly. He quickly released the tentacle, but the monitors up above their heads—placed so that the eyes of a Salik could comfortably read them, not the eyes of a Human—flickered and changed, a symbol appearing. Both men froze while Ia carefully pressed down and up in three spots, two of them thankfully close together. The screen returned to its normal view.

At her nod, they returned their hands to their starting positions. "Okay . . . on the letters countdown. Charlie . . . bravo . . . alpha . . . *One!* And . . . *two!* And . . . *three!* Good job!"

They lifted their hands away, Natmah surreptitiously scrubbing his fingertips against the edge of the console below the sensitive zone. Ia noticed it peripherally, but it wasn't important. Most of her attention was on the rising blue bar on the center right screen. It gradually darkened, slowly turning purple. Orange lights started flashing, and an almost musical alarm started wailing up and down. Reaching down, she grabbed two of the tentacles and lifted up on certain spots, then pressed down on a third control. The indigo violet hue stalled and stabilized, and the Salik version of a klaxon cut off, though the orange lights still flashed, clashing with the greenish hue of the overhead lights.

"What did we just do, sir?" Kipple ventured to ask as she sighed and straightened.

"We just increased the gravity field in every other part of the ship that still *has* gravity. Specifically, to 3.1Gs Standard. I can guarantee that any unsuited Salik within range of the weaves under the deckplates is flat on their front or back at the very least, and most likely suffering from broken flipper-joints . . . and struggling just to breathe. The suited ones might be upright, but they're struggling just to breathe, too." She looked away from the monitor and smiled grimly at the others, including the unnerved Culpepper. "Salik are lightworlders, like the Gatsugi. Their bodies are not designed to stand in anything heavier than 2.5Gs max for anything longer than a handful of seconds. The only reason their gravity weaves go higher than that is for the insystem safety fields, to help counteract abrupt acceleration forces. The moment I realized their lightworlder physiology had a weakness, I asked an engineering friend versed in Sallhash how to disable the standard Salik overrides a few years back."

"Well, that's just fine and dandy for *you*, sir," Private Bissel retorted, "but the rest of us are lightworlders. You could stroll out of here at any time, but *we're* stuck in here."

"Yes, we are, Private, but only until we're rescued. It'll take a few hours, but most of the Salik will have passed out or died from oxygen deprivation by then," Ia told him. "I need to stay in here and monitor the controls, since I'm the only one fluent enough in Sallhash to try something like this. But I need two of you to volunteer to go back into the boarding pod, and cycle through the other airlock. There's a chance there were suited Salik in the non-gravitied parts of the ship. We cannot afford to let any survivors blow a hole in that pod. Not when it's the only thing keeping the air in *this* section of the ship."

"I'll go, sir," Kipple volunteered, heading back toward his mechsuit.

"And I'll go," Lee volunteered, hefting her oversized rifle.

"Good meioas. It won't be more than a couple hours at most," Ia promised her crew. "The fleet knows we encountered two Salik ships, and launched boarding pods. They'll be coming in force to read the lightwaves and look for survivors. Use your suits to broadcast on lightwave bandwidths about our situation. I would try to figure out the communication system on this ship, but I suspect that the comm systems are probably boobytrapped with passcodes, to prevent their enemies from figuring out what frequencies they use."

Nodding, both meioas headed for the side chamber where the rearmost of the two boarding pods had clamped onto the enemy ship. Ia lifted her chin at the monitors overhead.

"Natmah, keep an eye on that screen. If *anything* on it changes, tell me at once," she ordered. "I need to check on Private Dixon again."

Crossing to the woman on the floor, Ia knelt at her side.

When Ia touched her face, Dixon managed to pry open her eyes. "I . . . heard you . . . sir. I held on . . ."

"Good meioa," Ia praised. "Keep it up, and I'll take you back into the fold as soon as your leg's been restored."

A twitch of her lips might have been a smile, or might not. Dixon parted her lips, breathed in deep, then stiffened. "How . . . how bad, sir?"

Ia didn't sugarcoat it. "You've lost everything from the knee down, right side. But I cauterized it fully. Of course, this means they'll have to cut off the dead flesh, and then you'll probably have to spend four or five months stumping around with your leg in a goo-cast."

"If they . . . get in here . . . shoot me first," Dixon muttered.

"Like hell I will, Private," Ia countered. "I'm shooting *them* first! You'll just have to wait for your turn, like everyone else."

That provoked something closer to a hint of a smile than the first one. Patting her on the shoulder, Ia rose, glad the other woman would live. Helia Dixon was very, very good at repairing and working with force field technology.

Ia intended to recommend the private be placed on board one of the capital ships patrolling the Blockade after the first month of regenerative healing had begun; on a capital ship, she could stump around and still do her job. From there, things would start to fall into place for the other woman. With the right roll of the percentages, Ia would be getting a better-trained, combat-ready force field tech, one used to the needs of a much bigger vessel than a Delta-VX, and a force field tech who was comfortable serving under Ia and her sometimes unorthodox ways.

She looked at the others, Kipple sealing up the last panels of his suit, Lee waiting by the door that led to the pod, Bissel and the others.

"Remember this trick, and try to think of others for situations like this. There are *always* options. Even giving up and allowing yourself to be captured is technically an option," she added, earning a few odd looks. "Between the moment of being captured and the moment of being eaten, there *is* the possibility that you can escape. But do try to find other ways, first. Your duty as soldiers is to complete your mission. My duty as an officer is to see the mission is completed with the greatest effect for the least loss of lives and supplies. I cannot do that without you.

"Now, let's keep an eye on our situation, inside and out. We still have a few more hours before we're out of this mess."

MARCH 11, 2495 T.S.
SYSTEM'S EDGE
SS'NUK LULK 53

Part of one of the outlying star systems beyond the Blockade dropped off her internal radar. When Ia finally realized it was missing, she discovered why. Sort of. Ia already knew it was one of the secret Salik military bases, but not one that she could reveal to her superiors, so she hadn't kept more than a peripheral awareness of it in the back of her mind. For one, there was no way to reveal it, without revealing her own abilities. That, she could not yet risk. For another, after the third week, the blank spot started to move away from the hidden base.

Whatever it was, it stayed away from inhabited systems, tracing a snaking course between stars at FTL speeds. She knew it was "missing" because anything to do with that part of space/time had turned a misty, impenetrable shade of grey. The problem was, *any* deviation from the expected was a danger to her mission. The base, she could still leave alone. This blank spot was the problem.

It was almost as if the Salik had developed their own version of Meyun Harper. Which was impossible, because there was no way in a slimy hell that Ia would ever fall in love with one of *them*. Yet whatever-it-was acted just like a Meyun-style void, thwarting her ability to predict its immediate surroundings, and being detectable mostly only because of the fact that it left a bubble-shaped void in the waters of Time.

Now she sat on the edge of a system the void would soon skim. It had taken her four weeks to both build up the courage to confront that void and find a spot in her patrol schedule where she and her crew weren't actually needed. The risks of the unknown it represented had to be confronted, however. If she didn't, many, many more voids would pop up in the near future, that much was clear. That would threaten to unravel her careful weaving of the coming wars, and *that*, she could not allow.

Taking the *Audie-Murphy* two full star systems beyond their assigned patrol zone would raise numerous eyebrows among her superiors. Doing so without reporting their new position the moment they emerged from hyperspace would raise even more. It was a double-violation of procedures that could get her into serious trouble.

Waiting in the dark, with most of the ship's systems shut down to minimize their lightwave signature, Ia practiced her excuses over and over in her mind, fine-tuning them depending upon each version's shift of the probabilities.

"Sir?" Corporal Kipple finally asked from his position at the engineering station. "Shouldn't we be changing duty shifts by now, sir? It's been two and a half hours."

Ia shook her head. In the next few minutes . . . more or less . . . the epicenter of that blank spot would reach this point and stay here for a little while. Probably to refuel, considering they'd emerged perilously close to the thin band of ice chunks floating in the system's Oort cloud zone. "Stay alert, and stay at your posts. Eyes to the boards, thoughts on your tasks."

"What *are* we waiting for, sir?" Culpepper asked, his tone skeptical. He was another rising problem, but one that would be easy enough to deal with, sooner or later. If they survived whatever-it-was that was headed their way, that was. She had placed him at the ship's systems post, since he was very good at multitasking in a crisis, but there was no way she would've let him get near the gunnery controls. That position was covered by Private Sikmah.

For the first time since she was a child, Ia felt the urge to chew her nails. She refrained; any show of nervousness on her part would make her bridge crew equally unsettled. Or rather, more unsettled. Culpepper's question needed to be answered with the same unflappable calm she had displayed on all other, more temporally visible occasions.

Plus, she decided, *it might help cover my asteroid if my crew knew my "reasons" for deviating so far from their orders.* "I've been having dreams, for the last few weeks. A very strong and disturbing dream. The world *I* come from, you learn to pay attention to repeating—*Holy!*"

Her shout startled the bridge crew. Zapping out of faster-than-light in a flash that lit up their primary screens, a huge monstrosity appeared. Simultaneously, a wave of white static overwhelmed Ia's brain. Gasping in pain, she curled over against her restraints. Her left hand was still stuck in the flight glove, and instinct kept it carefully still, but her right came up to clutch at her forehead in a futile attempt to contain the pain.

The problem wasn't physical, however. It was psychic. Gritting her teeth, Ia forced herself through her grounding and centering exercises, pushing up stronger, harder shields—until that made things *worse*. Quickly backing off, she let go of all efforts to use her abilities. Only then did the pain recede, leaving her mind-blind and reeling. Grabbing for the only thing that made sense, her physical senses, she stared at the screens displaying the object now coasting toward them, slowing no doubt to collect ice from the fragments of old comets giving them a scrap of cover.

It was wrapped in the dark grey, mirror-polished contours of ceristeel plating, of all treacheries, but bore the distinct configuration of a Salik warship, like a flattish, elongated, five-lobed star. If a warship could be four times the largest seen to date, that was. It almost qualified as a Battle Platform in size . . . and the moment Ia realized *that*, she knew out of sheer, paranoid instinct that it *could* take on a Battle Platform.

"Holy *shakk* . . ." Culpepper swore, staring at the ship bearing down on them.

"*Ah*, sir?" Private Sikmah asked from his position at the gunnery controls. "It's headed straight for us, sir. We have maybe two minutes before we're in range of its guns. What do we do, sir?"

"We . . . we have to destroy it." Ia murmured, staring at her screens. It was the only thing she could think of to do.

All three men choked. Kipple recovered first, spluttering. "*What?* Sir, have you lost your *shakking mind*? That *ship* will eat us for lunch, never mind the Salik who built it!"

Her resolve firmed. Ia didn't take her eyes off her primary screen. "Corporal, we *have* to destroy it. That thing is big enough, it can take on a Battle Platform and *win*." Switching on the ship's intercom, she broadcast to the rest of the crew. "*All hands, this is Lieutenant Ia. You have twenty seconds to* *lock and web yourselves in place, mark! Engineering, you have twenty-*five *seconds to bring all systems back online, mark!"*

"You're *crazy!"* Culpepper argued as lights started coming back on across their boards. "I didn't sign up for a *suicide* run!"

"Neither did *I*, Private," Ia snapped, bringing her right hand back to the controls. "Eyes to the boards, thoughts on your tasks. *All hands, brace yourselves!"*

Her head still hurt, but it didn't matter. Nothing mattered but the wild scheme that was their one shot at survival. Flexing her fingers in the glove, she hit the thruster controls with her free hand. There was no way they could escape from a dead stop, not when pointed nose-first at a ship that was headed almost straight toward them. No way they could escape detection, either. Any moment now, the Salik version of lightwave analysis would pick up their own existence, and the Salik version of capital ship guns would turn toward them.

The only choice left was to confront their unexpected, utterly unwelcome problem. Now, before they were noticed.

"Sir!" Kipple called out as the *Audie-Murphy* picked up speed. "Do I send a message to the Fleet?"

"Send our coordinates and emergency beacon *only,* then cut all power to the hyperrelay and shunt it to the hyperarray. We don't have time for anything else. *Engineering, give me every last scrap of spare power to the insystem thrusters and the* aft *shields in twenty seconds!"*

"Sir . . . we're headed straight for that warship," Sikmah warned her, eyes on his screens. "When do you want us to fire, sir?"

"Negative. *All gunnery pods, shunt all power to thrusters and aft shields. I repeat,* all *power to thrusters and* aft *shields— dammit, I said* aft *shields, Gundrich, not fore!"* Ia snapped into her headset mike, seeing the wrong set of telltales lighting up around the second of the two miniature ships displayed on her second tertiary screen. Her fingers danced across the controls. "Warming up the hyperarrays."

"Sir, we're not going fast enough!" Kipple protested. "We don't have enough room—the wormhole will collapse on *top* of us!"

"Sir, the Salik warship is powering up its lasers!" Culpepper warned her, his voice overlapping Kipple's. "Projectiles launched!"

"Not on *us*, Kipple," Ia half growled, half prayed. Head aching from the instinct to try and use her gifts, she danced her right hand over the controls, warming up the hyperjump dish at the nose of the *Audie*. The Salik ship loomed huge in her primary screen, the distance between her tiny vehicle and the behemoth shrinking rapidly. *"And lo, I followed the will of the Prophet, for the Prophet was never wrong!"*

"Message away, sir—*Sir!* We're—*Ungh!*" Sikmah cried out, just as Ia swirled the paired ships, dodging the incoming missiles in a spiral that swapped port and starboard. Her hand danced again, warming up the nosecone on the *Murphy* half. Sikmah's voice rose into a broken squeak. "Sir, we're going to *hit them*—!"

Ia sparked the hyperrift with a smack of her thumb and scraped the thrusters down with her fingers, shifting all power to the dorsal panels on the *Audie*. That, combined with the snap of her left hand, flipped them over and shoved them downward just enough to get them angling off-course from that spark of light. Golden white energies swirled into existence right on the nose of the enemy craft. Brighter, redder lights exploded as they rushed past, skimming so close to the underside of the alien ship that the collision klaxons blared. Kipple shouted, and Culpepper screamed, clutching at his harness, while Sikmah choked on a curse.

Snapping the heel of her left hand in the thruster glove as they flew past, right hand cutting the thruster grid for just a moment, Ia flipped the *Audie-Murphy* once more fore to aft, and sparked the second hyperrift onto the rear of the behemoth as they flew by. It, too, exploded, the view shifting from her primary screen to her third tertiary. Pulling out of the snap before they could tumble off-course, Ia shoved her fingers up the power controls, pouring everything into the rear thrusters.

The second hyperrift swirled open, then imploded onto the engine section of the Salik ship, triggering a cascade of explosions that raced back to meet the first implosion and its own chain reaction. Energy met energy, as the abruptly compressed matter created a pair of very brief, very bright balls of artificial fusion. Her third tertiary screen, the one showing her the view of everything behind her, blossomed golden white, then blacked out as the sensors protectively shut down.

A second and a half later, the fireball caught up with them, vibrations rumbling through the ship as the plasma molecules strafed their hull. *Pings* and *bangs* and *crunches* warned them of debris hitting the paired ships. With the debris came a release from her headache so abrupt, it was almost a new pain of its own. Dropping waist-deep into the timestreams, Ia flexed and flicked her hands blindly, dodging the wreckage of the ship hurtling upon them from behind.

She dodged most of it—the worst of it—but not all of it. A final hard *clannnng* was followed by the rumbling shriek of tearing metal. Instinct made her hit the emergency release clamps. The *Audie* parted company roughly from its twin, sending both ships into a tumble. *"Yeoman Bunker, take the* Murphy*! Shields to all sides!"*

The *Audie* jolted again, triangular wings catching on the plasma waves still burning out from the condensed remnants of the warship. They tumbled roughly, almost helplessly. Ia tried to guide the ship, but with the shields still imbalanced, the ship took increasing damage, burning off thruster panels and shorting out sensors. She did manage to slow most of the spin, turning it into a slow tumble, but couldn't stop their forward motion. Lights winked and blinked on the bridge, and the gravity plates beneath the decking stuttered, threatening everyone with nausea.

"All hands, gravity off. I repeat, gravity is off *inside the* Audie,*"* Kipple announced, broadcasting the warning to the whole ship. The bridge suddenly went weightless. Hair floated away from heads, limbs drifted away from keyboards, bodies bumped against restraint belts.

"Thank you, Corporal," Ia muttered. The weaves had a limited range, just a dozen or so meters. They were also monodirectional, which meant if they weren't balanced just right, they could stress the ship in odd ways. Given the battering the *Audie* had just taken, it was safe to say that any extra strain on the hull or its interior should probably be avoided. As much as Ia wanted to check the timestreams to be sure, her head throbbed too much to try, now that the worst of the emergency was over. As it was, she was now beginning to feel other pains, strained tendons and bruised flesh from being jolted in too many directions. Physical aches as well as psychic ones.

"Okay . . . Is everyone on the bridge alright?" she asked. "What's the status on the rest of the crew?"

"*Ugh*," Sikmah muttered. "I'll live, if that's what you meant, sir."

"I'll live, too, sir," Kipple reported.

"What the *shova v'shakk* did you *think* you were *doing*?" Culpepper railed at her, tugging at his restraints. He didn't remove them, but he did use them for leverage so he could turn and glare at her in the weightlessness of the bridge. "You almost got us *killed*!"

"Watch your language, Private!" Kipple snapped before she could. "If you hadn't noticed, the Lieutenant just *saved* us from certain death!"

"I don't *shakking* care!" Culpepper yelled. "I am going to have her hide hauled up for *reckl*—"

Ia stabbed her mind into his, knocking him unconscious. It gave her a raging headache to do so, one that squeezed her right eye shut from the blinding pain that seared like a migraine, but the abrupt silence, both physical and mental, was a relief.

Ia cleared her throat. "I think the, *ah*, excitement was too much for Private Culpepper. Hopefully he's just passed out. Status report. Sikmah, anything on the scanners?"

Kipple blinked and pushed to the side, reaching out for him. He snagged a wrist with his fingertips. "His pulse is still there. Let's hope he didn't have a heart attack. Trying to do chest compressions in zero G sucks."

Turning back to the few screens still flickering with life, Private Sikmah took a few moments to study the readings. "Several of the sensors got burned out, but since we're tumbling, sir, I'm getting something of a reading all around. I think the *Murphy* is off to, *uh* . . . well, to one side by about half a klick, maybe a bit more. It's hard to give a heading when you're spinning and half the ship is lightspeed blind."

"Any immediate threats to our vicinity?" Ia asked him.

He studied his few functioning screens for a minute, then shook his head. "No, sir. Nor to the *Murphy*. There are still chunks of the enemy ship floating around, but I'm not getting any energy readings from them. The pieces seem to be traveling on an explosion trajectory only, sir."

"All hands on board have reported in, sir. Internal comms are working, and we have no serious injuries on the *Audie*," Kipple reported from his station. In addition to engineering, he had taken up Culpepper's job of monitoring the other ship functions. "Thrusters are spotty at best, I'm afraid, but the hydroengines are still good, so aside from the lack of gravity, we do have power. Lifesupport's a bit mucked up, but otherwise functional for now. And . . . we do seem to have external comms, still. At least, here on the *Audie*."

"Confirmed, Lieutenant. I can try to contact the *Murphy* if you like, sir?" Sikmah offered.

Ia removed her hand from the control glove and unbuckled her restraints. Maneuvering carefully in the weightlessness ruling the bridge, she pushed herself toward Culpepper's chair. "Do so. I'm going to check on Culpepper, here, make sure he didn't have a heart attack or whatever. Get ahold of the *Murphy* if you can and see what condition she's in. Then see if you can raise the Fleet—you *did* get a message off before things fell apart, right, Sikmah?"

"Yes, sir, I had just enough time to send coordinates and the emergency beacon before shunting power. If nothing else, they'll send a ship to investigate that much. Five, maybe seven hours, and they'll be along to catch our lightwave info, and see the rest of it," he offered. "On the upside, sir, both ships' directions are carrying us out of the Oort plane. There aren't any major stellar body threats for the next . . . eighty million klicks?"

Ia nodded in acknowledgment, clinging to Culpepper's harness with one hand, the other on his throat. Ostensibly, she was checking him for signs of stress-induced trauma. Psychically, she was reducing his urge to haul her up before a Board of Inquiry. She would have enough problems explaining the deviations in their patrol; she didn't need him pouring oil on the blaze.

It was tempting to "correct" his behavioral problems. Not that she enjoyed meddling with other people's minds, but it was an option. Ia restrained herself; that was a problem for the near future, and one that would have to be corrected in a different way.

Not that she knew what the Salik had done to meddle with *her* mind. The amphibians were mind-blind, giftless, psychically null. *How* they could have blocked her abilities—*her* abilities—was still a complete mystery. *Who or what could they have on their side, working for them? A Feyori? No, that wouldn't make sense. They're even stronger than I am . . .*

At least the grey mist was gone. Enough to let her know that there was at least one chunk of that ship with a surviving databank core, and that in that core lay the coordinates for the base where this ship had been built. It probably would have moved on by the time the Alliance could get their hands on that databank, but there was a chance it would still be there.

That base just moved up from "unnecessary" to "vital" on the confrontation list. Someone needs to figure out what that mind-blocking effect was. Find it, and put a stop to it. Psychic abilities, and not just mine, are what will help us win the coming wars. The possibilities for many more blank-bubbles still existed in the timestreams, now that she knew what to look for, and the very real probabilities that their sheer presence would disrupt her work. But now there were viable streams that would connect to those blank-point whatsits. *And . . . yes, I think some of those streams will be mine to pursue. I'll have to readjust for the other ones, too.*

"Everyone on the *Murphy* is still alive, sir," Sikmah reported, recapturing Ia's attention. "Private Gundrich has a concussion and a broken arm, but otherwise they all survived. They have no thrusters and are in a tumble that's faster than ours, but they do have one functional laser pod, and they do have gravity."

"I'm glad. Tell them they can rig the escape pod to fire its thrusters for stabilization," Ia instructed her comm tech. "If they time it right, they can slow their spin and have some minor maneuvering capability—have them check their deadhead direction for obstacles and use the pod to miss whatever might be in their way. Other than that, they'll just need to hang on and wait, the same as us.

"After you do that, try your best to raise the cavalry, Sikmah," she ordered him, pushing back from Culpepper's chair. She twisted as she drifted so that she could catch herself on her own station and not bruise anything further. "The faster we can get hold of the Fleet, the faster we can expect a rescue. Freefall is only fun up until you have to go to the bathroom."

Her dry quip made him smile, raising his and the others' morale a point or two. "Aye, sir."

MARCH 16, 2495 T.S.
BATTLE PLATFORM *MAD JACK*
SIC TRANSIT

Commodore Deng sighed and gave the woman standing At Attention before him a hard look. Lifting his hand, he pinched thumb and forefinger half a centimeter apart. His words were pitched too low for the pickups to broadcast his warning across the auditorium. "You know, you came *this* close to getting flogged for insubordination, Lieutenant Ia."

"I know, sir," Ia returned crisply, if quietly. "As I told the Board of Inquiry, I do accept full responsibility for the consequences of my actions, sir. But every Human has at bare minimum a baseline level of gut instincts, sir, and my guts were *screaming* about the dreams I had, and where I come from, you pay attention to dreams that are that strong, sir. Particularly when they repeat. Prophetic visions plague everyone on Sanctuary, sir, as I'm sure you've heard about in the news Nets recently."

The watching audience of soldiers and attached civilian personnel waited patiently for the two of them to speak loudly enough to be heard. So did the viewing membership of the Terran Space Force attuned to the Commendations and Corporal Punishments channel of the military news Nets. Commodore Deng continued to speak quietly to her.

"Well, your hunch did pay off. If you didn't have such a long-standing record of your hunches paying off, you'd be flogged. As it is, you do *not* have a record of reckless behavior . . . and given how that balances your actions in this matter," he stated, raising his voice so that his next words were picked up and broadcast, "it is the policy of the modern Space Force to reward good gut instincts and innovations which lead to outstanding successes."

Picking up the first of the boxes on the salver carried by an aide, he flicked open the lid.

"It is therefore my duty to present to you the Screaming Eagle, for the extraordinary act of piloting a ship with such skill that you *missed* an OTL hyperrift, sparking two of them on the bow and stern of an enemy capital ship, and for successfully escaping most of the subsequent blast."

"Thank you, sir." Ia accepted the award with a salute. It wasn't her first Screaming Eagle, but it would probably become one of her most famous.

He picked up the next box. "It is also my duty to present you with the Compass Rose, for an absolutely outstanding, extraordinary act of engineering. It takes brains to realize that there *are* options for success even when you are so heavily outmatched that it would be like . . . like a *fly* looking at a horse and deciding to kill it, not just land on it and try for a bite. It took brains to realize you *could* kill the enemy's ship, and do so with the one means, however dangerous, at your disposal. And it took brains to realize that one rifting might not be enough . . . though our tech meioas have grumbled to no end that you barely left them enough rubble to sift through."

"I couldn't take the chance the aft cannons would stay intact long enough to shoot us down, sir," Ia confessed. "With the enemy ship too close to escape, I knew I had one chance to get myself and my crew away from death's door."

"Well, you chose wisely. And you piloted well enough to *keep* your crew and yourself alive." He handed over the box, returned her salute, and reached for the next. "To accompany these, your superiors bestow upon you the Target Star, for successfully shooting down an enemy ship . . . since there's no doubt who pulled the trigger on this kill."

Another exchange of salutes and commendations.

Deng picked up the next two. "However . . . for the awarding of the Skull and the Crossbones, just like your crew, you get only one of each. We have no idea just how many enemy officers and noncoms were on board, so that's the bare minimum we can rightfully hand out. You didn't leave all that much intact, Lieutenant."

"I'm sorry, sir," Ia apologized again.

"You should be," he stated blandly. "I could use a hundred more officers like you, and a hundred thousand soldiers. Hell, we could use a million. Though if you go off-patrol again without advanced warning, you *will* be flogged."

"Understood, sir." Accepting the last two boxes, she balanced the lot in the curve of her left arm and saluted him one last time. "Thank you, sir."

"Thank *you*," he acknowledged. "You and your crew are on a full week's Leave," Commodore Deng added, lifting his chin at the members of the *Audie-Murphy*, who were bruised but beaming, having received their own awards for their participation in the short but effective battle. He returned his attention to Ia. "Hopefully by then, the TUPSF *Audie-Murphy* will be fully repaired. Try not to scuff the polish the second you leave this Platform on your next patrol, soldier, or I'll take it out of your pay."

"I'll do my best not to, sir," she promised. "I'll leave that up to the enemy, and take it out of their hides."

MAY 29, 2495 T.S.
K'KATTA MINING SHIP *NN K'K'TIKUTT T'WII*
ATTENBOROUGH EPSILON 14 SYSTEM

The call came when Ia was in the forward cargo hold, examining the bars of refined minerals strapped into their carrying cradles.

"Lieutenant! This is Private Myang—Private Culpepper's going crazy, sir!"

Ia touched her arm unit. Private Adriene Myang—no relation to the more famous Admiral-General Christine Myang—was the newest member of her crew. *"Acknowledged, Private. What's your location?"*

The K'kattan captain chittered. His translator box rendered the clicks and whistles into Terranglo, since his race could not physically form over half the sounds the other sentient races could. "Is something wrong, Meioa Guardian?"

"I'm not sure, sir," Private Myang returned in Ia's ear, forcing her to concentrate through the alien's chitterings. *"Ah . . . here's my transponder—I'm not used to the layout on these ships, yet.* Holy—*Private Culpepper, put your weapon down! I said, put your weapon* down! *I'm recording this, sir!"*

Flicking open her arm unit, Ia tapped in the command that placed Myang's transponder overlaid on a map of the K'kattan vessel and turned her arm toward the alien. "We need to get from here to *there*, fast."

"This way, Guardian!" the captain chittered, and scrambled for an oval opening high up in the hold. Not much on a K'kattan ship was designed for the convenience of Humans and other bipeds, but there were handholds and footholds, and the captain had thoughtfully lowered the gravity to 1G Alliance Standard to comply with and ease the inspection process. That made climbing after him a lot easier for Ia. It also helped that she wore only body armor, and not the bulk of a mechsuit, which wouldn't have been able to maneuver in such tight quarters.

Scrambling through the tunnel-like corridor after him was much more difficult, since they were barely a meter and a half high, forcing Ia to crouch or risk smacking her head on the claw-hold grips. From there, it was another climb, this time straight up, then a side tunnel to one of the crew's private quarters. They could hear a *skreeling* sound, the piercing cry of a K'katta in pain, and shouting in Terranglo.

"I *said*, put your weapon *down*, Private!" Myang snapped, her voice high and tight. Laserfire hissed, and the K'katta screech-yelled again. *"Private!"*

Ia ducked inside and straightened. The ceiling was comfortably higher in here, mainly because the alcoves of the crew nests were stacked three high. Private Culpepper had aimed his HK-70 rifle into the middle alcove, where one of the aliens huddled. It—she, from the pale coloring of her chiton-fur—was missing part of one limb. The grin on Culpepper's face was not a pleasant one.

"Sir!" Myang protested. Her own rifle was pointed at her teammate's back. "He won't put his weapon down!"

"This *bug* is holding out on us!" Culpepper growled through his grin. "It's got a sack of contraband in its hidey-hole, sir, and it won't let go!"

"Private Myang, lower your weapon," Ia ordered, her voice loud but her tone calm. Her hand dropped to her laser pistol, flicking the safety switch as the weapon rested in her holster. The faint whine of the e-clip warming up was lost under the noises being made by the injured alien in her bunk-like nest.

The black and ceristeel muzzle in the private's hands dropped, but more out of surprise than compliance. Myang blinked at her. *"Me, sir?"*

"Guardian, I must protest!" the captain chittered at Ia, while his crewmate shuddered and keened, a thin trickle of blood seeping from the edges of its cauterized wound.

Ia ignored him. She flicked her hand at Myang, motioning the private back. "Private Myang, you never draw a weapon on a fellow soldier unless you are prepared to follow through. Private Culpepper!" she snapped, catching the other soldier's attention. "You are in *violation* of Blockade protocols. Drop your weapon and put your hands on your head. You have five seconds to comply. *Mark*."

"*I'm* not doing anything wrong, sir!" Culpepper retorted, gun still trained on the quivering alien trapped in its nest. "*This* piece of filth wouldn't—"

Ia, silently counting down during his protest, pulled her pistol from its holster and pulled the trigger. Dark red seared a smoking hole in his left buttock, just below the ceristeel plating of his body armor. Culpepper screamed and whirled to face her, hopping a little from the pain.

"You . . . you *shot* me!" he protested, eyes wide.

She flicked the muzzle of her laser pistol up, pointing it straight at his face. "Yes. I did. This is *not* a negotiation, Private, nor is it a discussion. You did *not* comply with a direct order from your superior, and have violated one of the Fifty Fatalities because of it, Private Culpepper. You will now drop your weapon and place your hands on top of your head. Be advised, my next shot is aimed to *kill*.

"You have five seconds to comply. *Mark*."

He wasted three of them gaping at Ia. Her gun and her gaze never wavered. Blinking, he hastily tossed the rifle on the ground and clasped his hands over his helmeted head. Private Myang quickly stooped and dragged the rifle away from his feet, slinging it by its strap over her left shoulder.

"Strip," she ordered, weapon and attention still focused on him. Hesitantly, he shifted his hands to the chin-strap of his helm. Ia lifted her chin, clarifying her order. "You will strip *completely*, and submit to being zip-bound, or you will be shot in the head, soldier. If you do comply, you will be taken back to the *Audie-Murphy* and placed in the brig for the remainder of our patrol. You will face a Board of Inquiry regarding your actions, and submit to thorough psychological examination. And if you are *lucky*, you will be dishonorably discharged and fined for the cost of the reparations both to regenerate this meioa's injuries and to recompense her suffering."

"But, sir! That bug has a bag of contraband wrapped up in that . . . cocoon thing!" he protested, starting to point into the nest alcove.

"You will return to stripping, Private, or by the laws of the Blockade, I will shoot you until you are dead!" Ia snapped, her gun arm still aimed at his face. "You have *thirty* seconds to completely strip to nothing but your skin. Mark!"

He blinked, eyes widening, then began struggling out of his body armor. She gave him three extra seconds, since he was trying to comply, then lifted her chin to the side, at Myang.

"Private Myang, zip the prisoner and haul him back to the brig. I'll take the rifle and secure his other belongings."

"Uh, sir . . . we kind of had to *climb* to get up here? If I zip his hands behind his back, he won't be able to get back down, and I can't carry him," Myang pointed out.

Ia had forgotten about that. She had only dipped into the timestreams far enough to ensure that Culpepper would comply, once she shot him the first time. Rolling her eyes, she shrugged. "Fine, *I'll* take him back. Zip his hands behind his back, bind his ankles together, and add four more around his waist. I'll need a handle." She turned back to the K'katta at her side. "Captain, I acknowledge that it is the responsibility of the Terran Space Force to make reparations. On behalf of the Space Force, I apologize for the gross misconduct of this soldier.

"I'm afraid we do not have the right medical supplies for healing K'kattan injuries on board our own vessel," Ia added, glancing at the figure still huddled inside the bunk-nest. "But I can summon a capital ship, which should have the right supplies and trained personnel. Or I can give you clearance to head for the nearest Terran Battle Platform or K'kattan Battle Nest, whichever you prefer," she offered to the dark brown alien at her side.

"We will accept the capital ship offer," the captain chitter-translated. "It is likely to be fastest."

"But—sir, the pod thing!" Culpepper protested, peering over his shoulder as Myang finished binding his hands and stooped to hobble him. "It's full of blue poppers!"

Sighing, Ia dug her scanner out of her pocket. Flicking it on, she aimed it into the nest. The scan confirmed the presence of the drug after a few seconds. "Yes, Private, it *is* a sac of drugs. But blue poppers are not illegal for the K'katta to possess because to them, it is *not* an hallucinogen. Their physiology reacts to it like it's nothing more than a triple-shot caf'. Drugs are an *internal* matter, Private, regulated by the sovereign rights of each sentient government. You were to report its presence, nothing more."

"And that gave you the right to *shoot* me?" he demanded, swaying as Myang tightened the second of the zip-ties around his waist.

"Did that sac of poppers give you the right to shoot that alien?" Myang growled, shaking him a little via the straps in her hands, before reaching around to apply a third one. "I think not!"

Ia answered him as well. "No, Private Culpepper. Your *refusal* to obey a lawful, direct order given to you from your commanding officer here inside the Salik Interdicted Zone gives me the right to shoot you. It's right there in the protocol regs for the Blockade zone," she reminded him, gun still trained on his face. "Discipline *must* be maintained while serving on Blockade duty. There will be no necklaces made of ears, no collection of severed legs, and *no* unstable soldiers serving in this zone. Not at *my* post. Not on *my* watch."

"The prisoner is secure, sir," Private Myang informed her, tightening the last strap around his waist. "I'll gather his things once you have him."

Holstering her gun, Ia nodded at Myang. "Acknowledged, Private." She turned her attention to the other Human in the cabin. "You're lucky I am strong enough to carry you, Private Culpepper. Given how angry I am with you, I'd be tempted to just kick you down the nearest access shaft, and let you take the damage that would result.

"But unlike *you*, I am in control of myself, and I will abide by the rules and regulations of Blockade Patrol." Hooking her hand through the ties circling the middle of his back, Ia heaved him off his feet. Ignoring his grunt of pain as the plexi ties bit into his stomach, she hauled him out of the alien crew quarters like he was nothing more than a sack of garbage.

CHAPTER 18

Yes, I would have indeed shot him. With Private Myang's recording, there would have been no doubt as to his loss of stability, and no doubt as to Private Culpepper's violation of Fatality Five, Disobeying a Direct Order. Those two circumstances make it permissible— and even required, when combined—to quickly remove the threat of an unstable soldier by any means necessary while on Blockade Patrol.

But I am very glad it was not necessary. I am glad he was the only unstable member of my various rotating crews in the Interdicted Zone. You see, I am not inclined to waste lives needlessly. Not just because it is my duty as an officer to preserve as many lives as possible while carrying out a particular mission, but because my conscience as a sentient being will allow nothing less.

. . . That does bring up the end of my Blockade career, doesn't it? People like to say that falling from one danger into another, greater danger is like going from the frying pan into the fire. Unfortunately, when the Salik are involved, it's more like the other way around.

~Ia

AUGUST 11, 2495 T.S.
PIRATE SHIP *STELLAR LONGEVITY*
NUK NUK 117 SYSTEM

Timing was everything. So were decisions.

There was the decision to hurry through the inspection in the previous system. The decision to give the order to jump immediately to this one, while Ia and her boarding crewmembers were still in the pods, just after they reattached to the backs of the *Audie* and the *Murphy*. The discovery of a lone pirate ship just a short flight away from their reentry point, and the command to attack and destroy its defenses with a shorthanded gunnery team.

The decision that the ship looked "sufficiently shot-up" wasn't Ia's, but then she knew that her junior officer for this patrol run, Lieutenant Second Grade Linsey Odingaarde, would make a bad call. Yes, the gun turrets had been successfully destroyed, but not nearly enough of the FTL panels.

Still, it was definitely Ia's decision to agree to launch the pods back out again. Or rather, just the one, since there was a slight hang-up in the launch mechanism for the other pod. A flaw that she created carefully via electrokinesis. It delayed the other pod's launch by a full six minutes, which was enough time for her pod to land and start carving an entrance into the other ship. The second pod therefore landed on its chosen section of hull just as Ia stepped into the still-hot opening carved beyond the pod's airlock, and began its sealing process just a little bit too late. Timing was everything.

"*Holy—!*" Lieutenant Odingaarde shouted in their headsets. "*The FTL panels! They're firing up the FTL panels! Disengage! Disengage!*"

Turning, Ia hooked her mechsuit hand around the edge of the pod entry and smacked the emergency release button. Yanking her arm back hard and fast, she slammed her hands into the walls above her mechsuited head, bracing herself. The pod slammed its airlock door right in Private Knowles's face, and blasted its sealant foam. A lot of air rushed past from the loss of that seal, but the bulk of her mechsuit, braced between arms and legs, kept Ia anchored in place.

Warning sensors beeped, letting her know the laser-carved

entrance was threatening her servo-fingers and mechanized feet with excessive heat. The stars were now moving beyond the oval cut into the side of the smuggler's ship. Only slightly, and more from a course change than from actual, fantastical speeds, but it did confirm that the ship's thrusters were indeed warming up. It also meant that, mere minutes from now, they would be moving fast enough to exceed the speed of light.

Even at just a quarter of that speed, the sheering forces caused by leaving the field's zone would be enough to rip anything apart. The hole she stood in was too small to need worry about the field divoting inward around her—the probabilities put it at less than a hundredth of 1 percent—but it wouldn't be a comfortable place to stay.

Which means the only way out is to go in, and the only viable option for survival is capture. Which puts me right on schedule. Carefully turning around, Ia worked her way further into the ship until she stood at the brink of a cargo hold, partway up the wall . . . and found three p-suited sentients, two Humans and a Tlassian, struggling to haul a heavy metal plate along one of the aisles between crates and canisters of unlabeled goods.

The Tlassian was the first one to spot her. He stilled, his tail twitching inside his suit. The others tugged on the plate for a moment more, then followed his line of sight, peering up through their half-silvered helms. They froze as well.

Taking advantage of their hesitation, she jumped down from the hole, aiming for the aisle they were in, which was offset from the hole by barely a meter. Using her boot thrusters to brake her fall, she landed with a *clunk* that she felt up through the legs of her suit. Once she had her balance, Ia just walked up to them.

Her heads-up scanners showed the plate was mostly ferrous, high in steel content. Activating the electromagnets in her mechsuit gloves, she pressed the palms to the metal with two *clanks*. Lifting it out of their hands barely strained the suit's capacity. They stared, taken aback, then followed her warily as she walked back up the aisle, then scattered out of her way when she put her back to the wall and burned her boot thrusters a second time. That strained the thrusters, but leaping was not an option, not with such a small hole for a target, nor while carrying such a heavy metal plate.

The suit's sensors were a godsend, letting her shift subtly. The moment she could catch her heel on the rim, she pulled herself into the hole, cutting the thrusters. She didn't pull the plate in after her, however. Leaving a gap of almost a meter, she used the eye-blink interface on her heads-up display to disengage her inner helm from the outer one, and cracked open the suit.

From there, it was a matter of grabbing onto one of her own suit arms and dropping to the now mostly cooled edge of the hole while she stripped off her arm unit and tossed it into the mechsuit's cavity. The moment it landed inside and clattered down into a leg cavity, Ia electrokinetically resealed the suit. There was no way she could allow anyone on this ship's crew access to either mechsuit or arm unit technology. Some rules and regs, she would break, and had broken. Letting military tech fall into enemy hands was very much not necessary, so this was not one of them.

From the front right thigh pocket, she grabbed a grappling gun and a small hand-welder. From the front left compartment, a belt hung with a holster and a shrapnel grenade. Even standing several centimeters back from the opening, the suit's arms were long enough to give her plenty of room to maneuver. The sight of the stars slowly shifting beyond the suit was an unnerving one; that meant they were now traveling at least half the speed of light. She didn't have much time before the transition came. Ia quickly slung the belt around her grey-suited hips, holstering the welder.

Aiming up through the crack between hole and panel, she shot the grappling gun up into the struts bracing the ceiling of the cargo hold. The motor on the oversized gun had no problem lifting her minuscule weight; it was meant to lift a soldier in halfmech armor, and possibly even one in full-mech. Lifting herself up through the opening, she reached out with her mind the moment her feet cleared the hole. The suit retracted its arms, pulling the slightly larger panel up against the bulkhead of the cargo hold with a *clang* that vibrated through the ship and down the wire, making her sway a little oddly.

Kicking her heels, Ia played out the line, swinging until the magnetic soles in her feet clipped the panel and stuck, allowing her to pull herself in close. Drawing the welding gun, she zapped the edge of the plate in six spots, then reached out once more with her mind. None of this would have been possible without her electrokinetic gifts; if the other pod had made it to the ship, one of her crew would have been stuck on board alongside her at the very least, and that meant at least one mechsuit would have fallen into enemy hands. But with her gifts, she was able to close her eyes, concentrate, and program the mechsuit—arm unit safely tucked inside—into releasing its electromagnetics.

Guiding the suit backwards, she made it leap out of the hole. There wasn't even a thump, since the warp panels instantly pushed the suit away from the ship, shredding it to dust. There was, however, a bright flash that seeped through the unsealed edges, letting her and the three crewmembers down below know that they had crossed the lightspeed barrier. Rappelling down, Ia kicked off one of the crates, landed in the aisle, and turned to find two more pirates had joined the first three. Pirates who were armed.

Turning the welder gun sideways, showing that it was just a welder and not a laser pistol, she slipped her hand free of the grappling gun and down to her waist. One of the armed smugglers motioned with his weapon, clearly wanting her to drop the welder and put her hands up. The welder dropped to the decking in a clatter that was felt rather than heard, given the lack of air in the hold, but when she lifted her pressure-suited arms above her head, the grenade was visibly gripped in her other hand.

They froze. Ia wriggled the gloved fingers of her empty hand, then lowered both arms. She had the advantage now, and they knew it; if they fired on her, the grooved grenade could go off, catching *all* of them—clad only in p-suits, which were tough, but not that tough—and shredding their meager protection against the airless state of the cargo hold, killing them slowly if the blast didn't kill them outright.

Once she was sure they wouldn't move, Ia stooped and picked up the welding gun again. Stepping forward, she offered it handle-first to the Tlassian. He hesitated a moment, then took it from her and edged toward the patch on their hold, focusing on it as the greater priority right now. Gesturing for the others to go ahead of her, Ia slowly herded the remaining four back up the aisle toward the inner airlock separating the hold from the rest of the ship. She even made sure they cycled through first, flicking her p-suit-gloved fingers in pointed instruction.

Aware that the small reoxygenation pack on the back of her suit wouldn't last forever, Ia cycled herself after them. Two more armed crewmembers awaited her. They didn't wear pressure suits, but they did bring the known count of Humans and Tlassian up to five and two respectively, albeit with one of the saurians left back in the cargo bay.

It was still a standoff, however. They had plenty of guns, but she had a military grenade, and they were all in close quarters. Lifting her free hand to the controls on her neck-ring, Ia unsealed her suit and flicked back the front faceplate, allowing her to breathe the air of their vessel. It also allowed her to speak.

"Thank you for not shooting recklessly," she stated dryly, if politely. "It seems, given our current standoff, a little bit of negotiation is in order."

"Alllll *we* have to do issss retreat and fire uponnn you from a dissstancsse," the pistol-wielding Tlassian in the corridor with her hissed.

"Neh-yah-veh," she agreed, using the V'Dan equivalent of *more or less.* "But I'll be blunt and admit I'm worth considerably more to you alive and unharmed."

"Shakk sh'keth," one of the Humans scoffed. His skin was too dark a shade of brown to tell if he was Terran or V'Dan. From the faint hint of an accent, Ia guessed it was the latter. "Th' military doesn't ransom anybody!"

"I'm not talking about the Terran Space Force," Ia informed him. "I'm talking about the Salik. It seems they have a very large bounty on my head. Naturally, the offer's only good if you trade me to them while I'm still very much alive, intact, and unharmed."

They stared at her. The male who had cursed blinked. "You . . . *want* to be sold to the Salik?"

She poked her free thumb over her shoulder at the airlock door behind her. "I noticed some of the crates you were hauling were stamped with codes for hyperrelay components. Since the rest of the Alliance can get their hands on such parts fairly cheaply, that means you're smuggling them close to the Interdicted Zone for a purpose—in other words, for the Salik, or at least for those who trade with them. Since you have Salik contacts, this means you're capable of looking up my ident through those contacts and discovering that they now have a bounty on my intact, unharmed, fully alive body, traded kilo for kilo in solid platinum. That's enough precious metal to buy a second ship . . . or outfit this one with far better engines and guns than the *sh'keth* you're currently running."

"Rrrunninng, until *you* sssshhot it up," the Tlassian hissed, lifting his gun a little higher in threat.

"Yes, well, I wasn't in charge of *that* decision," Ia drawled. "If I had been, your FTL capability would certainly not still be intact, and you'd be running and screaming from the advance of my full boarding party. As it is, my second-in-command is going to face a Board of Inquiry for losing both her CO and this ship."

"*You're* the CO? Commanding Officers don't lead boarding parties!" a new Human scoffed, this one a female. She wedged her way forward between two of the suited Humans, confronting Ia with her hands on her hips. Petite and Asiatic, hair cropped short and only modestly pretty for a Human, she could have been any of a hundred thousand women Ia had seen in her travels through the known galaxy. She carried herself with an air of absolute authority, however, and the rest of the crew backed off a little, deferring to her.

"I lead from the front, mcioa," Ia stated. She bowed slightly, grenade still visible in her hand. "Allow me to introduce myself. I am Lieutenant First Grade Ia, ident #96-03-0004-0096-0072-0002, and I am assigned to the command of the TUPSF *Audie-Murphy*, one of the Delta-VXs flown out of Battle Platform *Mad Jack*. I am personally responsible for the tracking, capture, and destruction of twenty-three Salik vessels . . . including single-handedly shooting down one of their rare capital ships.

"They *want* me, First Officer Veng, like you would not believe," Ia added, watching the woman jump slightly in surprise at hearing her name. "They're willing to *pay* to get their slimy little tentacles on me. Specifically alive, intact, and unharmed. And *you* are going to deliver me to them for a very substantial fee. Now, you can spend it however you want; I don't care. So long as you hand me over to the Salik, alive, intact, and unharmed, I honestly do not care about you, your ship, or your crew. You can go about your business as soon as I'm done with you."

Veng eyed Ia up and down. "You're *shakking* crazy. No Human *wants* to get eaten by th' damned frogtopussies!"

"I didn't say they'd get to eat me," Ia countered, shrugging slightly. "Just that I need to be handed over to them. This is an opportunity I cannot pass up, given my standing orders. You *will* sell me to the Salik. All I ask is that you don't actually *tell* them that I want to be sold . . . because if you did, they'd kidnap you and your crew out of paranoia, and then *you'd* be on the lunch menu, too." She shrugged eloquently. "In good conscience, I could not allow that. So for the time being, while you look up the bounty on my head, you can lock me up in the unused crew quarters on Deck 5, portside, cross-corridor Charlie."

"How did you . . . ?" Veng asked her, blinking.

"How did I know about the unused crew cabin?" Ia asked her. "*My* contacts heard about your ex-crewmate Connors leaving the ship, and from there, tracked down information on where he had been staying," she lied calmly. "Your lightspeed broadband comm panel's scrambler code has been cracked. You might want to get that changed out as soon as you can."

"But why do you need to be sold to the *Salik*, of all species?" the first officer repeated, shaking her head. "I'll admit we'll sell them a lot of things, since they pay through their nostril-flaps for it . . . but a living sentient?"

Ia smirked ever so slightly. "That's need-to-know information, meioa, and *you* do not need to know. In fact, you don't *want* to know. Trust me."

Several whispers behind her, sibilant with the hisses of the Tlassian language, told her the crew was discussing her insanity. The translation of their exchange was more or less wondering if Ia was secretly a Salik agent. Ia knew there were such agents in the military, though not as many among the Terrans as the Salik could've wished.

Veng touched the headset hooked over her ear. She lifted her chin at the taller woman. "Fine. It's your funeral banquet. But you strip to the skin. I want to make sure you're not here to sabotage our ship. It's funny, but I don't really *trust* TUPSF officers."

"Only if you give me something to wear in exchange. P-suits aren't comfortable in the long term. *Ah-ah*," Ia reminded both her and the others as they shifted toward her. She gave a little wave with the hand still holding the grenade. "No touching. This is nonnegotiable. You touch me, I break things. And I'll keep this grenade up until I'm sold, to keep you honest. Oh, and I'd like something to eat when I get to my 'guest quarters.' A ration packet will do; it doesn't have to be anything fancy. With luck, I won't be here long enough to be a burden on your resources."

"You can't hold on to that grenade forever, meioa," the V'Dan crewmember warned her.

Ia looked over her shoulder at him. "I survived all seven days of Hell Week in the Marines, Basic Training, meioa. *All* seven days. I can do anything I need to do. My advice? Don't get in my way, and I won't hurt you. Now, as I said, I suggest I be 'locked away' for your own safety while your captain and first officer investigate the bounty on my intact, alive body. But don't delay. Their offer has a narrow window of opportunity."

"Fine. You heard the meioa," Veng ordered her crewmates. "No touching, until we know if it's true. That also means *you*, Svass. Give her room to pass, the lot of you. If you force her into a fight when she's trying to be polite, I'll point and laugh at whatever she does to you. As for *you*, prisoner, move *that* way. If it's *not* true, Svass is only the first one who'll have a shot at your pretty little backside."

The members of the crew parted, and Ia politely passed through untouched. She skirted carefully around the Tlassian as she did so, keeping well out of his reach.

Not all of the Alliance races were bipedal, and not all of the Alliance races shared the same physiological traits. Some things did translate, somewhat. Solaricans and Tlassians and Humans reproduced via similar methods, and enjoyed similar pleasures while doing so. Gatsugi physiology was too different to be compatible, and K'katta, Choya, and Salik didn't breed unless they were in heat. As for the Dlmvla, they breathed the wrong atmosphere, and the Chinsoiy lived in an environment radioactively toxic to the other races. Both situations made such speculations impossible. But among the first three races, certain activities *were* possible, if one were perverted enough.

It didn't take long to get to the right deck and cross-corridor. The cabin was as small as precognitively advertised. The amount of floor space was the same as the area covered by the double bunk beds, and the bathroom was little more than a closet with a toilet and sink. Ia didn't care, though. She turned to thank the first officer, only to find Veng pointing a gun at her.

"Strip. You're clearly carrying something around your right ankle, and I want to know what it is," Veng ordered, nodding at the bulge beneath the silvery grey material.

"Bring a set of clothes, and I'll show you," Ia countered.

"No game. I'm not leaving you alone to pull some sort of James Bond device on me and my crew," the other woman countered.

"It's a bracelet. Well, technically an anklet," Ia corrected, once more lying through her teeth. "I cannot remove it, because I put it on when I was a kid and couldn't get it off again. Besides, all you have to do is call on your headset and ask someone to bring you a pair of coveralls. You don't have to leave this cabin. Now, we can play this game all day, Meioa Veng . . . but I really am what I seem to be."

"And that would be?" Veng asked, one brow lifted skeptically.

"A soldier with a crazy idea, and the abilities to carry it through. All I need is for you to cooperate . . . and in exchange, I'll give you five sets of navigation coordinates to go hide your ship for the next six weeks, because you're going to *need* to hide for at least that long," Ia told her. Veng frowned, so she explained. "The moment you took off with me on board, you tagged this vessel across the entire Space Force as kidnappers. Every port will be looking for you, for the bounty on your heads.

"*However*, it should only take me two and a half weeks to do what needs be done, then I'll be back, and within another two and a half, I'll be able to clear your names with the Command Staff," Ia told her. "Give another week or so for word to spread that the bounty's no longer valid, and you'll be free to go back to business as usual. *If* you really want to. I make no guarantees against capture or destruction if you do, however."

Veng snorted. "*You* have contacts in the Command Staff? Yeah, right. More like you'll leave us deadheading into the dark, meioa. Particularly since you *won't* be coming back."

"Then if nothing else, do not delay in checking out my ident with the Salik," Ia said. "I weigh just over one hundred four kilos. That's a *lot* of refined platinum. You could easily buy off an Independent Colonyworld to give you and the rest of the crew asylum. Maybe even turn privateer, and be semirespectable."

Veng gave her a wary look. She seemed to be considering Ia's offer. Finally, she touched her headset, activating it. "What's that ident number, again?"

Ia gave it to her. She waited patiently as Veng gave the orders for a spare set of ship coveralls to be brought down, too, then stripped out of the pressure suit—carefully, still holding the grenade in one hand at a time—until she bared the crysium on her ankle. Translucent peach pink, it was just clear enough to show it was just a thick ankle cuff. "Satisfied it's not some bizarre device?"

"No, but it'll do." Tossing the coveralls on the lower bed, Veng picked up the p-suit and started to back out of the cabin. She paused one last time. "*Why* do you need to be sold to the Salik? That's what I don't get. Since you don't have any gear or weapons with you, I can only think you're working for them. But if you were, why the ruse of being sold?"

Ia, stepping into the coveralls, looked up at the other woman. "I see you wear a cross," she observed. "I trust that you're familiar with the story of David and Goliath?"

Veng snorted. "Of course I am."

Ia shrugged into the sleeves and started fastening the front. "Well, I am *very* good with a sling, meioa. I suggest you don't get in the way of my cast."

"You are *beyond* crazy, meioa. Maybe the Salik *do* deserve to eat you." Stepping outside, Veng locked the door.

Touching the panel with her hand, Ia sank her mind into the locking circuitry. It wasn't the familiar military model, so it took her a few minutes to figure out and change the code. The moment she was secure, she retreated into the closet to use the facilities. The 6 percent probability that that one perverted Tlassian would want to get in there was now successfully cut off, leaving her relatively safe for the time being.

Ugh. *Too many hours stuck in a pressure suit, even if I didn't drink a lot before I went in. And I'd better dig into the*

*emergency rations in the locker above the toilet so I can have
something to eat and drink, since the probability is high that
these pirates won't be inclined to feed me. Not that the Salik
won't feed me. They'll be taking pains to keep me alive once
they get their suckers on me. But it'll be almost two weeks of
being stuck in a cell at FTL speeds with the Salik version of
food before we'll reach Sallha.*

*If I'm lucky, they'll have Terran ration packets, which are
tolerably edible if nothing else. If I'm not . . . I cannot afford
to starve to death, however terrible Salik prisoner rations
might be. I need to be healthy when we get to the Salik
homeworld.*

*At least I know from the timestreams that they won't waste
good sentient flesh by offering it to their livestock. I'm not sure
I could stomach adding cannibal to my list of crimes committed
for the Future.*

. . . Heh. "Stomach . . ."

At least she had her sense of humor to keep her from getting
bored, warped though it was.

AUGUST 23, 2495 T.S.
SALIK VESSEL
SIC TRANSIT

They took away her clothes of course, and hissed and burbled
in puzzlement over the smooth mineral permanently encasing
her shin. But that was alright; Ia had never been body-conscious,
not growing up with two brothers in her family's small home.
The clothing had been more to keep warm in the cool, dry
environment of her first set of captors, and shield herself from
the gaze of certain male members of the pirate crew.

Salik vessels were kept several degrees warmer and very
humid for the biological comfort of their crew, which for a
Human meant clothing wasn't necessary. As far as her alien
captors were concerned, clothing could be used for self-
strangulation, which would ruin the purpose of taking prisoners
alive. Having paid so much for Ia, she was given an "honor
guard" of two Salik males to watch over her, the sole prisoner
on the first of the ships bringing her via circuitous routes to

within OTL-jumping distance of Sallha, but otherwise she was left alone in her cage.

On the second ship, there were five Humans, two Solaricans, and three Gatsugi, all kept in tight-gridded cages that were just large enough to stand up in or stretch out and sleep. Like sentient-sized pet cages, they came with a waste bucket and a water dispenser permanently fixed to the interior. More prisoners arrived every day or so, including two K'katta, filling up the long, cargo hold–style brig.

Ia didn't talk to the other prisoners. There was nothing she could say to them, nothing she could do for them. They were meant for the various regional governors to eat, celebrating elsewhere across Sallha. Ia would be taken to their greatest underground military citadel, to be served with the rest of their most important war-food.

This mission wasn't about rescuing people. It *hurt*, knowing there was nothing she could do for them. No false hope she could give the others. Their fates were sealed. As the second Salik ship slipped its way carefully through the gaps between stars to the rendezvous point, all Ia could do was sleep, exercise to keep herself in shape, and meditate on the many needs of the future. Submersing herself fully onto the timeplains was the only way to block out the furtive whispers, the dull curses, and the different kinds of species-specific weeping of the others.

The captain of the ship came to see her on her second to last day aboard. So did the ship's medical personnel, performing tests through the bars to make sure she was biologically safe to eat. After they burbled their findings to their commander and moved on to the next prisoner, he moved up to the bars of her cage. Ia didn't pretend to ignore him. She didn't have the refuge of retreating into her own private mental madness, like some of the other prisoners had done; the timeplains were even less pleasant than reality, but they were necessary.

"Hhhew are a strrange Hhewman," the captain hissed in Terranglo. "Hhew do not cry, hhew do not curssse. No ssstressss. No fffearrr. Yet hhew ssseem to be hhhere, rathhher than lossst."

He uncurled a pair of tentacles, writhing them slowly to indicate the reality around them.

"Where else should I be?" Ia asked, meeting his bulging-eyed gaze calmly. She didn't move from her position, seated with her back against the bars that butted up against a cage holding a nervously chirping K'katta. They had taken away the alien's translator box, leaving it unable to communicate clearly with anyone but its own kind.

"Nnnot hhhere." Crouching easily, since his backwards-bending leg joints permitted it, he ducked his head a little and gazed at her more directly. First one eye, then the other. "Wwwhat do hhew wwannnt, Hhhewman?"

"What do I want?" Ia repeated. "What do you expect me to say? Should I say that I want your head on a pike, as a warning to the rest of the galaxy to never let one kind of hunger spill over into the other? Is that what you want to hear?"

"Yessss," he hissed, baring the points of his front teeth. "*There* isss the annger I exsspected . . . annger for my kinnnd."

Shifting forward onto the balls of her feet, Ia shuffled up to the front of her cage. "There's only one problem, meioa. I *don't* feel anger when I think of you. I *don't* feel rage when I look upon you."

His slit-pupiled eyes flicked in their sockets, shifting around before refocusing on her. "Wwwhhhhat, thennn, do hhew feelll?"

Looking into those eyes, Ia gave him the truth. One that she had carried inside of her since that fateful morning as a teenager, when everything had changed.

"Pity."

He hissed and reared up, finger-tentacles flailing wide as if in preparation to grapple and strike. It was, she knew, the worst possible insult she could have given from a xenopsychological view. Salik pity was not based upon any sense of compassion, unlike the kind of pity found in most of the other sentient races. Pity was not gentle regret, in their lexicon.

No, the Salik lived for the hunt and the kill. They valued the tough, the difficult, and the dangerous as their most worthy opponents. Pity, to the Salik way of thinking, was what one felt for a foe who was discovered to be unexpectedly weak. Pity was a disgusted dismissal on top of disgusted regret for any effort wasted upon their unexpectedly pathetic target.

In a twist of irony, Ia meant it purely in the Human sense, yet his reaction in the Salik sense was the one she needed. Hissing at her again, he backed up and dismissed the very idea with a curling spiral of one tentacle-hand. Rage widened his pupils and his leg muscles flexed beneath the fitted material of his species-equivalent of a p-suit, as if preparing to leap. Recovering after a moment, he hissed again, this time in satisfaction.

"Yyyessss . . . It isss said in your ffiless that hhew hhhunt yyour opponnents psssychollogically. Hhew are a mmmore cunning ffoe thannn I exsspected," the captain observed smugly.

Ia gave him a sardonic look. "Eat me."

A strange sound gurgled out of his throat. Salik laughter. "Ssssuch a prize iss nnot for me. Hhhew are meant for genn-eralss, Hhewman."

"Good. I look forward to it." Ia knew their conversation was drawing the attention of the other captives. "I have a few things I want to say to them before I die."

"Hhhhow bravve the bite you will be," he mocked, *pop-pop-popping* in lip-smacked mockery.

"How starved for a decent meal *you* will be," she mocked back. "I'm glad you know your *shallow* rank."

He almost reared up again at that, but subsided. "Hhhew will *nnnot* provoke mme."

Turning, he left, smacking his lips occasionally to the right or the left as he passed the rows of cages. Shuffling back to her former position, Ia rested against the bars. She had passed his test. Ia couldn't be anything *but* calm despite the gravity of her situation; she had trained herself long and hard to suppress and set aside her fears so that she could act in the right moment and the right way without hesitation. Such calm was unnatural, however, and had called into doubt her worthiness of being Salik prey.

Now the captain had no doubt of her prize-value, and would report as such, permitting her to be passed along. Now she would be in the right moment to be able to do things in the right way. Now she could relax in truth, awaiting the transfer to the hypership that would jump them down to the Salik home-world unseen by Blockade forces.

. . . I wish I could have seen the surface of their homeworld. We named ours after the dirt and the ground upon which we walked. They named their world Fountain, and decorated it with a million gorgeous waterworks. What a real pity it will all be laid to waste, soon.

The medical techs continued their scan of the various prisoners through their cages. The K'katta in the cage behind her chittered something, then fell silent again. The Solarican to her right rumbled and spoke.

"Is it wise to prrovoke them, meioa?" he asked her.

"I'm not afraid, if that's what you mean. I really wish I could rescue you," Ia replied, glancing his way. "All I can wish you is a swift death, and maybe the chance to break free and take some of them with you."

He *huffed* in mirthless laughter. "You mean, alll I can hope is to give them a massive hairrrball when I die."

Ia chuckled. It was gallows humor at best, but it was funny. "Whereas I, ungrateful guest that I am, forgot to bring my very own bottle of *fllk* dipping sauce. How 'tasteless' of me."

Caught off guard, he sneezed in laughter, lips pursed in the smile of his kind. Grinning, she rested her head against the bars, enjoying the rare bout of mirth, until it faded with a sigh. Closing her eyes, Ia returned her mind to the timestreams, making sure she knew all of the steps to be taken in the days ahead.

There was another blank spot coming, one in the banquet hall itself. One which worried her, though she knew there was a high probability that she'd achieve her objectives—most of the good potential-probable stream paths led out of the mist, of the ones she had marked as necessary to achieve. The more she probed at it, however, the more it felt like that capital ship had felt, like a headache from too much noise. What *that* meant, she didn't yet know, which meant she had to be ready for almost anything.

I just hope whatever it is that's generating these mist-bubbles is something I can deal with. This banquet is too important for me to fail.

CHAPTER 19

Yes, I actually did pity the Salik, back when I was in the Navy. By their own arrogance, their own pride, their own species-centric blindness, they condemned themselves. One way or another, they were bent on a course of self-destruction. Those races who do understand and value cooperation between each other's kinds are stronger because of our cooperation. Stronger because of our diversity, though the Salik looked upon it as species impurity.

I've always pitied them. Always felt sorry for them, knowing what I knew. Neither did I hate them for clinging so stubbornly to their nature and their beliefs; I just felt sorry for them. And I'll point out how I went out of my way to try to warn them, even as I did what I had to do. The rest . . . well, they were the ones who were choosing to go to war.

Good or bad, right or wrong, all of us must live with the consequences of our choices.

~Ia

AUGUST 27, 2495 T.S.
BANQUET HALL OF THE GRAND COMMANDERS
SALLHA

They chained her up about a third of the way back from the dais holding the highest-ranked members of the top brass. Everything else she had done would have earned her a frame at the back of the room, but blowing up a capital ship as she had, well . . . she was up here. Ia wasn't "worthy" enough to be their most prized meal, a fellow Human who would be set free in a contemptuous gesture of superiority to "fight" for survival against their Grand High General, but she was worthy enough to be here. That was the important part.

She did her best to ignore the swerving eyes and licking, smacking lips of the Salik generals nearest her while the others were brought into the hall and chained into the eating frames. They hissed and burbled in quiet little comments, studying her limbs hungrily, but none of them uncurled a tentacle-hand her way. No one would eat any of the prisoners until the Grand High General—the actual term in Sallhash was difficult to translate—had caught and taken the first bite out of his prey.

Instead, she filled the time by closing her eyes against the vision-straining hues of the blue green light shining down from the great glass globe overhead. Turning her attention inward and up, Ia focused on the locks of the manacles holding her arms straight up, her feet barely touching the floor. Some of the others struggled, some sobbed or hissed, and a few chittered. Announcements of each captor's "crimes" against the Salik gurgled through the hall, inducing temporary lulls in the aliens' various incidental conversations. The noise of nearly a thousand nostril-flaps whistling and all those lips smacking followed each introduction, since the Salik had no hands to clap in applause like some of the other races.

The headache came back as the first psychic captive was led into the chamber. Wincing slightly—the pain wasn't serious, but it was noticeable—Ia peered over her shoulder, trying to find the source of the annoyance. The Solarican being carried into the room, wrists and ankles tied to a pole like some sort of primitive tribal sacrifice, had a strange contraption strapped to her head. It was connected via cables to a heavy box being wheeled by a Salik guard behind her. Warily, Ia probed toward the box electrokinetically. Her headache immediately increased.

That's very strange . . . That's a machine! *How is a* machine *able to give me a psi-induced headache?*

She probed warily, precognitively, dipping just far enough into the timestreams to see the fog spreading outward as an aura-overlay on the real world. Specifically, from the crown-thing on the alien's head, not from the box, though the box and its cables did radiate a bit of mist-glow uncertainty. *So . . . if they've put this thing on her head, and I know from when we get out of this that she's a Seer, their term for someone with psychic abilities . . . then the machine is generating some sort of . . . of psychic-ability dampening field?*

That made sense. That made a horrible lot of sense. It also made sense as to why blowing up a capital ship armed with one of those things placed her so close to the dais, rather than at the back of the room for all her other crimes against the Salik nation. The generation of that much psi-nullifying energy, enough to block *her* abilities, would have indeed required the resources of a capital ship. By comparison, this little machine was a mere nuisance.

Until they brought in the second psi, and a third, and a fourth. Each machine ramped up her headache and spread another patch of fog into her mental awareness of the large underground hall. Quickly, before the fields grew too pervasive, Ia wrapped her hands around the chains holding her up and unlatched the manacles at wrists and ankles. She carefully held still, not wanting anyone to realize she was free, but unlocked herself subtly all the same.

One of the machines passed close by her eating frame. Carefully craning her head, Ia studied it. The head-thing was firmly strapped onto the crested skull of the priest-caste Tlassian. The machine had the usual sucker-controlled buttons, smooth and seamless, and very difficult to pull up on telekinetically. *By its very nature, the machine itself would no doubt block any electrokinetic attempts to interfere with it, and probably—*

—Aha! It's plugged *in! That's how they can fit on all the different skull caps, for different alien head configurations. The machines are the same, but the* helmets *are interchangeable, and it's the helms that cause the radiation effect.* Biting

her lip to keep from crowing, Ia focused on her pain to clear the joy out of her nerves. Pleasure could be just as distracting as fear, and the next few minutes would be vital. Mindful of her loosened manacles, she looked around the chamber, identifying the exact placement of each of the anti-psi machines and the sockets for their suppression helmets.

This would not be that much different from playing the wall harp back home. A little harder thanks to the fog, but not by too much. Confident she knew of each plug's placement, Ia relaxed. Instead of wrapping her mind around a dozen or so picks, she wrapped them instead around the base of each wire. The strain of holding on to them in spite of the fields' dampening qualities was about as bad as the strain of holding herself up by her chains without moving. Bearable, but not something she'd care to do forever. She closed her eyes and rested as much as she could, given the two problems at hand, balancing tension with what would look to her captors like resignation.

An extra-long speech in Sallhash warned her that the parade of prisoner-meals was coming to an end. Opening her eyes, she watched the Salik guards carry in yet another pole-bound prisoner. This one was their last prisoner, the greatest enemy the frogtopusses had managed to get their slimy tentacles around.

The naked, struggling, grey-haired and grim-faced woman was none other than the long-missing Admiral Jenka Viega, former Fleet Commander of the Blockade. Viega had been presumed killed while traveling on an OTL courier over four months ago. Despite her long captivity, she looked as if she had kept her middle-aged body fit and her spirit strong, judging by the curses she flung in Spanish and the flexing of her muscles against her bonds.

Her fighting spirit seemed to rouse some of the other captives. Several strained against their bonds, craning their necks to look at the woman. Breathing deep, readying herself, Ia watched as the admiral was set on the platform and her ankles were unbound. Ia knew the older woman was just waiting for her wrists to be freed before she intended to lash out, and hopefully take down the Grand High General before she died. Ia didn't intend to give the older woman that chance.

"Excuse me, meioas!" she called out, tightening her gut to project her voice over the hubbub in the hall.

Ia let go of the chains, freeing her hands from their restraints, kicking her legs to shake off the ankle cuffs binding her feet to the floor. The Salik around her hissed in surprise, too stunned by her sudden escape to move. Without hesitation, Ia turned her drop into a bound, striding quickly straight for the main platform. Hisses followed her progress, with some of the aliens rising from their cushion-seats.

Given that Sallha's gravity was barely .71Gs Standard, Ia reached the platform in mere moments. The Grand High General hissed and gurgled at her approach, no doubt something about personally eating the guards who hadn't secured her chains. She spoke again as he started to raise one set of tentacles in her direction.

"I hope you don't mind, General, but I went to a *lot* of trouble and expense to attend this little party. I am here to try to save your lives," Ia told him firmly, letting her volume echo her statement off the ceiling and walls.

Her words arrested him in mid-command. Curling his digits, he licked his lips. "Hhheww . . . wish to sssave *our* livvesss?"

Silence fell. Those Salik who had risen sank back onto their seats. Once again, alien psychology was now on her side, playing into her hands. With such a bold, bold statement, Ia had proven herself worthy in their eyes to face up to their leader . . . though perhaps not yet worthy of being eaten by him.

Chin up, shoulders level, Ia returned the taller alien's gaze calmly. "Yes. I do wish to save you. I am here to give you Deep Warnings, as your people put it. If you insist on going to war with us in the next few years, your *entire* race will perish. Generals, workers, males, females, tadpole-children and kraken-crones, *all* of them will vanish from the future of this galaxy. Knowing that will happen, I could not in good conscience remain silent, thus I arranged to be captured and brought here.

"You will perish to the last scrap of your species' existence," Ia stated, holding his swivel-eyed gaze. "Your rivers will run dry, your lakes will lie still, your waterworks will cease to drip, and the roar of your oceans will be silenced forever, *if* you go to war in the next few years. You have my Prophetic Stamp on that."

The Grand High General snorted. He wheezed through his nostril-flaps, eyes flicking this way and that before refocusing on Ia's face. "Hhheww are misstakenn, Hhhuman. We go to war in the nexst fffew *hoursss!*"

Ia ignored the alien version of laughter gusting through the hall. Instead, she yanked on the plugs of every machine within her grasp. If their headaches were anything like hers, the sudden cessation of pain in the other psychics' brains would force them to take a few moments to recover. Prepared for it, Ia ignored the backlashing ache in her own head. Focusing while the Salik around her mocked her words in babbles and hisses, she shifted her mind to target every single weapon being carried by the ten guards on the platform, followed by every manacle within range. It would strain her abilities, and she would have to unlock the whole room in a series of waves, but it was the best she could do.

She knew the Grand High General was permitting her to speak as a show of power over such insolent prey. She needed that arrogance, because she had to *try* to warn them, to salve the burning of her own conscience before taking up the burdens of her coming duties. When the laughter-wheezing finally died down, Ia spoke again.

". . . So. You will not change your mind? Even knowing that it *guarantees* the destruction of all of your people, and all your worlds, leaving you nothing more than a fading, pitied memory?"

He uncurled a tentacle at her, wiggling the tip in admonition. "There isss *nothing* hhew can do to usss. *We* are mighty! And hhhyouuu are *prey.*"

Holding up one finger upright toward him—the Human gesture was ironically similar to the Salik version of *please wait*—Ia looked over her shoulder at Admiral Viega. "For the record, sir, I *did* try to warn them. I honestly tried. Please stand witness to this, in the coming years?"

Viega frowned in puzzlement. She opened her mouth to speak, but was interrupted. Not by the scornful whistle-laugh of the head of the Salik military and his fellows, but by another set of sounds. The clanking and locking of every door around them, sealing them into this room. Hard on the heels of that came other sound.

Stunner pistols flew out of holsters and *pop-popped* out of suckered grips. They flew into suddenly freed fingers as manacles snapped and clattered. Solaricans roared, K'kattas chattered, and Gatsugi keened, some flushing rage-violet, others staying a sickly yellow-fear. Salik leaped up high and slammed down on their freed meals from overhead—only to find themselves batted off-target by Ia's mind, and more, aided by the other psis in the room. All of this took energy, some of which she siphoned from the crystal still encircling her leg, softening it so it could flow up her shin.

"Hhhheewww!" the Grand High General hissed, crouching in preparation to spring onto Ia. "Hhheww did thissss!"

Humans screamed, in rage and in pain—and the shadows in the room danced abruptly under the billowing pillars of bright yellow red fire that erupted. The other psis were rousing and fighting back. Chaos now ruled the hall. "*Hhhew* willll die!"

He leaped at her. Liquid crystal darted up from her leg to her fist, hardening just in time for her to punch him in the mouth. Not in time to stop the force of his pounce, but enough to break his sharpened teeth and thrust him, mouth and body, off to the side. Landing hard on her back, Ia grunted and rolled, using the momentum of her fall to haul her heels over her head.

Shoving back to her feet, she reshaped the blob cupping her fingers. She knew this banquet was being recorded and broadcast, and spat out one of the few words she knew she could pronounce in Sallhash. "*Pthaachsz!*"

Toothless.

Pupils dilating wide at the insult, the Grand High General spat blood from his mouth and reared up to leap at her again. Ia swung back her sword in preparation for a coup de grace.

"Lieutenant!"

The warning came too late. Weight struck her from behind. Teeth clamped into her left shoulder in aching, piercing, concentration-shaking pain. Clenching her jaw, Ia swung anyway, beheading the leader of the Salik forces. His body, caught midleap, knocked into hers, staggering her back into the Salik general literally trying to chew off her arm.

Stunnerfire washed over both of them. Ia squeaked as his jaws locked tighter, body sagging in electrostatic-induced slumber. Gasping against the pain, she slashed awkwardly over her right shoulder, hooking her wrist as hard as she could to make sure the monofractal edge cut through his skull without cutting into her own flesh. Scuffling forward as his body sagged, she aimed a second, even more awkward strike. It swept from behind her head, severing most of his body from his face. A third twist let her cut off the last bit of flesh holding his body to his jaws. That freed her just in time to turn and slash, gutting the next Salik.

Whirling to face the rest, she found them slumped unconscious on the dais. The Fleet Admiral spun around as well, facing into the bloodied crowd. A frustrated growl escaped her. "I can't *hit* them without . . . *Gaaah!* Why can't this be a *laser*?"

There wasn't time for subtlety. What Ia needed was a hundred small shards, and the nearest source was the great globe of the light-fixture overhead. It was a magnificent piece, stained and shaped to replicate the many islands and seas of Sallha. Ignoring the pain in her shoulder but wincing in regret for the chandelier's loss, Ia flung her telekinetic might at the great globe from two sides, like two giant, invisible hands bashing together.

Glass *crashed* and fell. She caught most of it, the larger, sharper chunks, and sent them flying through the air like oversized harp picks. Instead of plucking strings, however, she plucked out throats. It was a sickening symphony of spattering, splattering red. Bodies fell, and the sounds of combat faded. Drawing in a deep breath, she shouted to catch the attention of the survivors.

"Listen up!" Heads turned her way. "We have *two minutes* to grab all the survivors and get the hell out of here before the Salik send in their reinforcements! Search for survivors—you *know* what'll happen if they get left behind! Find people, and move toward *that* door!"

She pointed with her sword, and seared a line of electricity across the upper edge of its metal frame. Those who were still on their feet scrambled to look for survivors. Fire still crackled and seared, spouting up from the bodies of the fallen Salik off to one side of the huge hall. Ia stabbed for the pyrokinetic's mind with her own; now was not the time to let him go rogue. As it was, he was perilously close to self-combustion, with the very air around his naked frame showing wisps of smoke.

(Control *yourself, Michaels! Lock down your gifts; we don't have* time *for you to burn down their world just yet!*) Out loud, Ia added more orders to the rest. "Tllaanva, Ssthikit, grab one of those damn anti-psi boxes, and keep your helmets with you," she ordered a pair of priest-caste Tlassians. They flattened their spiked crests in dismay, but moved as she asked. Ia addressed the other psis. "Everyone, keep your helmets! We need to know what those things are and how they're made—*move* it, people! *One* minute."

"I trust you know what you're doing, Lieutenant Ia?" Admiral Viega muttered, following Ia as she moved across the blood-slicked platform toward the stunned bodies of the high generals. "Because unless you can pull off an even *bigger* miracle than this . . ."

Ia slashed through the spines and throats of the sleeping generals, making absolutely sure each one was dead. She didn't bother to ask how the admiral knew her name. The reputation that had earned her a place at this banquet had been earned among her fellow Terrans, and earned long before the four months that Viega had been missing.

"Trust me, sir," she muttered, teeth clenching as the swiping of her right arm shifted her left shoulder painfully. "I know *exactly* how to get us out of here—done. Move it, Admiral!"

Turning away from the last of the bodies, she sprinted off the dais, heading for the indicated doors. Running wasn't easy, not with her left arm clenched across her bare ribs, though turning her sword into a bracelet helped free her good arm for balance. Overturned end tables and scattered cushions were the least of their hazards; broken glass mingled with bloodied bodies, most of them Salik but not all. Ia detoured toward a stunner-slumbering body trapped between two throat-gouged enemies.

Heaving the unconscious Gatsugi out of the pile with her good arm, she dragged him as far as two of the Solaricans, a pair who looked like they were about to turn catatonic with shock at the gore and death surrounding them, and dropped him at their feet.

"You two, carry him. Don't let him die here," she ordered.

They flicked their ears back at that thought and quickly stooped, heaving the alien into a carrying position. One was missing half her tail, the other bore Salik teeth marks on his arms and shoulder, his body-fur streaked and matted with blood, but they picked up the unconscious Gatsugi without hesitation.

"The doorr is lllocked!" one of the other felinoids called out. "We're trrapped in here!"

"No, we're not!" Ia called back, freeing another sleeping, injured Alliance member from the blood and gore strewn across the floor. Viega quickly took over, directing a pair of muzzled Tlassian warrior-castes to grab and lift the curled-up K'katta.

"The door is still locked because *I* locked it. There are fifteen guards piled up behind it, and we need to be ready before it's opened."

"How can we be ready for something like *that*?" one of the other Humans demanded. "We're naked, some of us can barely walk, most of us are bleeding, and only a few of us have weapons!"

"*I'll* be ready for it," Ia promised him. "I'm going to open the door, kill the guards, and then we're going to run about half a klick. Do *not* let anyone get left behind—don't touch that!" she added as one of her fellow Humans reached for the segment of head and jaws still clinging to her left shoulder. "One of his teeth is right next to my brachial artery. Pull it out and you'll kill me. I'd rather not die today—get that Solarican!"

Pointing off to the side, she gestured for two of the survivors to grab the dazed felinoid standing alone amid a pile of throat-gouged bodies. Not waiting to see them comply, she carefully shifted the bracelet off her wrist and over to her left hand, then curled her arm up at the elbow just enough for her needs. The movements shifted the teeth jammed into her shoulder, but they were necessary. Subtly spinning the glob of crysium in her grip, she nodded at the Tlassian by the door.

"Ready? Open it in three . . . two . . . *one* . . . !"

The lock snapped open with an audible *clack*. Startled, the Tlassian grabbed the edge of the door and heaved. So did Ia, but with her mind instead of her muscles. The spinning glob of crysium snapped up and out in a shield, catching the laserfire aimed their way, glowing brightly where the laser from their weapons struck the nearly transparent pink material.

Everyone flinched back, except for Ia. Her attention was spent on absorbing that energy, preventing the thin shield from overloading. The only place to store it, however, was inside herself. The strands of her white hair started to rise away from her face, triggered by the conversion of photonic to kinetic to electric energy.

"*Dios mio*," she heard Viega mutter. "What in God's Name *is* that stuff?"

"Now is not the *time*, Admiral!" Counting down to zero, Ia twisted her whole body to shift the shield aside, since she couldn't move her left arm that much, and flung out her right arm. Tendrils of miniature lightning *cracked* down the corridor in reply before swerving back. More laserfire scored on the shield, bright yellow and overcharged, darker orange and ugly. Somewhere in the corridors beyond, more guards were headed their way. They were running out of time.

Time.

The timestreams dragged her briefly under. For one moment, she ignored the lasers brightening the shield not just in dots of light, but in broadening patches of peach gold color. Instead, she saw with her inner eyes a much larger box being hauled up from below, grey and ugly with the hint of impending, future mist, though it was not yet active. But the box had to come up an elevator shaft, and in that shaft were safety cables and safety latches, and a host of interior safety fields.

Ia ruthlessly ripped them out, drawing on her tenuous, laser-peppered shield for enough energy to work at that distance. The startled whistles and gurgling *skreels* of the crew hauling that box into the elevator couldn't be heard at this distance, but the faintest of crashes as it dropped did vibrate through the floor. Twisting the shield aside, this time Ia grabbed and flung shards of bloodied glass with her mind. Bodies gurgled and dropped as the slivers darted past, while doors slammed shut in their wake.

Breathing hard from the effort, Ia gathered her energy. "Right . . . That should do it. Everybody, move out! Viega, Jophuran, Michaels, Chong, form a rearguard. Krraul, K'sith, you're on point with me. No one gets left behind!"

The pain in her shoulder grew steadily worse. Ia had at least two splinters of glass in her right foot, making her half run, half lurch. She had only the one bite wound, but it stank of blood, both Salik and Human, as well as other things. Slowly, the shock-locked muscles of the general's jaws relaxed, allowing more of her own vital fluid to seep free.

They reached a bank of elevators, and an emergency stair-well next to it. Sweat beaded on her skin as they jogged further down into the depths of the complex. Her head swam from the effort of keeping doors and shafts sealed shut against the advance of the furious Salik forces trying to get at them. Her teeth ached, clenched tightly against the urge to groan, and her skin crawled, hyperaware of each drop of blood she was losing.

Somewhere out there, lesser generals were tracking their progress. Somewhere out there, orders were being given to set the docking bays to self-destruct. Somewhere out there, Salik technicians flung Sallhash curses at Ia's blood-streaked white hair as she slid doors open and shut, navigating them almost sightlessly all the way to the hidden gantries of two courier ships. Both were visible through the thick plexi windows looking into the vast bay, suspended from gantries above rows of similar ships.

One was entirely Salik in design, while the other was a captured V'Dan vessel. Unlocking both of them with a thought, Ia turned and started pushing bodies randomly toward the open doors with her good hand. "Get inside and strap yourselves down! Use every space you can think of! We have only two pilots, and not enough time to look for a third ship! *No* one gets left behind, got that?"

Admiral Viega pushed herself forward through the limping, bleeding bodies. She almost grabbed Ia's injured arm, but caught herself in time. Instead, she demanded, "Who is the other pilot?"

"*You* are, sir," Ia told her superior, flicking her hand to point people to either side. Most of her attention was focused on counter-commanding the frantic coding of the hidden base's technicians, but she spared enough awareness to look Viega in the eyes.

Viega returned that stare with fierce embarrassment, hissing, "Lieutenant, I haven't piloted an OTL ship in *fifteen years.*"

"Sir, do you trust me?" Ia asked. Viega blinked. Ia repeated her question with terse emphasis. *"Do you trust me?"*

"I . . . Yes, I do," Viega finally swore.

Before she could babble anything about Ia having gotten them this far, Ia clapped her fingertips to the side of the admiral's grey-haired head, holding it in place. "Then *trust* me, and this will work."

Stabbing into the older woman's mind, Ia laid the patterns of what must be done. *Thus,* and *there. This* and *that . . .* and just enough V'Dan to cope with *these* counter-possibilities. It took maybe five, six seconds of real time, though in the speed of the timestreams, Ia spent more than a minute to lay her contingencies. Releasing Viega, she nodded.

"Take K'sith with you," Ia ordered, lifting her chin at the V'Dan male helping sort the escapees into the two different ships. "He knows the comm and ops, and can be your backup, even though he isn't a pilot. Do everything *exactly* as I have showed you, and you'll get everyone out of here. Now, get to your ship!"

Viega turned to go, then turned back with a scowl. "Would you stop ordering me around?"

"Would you stop lagging behind?" Ia shot back. She cut off the former Fleet Admiral with a flick of her hand. "You know as well as I do, *sir*, that the officer in charge of a rescue mission is the *only* officer in charge of said mission! Now get in the V'Dan ship and get ready to undock. I can only hold off the Salik techs for another five minutes before they burn enough holes through their own blast-doors to manually blow up this place!"

A tight smile quirked the corner of the older woman's mouth. "If we weren't in the middle of a rescue operation, you'd be perilously close to insubordination, *Lieutenant*."

"Well, I'm in a lot of pain right now, *sir*, so I'm perilously close to *not caring*. Go!" Ia ordered, lifting her chin sharply in the direction of the last of the bloodied bodies boarding the ship to her left. Turning, she counted heads, making sure the last of the stragglers got on board.

Everyone was making sure that everyone else got on board. Herding each other, reassuring each other. Bloodied, battered, scared, but working together. The possibility of freedom had snapped even the worst of them out of their fear-generated stupors, leaving only the unconscious unable to help effect their own rescue. More stunned bodies had been found than the ones Ia had dug out—almost all of them, in fact.

Almost.

But I could only save the most important souls, the . . . the ones with the greatest impact . . . No time. No time *for this!* Gritting her teeth against the ache of regret, she scrubbed with the back of her right hand at the tears blurring her tired vision and followed the last of the escapees into the Salik-built courier.

Turning at the airlock, she called across to Viega, "Remember, Admiral, *you* have to go first. I'm the only thing keeping the enemy at bay!"

A flip of her hand was Viega's only reply. Ia let her go. Her head was starting to ache badly, enough that it was noticeable against the pain in her foot and the agony of her shoulder. Mist was beginning to close in again, and—the mist. Ia stopped in the airlock, eyes widening. *They . . . they're cobbling together another mass anti-psi generator. It's going to block everything I do!*

Her head swam with snatches of possibilities. Forcing herself to move, attention more on skimming the timestreams than on her physical surroundings, she fumbled her way into the cockpit. Her best choice—the one that would buy everyone in the Alliance the most time—was deceptively simple. This entire underground base was wired to explode in the event of discovery by Alliance forces. All she had to do was trigger every last one of those devices . . . and then hold off the final leap of the detonating electrons.

The trick was doing it under the onslaught of increasing interference from those infernal creations, holding on just long enough for all of them to escape.

Somehow, she made it to the pilot's seat, half blind from the massive division of her attention span. The Salik version of seating wasn't comfortable, more like straddling an awkwardly curved bench than anything else, but at least the restraint harness was the same four-point strap system. The only problem was, she couldn't do it manually, not with the Salik jaws still clamped to her shoulder.

"Hey, aren't you going to strap in?" That came from the Human seated behind her and to her left. To either side sat one of the rescued Solaricans—the one with the bloodied, half-eaten tail, using her own weight for a compression bandage on its end—and the V'Dan, still wearing one of the anti-psi crowns strapped to his head.

"I can't move my left arm," Ia muttered. "And I can't exactly spare the attention. I'm juggling chain saws, tap-dancing on coals, and yodeling before a tone-deaf audience, here."

"I'll do it." Unstrapping himself, he leaned over her position, carefully strapping in three of the four points. The chunk of severed head cupping her shoulder interfered too much with the fourth strap to have placed it. The psi grimaced, but didn't try to latch that strap. "Sorry, meioa; I'm a xenopath, not a biokinetic—hang on, I'm almost out of your way . . ."

Ia didn't have to be able to see the console to activate it, let alone reach it. Not that touching it would have mattered; it was designed for Salik suckers, after all. Pulling and pushing telekinetically on the controls, Ia started the engines, then activated the comm system, hooking it into the other vessel so she could address everyone.

"This is Lieutenant Ia. All hands strap in or wedge yourselves flat against an aft wall. We have to slingshot out of here, in order to achieve sufficient speed for OTL escape velocity. Acceleration forces will exceed 12Gs Standard for a minimum five seconds. Most of you will pass out. Some of you will suffer broken bones. I repeat, wedge yourself flat against an aft wall if you are unable to find secure seating. We have room for two K'katta on the aft wall of the cockpit in the Salik vessel. Admiral Viega, launch the second you are ready. Ia out."

The door to the cockpit slid open. Two K'katta scuttled inside and climbed up the back wall, using both the freefall handholds and the projecting corners of the various instruments to cling to the surface. Their multilegged knees projected past the edges of two of the three seats, with their torsos not quite wedged in place.

The V'Dan, strapped back into his seat, winced and lifted a hand to his metal-wrapped brow. *"Sh'kathek v'shakk!* It's coming back—that machine is coming back online. I'm not even plugged into it, and it's getting to me!"

She could feel her control starting to waver, her sphere of influence slipping at the farthest edges. Ia flicked on the comm again. *"Viega, you have* three *seconds to launch, mark!"*

The other ship disengaged from its docking pylons. So did Ia's. Unlike the V'Dan vessel, which dropped down onto the launch cradle on automatic, Ia piloted her ship manually. Or rather, in a mix of telekinetics and electrokinetics. Positioning it right behind the V'Dan vessel, she fired the forward pair of grapples, clamping onto the back of the other ship. That caused both ships to jolt, but the launch cradle holding the V'Dan ship didn't show any signs of strain.

"Lieutenant, what the hell *are you doing?"* Viega demanded over the comm. *"You are* not *the reincarnation of Shikoku Yama!"*

"No time, Admiral," Ia shot back, warming the thrusters. The edges of effective range on her psychic abilities slipped further, contracting abruptly. She pushed as hard as she could

to the front, striving to hold off the enemy long enough for them to escape. *"Launch!"*

Light flared beyond the observation windows. Both ships finished descending into the launch tunnel and started moving forward, one by machinery, the other by tow and by thruster fields. The *ping-ting-tang* vibrating back down the cables to the Salik vessel rose in volume, an eerie aural counterpoint to the thrumming of the engines. If those cables snapped at the wrong moment up ahead, what she had done to the Salik capital ship would be done to them. Yet if she accelerated too much at the wrong moment, she would drive the nose of this ship up the backside of the other, cracking both vessels wide open. The probabilities were not all that good.

Surrendering to the racing flow of Time, Ia let her precognition pull her under. The cradle snapped forward, launching the V'Dan vessel. The Salik ship roared with the pulse of attitude jets as well as thruster fields, the twin cables jerking the ship that much father. A frantic corner of her mind programmed the controls with autopilot instructions, but most of the rest was focused on holding back the explosions brightening the windows of the observation bays.

Behind them, the windows exploded, billowing atmosphere and fire into the launch tunnel they had just left. Giving up, Ia released her hold on the self-destruct mechanisms; it was too late to stop their escape. They launched into the great chamber, thrust so hard at the end by the cradle that the edges of Ia's physical vision blackened and drained.

"Opening the rift!" Viega shouted over the comm, her voice showing the strain of her fight to stay conscious under the heavy pull of their velocity. Sparks shot forward from the lead ship, arrowing in and impacting together in a collision of spinning, exotic, highly charged particles. Both ships, one flying right behind the other, cables ever so slightly slack, vanished into the swirling maw that opened in the middle of the vast, vacuum-drained chamber.

Time warped and jolted. Nausea and fever flushed through Ia's body, forcing blood out through her teeth-punctured wounds, weakening her in a head-spinning rush. It wasn't a lengthy jump; maybe five seconds at most, just far enough to get them to the next star system.

Ia had implanted the exact coordinates for one of the nearest Blockade Fleet stations in Viega's mind, one that had the facilities to treat all the races of the Alliance. She had also programmed her ship to reverse its thrusters the moment they emerged, slowing both vessels before they could race past the giant, spine-covered, ceristeel-plated egg. Thankfully, the cables held; they creaked and groaned, the strain vibrating palpably between the two vessels, but they held.

She knew they had to get the ships docked. The problem was that the cabin spun every time she opened her eyes, making it difficult for Ia to concentrate. Waves of heat flushed through her body, leaving behind contracting muscles that shuddered and ached. Spots studded her skin, and her shoulder was visibly swollen and red. Everything hurt so much, she wanted to cry. But there were over three dozen sentients crammed into this ship, many of them suffering from OTL-shocked injuries of their own.

There was no way the others on board could dock this ship; it would be too dangerous for them to try. Struggling against the disorientation, the fever and exhaustion, Ia focused her thoughts down onto the exact sequence of steps needed. The first step was closing her eyes to block out the distraction of sight. She could hear Viega broadcasting on the comms that they were two ships full of escapees in need of immediate medical aid, so that was one of her other concerns handled.

The next step was to release the grappling clamps; if things went sour, and there was too high a probability that they would, the last thing Viega would need was a deadheaded ship right on her tail, not if it had been fifteen years since the other woman had last piloted anything. A flick of Ia's mind managed that much, leaving the cables trailing ahead of them, but the effort increased the dizziness in her head. Belatedly, Ia realized most of her kinetic inergy, the fuel for her gifts, was pouring into her biokinesis, trying to keep her septic infection at bay.

Slag . . . this is going to cost me . . . Focusing tighter, she opened the comm, broadcasting to the Solarican Battle Platform. *"This is Lieutenant First Grade Ia . . . TUPSF-Navy, requesting emergency sentientarian aid. I am . . . I am piloting the Salik vessel. I am going to attempt to dock at Krrim Rau . . . gantry 17, but I will need help. I am injured and suffering . . .*

from OTL-accelerated septic shock. Some sort of . . . Sallha-native bacteria."

Her concentration wavered. Every time she shuddered, the force of her contracting muscles ground the teeth of that lower jaw deeper into her shoulder blade. Ia struggled to remember what she was supposed to be doing.

"We have . . . thirty-eight injured on board this vessel. I repeat, I am . . . dock at Krrim Rau 17, and . . . need grappling." Nausea welled up, threatening to escape her throat in a most unpleasant manner. She swallowed, panting. *"I . . . don't feel so good . . ."*

"Lieutenant, hang in there!" she heard Viega order. *"You dock that ship, Lieutenant Ia! You hear me? That's an order, sailor!"*

A hand cupped her forehead. It was the V'Dan male, offering her a very precious, very intimate gift. (*Take my energy; I offer it freely. If you're strong enough to do everything you just did for us,*) he told her, (*then I know you can take it and use it—take it! I'm Pathic, not Kinetic. It's a Saints-damned Salik ship. I can't fly this thing for you!*)

"Lieutenant, you are deadheading past the Solarican Warstation! Don't you dare *give up on me, Bloody Mary, not here, not now! Stop your drifting and dock that goddamn ship!"*

Ia latched onto the KI of her fellow psychic. Vaguely aware of his unrestrained state, she flexed the dregs of her third strongest gift, her electrokinesis. The thrusters hummed in a faint, pulsing rumble, altering their drift.

"Sallik Courrrier, this is Warstation Nnying Yanh. Correct yourr course to Krrim Rau 22," the Battle Platform instructed her, naming a different docking gantry. *"We have salllvage crew already in place for that gantrry. Slow speed and pre-parrre for grappling."*

Another nudge of her mind swayed them in that direction. It took most of her strength—hers and the inner energy donated from the V'Dan at her side—to slow the courier. The moment everything lined up, Ia poured all of her spare energy into her mental walls. The V'Dan took that as his signal to let go of her forehead, moving back to his chair.

He grunted as the grapple pods struck the courier, jolting it hard enough to knock him into the waiting alien seat. The blow also dug the teeth into Ia's upper back a little harder. Teeth clenched tight, muffling her groan, Ia forced her body to stop trying to heal itself. As life-threatening as septic shock might be, leaving her precognitive gifts unlocked and unguarded was the far greater threat. Physicians and paraphysicians would have to physically touch her to treat her injuries and cleanse the bacteria infecting her blood. She could not, dared not allow the timeplains to drag them under, not while she wasn't coherent.

Even with modern medicine throttling the death rate down to a fraction of a percent, it still would take weeks to recover from sepsis. Knowing the Solaricans would reel in her ship, that she and the others would receive enough medical care to survive, Ia focused on wrapping her mind into a tight, protective little shell. It took the last dregs of her strength, but that was alright. She had successfully saved all the lives that she could, and that was all that mattered.

For the moment, the timestreams were safe. For the moment, she could rest.

SEPTEMBER 1, 2495 T.S.
SOLARICAN WARSTATION *NNYING YANH*
SALHAIT SYSTEM

> *Nnnyaaao, wann yan sieeeeh,*
> *Llun guon yiell-yoowoou*
> *Iiieh! Iiieh! Rrrral ff'tah*
> *Kundieh, kundieeeh, ff'tah*
> *Gun rr'liiiehh nyielloouuu!*
>
> *Twaaan l'ooo wau-urgahhh*
> *Llun guon yan-miii-iiiehh*
> *Iiieh! Iiieh! Rrrra—*

"What the *hell* is that infernal racket, Lieutenant?"

Expecting his arrival, Ia looked up to see Rear Admiral Duj, commanding officer of Battle Platform *Mad Jack*, standing in the doorway of her infirmary room. Behind him were two aides, plus the Solarican doctor treating Ia's condition. The noise he referred to was not the faint hum of the dialysis machine, nor the rhythmic beeping of the scanners monitoring her condition. The yowling he referred to came from the radio commchannel built into the frame of her infirmary bed.

"It's Solarican singing, sir." Arm somewhat hampered by the intravenous tubing strapped to it, Ia politely turned off the broadcast she had been enjoying.

Between the feeds for the dialysis machine on her right arm and the regen-packs strapped to her left, she didn't have much mobility at the moment. At least the cuff of her crysium bracelet-and-sword was back down around her right ankle once more. Ia lifted her burdened arm a little higher in indication before lowering it back to her gown-covered lap.

"Please forgive me for not saluting, Admiral. I'm a little tied up at the moment. Or rather, tied down," Ia quipped. "Unfortunately, modern medicine can't cure everything immediately."

"You're forgiven," he stated crisply, approaching her bed. "But only for that much. After reviewing all the reports we've collected over the last five days regarding your little escapade, you are in so much *trouble*, soldier, that I cannot . . . even . . . Doctor, why are you growling at me?"

"You arrre about to strrress my patient, Humann," the Solarican answered, his voice low, his mane half fluffed. "I have finnally contrrolled her blood prrressure. You will *nnot* aggravate it."

"It's okay, Doctor Miian," Ia reassured the alien. She didn't pretend ignorance as to the purpose of the admiral's visit. The time for pretending was finally over, even if there was still some need for discretion on certain subjects. "He's just posturing. He can't actually do anything to me."

That earned her a hard look from her superior. "You are *perilously*—"

"Perilously close to insubordination," Ia interrupted him. "Yes, sir, I've heard that before. Specifically while rescuing *your* superior, Admiral Viega. Would you like to know what that song was about?" she asked, changing the subject. From the blink Duj gave her, it threw him out of his plans to half threaten her. She forged ahead while he was still trying to shift mental gears to keep up with her. "That was a war song. In specific, a war song about *me*. It's one of the highest points of praise a Solarican can bestow upon another, to compose and perform a song praising their deeds.

"In specific, it was the fifth brand-new song I've heard about me since I woke up today, Admiral," she stated dryly. "That's not counting the three from yesterday, and the three the day before that. I don't know if there were any others before that point, since I was still a bit out of it from the sepsis-fever. But that still makes eleven songs, and the day is barely half over. What that *means*, Admiral, is that I am a war hero to these people.

"In the face of such open and widespread admiration, not to mention the doctor's legitimately expressed concerns," Ia told him, nodding briefly at the waiting, ginger-colored physician, "perhaps it would be more diplomatically useful if you dropped the posturing and spoke only of what really brought you all the way out here from your post, sir?"

For a moment, it looked as if the rear admiral's blood pressure would be a concern, rather than hers. He drew in a deep breath after a few seconds, letting it out slowly before he spoke.

"Very well. If you insist on playing it *that* way, Lieutenant, I am here to interrogate you on exactly what you did on Sallha, and how you did it. You are charged with Fatality One, Committing a Civilian Crime, via the failure to register your abilities as a psychic, and . . . Why are you laughing, Lieutenant?" he asked her, dark brown eyes narrowing. "Do you think these accusations are a *joke*?"

Chuckling, Ia shook her head, rustling the synthetic fibers stuffed into the Solarican-style pillow supporting her head. This wasn't the best time for her sense of humor to rear itself, but she did find it amusing. Sobering slightly, she smiled wryly. "Oh, but I *am* registered, Admiral. I have been registered as a psychic since I was a young child. And that registry *is* listed in my military records. I listed it the day I joined the Space Force as a recruit in the Marines. It's hardly *my* fault that the *details* behind that listing have been overlooked for so long."

His mouth opened and closed. For a moment, Duj was utterly speechless, then he flipped open the lid of his arm unit, no doubt to call up her file.

"You'll find what you seek under my religious affiliations,

sir. As you will see, I am listed in my Service file as an ordained priestess of the Witan Order, Zenobian Sect, as duly registered on my homeworld. By charter, all duly ordained members of the Zenobian Sect, whether they're naturally psychic or simply trained, must undergo basic psi training as well as religious instruction. To maintain their rank in the Order—including my rank—we must undergo the same yearly ethical exams required of all duly registered psychics . . . whether or not we have any.

"By the *Terran* charter, as a psychic, I am required to be registered with a duly authorized organization. Such as the Witan Order, which includes its subsects. By the Space Force charter, I am required to list proof of that registration on my Service record . . . which I have done . . . and by both charters, I am required to undergo yearly ethical examinations. Which are all on record with my Order, undertaken and filed every nine to eleven months, depending on when I could meet up with my examiners. Those examinations place me *well* within the mandatory once-a-year examinations required by law."

He swapped his attention between her file and her face as she spoke, a frown pinching his dusky brow.

"For the record, sir—and you can subpoena those records from the Zenobian Sect, if you like," Ia added, "I have undergone yearly ethical testing since I was a young child. Admittedly I had to have my fellow psis come out from Sanctuary to meet with me for my yearly examinations once I enlisted, but I have been duly examined each and every year . . . and I *have* passed my ethical examinations, each and every year. Any court— civilian *or* military—would be forced to drop that charge the moment they looked at all the facts of the matter. Fatality One does not apply, sir."

"But you cannot deny that you have *hidden* your abilities from your superiors," Admiral Duj countered.

Ia flicked another glance at the Solarican. "Not from all of them, sir. But with respect, sir, that's a matter of internal security. It is not something that should be discussed while I am under constant surveillance by foreign medical service—and before you try to arrange it, Admiral, no, I cannot be moved back to the *Mad Jack* just yet. I cannot even walk to the head on my own without the risk of falling down, right now."

"Sepsis is too danngerrous to meddle with durinng the

rrrecovery phase," the Solarican doctor growled. Admiral Duj turned to face the felinoid as he continued. "If she is not fully curred before leaving our constant surrveilllance and care, she could rrrrelapse and *nnot* know it untilll it is too late. I will *not* be the doctorrr who allowed the Herrrro of the Banquet to die because I did nnot do my job."

"Doctor Miian is considered one of the foremost specialists in Human medicine within the entire Blockade Fleet," Ia stated quietly. "Even among Human doctors, he has a stellar reputation for successfully treating our kind. As soon as the medical staff realized how bad my condition was, they put him on my case, as well as five of the others. Any doctor on board the *Mad Jack* who knows anything about *this* doctor's reputation would agree that we're in extremely competent hands . . . and they will tell you that in cases of OTL-accelerated bacteremia sepsis, there is *no* such thing as being too cautious or too careful."

"We arrre still growinng her a new pair of kidneys, and have alrrready replaced her spleen," Miian stated, lacing his claw-tipped fingers in front of his chest. He licked his lips and attempted to speak more clearly in Terranglo, though some of the rolled consonants still came through. "The next trransplant will take place in two days. Thenn she will undergo a two-day rrrecovery period before beginning physical therrapy. Given she is a heavyworrldor like us, the rrrecovery rate is more than double the stanndard, as we will be moving her to the grrravity acclimation ward to slowly help her rrregain her strength. Her healllth must be carrrefully monitored to make sure she does nnot rrelapse."

Duj glanced between the Solarican in the doorway and the Human on the bed. His two aides were carefully looking elsewhere, trying not to catch their superior's attention. Duj finally focused his attention on Ia. "Do not assume you will escape that interrogation, Lieutenant. You *will* recover."

"I know that, sir . . . but it won't be conducted by you, Admiral," she told him. There was no need right now to keep silent on the facts of the near future, and a need to prove to the rear admiral that she knew that near future. "The Terran Space Force has already received two requests for intergovernmental recognition of my actions on Sallha, including a directive from the Empress of the Solaricans. More are coming in from the other alien governments as we speak. Four days from now, arrangements will be made across the diplomatic channels for an Alliance-wide commendation ceremony, which will take place in eight days.

"*Six* days from now, the Command Staff of the Space Force will order me to report to them in person on Earth as soon as I am healthy enough to travel, to give them a full accounting of all my actions, and in specific, all my motivations for joining the Space Force. But I probably won't be judged healthy enough to endure the rigors of travel for at least two more weeks beyond the ceremony, and not back to my full health for a month. Your visit is appreciated, and a testament to your willingness to defend the letter of Space Force law, sir," she concluded, closing her eyes. "But your orders as they currently stand will *not* be the same by the time I'm healthy enough to be questioned."

"You seem to be responding just fine to my questions right now," he pointed out.

A snort escaped her. Ia pried open her eyes again, glancing his way. "My will is astronomically strong, Admiral, but my reserves are dangerously low. Just because I lasted all seven days of Marine Corps Hell Week doesn't mean I didn't pay for it by the end. I was healthy at the time, back in Basic. This time, I'm most definitely not. I have maybe ten more minutes before I'll end up falling asleep again . . . and that's pretty much all I have been doing."

The machine whirring at her side beeped. The Solarican physician stepped around the admiral, moving close enough to read the report. "Twelve morre Terran minutes Stanndard, then this session of dialysis will be complete. Would you like anything to eat beforre your nap?"

"No, thanks. I'm not hungry," Ia demurred.

The dialysis was important for keeping her blood clean. It even balanced her endocrine system, keeping her relatively healthy. But the on-off cycle of blood cleansing exhausted her energy reserves and left her feeling slightly nauseated. However, the doctor's ears lowered and his eyes narrowed, fixing her with a stern look that translated fairly well across the species boundary.

She sighed and rolled her eyes. "Fine. A glass of juice and some crackers."

Rumbling in his native tongue, the Solarican doctor murmured instructions into the headset clipped around one pointed ear. "They will be herre in thrree minutes, along with cheese for prrrotein. You will eat it all, to regain your strrrength. I must check on the otherrrs soon, but you will eat firrst."

"The others?" Duj asked, curious.

"The pyrrrokinetic is still suffering from psi-induced feverr. Until a Human parapsychologist arrives and begins the healing of his emotional wounnds, it is all our Seers can do to contain his gifts," Miian explained. "The sergeant is still in physical therrapy, learning how to walk with a prrosthetic while his foot is being rrregenerated, but will be released soon. The other thrree are rrecovering from sepsis trauma. Llieutenant Ia's case was worrsened by KI shock, from exercising too many Seer gifts all at once, but she is nnot the worst of my sepsis cases. She, at lleast, is mostly intact.

"I must ask you to go now, Admirrral," he added. "So long as yourrr Warstationn is in the same system, you will have opportunnnities to come back and speak with my patient. But forrr now, she *is* my patiennt. Yourr authority overr her has been temporarily superseded."

Irritated but thwarted, Admiral Duj gave Ia one last, dark look and left, his aides following in his wake. The Solarican busied himself with checking her monitors as the trio of Humans left.

"Thank you, Doctor," Ia murmured. She thought about reaching for the bed controls, but she hadn't lied; the treatments required for her illness were wearing her out. "Could you turn the comm radio back on? I was enjoying the music."

Doctor Miian sneezed in Solarican-style humor. "Now I *knnnow* you're delirious. Verrry few Humans like Solarrrican-style singing."

"I like all kinds of music," she murmured. "There haven't been a lot of opportunities for enjoying it in the last few years, not on Blockade Patrol. Even when we were on Leave, there've been precious few minutes for anything fun."

"Funn?" he asked, checking her pulse with the pads of his fingers, mindful of his claws. "Funn, like what?"

"I miss singing. I miss playing music simply for the pure pleasure of it. Even in the Marines, we got to sing. But not on

Blockade Patrol." Her brow creased in memory. "Now, I can't help but think of what I did to all those Salik throats, plucking them out like . . . like demented harp strings."

"We have rrreceived a rrequest for a visit frrom a Chaplain Bennjamin," the Solarican observed. "She says she is worried for yourrr mental and emotionnal health. She is rregistered as a psychologist as well as a prrriestess. Perhaps you shoullld see her?"

Ia sighed and stared up at the ceiling, where some Solarican nurse, in a fit of whimsy, had hung a miniature ball of string. "Perhaps I should. But not until after I've received my new kidn—*Ungh!*"

"What?" Miian asked, bending over Ia in concern. "Wherrre does it hurrt?"

She grimaced, unable to lift a hand to her head, thanks to the tangle of tubes strapping her down. "They're—*oww*—playing with that damned *machine* again. Trying to figure it out. I wish they'd stop. I won't be the only one with a headache. Every Seer and psychic within sixty *kesat* of that thing will be hurting."

"You knnow what it is?" he asked her, ears flicking in curiosity.

"Oh, thank god, they shut it off again," she muttered, relaxing as the headache vanished. "No, I don't know what it is. But I do know something of what it does. That thing is more dangerous to the Alliance than even I can foresee. The only weapon we have against it . . . is knowledge . . ." Ia yawned, tiredness creeping up on her again.

"No falling asleep, Humann," her doctor admonished her a few moments later, nudging her right shoulder. The left one was still encased in a sleeve of regeneration packs, patiently removing the last of the scars from her multiple puncture wounds. "Wake up, your snnack has arrrived."

Dragging in a deep breath, Ia opened her eyes. She sat up a little more and reached for the items on the tray the brindle-furred nurse was swinging into place. Nauseated or not, she had to eat to refuel her body. The Command Staff would be expecting her to head their way in roughly fourteen days. She needed to be ready to travel in just under eleven.

Sipping at her juice, Ia let her mind drift back to the anti-psi machine. "I'll need to take it with me."

"Take what?" her physician asked as she ate.

"The machine we brought back—*Nnyam ma'fau krrruu, k'in krramzhann l'ingh rruowel mnaa*," she added, shaping the words as best she could.

Miian snorted, watching her bite into another of the cheese-topped crackers the nurse had brought. "Yourrr accent is almost as atrocious as yourr claim. What makes you thinnk we'll let you take it as yourrr warr-prize?"

"I destroyed an entire enemy encampment the size of this Warstation," Ia reminded him. "I personally cut off the head of their Grand High General, an act witnessed by many of the survivors, all of whom I rescued personally. I am responsible for the deaths of hundreds of high-ranked enemy officers. I have struck a blow so hard and deep into the chest of our enemy, it will take them almost a year—a Solarican Standard year, never mind a Terran—to recover. I have done such great acts of courage and valor, I have earned the right to be ranked as a War Princess, with all the privileges, power, and wealth such a position entails by Solarican law. Even as a foreigner and an alien, I have earned that much. It isn't official yet, but it will be. Yet all I want is that box, and at least one of the Human-shaped headsets to play with."

"I will pass along your rrrequest," he murmured. "But I cannnnot guarantee it will be honorred."

"Tell them they have my personal word of honor that I will make sure all findings are shared with the Royal Seer's Council regarding that machine," Ia told him, picking up her cup again. The tangle of tubing forced her to move carefully, but she still managed to salute him with it. "Remind them that this is the same code of honor that made damned sure I rescued every single being that I could, backed by the same determination that blew up that installation. They have my word of honor, meioa."

"I will lllet them know," he murmured. "But firrrst, you must eat. That is an orrder. Even a Warrr Prinncess must obey herrr physiciann when she is ill."

Tired but knowing he was right, Ia picked up the next cracker on her plate.

CHAPTER 20

Most of us understand the concepts of honor, courage, cooperation, and the tenets of sentientarian aid, of saving lives, maintaining dignity, and alleviating suffering through acts of sharing and compassion.

The Alliance works because we recognize these qualities in each other. Yes, the Salik War and its subsequent Blockade formed our initial purpose for cooperating with each other, rather than contending or conflicting over the last two centuries. Yet the reason *why we still get along and still work together so well after all these years is the realization that we are at heart—or whatever passes for the heart—the same as our alien brethren deep down inside.*

Whenever the Alliance as a whole agrees upon a thing, it is therefore a most powerful realization. Powerful, and humbling. Even if you knew it was coming, as I did. But as important as it has been to make sure people know what I am capable of doing—so that they can trust me enough to let me do more of it—it isn't about my abilities. It has never been about my abilities. It's about the fact that I use *them, and most importantly, why.*

It has always been about saving lives.

~Ia

SEPTEMBER 6, 2495 T.S.

"Do you feel like talking about it?"

Silence.

"You do know you can talk to me about it . . ."

More silence.

"Are you *sure* you don't want to talk about it?"

Nothing but silence.

"Well, then. If all you're going to do is *pout* over it—"

"I am *not pouting*!" Bennie snapped, finally breaking her sullen silence. "I am *sulking*. There *is* a difference, you know."

"Okay, so you're sulking," Ia agreed, holding up her right hand. She still had two intravenous tubes hooked to the veins in her left arm, but mostly to run it through a bacteriometer to make absolutely sure her blood was clean. "Do you want to talk about *why* you're sulking? Or do you just want to grump and glower a bit longer?"

Bennie muttered something under her breath. At Ia's inquisitive look, she repeated it a little louder. "Grump and glower."

"Alright. Do let me know when you're finished, so we can talk it over and work through why you're so mad at me," Ia stated calmly.

The chaplain gave her a dark look. "Excuse me? Where did you get *your* psychology degree?"

"School of Hard Knocks, magna cum laude," Ia quipped deadpan, picking up her cup of caf' for a sip. Her blood pressure had stabilized without the need for further medicine the day after her newly grown kidneys had been implanted, but this was her first official cup of caffeine since then. "I would've been valedictorian, but I'm terrible at speech-making. Definitely long-winded, but nowhere near flowery enough."

Bennie chuckled in spite of herself. "That's for certain— dammit, Ia! I *knew* you were hiding something from me, but *this*? A psychic? And one *hell* of a psi, given all the reports I've heard. Telekinesis, electrokinesis, telepathy, biokinesis—what *else* are you hiding under all that white hair?"

Swallowing the semibitter liquid, Ia set her cup down with a sigh and a *click*. "Quite a lot. But I had very good reasons for hiding it as much as I did. Now I don't have to hide it anymore . . .

not that I *could* anymore, given all those reports that you've heard."

Bennie shifted in her chair, arms still crossed over her chest and looking very much like she was still sulking. "I had to call your parents, to let them know you'd been kidnapped. And then . . . then I had to call them again. They caught the pirates that kidnapped you, and the villains confessed that they'd sold you to the Salik. I had to tell your *parents* that you were now listed as Captured, Presumed Et. That is absolutely the *worst* task I or any other officer in the history of the Blockade has ever had to do!"

"I know," Ia murmured, not unsympathetic to her friend's pain. "I knew a long time ago that I needed to be captured at that point in time. *And* that I'd get myself and most of the others out alive."

A snort escaped the older woman. Bennie swiped a hand through her auburn locks, revealing the grey streak forming at her temple. "Well. That does explain why they were so *calm* when I called and told them you'd been captured. At least, I'm presuming there's some correlation between the two."

Ia looked across the room at the fake window projecting a computer-generated view of a lightning-teased forest from her homeworld. She had been upgraded to the gravity ward that morning, though the pull of gravity was not yet more than an easy, gentle, 1.2Gs, something even Bennie could tolerate.

She had also been given the best amenities the station had to offer, thanks to her newly minted heroism in the Solaricans' eyes. Some of the amenities were felinoid-specific, such as the all-body dryer nozzles built into the showering stall, but most of it was familiar enough to translate over to standard Human needs. It was a vast change from living naked for two weeks in an animal cage, waiting for her one chance to avoid being eaten alive.

"When I was three . . . I told my mother that she was pregnant with my little brother Fyfer, the day she conceived," Ia confessed quietly. "She didn't believe me. I told her my little brother would grow up short, and cute, and have curly dark hair. Three months later, a routine examination determined his gender. And when he was born, he was born with tufts of curly dark hair. He is now one hundred forty-eight centimeters tall, over thirty centimeters shorter than our older brother, and he still has dark curly hair."

"I've seen pictures of your brother Thorne. He has dark, curly hair, too," Bennie reminded the younger woman on the bed. "That much wouldn't have been difficult to guess."

"Thorne was born with lighter hair, almost blond. It only darkened as he got older," Ia stated.

Needing to get up and exercise some more, to push herself to get back into shape, she swung her legs off the bed and stood. Her abdomen was still tender, but at least she had her kidneys again. Doctor Miian had offered to regrow her ovaries as well, but Ia had demurred. She had grown used to not having any biological worries in that department. Most of her energy these days was being spent on keeping herself alive, anyway. Adding children into the mix was not an option for her.

"When I was an infant," she continued, "I would stop crying shortly after my mother began heating up a bottle of milk. If she started to put it away again, I'd start crying again, and stop when she resumed her task, even if I was in another room," Ia stated, carefully swinging and stretching her arms, mindful of the bacteriometer and its tubes. She could now wear pants instead of a gaping hospital drape, but her shirt was a poncho-like thing that snapped in place under her armpits. Grimacing, she flapped her elbows and muttered under her breath as the fabric fluttered. "I feel like a chicken in this drape-thing . . ."

"What are you saying?" Bennie asked skeptically. She ignored the younger woman's quip, still fixed on the previous topic. "That you're some sort of precocious clairvoyant?"

"Precognitive," Ia corrected, bending her legs in shallow squats. A few more minutes of this and she would begin to sweat. Too much bed rest had left her weak. "Not clairvoyant. Every step I have taken since my abilities matured at the age of fifteen, I have undertaken with full foresight and careful planning. I *knew* I would be captured. I *knew* I would be at that banquet as one of the main dishes. I *knew* I would be able to free all those people and destroy that installation. Just as I knew I would be doing most everything else I have done in my military career. Not always *exactly* what I would do . . . but I knew I would do it."

Another snort escaped the chaplain. "*V'shova*, Ia. Nobody can foresee that much. Precognition is the *least* reliable of all the psychic abilities. Nebulous visions, metaphoric meanings, flashes of moments . . . and most of it can be derailed or avoided by making different choices. Even the Inner Circle of the PsiLeague won't pay that much attention to foresight warnings unless a minimum of twelve precogs all agree."

"Actually, it's only six who need to agree," Ia muttered. Bennie shot her a mock-dirty look. Sighing, Ia shifted to walking in place, swinging her arms and lifting her knees. "Look, just don't close your mind, that's all I'm asking. Dr. Miian has agreed to let me help run some of the experiments with the anti-psi machine we brought back. It'll take place after the commendation ceremony. I'd like you to come along and stand witness."

"Stand witness to what?" Bennie asked her.

"They've gathered several members from the various psychic organizations across the Alliance. The PsiLeague, the Seer's Council, the Nesting of Minds . . . I have some ideas of my own on what to try with the machine," Ia admitted. Her efforts were starting to make her sweat. "Part of what we're going to do is compare the machine to a KI monitor, and see how much the one can pick up through the interference of the other, as a way to gauge just how strong the nullifying field is. While we're doing *that*, the PsiLeague has agreed to give me an official rank testing, since all the various organizations have agreed their tests are the best benchmark for such things."

"Well, it *was* the founders of the PsiLeague who developed the first psi-sensitive monitor," Bennie muttered. "Alright, I'll come along. But only to hear the results of your testing."

Sitting back down on the edge of her bed, Ia picked up her mug and sipped at the cooling brown liquid. She sighed and set it back on the tray. "Part of me knows I'm going to take several more days to recover, even at my best pace. Part of me is just damned impatient to get back to full strength."

"Well, don't push yourself into a relapse," Bennie warned her. "Dr. Miian is kind of cute for a felinoid, but I hear he's already engaged."

Ia chuckled at that. "Bennie, I had *enough* problems with my one failed attempt at a relationship. What makes you think I'm going to go throw myself into another?"

Lifting her own cup to her lips, the chaplain paused and made a few *bok bok bauk* noises under her breath.

"I will *not* be provoked," Ia muttered. "Listen, once we're done with this visit, I want you to go back to the *Mad Jack* and pack up everything. Your office, your quarters, all of it."

Bennie choked on her caf', coughing hoarsely. When she had regained some of her breath, she wheezed, "Are you *nuts*?"

"Maybe. I want you to put in for a solid week of Leave, starting September 10th. Tomorrow, the Command Staff will send orders that I am to report to them in person as soon as I have medical clearance to leave. Those orders will be rendered all the more urgent once I've undergone my rank testing. Everyone who'll be here to examine it is working for one or another of the military forces in the Alliance. Well," she amended, thinking ahead, "almost everyone . . .

"Anyway, when I head to the Tower on Earth, I would like you with me. If nothing else, for damage control," Ia muttered under her breath. "I have one last, big battle to fight, before everything changes. Unlike the Salik one, the probabilities for success are far less certain. Less than sixty percent. If I do succeed, I'd like you to come with me on my new assignment. If I fail . . . I'm going to need you to contact somebody for me, and make sure they get in to see me."

"Get in?" Bennie repeated. "Get in, where?"

Ia gave her a level, sober look. "The Tower Dungeon."

The chaplain stared. She stared until she finally blinked and drew in a breath. "You're . . . going to try something that will risk you getting thrown in *prison*? What the hell are you going to do, Lieutenant?"

"An extremely rare Yamaneuver," Ia said. She didn't bother to explain which one, though she did respond to the chaplain's dubious look. "Bennie, what is the one thing that you *know* I will do, regardless of the consequences to myself?"

She rolled her eyes, sagging back in her chair. This was an old discussion between them, one that was all too easily recited. "You will do your damnedest to save lives, because that's the only way you can live with yourself." Bennie slanted her a sardonic look, mouth twisting in wry amusement. "You're like some God-damned martyr, meioa. Except you thankfully keep coming out of these situations alive."

Picking up her cup, Ia saluted her chaplain with it. "Hallelujah, Sister. Amen to that."

SEPTEMBER 9, 2495 T.S.

Once again, she stood before an audience of military personnel. This time, it was a mixed audience, containing both Human factions, Solaricans, Tlassians, Gatsugi, K'katta, and even a few Choya. She hadn't actually rescued any Choya from the suckered grasp of their mutual enemy, but that was believed by the rest to simply be a matter of Salik preferences; with their copper-based blood, the Choya "tasted bad" to Salik sensibilities.

She knew why. The average Choyan soldier, the ones sitting in the auditorium, they had no clue, but their top military and government leaders had made a devil's pact with their fellow amphibians. That was a problem for another day, though Ia couldn't quite stop worrying about it. *My schedule never clears . . . It just scrolls down to the next week's disaster, and the blank spots fill up as fast as a thought. At least I've pushed back the start of the next Salik War by several months. They're still scrambling to fill in the gaping holes in their top echelons, thank god . . .*

The K'kattan ambassador gestured for her to kneel for a fourth time. Lowering herself, Ia rested a palm on the floor as she ducked her head, permitting the dignitary to toss another thin, silk-like sash over her head. His arachnoid race didn't wear much in the way of clothing, unless the ambient conditions of temperature and weather or a lack of atmosphere demanded it. But they did decorate themselves and each other with colorful sashes, tassels, and ribbons. Alien or otherwise, their war heroes were no exception.

Clicking and whistling, the K'kattan envoy chittered, letting his translator box explain the honors bestowed. "And this is the Sash of Sentientarian Aid, specifically bestowed upon those aliens who go out of their way to render assistance to our kind. Thank you, meioa. May there always be such acts of compassion, valor, and honor exchanged between our kinds."

"Thank you, Ambassador." Dipping her head, she carefully rose back to her feet. Though she had regained much of her illness-sapped strength, the weight of the medals now pinned to her jacket—all of her medals, pinned in place for this very formal occasion—made it feel like she was wearing the upper half of her weight suit instead of her Navy Dress Blacks, her

most formal uniform with the blue stripes down the black
sleeves and matching pant legs. A uniform she would have to
remember to take with her.

"Go forth onto the plains of war," the alien chitter-translated,
giving Ia one last benediction, "but may you one day retire in
peace and long life in the trees, Guardian of the Terrans."

"Thank you, Ambassadorrr Ch'chullwik," the master of
ceremonies stated. Sent all the way from the Solarican homeworld, Prince of the Blood Nazrrin gestured for the last set of
presenters to step onto the stage. "War Prrincess Ia, I prrresent
to you the Secondaire of your own goverrnment, Meioa Justinn
Mandella."

The tall Human strode onto the stage with the same confidence as the last Secondaire Ia had faced. Prince and Secondaire exchanged murmurs in greeting, touching palms and
pursing their lips in Solarican-style smiles, then Secondaire
Mandella faced Ia, his lips still closed but now stretched wide,
Human-style. "Lieutenant Ia."

She saluted him. "Secondaire, sir."

He returned the salute, then clasped his hands in front of
his waist. She knew it had to be a calculated gesture; no protocol
cabinet member would have allowed him to board an alien
station without informing him of the various possible interpretations for common body gestures. It was the Solarican version
of crossing his arms over his chest, one which could be inter-
preted as either stern or playful . . . and among the Gatsugi
could have meant anything from mere hunger to the symptoms
of cardiac arrest. "Lieutenant First Grade Ia. You have a bad
habit of doing heroic things, don't you?"

"Sir, no, sir," Ia denied. "I simply did what anyone else would
do, sir."

"What anyone *would* do, were they in your shoes," Secondaire Mandella agreed, emphasizing her choice of words, "but
not necessarily what anyone else *could* do."

A gesture from the Secondaire brought a black-uniformed
lieutenant up to his side, a silver tray in the other man's gloved
hands. He was a match for the uniformed sergeant standing
behind Ia's shoulder, carrying the tray burdened with the para-
phernalia of her honorifics from the other governments.

"For your acts of extraordinary psychic service . . . simply

extraordinary . . . it is my privilege to bestow upon you the
Blue Heart," he informed her, opening and displaying the dis-
tinctively shaped medallion. Eyeing her jacket, Mandella
snapped the box shut. "Normally, I would pin this on your
jacket, since our records show this is your first official Blue
Heart, Lieutenant. But it seems you lack the room to display it
on your chest."

"Sorry, sir," she apologized.

"Are those all of your medals?" he asked, lifting one brow.

"Sir, yes, sir," Ia replied, straight-faced.

Curious, he arched a brow, looking her over from head to
toe. She turned around crisply, toe tucked behind heel, and
displayed the ones carpeting the back of her jacket. Another
about face allowed her to face him again. The only spots not
covered in medals were an inch or so from the bottom of the
jacket hem, her collar points and shoulder boards—reserved
solely for the silver bar of her rank—and the actual lapels of
her jacket, save that the left one held her Star of Service from
two years before. The only medal that ever went on the right
lapel face was either the Red Heart of an honorably retired
soldier, or the Black Heart, for service unto death, which was
only ever pinned in place postmortem.

Facing him again, Ia spoke. "I won't stop saving lives, sir . . .
but I may have to ask that my superiors stop recognizing me
for it. As you can see, I'm sort of running out of room, sir."

The corner of his mouth quirked up. "I'll just pass a note to
the Command Staff to look into designing a floor-length Dress
Coat. In the meantime, consider this duly pinned."

"Sir, yes, sir," Ia agreed, accepting the box from him.

"And this one, the White Cross, for rescuing a fellow sentient being. *Six* White Crosses, one for each member nation
of the Alliance whose people you rescued, the Solaricans, the
V'Dan, the Tlassians, the K'katta, the Gatsugi, and your fellow
Terrans . . ."

Accepting each box, she stacked them on the tray carried
by the sergeant standing stoically at her side. Other awards
passed through her hands, Ten Skulls, for known, confirmed
kills of high-ranked Salik generals. Crossbones for the lesser
ranks slaughtered when the base was destroyed. A Rearguard
Star, for being the last of the two ships to flee, holding off the

enemy's counterattacks with her abilities, and another Screaming Eagle for successfully tailgating Viega's vessel through
that hyperrift without destroying either ship. A White Heart
for rescuing herself, and a Purple Heart for the injuries she had
suffered.

"And finally, most importantly," Secondaire Mandella presented, "the highest peacetime honor the Terran government
can bestow. As much as we have made it a standing practice
of honoring the honorable and extraordinary efforts of the
meioas in our Space Force and its Branches, it is a very rare
individual who goes so far above and beyond the call of duty
that they risk not only life and limb for their fellow soldiers,
but risk life and limb for the civilians and soldiers of all our
allies.

"Like its wartime counterpart, the Medal of Honor, the Star
of Service is not bestowed lightly, Lieutenant. You have earned
this—*again*—literally through the efforts of your blood, sweat,
and tears. May all who see you and hear of your deeds draw
courage and inspiration from your shining example of what it
means to be a true and honorable soldier of the Terran Space
Force. Lieutenant First Grade Ia," Secondaire Mandella told
her solemnly, "I salute *you*."

Lifting his hand to his brow, he matched actions to words.
It was a breach of protocol, and Ia knew precognitively that he
would catch quite a bit of flak from the Command Staff for it,
as well as some political repercussions from the more conserva-
tive factions in the Terran United Planets. The Secondaire and
the Premier *never* saluted anyone in the military first. They
were the Commanders in Chief during times of peace and war,
respectively; others saluted *them* first. But he saluted her now,
in a broadcast that was being streamed not just to the Terran
worlds, but to every other world in the Alliance.

Blinking hard, Ia saluted him back. When she lowered her
hand to accept the last commendation box, she found herself
pulled into an embrace. Under the cover of patting her back,
the Secondaire murmured into her ear, "You *do* realize you'll
have to face a Board of Inquiry regarding your gifts, right?"

"Sir, yes, sir. I've already prepared my defense, sir," she
murmured back, strengthening her mental walls to keep from
foreseeing his future. She couldn't block out the sincere

admiration lurking behind his words, though, forcing her to blink rapidly a second time.

"If I can arrange it, I'll be there to speak on your behalf. You may not have followed the letter of the regs, but *no one* will be allowed to deny or set aside the *results* of your efforts." Releasing her, he handed her the Star of Service box, speaking aloud for the broadcast pickups once more. "Remember this day, Lieutenant. Let it be an inspiration to you and to those around you. May the soldiers of *all* nations look to you as their role model in the years to come."

That's the idea, sir, Ia thought, though she kept it carefully under shield, mindful of the other psychics on board. She saluted him one last time, shoulders back and chin level. *The salvation of the Future is counting on it.*

SEPTEMBER 10, 2495 T.S.

The aching, nauseating pain ceased abruptly as the mind-blind technician manning the sucker hands on the machine carefully tugged and pushed, shutting it off. Everyone else let out a sigh of relief, or the species-equivalent. From her perch on the table serving as her podium—since the knee-joints of most K'katta barely reached one meter high, rendering them rather short in the presence of the other sentient races in the room—Meioa Nik'ikk addressed the others, her translator box projecting her words in Terranglo over the chittering of her native tongue.

"Thank you, that should be enough for now. We now have enough information to calculate a baseline formula for the rate of interference. Meioa P'hrrn, have you calculated the numbers?"

The Solarican psi in question nodded and stood, writing pad in her hands. "Based on the technician's calculllations, compared to PsiLeague rrratings, this machine blocks our abilities at a rratio of nearly four-to-one. At full strength, anyone of lless than eighth rrank is completely blocked . . . but that is due morrre to the painn of this machine, since at Rrrank 2, they could still technnicallly use their gifts to a tiny poinnt."

"We know that prolonnged exsssposure overwhelms the pssssi," one of the crested Tlassian priest-castes in the room hissed, his crest-spikes dipping in displeasure. "Even our ssstrongest priestesss among the captivess could not concentrate passt the first half hour, and ssshe iss Rank 16. In short durationss, I can usse my Rank 15 sskill at almost a Rank 4 rating in spite of this machinne, but not for very llonnng."

One of the grey-clad Humans snorted. "Smack anyone with a headache that strong for that long, and see how well *you'd* function. We need to figure out how to counter these damned machines. It doesn't matter if it's a Kinetic, a Pathy, or a Clairancy, or one of the wild gifts, these devices interfere with *all* of it. Our psychic abilities are the one thing the Salik *don't* have, the one weapon in our arsenal we can still hold over their slimy heads. But this machine changes all of that."

Nik'ikk lifted one leg, claw-tips snapping against each other to catch everyone's attention. "We will discuss that later. Meioa Ia had requested that, once we have ascertained the dampening field's strength and effects on a KI meter, we test *her* for an official ranking."

"Can't we do that later?" another Human complained. This one was clad in the dark red uniform of the V'Dan military. "The problems posed by this machine are far more important than someone's mental *ego*-stroking."

Rising from her seat, Ia moved toward the center of the room, where both the KI machine and the anti-psi generator sat on a pair of carts. Still a bit weak, she moved slowly, but she moved. "As much as I'd agree with you, Meioa Jin-Palu, this machine will be necessary to help successfully gauge my rankings."

"What I/myself want/need to know/grasp/understand," one of the Gatsugi psis spoke up, "is who/what authority made/gave you/you/you the right/privilege of ownership/control of/over this/this thing/machine."

"I will answer that question, meioa, *after* I have been tested. First, I need my gifts officially ranked," Ia told them. "I know *what* they are, and I have an idea of their strengths, but I have not been officially, formally tested. For reasons you will soon see."

Reaching the bench seat the other volunteers had used, Ia settled onto it. Each wave of headache-inducing interference had weakened her temporarily, but with her reserves slowly regaining strength, she had managed to bounce back a fair bit.

This, however, would leave her weak and sweating once it was done. Nodding at the technician, she gave him silent permission to wire her forehead and hands to the KI monitor, a necessary precaution to prevent her testing from picking up too much interference from the others.

"We'll do this in reverse order, from weakest to strongest gift," Ia stated as he applied the sticky patches to her skin. "I need a volunteer from one of the other species to test my Xeno-pathic abilities."

One of the Gatsugi volunteered. Of all the other species gathered in the room, their thoughts were least like a Human's. Only a Choya or a Salik would have been more different among the oxygen-breathing, carbon-based sentiencies, but neither race had psychic abilities. When the four-armed alien settled onto the bench across from her and had composed himself into a light shade of calm-blue, the Solarican technician instructed Ia to begin.

"First test. Conntact the meioa-o's mind from a distance."

"I'm not very good at the non-touch-based Pathies," Ia muttered in warning. Breathing deeply to center herself and settle her thoughts, she reached out, sensing the Gatsugi's whirling cascade of thoughts. The alien obligingly kept his mental walls lowered, but did not reach out to her in any way. Politely, she kept to his surface thoughts. Not that she could have read much of anything at a greater depth; Ia simply wasn't that strong.

"Rrrank 4," the technician stated. "Now, trrry it via touch."

Shifting forward, Ia held out her hand. The Gatsugi extended one of his lower arms, four digits meeting five. His flesh was cool-calm, his walls still down, his thoughts a swirl of polite welcome. (*Greetings/Salutations/Hello . . .*)

(*Hello/Hello, thank you/my gratitude,*) she returned, shaping the thought along his alien patterns. She had practiced a little bit by reading Salik minds during her various boarding sorties, increasing her original rank, but hadn't been able to practice a lot, nor all that much on the meioa's own species.

"Rrrank 6," the tech concluded as Ia and the alien released each other's hand. "Next?"

"Biokinesis, others. Xeno or otherwise, it's the exact same," Ia stated. "My ability to affect others is several ranks below my ability to affect myself."

Nodding, the Gatsugi picked up one of the sterile razor packets on the table. Opening it with his upper fingers, he made a small, careful cut on the palm of one of his lower hands. Ia cupped his injured hand in hers and focused, pouring some of her personal energy into his biology. The bleeding slowed and the centimeter-long wound clotted faster than it would have on its own, but not by much.

"Rrank 5," the technician asserted. "Test your ownn biokin-netics, pllease."

Picking a fresh packet, Ia obediently cut her own hand. Compared to the headaches induced by the Salik machine, the pain was a minor annoyance at best. She had it sealed and headed toward pink in half the time of the other cut, giving her a rating of Rank 9.

The technician remained unaffected by the sight of her blood. Undoubtedly he was used to it. The technician was an honorary member of both the Seer's Council of the Solarican Empire and a technician in the employment of the PsiLeague of the Terran United Planets. Mostly because both organizations' charter rules stated that a non-psi should be the one to operate the testing machinery, guaranteeing non-interference with the results.

Of the thirty-plus beings occupying the chamber, only Chaplain Benjamin and four of the Solaricans—the technician, the two guards at the door, and a male felinoid who had come in with a cart loaded with fresh cups and pitchers of water—were not there as gifted representatives of the various psychic organizations in the Alliance.

To test her telepathic abilities with the minds of her own species, another volunteer took the place of the Gatsugi, a Human clad in the dark red uniform of the V'Dan Empire. This was a gift she had exercised even less than her xenopathy, and it showed during the testing. With a touch, it was a 7; without, it was merely a 5.

"Annny otherr gifts?" the Solarican technician asked her.

Razor still in hand, Ia nodded. "Pyrokinesis, telekinesis, battlecognition, electrokinesis, postcognition, and precognition."

Scoffing noises erupted across the room. Even the chairwoman of the meeting, Meioa Nik'ikk, chittered skeptically. Her translator box obligingly emphasized her disbelief in modulated Terranglo. "That would be three more gifts than the greatest of us! No one has just one ability, *yes*, but no one has *that* many!"

Ia let go of the flat, rectangular blade in her hand. It floated upward. So did Meioa Nik'ikk, the Human volunteer still seated across from her, a dozen other startled aliens, several tables, assorted chairs, and all the unopened packets of razors. This was one she had definitely exercised over the years, pushing it as high and hard as she could make the gift grow. Sheer survival had demanded she develop it to its fullest.

"Rrrank 17," the technician stated phlegmatically, though the tip of his tail twitched. "Is that sheer strrength, or manipulationn as welllll?"

Not wanting to exhaust herself, Ia set everyone and everything back down gently, sending the used razor into the biohazard bin. "Sheer strength. Manipulation . . . I used fifty, sixty glass shards to slit the throats of various enemy combatants back on Sallha. I could even play a full symphony on a concert wall harp, if one was available."

Craning his neck, the technician looked around the room. He pointed at the cart. "Lllevitate those cups, meioa. Individually."

Ia nodded. Three of the stacks of cups on the water-cart lifted up, separated, and whirled around the room over their heads. Four pitchers of water followed. Water sloshed and poured, angling in long arcs that made the sentient below them flinch, though every drop hit its target. Ia brought the display to a quick end, pouring the water back into the descending pitchers as the fifty or so cups came back to a rest on the cart. All save for one, which she topped up and floated her way.

"It is still Rrank 17," he confirmed while she caught the cup, sipping from it. "Next?"

She held up her left hand, and the air above it caught fire. That was gauged at Rank 8. She followed it, still drinking from her cup, by a crackle of miniature lightning that consumed her arm down to the elbow and glowed brightly enough to make everyone wince.

The technician, his fur fluffed by proximity to the static energy she was arcing, phlegmatically announced her electrokinesis as "Rrrrank 19."

The V'Dan male shook his head, staring at Ia. "That's impossible. Even Mama Mishka is only a Rank 18 at the highest. Is that thing calibrated correctly?"

The technician didn't even flick an ear at that. "We have alrrready ascertained that it is callibrated, meioa." He glanced at Ia. "Though I wonnder how her otherrr gifts rrrank, if these arre her weakest."

"The remainder are considerably stronger," Ia stated. She nodded at the Salik machine. "If you don't want your KI machine short-circuited from an input overload, you'll have to plug me into *that* thing first."

"Well, aren't *you* just full of yourself?" the Human quipped. He started to say more, but subsided under the weight of Ia's steady gaze.

"I think we'll have to forgo testing my battlecognition for now," Ia said once she was sure he wouldn't scoff any further. "I'm in no shape physically to get into a fight, just yet. Suffice to say, it's stronger than my electrokinetic abilities. Which leaves us with postcognition and precognition. I'll need a volunteer to help me test those abilities."

Meioa Nik'ikk addressed that. "Postcognition can be verified through object-reading, but precognition is . . . nebulous," she chittered. "Why would you need a volunteer?"

Ia looked at the arachnoid. "Come with me, and find out for yourself." She looked back at the technician and lifted her chin at the array of salvaged headgear sitting on the table behind him. "Hand me one of the Human-sized helmets, and plug me in. Set the machine to full strength. I'll try to make it quick for the sake of the others, but you'll definitely want it running before I begin."

He shrugged and twisted in his seat, selecting one of the wire-draped crowns. Taking the metallic, clunky circlet from the Solarican, Ia settled it on her head. She strapped it in place, then glanced at the K'katta heading the meeting.

"Well? Aren't you going to come over here?"

"I should remain neutral in these proceedings," Nik'ikk demurred. "Do we have another volunteer?"

The Solarican by the now quiescent water cart sneeze-laughed. "I will volunnteerr."

"*You* will not interfere with these measurements," Ia

countered sharply. She pointed at the Solarican server. "Guards, make sure that male does not leave this chamber. Keep your eyes on him at all times."

"You are rrrather presummptuous, Human," one of the higher-ranked Solarican psis countered, lacing her clawed fingers together as she stared at Ia. "What makes you thinnk you can give orrders, here?"

"Aside from the fact I am now a War Princess of Solarica, and we *are* technically in a war zone? You're asking the wrong question, meioa. You *should* be asking how *he* got into a closed meeting," Ia retorted dryly. "But that can wait. Right now, I need volunteers. Preferably more than one, so you can countercheck with each other on what you're about to see."

"Fine," the Human across from her offered, the one who had subjected himself to her attempts at same-species telepathy. "I'll do it. Nothing quite like a skeptical witness, wouldn't you agree? I'm certainly strong enough to think through the antimachine, provided we don't take too long. Anyone else?"

Two others volunteered, a Tlassian and a K'kattan. They moved up close enough that the K'kattan could touch Ia's blue-clad leg with a foreclaw and the Tlassian could touch her shoulder with his callused, scaled fingers. The Human scooted close enough to grip Ia's left hand. Nodding at the technician, Ia braced herself for the pain.

"Postcognition first," she stated, and winced as grey mist stabbed through her head the moment he turned it on. Gritting her teeth, she grabbed the minds of the three touching her and dragged them onto the timeplains, aiming each one into a point in that particular person's past. Specifically, a strong memory from each one's childhood . . . and then she swapped them, dunking the Tlassian into the Human's stream, the Human into the K'kattan's, and so forth . . . and followed them with a third swapping.

When they were reeling from that, she dragged them far, far into the past. Into the dawn of V'Dan civilization. Only for a few moments, though; mindful of her reserves, Ia didn't join them herself. She also let them see only a few moments of the event she had targeted before she pulled them out of the riverscene. A lift of her hand and a slash of her finger instructed the technician to turn off the anti-psi machine.

Her gaze wasn't on the volunteers, however. It was on the Solarican cart-pusher, who had slumped against the back wall, eyes wide and ears flat. If he had been Human, she knew he would have been pale and shaking. As it was, he did not look well.

Of the three volunteers surrounding her, the V'Dan was the most shaken. He gaped at her. "That . . . That was the Valley. That was the Exodus! I saw the *Exodus* . . . Everyone coming through the Gate of Heaven, animals, people . . . It was as clear as I see this room!" he exclaimed. "This wasn't holokinesis, was it? Some sort of illusion? It *had* to have been . . ."

Ia shook her head, looking at her fellow Human. "No illusion, meioa. Just pure postcognition, projected directly into your brain. Or rather, with your brain pulled into Time itself. You *were* there, seeing it through the eyes of one of the overseers of the Exodus from Earth. His name was . . . ?"

"Nahmed Ik Mann," the Tlassian confirmed at her prompting. "He wasss counnting flockss of sssheep . . . but thinnking about the earthquakesss back home. The tectonnnic shifting mentioned in the Book of the Sssh'nai. But before that, we sssaw our hatchling yearsss. The day I broke my firssst tooth, the meioa-e'sss firsst hunnt . . ."

The V'Dan shook his head. "No . . . no. It's a trick. It *has* to be a trick—holokinesis, telepathy, some sort of combination—well, not the first part, not my seventh birthing-day. I remember that day very clearly. But surely . . ."

Ia shook her head again, a slow back and forth that countered his denial.

The technician looked up from his portable workstation. "Based on the interferrrence from the Salik machinnne . . . my calculations place that gift, whateverrr it was, at approximately Rrrank 54."

"Confirrrmed," agreed another voice. It was the female Solarican a few tables away, the one who had double-checked his earlier calculations on the suppression rate of the anti-psi machine. "Her Postcognnnitive Rrrank is 54."

That caused an instant commotion. Ia endured it up to a point. When the noise threatened to give her a non-machine-induced headache, she grabbed for their attention with a short, sharp shout.

"*Enough!* . . . Calm yourselves, meioas. The KI machine *is* calibrated, the calculations *are* accurate, given the anti-psi machine's fully demonstrated interference capabilities, and I *am* that slagging powerful. Now, if you don't mind, my *strongest* gift has yet to be tested. So, if we could kindly have some peace and quiet?"

"The KI monitorr registerred her gift at 13.7," the technician stated in the silence that followed her words. "At the calculated suppression rate of approximately 3.9, the math places her Rrrrank at 54. These nnnumbers are slllightly approximate, meioas . . . but they do not llie."

"I saw the meter move that high myself, even with the anti-psi machine fully active," Nik'ikk agreed, shifting restlessly on the table serving as her podium, "but I do have difficulty believing it. Meioa Ia, you say this is *not* your strongest gift?"

"No, Meioa Nik'ikk. It is merely an offshoot of my strongest gift, like how xenopathy is often an offshoot of telepathy, or telepathy an offshoot of empathy," Ia confirmed.

"Demonstrate your strongest gift to us, then," the K'katta instructed her.

"Turn on the machine again," Ia instructed. The Tlassian touched her shoulder and the other K'katta her leg, but the V'Dan hesitated when she held out her hand. Lifting one brow, she challenged him. "Or are you afraid of what else you might see?"

Tightening his mouth, he placed his fingers once more in hers. Waiting just long enough for the machine to spew its counteracting waves, Ia plunged them back into the timeplains. This time she brought them in carefully, yanking them out of their streams quickly and sending them racing high over the streams, like a quartet of birds flying over a swamp-soaked briar patch.

This time, she showed them everything, if from a distance. Starting with their own mist-shrouded streams, she pulled back, and back, and back, revealing the near-infinite tangle of intertwining lives, and all their side-possibilities, in near-endless configurations.

Something *banged* at the farthest edges of her awareness. The mist vanished, giving them an even clearer view of all the interwoven pathways. Diving back down, Ia dropped each of them into their immediate future, giving them a glimpse of three memorable moments, of conversations later on that day, moments that would convince them beyond a doubt that she was indeed able to foresee what would and could happen.

Pulling back from those intimate views, she released each mind in turn. In turn, they each drew in a shaken breath, releasing her from their grasp. They also coughed. The circuits of the KI machine had exploded, overloaded when the buffering of the anti-psi machine had been switched off. A smoky haze now permeated the room. Ia looked at the technician, who was calmly rechecking his calculations on his workpad.

"Well?" she asked him, trying not to breathe too deeply. They were lucky the fire suppression system hadn't activated, but the smoke was dissipating. "What's my ranking?"

"I am . . . not completely surrre. The meter onnly goes up to 20," he informed her. "The needle smacked the farr side of the window. A baseline guess would be . . . 84? Prrrrobably higher, though. You, Meioa," he added, directing his next comment at the K'katta overseeing the meeting, "owe me a nnew KI monitorrr."

Meioa Nik'ikk dipped her body in the best approximation her species had for an acknowledging nod. "I will pay for it personally," she chittered, her translator box flavoring her words with the nuances of her meaning. "The experiment was worth the expense, in my thoughts. Shutting off the nullifying machine proved the excessive levels of KI emitted by this meioa-e exceed all prior experience. Whatever that gift is, pathic or clairant, it is . . ." She paused, then stated carefully, "It is *not* Human. Which begs the question of *what* you are, meioa-e."

It wasn't widely known in the Alliance where most psychic abilities came from, but these weren't the average masses. The meioas around her were the psychic movers and shakers in their respective militaries, and there was one blatant conclusion which would leap immediately into their minds.

"You're only half right, meioa," Ia confessed in the wary quiet following that statement. "My mother was and is fully Human." Lifting her hand, she pointed at the Solarican still leaning against the wall, looking ill. "But since I have no choice, I'll admit my father-progenitor was one of *them*."

The male felinoid leaning against the wall started and straightened upright. He looked around the room, eyes wide, ears back. "Me? How could *I* be rrrelated to him? I am not evennn the same species!"

Pushing herself up from her bench, Ia leaned over the still-functional anti-psi machine. One hand rested over the sucker hand, ready to push and pull on the controls to make it work. The other lifted into the air. Energy crackled between her digits in unsubtle warning.

"Confess the truth, meioa . . . or I will turn *this* thing on, and give it *extra* power," she growled.

His ears flattened full, and his teeth bared. "You wouldn't *dare*."

"You're here for the same reason we are. Because *these* machines are a threat to us all," Ia stated, while the other beings in the room glanced back and forth between the two of them in confusion. "But it's not the same threat for you as it is for us. This just interferes with our gifts, and gives us a nasty migraine. To your kind, this . . . this anti-psi energy acts like a *poison.*

"Doesn't it, *Feyori*?" Her accusation made him growl. Ia lifted her right hand higher, brightening the sparks of energy snapping between her fingertips. "Oh, no. Don't even *think* of trying to counterfaction *me*, Meddler. You and I do want the same thing, after all: to see the source of these machines tracked down and silenced. Cooperate, and we will assist you."

" 'We'?" he challenged her, pushing away from the wall and lacing his fingers together Solarican-style, like a Human would have crossed his arms. "You speak as if *you* werre a faction, Humann."

"My Right of Simmerings is not yet over," Ia reminded him. This Meddler wasn't the one who had posed as Doctor Silverstone during her recruit days as a Marine, but she knew postcognitively that Silverstone had told the others about her. She knew that this one was aware of her temporarily sanctioned presence in the Great Game he and his kind played. "My faction is my own, counterfaction to none. *You* will cooperate in this matter.

"It is in your best interest to do so, since this machine is a threat to your kind as well as to mine. Swear yourself in faction to me," Ia ordered him, "or swear yourself neutral, and go."

He glanced at the guards, who were eyeing him warily. Their hands were not on the stunner guns at their waists, but rather on the knives sheathed next to them. Physical weapons would not actually kill a shape-shifted Meddler, but Meddlers could still feel pain when wrapped in fleshy matter. And unlike a laser or a stunner, knives wouldn't feed a Feyori, either.

It didn't look like he was going to swear faction to her. Ia lifted her chin. "As you wish. We are neutral to each other. But your cover is now blown, meioa. You'll find a set of power outlets behind you. Take what you need, and *go*."

He studied her for a moment more, then unlaced his hands. Electricity arced from the wall sockets to his claw-tips, fluffing and sparking through his fur. The lights dimmed, and the hairs on everyone else started to rise in static response. A moment later, energy leaped across the room from several more outlets, slamming into the Solarican—and an eye-dazzled blink later, a large silvery soap-bubble floated in the air where the felinoid once stood.

The metallic surface swirled, darkening for a moment as it continued to absorb more arcs of energy from the wall sockets. Seconds later, it swirled further, as if turning, and soared *through* the wall, picking up speed as it left without hindrance. Wide-eyed and wary, the meioas in the room watched it go, their stunned silence speaking volumes.

The moment she was sure the Feyori had left, Ia slumped back onto the bench behind her. She rubbed a trembling hand over her face, exhausted. Not just from the efforts of proving her gifts against the nullifying ache caused by that infernal machine, but from the effort to seem strong enough to take on a full-blooded Feyori. A member of a race who could literally eat laserfire for lunch.

"So." The single chirrup from Meioa Nik'ikk fell into the silence blanketing the hall. She chittered again, the complex programming of her translator box analyzing and filling in the nuances for her. Mostly ones of scorn. "A Feyori *half-breed*. One who understands their pol—"

"Stop." Lifting her gaze from her palm, she glared at the spider-like alien. "Just *stop*. I will *not* let you poison the minds of everyone around you with *your* prejudices. *Think* about what I have done with my gifts, meioa. *What*, exactly, have I *done* with them?"

Her demand echoed off the walls. Righteous anger gave her

the strength to rise, the strength to cross the meters of distance separating them. Bracing her palms on the edge of the table serving duty as the K'katta psychic's podium-platform, Ia leaned her face between the foremost legs of the alien, bringing her head within biting distance.

"Have I destroyed cities? Have I slaughtered children? Have I brought wrath and ruin? No, I have *not*. I have saved lives, meioa, at the personal expense of great pain and multiple injuries. I have strived, meioa, to be a *good* sentient being. Courageous, honorable, and compassionate. I have not sought high rank, I have not sought political power, and I have *not* tried to manipulate the people around me just for the amusement of some half-incomprehensible *game*!

"I have laid *my life* on the line for my fellow sentients, over and over and over, and I will not let you try to twist my actions into anything less than what I have *proven* them to be, over and over and *over*!" she snarled, leaning close enough to those flexing mandibles that the K'katta swayed back a few centimeters. "So before you chirp one more *word*, you will either clamp your mandibles shut and lay *your* life on the line for others, as many times as *I have*, or you will shove your personal prejudices right back up your waste orifice! Is. That. Clear. Guardian?"

Crouched low, cowed by her verbal attack, the K'katta didn't respond. Slowly, arms threatening to tremble, Ia pushed herself back upright.

"I repeat, I am *not* a monster. I am not some sadistic, uncaring deus ex machina, sweeping in and out just long enough to carry out some incomprehensible plot to manipulate others. I am a mortal and fallible and *mostly* Human being, as I have *always* been. I may be more gifted than others," she allowed, "but that only means I have a few more tools to work with than the average being. I make mistakes, I get hurt, but I *try* to do what is right. What all of us—Human and Tlassian and K'kattan, *all* of us—agree is *right*.

"Now, if *that* is an unforgivable sin," she snapped, looking around the room, "then may God damn you all to hell, because my *birthright* is nothing more than one extra means to help me get it done."

Pushing away from the table, she headed for the door. Without a word, Chaplain Benjamin rose from her seat near the back and followed her. Ia paused a few meters from the exit and looked back over her shoulder.

"I don't expect any of you to be able to keep all of this to yourselves, but I'll remind you that the only reason why I rescued so many from Sallha is because the Salik *didn't* know about my abilities. And the less they know about them, the better. So I'll ask you to keep silent, and treat my Rankings as an Alliance secret . . . but I won't hold my breath.

"The Solarican government, which currently holds custody over the anti-psi machine, has agreed to give it into my control as my war-prize for destroying the Salik high command. I in turn will be handing it over to the Terran Space Force, Branch Special Forces, for a more detailed examination of its function. I don't care if you believe me or not," she added, her words edged with a slight, sarcastic bite, "but I give you my word of honor that any further research conducted on it will be shared among the member races of the Alliance, and used in *our* mutual fight against the Salik. I promise we will track down the scientists who created it, and stop them from producing more.

"Now, if you will excuse me, I am still recovering from my injuries. I am tired and need to go rest." Facing the doors, she found the Solarican guards standing in the way.

Ia stared at them. She turned her head slightly to the side, displaying the distinctive earring dangling from her right lobe. An earring bearing the royal seal and the Solarican symbols that marked her battle rank as a War Princess among their kind. They looked at it, glanced briefly at each other, and parted to either side. One of them even palmed open the door for her, politely letting her go.

Without another word, Ia strode through, Bennie following in her wake. Of all the races, the Solaricans themselves were the least skittish about dealing with the Feyori, mostly for reasons they refused to admit to the other races, though Ia herself knew. Unless and until a member of their imperial family revoked her status as a War Princess, Ia technically outranked nearly everyone else on board the Solarican Warstation. She was diplomatic enough not to abuse that rank, but if necessary, she would use it.

Bennie waited until they were in one of the nearby lifts before she spoke. "Well played, Lieutenant. Not just the bit about quashing any rumors regarding your 'birthright,' but the whole revelation of your gifts."

"Thanks. I think," Ia muttered. "But I'll have you know it's not an act, Commander. I'm *not* a monster, and the only thing motivating my so-called *agenda* is the chance to save lives."

"Relax, I believe you," Bennie murmured back. "And I'm beginning to believe *in* you. I'm not quite sure *where* your cause is headed just yet, but at least I know you'll do your best to keep it on the right track. You've earned my faith in you. Don't abuse it."

"Thanks." This time, the word was uttered with more sincerity. "I wish I could tell you where it was headed," she added as the lift car swayed to a stop, "but at this point, I'm still faced with my biggest fight."

The doors opened and a trio of Solaricans boarded, clothed in stained coveralls and carrying tool kits and scanner equipment. They gave the two Humans cursory looks, but otherwise ignored the aliens in their midst.

"I forgot to ask. Did you get everything loaded, this morning?" Ia asked Bennie obliquely.

"It's all stowed," the redhead confirmed.

Relieved, Ia nodded. They weren't on their way back to the Solarican version of an infirmary ward. Instead, they were headed for one of the docking gantries, where a civilian mail courier waited for them. Bennie had actually traveled on it this morning, flying from the *Mad Jack*, which had moved two systems away in the last few days, forced to return to its assigned position in the Blockade zone.

When the Space Force had learned that Ia had been sold to the Salik, her belongings had been prepared to be shipped back home to her family. Very few soldiers had ever returned from a formal CPE listing, before. Luck alone had caught and rerouted them back to the Interdicted Zone before the cases filled with her few belongings had reached the halfway point. Ia hadn't unpacked much of it, just enough to don her most formal uniform yesterday. The rest, Bennie had picked up and sent to the courier ship waiting for them.

Halfway up the docking ring, Bennie slugged Ia on the arm. Yelping, Ia cupped the bruised muscles. She had only placed that possibility at less than 10 percent. "What was *that* for?"

"You're the precog, Lieutenant. Or rather, the postcog. *You* figure it out," Bennie muttered.

Ia didn't have to guess all that much. "I didn't tell you about my father because I *couldn't* tell you, alright? *Think* about it, Commander. Meioa Nik'ikk's reaction was only the tip of the iceberg. Even if I quelled some of it, everyone is going to be looking over my actions with a microscope and a fine-toothed comb, wondering if I'm a monster."

"So why reveal your background now?" Bennie her.

"First of all, there is no way with a 'bare minimum' ranking of 84 that I *could* keep it quiet," Ia reminded the other woman. "Something like that would always raise questions about where I got that kind of power. Second, if it had been brought up earlier in my career, I'd have been drummed out of the Service out of misguided, baseless paranoia. But by now, it has been proven, over and over again, what a massive *asset* I am to the Space Force. They can't afford to let me go, and everyone knows it.

"And third, I *want* people to go over my record. I want them to take a good, long look at everything I have done. Nothing about me has actually changed. I'm still the same soldier I was before my background was revealed," Ia reminded her. "But I want my Service record, both the good and the bad, to be so fresh in the minds of the Command Staff that they'll have no choice but to *think* about all I have done so far, and all I could still do. Specifically, of what I could do for *them* in the future."

"That could backfire, you know," Bennie warned her.

Ia wrinkled her nose, glancing at her friend. "Why do you think I'm so worried about winding up in the Dungeon? Come on, we've a long way to go and a short time to get there."

"Are you sure you're safe to travel this early in your convalescence?" Bennie asked her. "I'm not a doctor, if you go into a relapse."

"Hello, precog?" Ia retorted, spreading her hands. "I'll be fine, don't worry. OTL might exhaust me silly, but that's it. Trust me, I'm disease-free. No more sepsis. At least, this year."

The look Bennie shot her was definitely not an amused one. The corner of Ia's mouth quirked upward anyway.

CHAPTER 21

*For all my courage on the battlefield . . . for all my willing-
ness to face a barrage of enemy fire and mortal fear . . . my
most daunting fight did not come when I faced down the
Salik in their own banqueting hall. It came a few weeks
later in a modest-sized chamber buried deep within the
heart of the safest place in the Terran Empire.*

*Yes, even I have trembled in fear when faced with the
specter of failure. I can predict everything with great accuracy, but I cannot* guarantee *everything I foresee.*

~Ia

SEPTEMBER 19, 2495 T.S.
THE TOWER, TUPSF HEADQUARTERS
EARTH

The weight of her fully pinned Dress Black jacket, bundled up
in her arms with the lining side out, was nowhere near as heavy
as the lump in her stomach. Ia glanced at the chrono on her
new command arm unit, which had been issued during her
convalescence, then paced nervously back to the corridor junction for another peek around the corner.

The staff desk was still manned by the same brass-eagled
major, still patiently going through whatever it was on his work-

station screen that lit up his Dress Greens uniform. Before he could glance her way, she paced back to where Bennie waited, ostensibly reading the history placard on the wall.

"You'll have to quit doing that," the chaplain stated under her breath. "He's going to get suspicious."

"He's already suspicious," Ia murmured back. "You don't sit any post in the Tower without looking for enemies, whether they're hiding in plain sight or lurking behind a potted tree. Particularly not in a post as sensitive as that one."

"I'm not lurking behind a tree. The tree is merely next to me," Bennie replied primly, nodding her head at the sculpted branches of the ficus next to the placard. "You're the one who looks like she's lurking."

"That's because I'm nervous," Ia muttered.

"What's there to be nervous about?" Bennie asked her. "Aren't you Bloody Mary, scourge of the Salik? Besides, between what you've told me, and what I saw of the reactions from those three volunteers, all you have to do is flutter your fingers and *show* them what they need to know. Right?"

The very thought made her stomach churn. Ia shook her head. "No. I cannot cheat. It *has* to be done the honest way."

"What is *that* supposed to mean?" Bennie asked, eyeing Ia with suspicion. "You promised me you've been playing everything as straight as you can, so far."

"And I *have*, as much as anyone could in my position," Ia replied. She started to say more, but fell silent. A few moments later, a trio of officers walked past, conversing quietly among themselves. She waited until they had passed out of earshot before continuing. "Bennie . . . the things I have asked of you, the things I haven't yet explained, you have understood and agreed to follow because you have *faith* in me. You have lived on the same base ships as me, you have served with me, you have seen me in in the classroom and in action on the battlefield.

"The men and women I am about to face have *none* of that personal level of experience to back up their faith in me." That wasn't entirely true; there were at least two people in the minutes ahead who did have at least some personal experience with her. But it was true enough in the general sense. "However, the things I must do in the future *will* have to be undertaken on the fly, without any time to spare to explain myself in advance.

"The Future *does* shift, even under my feet," she confessed. "I cannot win the battles that must be fought if I do not have their *trust* in me. And no amount of psychic legerdemain or mental chicanery will *prove* they have that trust in me, unless I win it blindly. The things I must do . . . I am facing a forty-one percent *failure* rate. But I have no choice I can live with, other than to try for my best shot at this.

"If I used my gifts, I *might* make it on my second-best chance, but second-best might not be enough. Particularly if I am accused of undue psychic influence, farther down the line. I *cannot* afford that kind of stain on my record." Another check of her chrono made her clutch her jacket to her stomach. "Two more minutes—promise me you will stay out of this?"

"Since I still don't quite know what 'this' is, you're asking for some of that same blind faith out of *me*," Bennie quipped. At Ia's chiding look, she relented. "Alright, I promise. And if they throw you in the Dungeon, I promise to come and visit you, as you have asked. But only if you tell me why it's so important for this . . . this Doctor Silverstone fellow to visit you in the Dungeon if things go nova in there."

"Let's just say he owes me two little favors," Ia muttered, thinking of the Feyori she had met in basic training, and the preparatory meddling he was doing right now in the lives of his twin sons. Twins she had predicted several years ago. "But that would also be cheating. I need to win this argument on my own, so calling on him is a last-ditch effort only—it's too important for me to win, Bennie. You have no idea how much. Enough *to* cheat, if in the end I must, but . . . that would create a host of new problems. I'd rather win through on my own. *If* I can."

"So stop fretting, go forth, and *win* it," Bennie ordered her.

Sighing roughly, Ia unfolded her jacket. She placed the black cap on her head and swung the heavily weighted material onto her arms. Shrugging into it, she focused on fastening the buttons. Bennie moved around her, adjusting the pins fastened to her sleeves and her back so that each medal and ribbon lay flat.

"You have an absolutely ridiculous number of awards and merits, young meioa-e, particularly for so few years on Border and Blockade Patrols," the older woman fussed. "If they cannot see the high value their own armed forces have clearly placed on you, then they don't deserve your faith in *them*. Faith is a two-way street, after all." A last adjustment of Ia's lieutenant bars, a slight twitch of the cap, and she stepped back. "There. God has faith in you. So do I. Now, go knock some of *our* belief into them."

Her warm words and her soft smile made Ia feel slightly better, but they couldn't dispel the knot of anxiety tightening inside her stomach. Squaring her shoulders, Ia walked around the corner. The major seated at the staff desk glanced up at her. He seemed to still be focused on his work, but she knew he was watching her carefully as she approached.

Except she didn't approach him, but rather the airlock-thick doors next to his desk.

"Excuse me, Lieutenant, but where do you think you're going?" he challenged her.

"I have an appointment to keep with the Command Staff, Major." Stopping in front of the doors, she reached for the security codes with her mind.

"The Command Staff is in a sealed conference, Lieutenant, and you are one step from being in a restricted . . . area . . ." He trailed off, frowning in confusion as the doors slid open in front of her. His hand reflexively grabbed for the pass key clipped to his waist, one of the physical components required for access on top of the ident scans, which she had not used. It was still there. "What the . . . ?"

Ia stepped into the small room beyond the blast-proof doors, literally an airlock. She could hear the major scrabbling for the weapon stored at his desk, and triggered the doors a second time.

"That is a *restricted area*, Lieutenant, and you are *not* auth—"

The panels sealed shut. Ia relaxed marginally; at least now she couldn't be shot in the back. Shot in the face, maybe, but not in the back. *One more obstacle,* she thought, working the security system electrokinetically. Part of her mind was keeping the emergency beacon paralyzed, despite the repeated thumping of the major's fist. Part of her mind was focused on opening the inner doors at just the right moment without any advanced warning signs broadcast to the inner chamber.

Part of her was focused on the potential fallout from the very risky decision to cut off any warning signals from inside the inner sanctum. The rest of her struggled against the urge to either turn tail and run, or double over and lose her lunch. Except she wisely hadn't eaten any. *That's the* only *wise thing about any of this. From this point on . . . the probabilities are stacked too close to each other to tell* which *way they'll go. And I daren't try to manipulate the system, not with a fellow psi about to watch my every move in there.*

The doors slid open in time for her to hear the voice of Admiral-General Myang, right on cue. ". . . brings us to the issue of who will command Project Tita . . . Lieutenant!"

Ia strode into the room, fear squashed, determined to be brave. The schematics displayed on the screens lining the round chamber flickered and blipped off. She lifted her hand in dismissal. "Don't bother, sirs. I've already seen it."

"Lieutenant Ia!" Admiral-General Christine Myang snapped. She was seated in the center of the bottommost ring of five tiers of horseshoe-shaped tables, the only person in the room clad in solid black. The others around her were clad in the Dress Colors for their particular Branches. The head of the Space Force scowled at Ia, face reddening. "You have *five seconds* to explain your presence here!"

"Actually, sir, it's supposed to be five minutes," Ia countered, feigning calm. It took conscious effort to keep from letting her hands tremble, or from balling them into fists. Right fingers flat, she lifted them to the brim of her cap, her eyes on the grey-haired woman at the center of her vision. "Lieutenant First Grade Ia, requesting permission to perform a Shikoku Yamaneuver, sir."

"I don't see a starfighter anywhere, *soldier*," one of the green-clad generals off to her left growled. "Request de—"

"Not *that* kind of Yamaneuver, General," Ia countered, cutting him off, fingertips still angled at her brow. "I'm referring to the Star of Service Yamaneuver, sir. And I *don't* mean the whitewashed, heavily edited version they teach to schoolchildren, sirs."

Myang studied her a long moment, then returned Ia's salute with a flick of her hand to her brow. "Do tell, Lieutenant. *Which* unedited version are you referring to?"

Ia dropped her arm and answered the older woman's question. "The one where the Command Staff *didn't* admit him willingly to their presence. The one where he broke into their sanctum because they *refused* to give him a hearing regarding his idea that the Loyalist AIs could be, and should be, used to infiltrate the Rebel AIs in order to bring the AI War to a swifter end. The one where he *spat* on his Star of Service, and said that if everything that his many medals represented weren't worth even so much as *five minutes* of the Command Staff's time, sir . . . then they could go straight to hell, and be damned for dragging the rest of the United Planets with them.

"The one where the shock of his actions caused them to rethink their stubborn closed-mindedness, and call him back into their presence to listen to what he had to say. *That* Star of Service Yamaneuver, sir." She held Myang's gaze without wavering. The others around the room were important, but the Admiral-General was the keystone of her plan. If Ia failed to convince *her*, the rest would barely matter.

"There's just one big flaw in your request, Lieutenant," an admiral off to her right stated. "We are not currently at war, and we are definitely not *losing* that war."

That turned her head. Ia stared at the blue-uniformed man. "Admiral Fulk. You may have not noticed, but the only reason why we *aren't* at war is because I personally went to Sallha to *stop* it. That was their Eve of Battle Banquet. As soon as they finished eating us, they were going to *launch* the next Salik War. If I hadn't stopped them—if I hadn't *slaughtered* their high command, at great personal risk—we'd be eyebrow deep in body parts and broken ships by now, sir."

"I don't think—" he scoffed.

"No, Admiral, you *don't* think." That came from the tier behind him. Ia lifted her gaze to Admiral Viega, who was looking a lot better than the last time she had seen the other woman. Healthier and fully dressed, Viega stared down at Admiral Fulk. "That exact same information was in my debriefing report, two weeks ago. My captors told me that six Sallhan hours after the banquet, they were going to launch everything they had at us . . . And my captors boasted multiple times during my incarceration just how *much* they had ready to throw at us. I know they didn't tell me everything, either."

"They still have those resources, sirs," Ia confirmed on the heels of Viega's words. "They just don't have the *leadership* to use all of it. Yet. But time will not stand still, gentlemeioas. Every second we waste here is another second they have to pull together enough competency in what's left of their leadership to resume being a serious combat threat. A very serious threat."

"Damn straight," Viega agreed.

"Admiral Viega, as your viewpoint could be considered rather biased in this matter, I must request that you remain silent until addressed," Myang stated, twisting to look over her shoulder.

"Aye, sir," Viega complied.

Myang returned her attention to Ia. "All you have said so far, Lieutenant Ia, is what the Dlvmvla like to call 'all wind and no breeze.' You have risked your life and your career to barge into a closed session containing Ultra-Classified information. Legally, I have every right to toss you in the Dungeon and throw away the key. Legally, I can have you flogged to the bone. *Legally*, I can have you hung until you are *dead*, Lieutenant.

"Now. Why don't you try to tell me why you thought it was such a *brilliant* idea to *shakk* away your career, today?"

The nausea was back, cramping in her stomach from sheer nerves. Ia struggled to keep it from her voice and her face. "I am here, sir, to hopefully help prevent you and your fellow Staff members from making a lethal series of mistakes."

That caused a skeptical outcry among the twenty-plus officers scattered around the room. There was enough room, there could have been eighty or more present, but the materials they were there to vote upon were not something the whole Command Staff had needed to know. Nonetheless, the furor roused by her claim caused enough noise for at least twice their number, if not more.

"A *lethal* series of mistakes?"

"*Who* do you think you are?"

"Of all the unmitigated gall!"

Ia opened her mouth to defend herself, but the two dozen or so generals and admirals in the chamber didn't let her. She could only make out a few of the outraged shouts and comments being aimed her way.

"You'd better explain yourself!"

"I've never heard anything so outrageous in all my career!"

"I don't see how she *can* explain it."

"If I were in charge of the Navy, I'd—"

"Sirs!" Ia shouted, cutting through their protests. "Admiral-General, could I *please* have my five minutes of *uninterrupted* time, so I *can* actually explain?"

The Admiral-General held up her hand. "Quiet, everyone!"

The others subsided. All, that was, save for one of the admirals wearing the grey uniform of the Special Forces. Leaning back in his chair, arms folded across his medal-sprinkled chest, he spoke in the silence following her words. "Technically, Lieutenant, if a single Star of Service was worth five minutes of our predecessors' time to Shikoku Yama, *you* should be asking for ten. You do have two of them."

"Fine. Ten minutes, then," Ia amended, seizing on his offer.

"You are no Shikoku Yama, Lieutenant Ia," Myang stated. "And this is no AI War . . . but you have earned your ten minutes. Spend them *wisely.*"

"Earned them?" one of the generals in the second tier scoffed. "Have you not read the latest report? She's a psi! She *manipulated* those medals onto her chest!"

"Clearly, *you* haven't read her files, nor the correlated reports of the events that *earned* her those medals." That came from a familiar face, General Sranna, whom Ia hadn't seen since the incident in the Zubeneschamali System, back when she earned her Field Commission. "Lieutenant Ia's personal incident reports are rather dry and factual, with no embellishments whatsoever. It is only when you read the *other* accounts, the ones from the other individuals involved in each case, that you get a glimpse of just how extraordinary her actions have been. More to the point, when you contrast the *vid* records of what she has done, versus what she reports, she *consistently* comes across as boring and factual, compared to the actual events."

"There's more to it than that," another general stated, this one in the brown uniform of the Marine Corps. Ia belatedly recognized him as the general in charge of the segment in which Commander Ferrar's troops served. "Every report she has filed on behalf of another soldier, making recommendations for granting them honors and medals, have been just as factual, if slightly more detailed, than the reports of her own accounts. Starting from her very first promotion to corporal rank, when

her actions and deeds caught the eyes of her immediate superiors, and all related reports wound up on my desk. Such self-
effacing accounts are *not* the acts of a self-aggrandizing
glory-hogger. Particularly not when she has so clearly done
more to help *others* gain rightful recognition for their own
heroism."

Ia unbuttoned her jacket, shifting the medal-weighted folds
aside so she could safely rest her hands on her hips. That bared
her blue Navy shirt, and the four colorful ribbon-sashes the
K'kattan government had bestowed upon her. "I do appreciate
the support, sirs. Particularly from you, General Sranna—and
it is good to see you looking so well after all these years. But
I will *not* allow the salvation of our future to be derailed by
any further sidebars, if you please. Not for ten full minutes."

"Excuse me, but you will *not*—" the Army woman protested.

Impatient with the delays, Ia snapped back, "Would you
please be silent and let me explain? I have *earned* those ten
minutes, and I will not have them pissed away just because *you*
want to talk!"

"You're not in the military to make friends, are you, Lieutenant?" Admiral-General Myang drawled.

Ia replied candidly, hands back on her hips as she looked at
the head of the Space Force once more. "No, sirs, I am *not* here
to make friends. I am here to help save innocent lives. Why are
you here?"

Deliberately, Ia looked around the room, meeting as many
eyes as she could in the silence following her demand. Only a
handful of them met her gaze.

"Get on with it, Lieutenant," Myang ordered, avoiding the
pointed question herself, though she did meet Ia's gaze.

Lifting a hand, Ia snapped her fingers. The screens turned
back on, surrounding them with images of the project they had
been about to discuss. More than one of the men and women
around her twitched a little in startlement at the display, though
not all of them moved.

"Project Titania, also known as the Godstrike Cannon, is
the culmination of several projects run by the Oberon Mining &
Research Consortium. A company which is partly a front for
the Terran military's efforts to research and refine increasingly
more powerful, more calorie-efficient laser weapons. The 67.19

percent caloric efficiency rating of the standard HK military rifle is *nothing* compared to the Godstrike's unprecedented 90.3 percent conversion rating.

"You've been patting yourselves on the back for the creation of the biggest weapon in Alliance history. The Godstrike cannon, at full strength, is indeed capable of cutting thirty kilometers down through the crust of a planet in one minute flat. But you have overlooked the two biggest flaws inherent in its design, and all the accompanying headaches those flaws entail," she stated.

Ia shifted the screens electrokinetically to a series of graphs detailing the quarter-scale test cannon's caloric output versus various targets. Myang sighed impatiently. "And those flaws are . . . ?"

Enlarging one of the charts, Ia explained. "The first one is so basic, we literally learned it *in* Basic Training, as one of the four Rules of the Range. In case it has been a few years, I will remind you of those rules: Always assume a weapon is loaded; Always point your weapon in a safe direction until you are ready to fire; Always keep your finger off the trigger until you are ready to fire . . . and *Always* be aware of what is downrange of your target. Just in case you *miss*, sirs.

"The caloric diffusion rate of the newest HK-72 laser rifle in the SAC, Standard Atmospheric Conditions, is almost three kilometers. But in *space*, its diffusion rate is almost half a *lightsecond*. Given that the Godstrike cannon is a raging forest fire to the HK's tiny little match, and that your technicians have been aiming at small moons and large comets for testing its strength, huge, thick targets that are impossible to miss, you have forgotten to consider carefully what that means in relation to the fourth Rule of the Range," Ia stated. She flashed another picture on the screen, this time an archive file from one of the Border engagements, between a Terran battlecruiser and a small fleet of pirate ships. "This brings into play the *second* fatal flaw in the cannon's design.

"Because of the massive amounts of energy required, and the refraction rate of the focusing crystal, it takes ten seconds to charge the Godstrike cannon. At the end of those ten seconds, under the current design, the cannon *must* be fired or it will overload and cause a potentially catastrophic thermal reaction that will overload the thermogenerators, send feedback into the hydrogenerators, and run the risk of blowing up the entire ship." She nodded at the screens around the room. "As you can see, a *lot* of maneuvering takes place in ten seconds in a standard stardogging fight. It is very difficult for even the best of combat-seasoned pilots to gauge exactly where the enemy will be, ten seconds down the road.

"The sheer caloric force of the Godstrike cannon makes the Fourth Rule *vital*, sirs, because even with the barest minimum burst, at one twentieth of a second, its diffusion rate in the vacuum of space is *four lightmonths*. It's even greater than that if the cannon is fired for longer than its shortest possible burst." Another flick expanded the view on the screen to a systemwide diagram. Ia streaked a line of white from the dot where the fighting had taken place to a point well beyond the system's edge. "Though it *is* possible for a combat-seasoned pilot to gauge where enemy ships might line up in the next ten seconds, ten seconds is nothing compared to 10.5 *million* seconds. That, sirs, is the number of seconds that will pass if the Godstrike cannon *misses* its target.

"I will also remind you that the caloric force of that cannon will require a minimum of seven medium-sized warships *or* three capital-sized ships in alignment to be able to absorb the force of a single, twentieth-of-a-second strike. If things don't line up just right, you will literally be endangering shipping lanes for *months* to come."

"So what, do you expect us to scrap Project Titania? Is that it?" one of the blue-clad admirals asked.

"Or do you expect to pilot it yourself?" the admiral in grey asked, arms still folded over his chest.

"I'm the only one who safely *can*," Ia answered the second man. She knew his name and his face very well through the timestreams, though they had yet to be formally introduced. "Yes, the Space Force has great pilots, but they aren't precognitives. And your typical military precognitives have spent their careers wrapped in cotton wool, not in combat.

"Very few of them are capable of predicting anything in the chaos of combat, because they are not trained to do so," Ia said. "They cannot focus that well, and they cannot predict most combat situations with the necessary level of pinpoint accuracy.

I am that capable. My entire service record *proves* that I am. That I *have*."

"Yeah, right," one of the brown-clad generals on the second tier snorted.

Ia stared at the older woman for a moment, then shrugged out of her jacket. Holding up the heavy, lumpy garment, she nodded at it. "*This* says I can. *Everything* I have done in the Space Force has been predicted. Every objective that I could safely meet, most of them under the heavy restrictions and hobbling parameters of my orders, which I have followed to the best of my abilities, I have met.

"Ironically, the reason *why* I was such a valuable war-prize to the Salik for their little prewar meal was one of the few times I deliberately disobeyed orders, sirs. I deliberately strayed far beyond my assigned patrol zone, and I successfully destroyed a major Salik warship, because I *knew* it was carrying some sort of psychic interference capability. With nothing but a Delta-VX at my command, I destroyed an entire enemy capital ship, one the size of a Battle Platform, *and* I got my dual ships and her crews out of that fight alive.

"Now, meioas. Imagine what I could do for you if I had your trust and your confidence backing me," she coaxed. "If *all* of my moves could be made that freely. Because we *are* going to war. You don't have to be a precog to see that much . . . and I can see that they are scrambling faster than anticipated to relaunch their war efforts against us. I am here to warn you that we will have barely half a year to get ready for the first wave of the coming frogtopodic tsunami, and you *will* need the Godstrike effectively wielded in combat to save the people on the shore. Scoff all you may want, *resist* all you may want . . . but I am your *only* shot at safely wielding it."

"You're rather full of yourself," one of the generals in green on the first tier snorted.

Ia lifted her jacket a little higher. "Am I?" She lowered it to her side. "Anyone else want to discuss the proof of my qualifications? Medal for medal, kilo for kilo, wound for wound? All I ever have done is my assigned *job*, sirs. But that job has *not* utilized my abilities to their fullest extent, yet."

Myang studied her. Lacing her fingers together on the curved surface of the desk in front of her, she leaned on her elbows and addressed Ia. "If you really are as strong a precognitive as the reports we've received have indicated, Lieutenant, then surely you knew Project Titania was conceived over three years ago. Given that, why wait so long before revealing your knowledge of it, and making this proposal now, of all times?"

"For one, you wouldn't have believed me back then, sir. I'll remind you that the roots of Project Titania started before the incidents at Zubeneschamali, back when I was a mere sergeant. For another, I didn't have any practical experience in piloting or operating a ship's gunnery systems at the time," Ia confessed dryly. "For a third, there are three major leaks in the upper echelons of the Space Force. Thankfully, none in this room, but if I *had* told anyone of my psychic abilities—aside from Commander Ferrar, who figured it out on his own—the Salik would have gotten wind of it, and they would have been far more prepared against me just a few weeks ago. If they'd learned what my true capabilities were, I would've been so covered up in those anti-psi machines, that they would've been hard-pressed to find a place to *bite* me.

"I still would have broken free, but more lives would have died that day. Possibly even Admiral Viega's. I couldn't risk that." She lifted her jacket again in indication. "I honestly don't care about these medals, sirs. I am honored to have received them, yes, but I'm not in this for glittery or glory. I'm in this to save innocent lives. You put me in charge of that cannon, and you give me enough leeway to do what needs to be done, and I will turn the tide of the Second Salik War for you—and I'll remind you that *this* time, we're on the same level playing field that the Alliance initially suffered before we Terrans joined the fray, with our hyperrelay communication arrays and our OTL traveling speeds. *This* time, we don't have those strong extra advantages. And with that damned machine being developed and manufactured out there, we don't even have the advantage of our psychic abilities, right now."

Sitting back, the Admiral-General folded her arms across her chest. "You make it sound like I should be giving you *carte blanche*, Lieutenant."

"To an extent, yes," Ia admitted. That caused several of the other men and women to choke and cough at her audacity. She ignored their affronted stares. "Give me the freedom to handpick my crew, and the leeway to negotiate my patrol assignments, and I will pull off miracles for you. That ship *cannot* be assigned to a specific route. It will be needed in disparate battle zones placed hundreds of lightyears apart . . . and *not* always where you'd think it will be needed. Out of a thousand hovering butterflies, very few people can predict which ones might start the next hurricane, let alone *will* start that hurricane, and do so with the level of accuracy that I can provide for you. That I *want* to provide, given the limitations of Time that are at hand."

"And who would you have for your handpicked crew?" one of the grey-clad women scoffed. "Half an entire Marine Corps division? The Troubleshooters? The entire Knifeman Corps?"

"No, sir—though I will need at least two Knifemen, a few Sharpshooters, and a handful of Troubleshooters on my crew," Ia stated. "Mostly only those who can be spared. I will not waste our resources by asking for those who will be needed far more, elsewhere. But I *will* need them. We have a very big, very immediate problem on our hands, and it is those damned anti-psi machines.

"Our psychic abilities have been one of our few advantages over the amphibious races," she reminded the men and women around her. "Those machines *have* to be hunted down and the source-points for their development and creation *must* be destroyed. Those machines will even slow *me* down . . . but they cannot *stop* me. I am therefore the best choice to spearhead the efforts to track them down. Unfortunately, I am only one woman, and I will need the expert help of others to find and destroy their production lines. This is something I know can be done during the shakedown cruise of the new ship, which kills yet another bird for you with only one stone's throw."

"And again, what size army do you expect us to grant you, in order to carry off such a feat?" the Admiral-General asked her.

"I only need a crew of one hundred and sixty, sir. Well, one hundred and sixty-one, if you count my DoI-appointed chaplain," Ia amended dryly.

"Impossible," the admiral in grey snorted. "That ship is currently designed to be run with a minimum crew of five hundred. You'd have to cross-train everyone in three other jobs!"

"I know. Which is one of the other reasons why I'm here *now*, before the interior has been finished, as well as before you've assigned the command of that ship to anyone else—this would've been easier if my name had already been on your list of possible captains," she half muttered, rubbing the bridge of her nose with her free hand. "I'll need three months to get the ship retrofitted to the right specifications, and to select and train the necessary crewmembers.

"Follow that with a two-month combination of shakedown cruise and anti-psi hunt, and we'll be ready to go to war a month before the Salik actually do. *If* everything goes according to plan," Ia amended. She shrugged slightly. "There is a twenty-three percent probability that the Salik and their allies will go to war a couple of weeks to a month early, which is why we'll need to *be* ready before they actually do—if you can arrange to stall the entry of those allies into the war front, all the better, sirs."

"The Salik *and* their allies?" one of the other Army generals asked. "Who in their right mind would ally with them?"

"Who do you think?" one of the Special Forces generals replied. He tapped something on the workstation console in front of him, and a list of names, grouped by species, appeared on several of the smaller screens ringing the room. "Not a single Choya was present at that banquet, waiting to be eaten, because the Salik find their blue hemocyanin blood to be literally distasteful. The Choya have decided they are tired of lagging behind the other races in various areas of technology and respect, and have chosen to ally with their fellow amphibians."

"They are overconfident that the Salik will leave them off the galactic lunch menu," Ia agreed. "Unfortunately, the Salik *will* leave them off of it, so long as the Choya are useful. And it's mostly been the Choya slipping various bits of tech and other commodities through the Blockade lines. I tried to stop what I could reach, but most of the time, I couldn't deviate from my orders."

"You make it sound as if you can predict their every single move for the next century," an admiral behind Myang muttered.

Ia shook her head slowly. "A century is as clear to me as a day, Admiral. Unfortunately, we don't have a century. We have a matter of months before the first tidal wave of war crashes over our heads, and only a handful of years before the second war hits."

"Second war?" Myang asked her sharply. "What second war?"

Holding up the fingers of her free hand, Ia listed them. "I am fighting four wars, Admiral-General. The first one is the return of the Salik and their plans for galactic conquest and lunch. The second one is the return of the *Greys*, sir, which will prompt the third war, which will be a civil war on my homeworld."

"The Greys?" Myang repeated, frowning at Ia.

"Yes, sir," Ia confirmed. "They will come for us *before* we are through with the Salik, when our best resources will still be needed for fighting back the amphibians, sir."

She paused to let that sink in. More than one of the officers around her blanched at the thought. Myang tightened her mouth for a moment. "And the fourth war?"

"I will tell you something nobody else in the Alliance knows, sir," Ia said. "The Greys are *not* from this galaxy. They originally came from a galaxy that used to exist in an area the astronomers call the Blight."

"*Used* to exist?" General Sranna challenged her.

"Yes, sir. Three hundred years from now, the ancestral enemy of the Greys, the ones who destroyed the Greys' home galaxy, will approach the Milky Way. They are . . . they're like a hive of wasps, is the best way I can express it," Ia offered, gesturing with her free hand. "They are traveling in a Dysun's Sphere, they are overcrowded—which is a frightening thought, to think of something that astronomically huge as *being* overcrowded—and they are looking to build a second hive.

"In order to build one, sirs, it will require the *entire* resources of a new galaxy. Our galaxy." She met his gaze soberly, and the gaze of the general next to him, and the admiral, and the gaze of the Admiral-General herself. "I promise, I will give you and your successors instructions on how to deal with them when the time is right. But in order for the Alliance to still be *around* to deal with them, we have to fight off the Salik, and fight back the Greys. Each war has to be fought in the right way at the right time."

"And your homeworld? You said you'll be fighting a war

back on, what, Sanctuary is it?" Myang asked her. "Is that why your brother 'mysteriously' won the biggest Lottery jackpot in Alliance history? To fuel an insurrection?"

"No, sir. That war will be started by the *other* side. My brother's money is being used to create defensive fortifications, and stockpile sentientarian resources," she explained. Ia held up her finger, cutting off the older woman. "Before you make any other accusations, sir, *think* of where Sanctuary is located. *Think* about it."

Snapping her fingers, she projected a map of the galaxy on the central viewscreen behind her. One which outlined the Terran Empire in blue, Sanctuary in gold a short distance away, and, directly behind it, a huge blob of silvery grey.

"My homeworld, gentlemeioas, is on the backside of Terran space, in the direction that the *Greys* retreated. It is, in fact, on the very border of Grey territory. The only things that will save my people from being *farmed* by the Greys are its extreme high gravity, and the xenophobic isolationism of its current ruling government. When the Greys do attack, this will fuel their paranoia to a near-catastrophic degree, to the point where they will destroy any starship, orbital shuttle, and even their own *space station* in the effort to cut themselves off from the rest of the universe.

"That money has been given by my brother to a nonprofit organization to make *sure* my planet can survive two hundred years of isolation behind enemy lines. You cannot evacuate them, either," she stressed as two of the generals on her right started to speak. "Aside from the sheer logistic improbability, and all those families stubbornly refusing to give up their first-worlder colonial rights, you cannot move the *children* of Sanctuary without adversely affecting their health. The gravitational differences between Sanctuary and Parker's World are too great.

"I could go into far greater detail as to *why* their continued survival on Sanctuary is so important," Ia dismissed, "but for now, I will only say this: What the people of Sanctuary are destined to become when it's safe for them to reemerge will be *vital* for the war effort three hundred years from now. It is enough for me, a daughter of Sanctuary, to know that they *will*

survive, and to help them in the only way I can, giving them
the funds to ensure they have the means for it.

"You and I have bigger problems on our hands right now,
Admiral-General," Ia told Myang. "Ones that are a lot closer
to *your* homeworlds. Things that *we* can handle, just as there
are things only my family and their friends can handle back
home. Let them handle it. We have enough troubles of our own,
right now."

Myang subsided. Her brown eyes studied Ia thoughtfully,
though the rest of her expression was shuttered. Ia lifted the
jacket still held in her other hand.

"Admiral-General, sir. You have been apprised of the two
hidden, lethal flaws of the Godstrike cannon. You have been
advised on how best to still utilize it, in spite of those flaws.
You have been offered a better than fair chance at neutralizing
the enemy's latest weapon, those anti-psi generators, and you
have been warned with plenty of time to prepare for the return
of an enemy so advanced, even the *Feyori* tread carefully near
their territory.

"I thank all of you for giving me these ten minutes and more
of your time . . . but arrogant as it may be, by the weight of this
jacket, and all the honor, effort, and regulation-constrained duty
that it represents, I *will* have an answer. Choose carefully,
Admiral-General Myang: Should I spit up a lung on all that *this*
represents, as my predecessor was forced to do? Or would you
have me put it back on and let me *fight* for you, as I *truly* can?"

Silence stretched between them. Two or three of the other
officers opened their mouths to speak, then thought better of it.
Ia tried very hard not to think, not to project, not to do anything
in any way which could be misconstrued as undue influence.
The man in grey on her right, second tier, was General Jolen
Phong. Head of the Psi Division of the Special Forces, and a
Rank 15 telepath, he was more than strong enough to pick up
on any stray projected thoughts. Ia carefully did not do that.

The Admiral-General sat forward, folding her hands on top
of one another on the curved tabletop between her and Ia.

"I don't care *how* many medals you may have earned, soldier.
I will *not* hand control of our most advanced ship into the care
of a mere Lieutenant First Grade."

Sick fear pooled in the pit of Ia's stomach. She forced her numb fingers to tighten a bit more on the collar of her heavy jacket, keeping it carefully aloft. She was quite sure that the Admiral-General's dark eyes didn't miss the sudden paling of her face, nor the clenching of her hand, either.

"I am therefore promoting you to Ship's Captain," Myang stated dryly, her brown eyes fixed implacably on Ia's face, watching her every reaction.

Ia swayed in relief, blood rushing back to her head, making her ears roar and the Admiral-General's next words sound a bit odd for a moment.

". . . But not without a cost," Myang was saying. "First of all, you will be moved into the Branch Special Forces and placed under the direct oversight of Admiral John Genibes."

The admiral in grey who had half challenged, half supported Ia dipped his head in acknowledgment. Ia barely spared him a glance, though she did give him a slight nod in return. She had already known that, *if* she won this fight, she would be working with him. The only doubt had been that very big *if*. The Admiral-General continued, forcing Ia to focus on the older woman's words.

"You will have to get *his* approval for any and all crew-members, and any and all changes to the ship, and you will coordinate and approve all patrols and special assignments through him. Project Titania has been under his purview since its inception. I don't care what kind of psychic you *think* you are, he knows all of it better than you do," Myang stated. She paused, then added, "Secondly, and more importantly, *Captain* Ia . . . you are hereby placed under a double indemnity clause for any and *all* corporal punishments assigned to your so-called handpicked crew. From a single stroke of the cane all the way through a Grand High Treason hanging, whatever your crew suffers, *so do you*. Is. That. Clear?"

"*Yes*, sir." Relief threatened to make her giddy. Somewhere in the back of her mind, the part of her that kept track of the flux of the timestreams warned her that there might be problems up ahead, but they were troubles she knew she could navigate. Ia repeated her orders carefully to let Myang know the message was fully received and fully understood. "I accept the double indemnity of responsibility not only for my own actions, but also for those of my crew, sir. I shall willingly endure without restraint or hesitation any and all corporal punishments assigned to them, as well as any I may accrue on my own, whether it's five canings, or five hundred, or being hung for Grand High Treason, sir."

"Good. I'm glad that you do understand the severity of your situation, and the price you will pay if you abuse it. Now, is there anything *else* you wished to discuss with us, soldier?" Myang asked mock-sweetly. "Or can we get on with our business? We do have two wars to prepare for, *if* what you said is true."

For a moment, Ia's mind went blank. She blinked a couple of times, drew in a deep breath, then shook her head slowly. "No, sir. I do think all the rest of the business regarding Project Titania can be discussed between Admiral Genibes and myself in another location, at another time. And I'll get you datafiles on everything I can safely foresee for you, Johns and Mishka notwithstanding. Oh—*ah*, you might want to send the all-clear signal through to the other side of this room," she confessed, blushing. "I've . . . sort of . . . *um* . . ."

"Been holding off the security forces just long enough to have your little Yamaneuver say, yes, I know," Myang finished for her. "Not all of the security measures built into this room are electronic." Flipping up her arm unit screen, she punched in several commands.

Project Titania vanished from the screens, and the airlock doors guarding the chamber slid open. Both sets of doors opened, revealing a team of armored soldiers, weapons at the ready. They peered warily into the room, clearly wanting to see what was going on first, rather than randomly opening fire. Lowering his gun only slightly, the major from the staff desk stared first at Ia, then peered at the men and women seated behind her. "Admiral-General, sir?"

"Stand down, Major," Myang stated. "Your diligence is commendable, but I sincerely doubt even a thermonuclear bomb could stop *this* woman from going wherever she thinks she needs to go."

Oh, I'm pretty sure a thermonuclear bomb would *stop me,*

one of the few corners of Ia's mind not dazed by her success muttered. *It wouldn't stop the Immortal One, but I'm not that strong a psi, thank god . . .*

Myang addressed Ia, recapturing her attention. "Be advised, Captain, that if you ever charge in here uninvited again, I *will* flog you myself. Stroke for stroke. For now, consider this a successfully accomplished Yamaneuver. I trust you will be too smart to brag about it to anyone. Dismissed."

"Sir, yes, sir. No, sir, I won't brag about this. And thank you, sirs, for listening to me. If there were any other way to have gotten my name onto that list—an *honorable* way—I'd have done it, sirs," Ia said. "You'll have my absolute best; I promise you that."

Mindful of the cap still on her head, Ia gave the Admiral-General a salute. Myang returned it crisply, then flicked her hand in silent admonition to go. Turning on her heel, she strode for the doors, ignoring the weapons pointed at her. The security team lowered their guns, shifting back to give her room to exit. Outside, across from the doors and desk, she found an unpleasant sight awaiting her return.

Oh, Bennie . . . I'm so sorry. I didn't think they'd go that *far with you.*

At least the chaplain was being released from custody; the zip-ties lacing her wrists and ankles together were being cut free by one of the Tower guards as Ia approached. The guard even offered her his hand, helping the older woman back to her feet. Smoothing back her auburn hair, Bennie faced Ia with a lividly curious glance toward the now shut double doors.

"Well?" she asked Ia. "I take it I won't have to visit you in the Dungeon? Or share a cell next to yours, for that matter?"

Still a little dazed, Ia opened her mouth, shut it, tried again, and finally found her voice. "I . . . got promoted. And transferred. I'm now Ship's Captain Ia, Branch Special Forces."

Bennie peered at her face, then at the doors several meters away. "You got promoted? All the way to a Ship's Captain?"

She shrugged almost helplessly, jacket thumping against her left leg. "I won, Bennie . . . I *won*."

"Well, you sure don't *look* like it," Bennie quipped, guiding her by the shoulders away from the staff desk and the dispersing guards. "Why don't we head for the nearest commissary, get you a nice cup of tea, or maybe a hot caf', and you can tell your Auntie Bennie all about it."

That snapped her out of her daze, if only from mild irritation at the chaplain's mock-patronizing tone. "I *can't* tell you 'all' about it. Not yet. Most of it's Ultra-Classified. But . . . I have a ship. I have *the* ship," Ia emphasized, thoughts turning back to the future. "The right ship. And all I have to do is fill it with the right crew, and the right—"

Her arm unit beeped. Ia flipped open the lid. A text message scrolled onto the screen.

"The official paperwork for your new promotion and cross-Branch transfer will be ready by 1400, Lieutenant. Meet me in my office. I'll trust you can find it, since you found your way in here. ~Adm. Genibes."

"Right," Ia murmured, closing the lid again. Her words to the Command Staff came back to her. Time *was* fleeting, and every second counted. She had too much to do, and too many wars to win. "Let's make that a meal instead of a drink, Bennie. I didn't eat any breakfast, and I'll have a lot of work to do, this afternoon."

"A *lot* of work, eh?" Bennie asked wryly. "Anything I can help with, or is that ultra-secret, too?"

"Oh, I fully expect you to come along with me for some of it," Ia sighed roughly. "I'll need a good chaplain for my crew—and I'll need you to be ready to save their souls while I'm busy trying to save everyone else's lives."

"You make it sound like you're about to drag your crew into hell," Bennie quipped. "But no single mission, however important, could possibly damn you all."

"If I don't get every step of this just right, then yes, we all are," Ia muttered. They stopped in front of a bank of lifts, and she pushed the button for the ground floor. Giving her friend a wry look, Ia shook her head. "I may have won *this* battle, Bennie—and I thank God I did—but I still have to win the coming wars."

Every single day, we have choices to make. What to wear, what to eat, where to go, who we will interact with, and how we will do it. But none of these choices can hold a candle to the choice, the impulse, the drive to serve others. To be a part of something greater than ourselves. To think first of the welfare of others, and then of our own.

It takes surprisingly little effort to think of the welfare of others. All it requires is a slightly higher level of consciousness, a higher level of awareness, to be able to move beyond the sole concerns of the self. How much more important is it when the welfare you are considering concerns the life or death of your fellow sentient beings? Is that something you yourself would consider?

As an officer, it is my duty to consider the lives and welfare of those around me. Not just of those placed in my command, but of those my soldiers can help, and those my soldiers must face. I know I will not be able to save every life. I am only one person, and there is only so much even someone like me can do. But I will put my own life on the line to save those that I can, and I will direct those under my command to do the same. We will fight to save lives. That is my promise to you.

I am an officer. That duty is mine.

~Ia